"THE BOOK IS FABULOUS!"

–Sherrilyn Kenyon,
New York Times bestselling author of the Dark-Hunter series

"*Dancing with Werewolves* is charming, witty, and utterly imaginative. A pure delight! Captivating characters, a new spin on the supernatural, simply delicious. Carole Nelson Douglas is wonderful and unique and always ahead of the pack."

–Heather Graham,
New York Times bestselling author of *Blood Red*

"A wonderfully written story with a unique take on the paranormal."

–Kelley Armstrong, author of *Bitten*

"In *Dances With Werewolves,* there aren't just scary things under the bed, but in it, too! Carole Nelson Douglas invents an amazingly rich world of shadows come to life, demonstrating yet again that she has one of the most fertile imaginations in fiction."

–Nancy Pickard,
nd Agatha-winning
rgin of Small Plains*

"C...................n a wild ride to the
V......................f your fantasies."

–Rebecca York,
USA Today-bestselling author of *New Moon*

From *Dancing With Werewolves:*

THE HEAT, THE NOISE, THE RHYTHM. It was getting to me. Moon madness. I let my hands slither down from his shoulders and undid the third button on his open shirt collar.

His eyebrow rose.

I swung my left hip hard into his right hand and undid another button.

Wolf whistles became a chorus, echoing around us from the hard wooden dance floor. *Olé*s echoed encouragingly. We were making a spectacle of ourselves, and I was now the main instigator. But the music was so engaging, so insistent.

On the next hip swing I undid another button. The skin beneath the shirt was as smooth and mocha-colored as a really great creamy latte and all this exercise was making me thirsty.

Ric suddenly swung me out, twirled my arms around myself and pulled me hard against him. My own crossed arms held me prisoner, pushing my back into his front, my cleavage into full focus as he looked down at me.

"The werewolves are dancing their paws off. Look."

Forced to take my eyes off him, off us, I saw that the Plexiglas flap had descended to the floor like a transparent iron curtain, dividing the dancers into Us and Them. Ric and I were on the tourist side. The transforming werewolves were circling madly in a salsa gone mad on the other side of the see-through barrier . . .

By Carole Nelson Douglas

Delilah Street, Paranormal Investigator

DANCING WITH WEREWOLVES

Carole Nelson Douglas

JUNO

Dancing With Werewolves
A Delilah Street, Paranormal Investigator, Novel

ISBN: 978-0-8095-7203-8

Juno Books
Rockville, MD
www.juno-books.com
info@juno-books.com

For Jean Marie Ward,
A world-class writer, journalist, and friend.

Delilah Street, Paranormal Investigator

DANCING WITH WEREWOLVES

Prologue: The Millennium Revelation

I saw Satan fall from heaven like lightning.
                                              –Luke 10:18

For the first time in the history of humankind, the turn of the millennium was tracked around the globe like an incoming comet zooming over the earth from the black night sky.

People everywhere joined to watch the exciting evidence of this invisible moment of time arrive. Exploding nebulas of fireworks in the midnight heavens marked its passage. Space satellites and television stations tracked its progress.

From the Pacific islands and Australia to China, where fireworks and gunpowder were born, to Europe to America, rockets were bursting in air, just like in the national anthem. They illuminated the edge of oncoming midnight.

A world globe stood next to the TV screen so we kids could track the necklace of fireworks circle the earth. On TV, men and women in exotic locales—Singapore, Sri Lanka, Krakow, Paris, New York City, San Francisco, Peru, Easter Island—sounded breathless and triumphant. They announced the magical millennium moment over their microphones as the thousand-year turn of the centuries overtook each of the world's time zones.

Even the littlest kids in the orphanage were allowed to stay up past midnight to watch.

The oldest at eleven, I thought that there could be no more delicious moment than standing under those glittering showers of light with a microphone like a lollipop in my hand, telling everyone all about it.

Oh, we had piles of bottled water and dry foods stocked in the basement, and all the residence's computer screens were darker than night. Primal fears underlay the outward celebrations of the millennium. Some people swore the year 2000 would bring technological chaos, or an old-fashioned End of the Word cataclysm. And I was living through it, a skinny, careful kid with no history who dreamed of making some, someday.

The nightmares hadn't started yet.

Mine. And everybody else's.

We all are so much older now, and not much wiser.

I'm twenty-four and hold that TV microphone in my hand on a windswept scrap of high plains turf called Kansas, reporting the continuing aftermath of that landmark night and its unexpected revelations.

Ironic, how all the pundits, religious and secular, had feared the wrong bogeymen when the twentieth century turned its hoary head over its shoulder to mark the end of the second thousand years after Christ with the sharp slash of a scythe. Before 2000. After 2000.

I'd been taught the religious implications, of course, and even back then had a reporter's dubious eye about ballyhooed adult events. Later, I understood it all even more.

The apocalyptic crowd had predicted Armageddon, the Antichrist abroad, raising Hell quite literally. The dark, evil dead would be drawn from their graves to battle the Lord of the Second Coming and His legions of shining angels.

World leaders had feared a terrorist cascade of bombs bursting across the globe to broadcast religious strife, anger, and hatred.

Computer geeks had predicted that Y2K, the Year 2000 in their geeky shorthand, would short-circuit computer programs the world over. The preprogrammed 0000s and 1111s would go berserk with the stress of recording the unprepared-for calendar shift to 2000, plunging us all back into the chaos of an abacus age.

They were all right in a way, and all wrong.

Instead—wonder of wonders—the lost, the legends, the outcast, the feared, the bogeymen and women of more simple-minded times, witches and ghosts, werewolves and vampires and zombies, oh my—rose from the grave-yard of myth, gradually demanding recognition, reveal-ing themselves as endlessly ongoing inhabitants of our same human planet.

It started with a few werewolf cub sightings. They were mistaken for feral children until a couple were captured in transition. Then came increased rumors of vampire bites. Air traffic controllers reported small flying bodies, relatively speaking. These turned out to be flocks of giant vampire bats migrating between South America and the other continents by night. By Halloween, witches were reported hot-rodding across the moon and scaring trick or treaters with candy-stealing fly-bys. These were just the show-offs. Previously normal citizens revealed weird, inexplicable powers. The Change became too general and global to deny.

Religious leaders were torn between dismissing them all as demons . . . or the benighted mentally ill. The divide between both conditions had always been hairline-thin.

Politicians wavered between rallying popular feeling against the new-old population . . . or registering them to vote.

Techno-geeks veered between calling them a bunch of hallucinatory Luddites . . . and wanting to get them online blogs.

I found myself with mixed feelings too, not sure whether I was destined to be a casualty of this bizarre new turn in human history, or its recording angel.

And then things really got weird . . .

CHAPTER ONE

"Authorities assert," I said clearly into the microphone I held, "that medical examinations will reveal this as just the scene of another rural juvenile prank, nothing more."

I held my position while the station videographer wrapped the take. *No moving.* You never knew when you were really on or off camera. A savvy TV reporter learned to freeze like a department store mannequin before and after filming a stand-up.

Of course I hadn't believed a word I said.

If you don't cooperate with the police in the early stages of a crime story, they'll cold-cock you later, just when everything is getting juicy. They'll cold-cock you anyway, just for the fun of it.

Speaking of juicy, the three corpses were bone soup inside their intact skins. No way does any weapon known to human do that. Yet the "authorities" were playing the incident like a frat-boy prank for the public. So this was just a semi-crime scene.

That scene was a Kansas cornfield and my mid-heeled reporter pumps were sinking arch-deep in clods of dirt or shit, depending.

"Del," the lieutenant said as soon as the day-bright camera light had turned off and we were all plunged back into a rural darkness where no crickets chirped.

Crickets always chirped in the spring country night, which was yet another sign that this was one eerie crime scene.

As the cameraman drove off in the station van to film another story, Lieutenant Werner, short, dark, and rotund, escorted me over the clods to the unpaved road, where a sleek black car stood shrouded in gravel dust. We had a working history, so I accepted his part gallant, part controlling male custody. Besides, that car was very interesting. Out of state license plate. Way more than unmarked police car class. Cool.

"Agent Edwards wants to talk to you."

Agent Edwards. Not the county agricultural agent, not state police. Fed. *Hello, Fox Mulder, maybe?* Just when you need a hero.

"Miss Street," the man said.

I nodded, unsold. Viewed in the headlights from his car, Agent Edwards was an East Coast yuppie, no hair below the tops of his ears or the back of his stiff white shirt collar. Cornfields were as alien to him as crop circles, but I knew a lot about both.

"You cover the 'paranormal crime' beat around here, I understand." Edwards put a sneer inside his quotation marks.

"I don't think you *do* understand," I answered. "What . . . bureau are you with?"

"Office of Rural Security. We handle uncooperative farmers on the mad cow disease issue, fertilizer thefts, anything that involves national safety. So all suspect incidents are a federal case. Media rights bow to national security nowadays. We demand your discretion."

"I know I have to give it, but that doesn't mean you can't tip me off early in return."

He nodded. Not a real "yes." As if I hadn't noticed.

"Miss Street, you know this community, this terrain. What do you think?"

What I thought was that Agent Edwards was a stupid tight-ass, but that didn't mean he couldn't be one of the

still-closeted supernaturals. He broadcast an air of "other."
Maybe it was just East Coast ego toward heartland hicks,
not the arrogance the supers often felt toward us mere
mortals. Then again, he could just be the usual officious
bureaucratic prick.

What I thought about the corpses would get me a strait
jacket in the state hospital, but I tested him. "The bodies
have been turned into creamed corn in a can, Agent
Edwards."

"Interestingly put, Miss Street. Why? How?"

"We've had a lot of crop circle activity lately."

"Rubes with rider lawn mowers. Pranks."

I might have told him. What I'd seen. What I'd put
together. The "rubes" comment killed it. I lived here.
Worked here. Maybe had been born here.

Suck grass, Fed.

I SAT IN MY CAR while everyone else peeled away into the
darkness, riding a pair of blazing headlights. Werner and
his partner were last. He leaned on my open car door.
Between the '56 Cadillac's width and the wide door, we
nearly blocked the two-lane road. Dolly and me. That was
the car's name. Dolly. She was built like a fortress. I often
needed one.

"You don't want to hang around out here, Del. Could
still be dangerous."

"Just gotta record a few notes while they're fresh." I
held up my lipstick-size machine. "I'll be okay. It's all
over out here, whatever it was."

"The Agri bastard is probably right."

"Aren't they always?"

Werner laughed. He was just looking out for me. That's
what was nice about living in a smaller city. A buzz came
from the police radio screwed onto Dolly's humongous
drive-shaft hump.

Werner nodded at it. "You're wired into us if you need anything."

"I'm okay, you're okay. Good night, Leo."

I watched his taillights fade into the absolute country night.

I'm not a particularly brave woman, but I am determined.

Once me and Dolly and the dark were an uncrowded three-way again, I left the car, toting a heavy-duty flashlight. Dolly's trunk could hold everything, including the kitchen sink.

The flashlight spotlighted the corpses' massive profiles. Three dead cows, their huge carcasses pulverized to broken bones floating in precious bodily fluids inside intact cowhides. Those intact hides were most unusual for livestock attacks; they usually involved cryptic mutilations.

I played the intense light over the ground markings. What Edwards had described as "moo-cow hooves wandering into a scene of punk prankery," I saw as local livestock blundering into a mysterious crop circle creation incident.

I'd also spotted some very non-bovine marks on the rough soil. Maybe the spooked animals had been stampeded into the crop circle by something.

My flashlight hit the highs and lows of the alien footprints. Not "moo-cow" hooves, but huge heavy foot*pads*. Way too big for werewolves, but what else pulled down adult cows except were-packs, or even natural wolves, of which very few were left?

I squatted to measure the tracks mixed in with the milling hooves.

Dinner-plate size. Clawed. Almost wiped away by some trailing . . . appendage.

Okay. Cow tails are scrawny and just long enough to swat away horseflies and not much else. This was almost a . . . a *reptilian* trail, making a long, S-shaped swath. Cows with lizard tails? Not even a rare were-cow could leave marks like that.

I stood. The cows had been attracted to the activity at the crop circle. Lights. Action. No camera. Something had followed and then slaughtered them. I'd get another station videographer out here in daylight to film the footprint evidence without the prying eyes of the authorities present. Even the local cops had a stake in not stirring up the populace with alien invasion or supernatural slaughter stories.

In less than half an hour, I was back in my rented bungalow, jubilant, rerunning the audiotaped *second* version of the stand-up I'd sneaked in under the noses of the local cops and the Fed.

"Authorities are perplexed by a crime scene where local cows apparently have been cooked inside their hides by forces beyond conventional firearms or other weapons. Found dead yesterday in a field outside of Wichita, Kansas. . . ."

Found dead.

Found live was the story of my life so far: I'd been found alive, from birth, but just barely.

Found dead always made a much better story hook.

CHAPTER TWO

After work the next day, the latest report on my story safely digitalized and under wraps for a debut on the evening news at ten, I crashed at home by seven that night. How does a weird-phenomenon TV reporter relax? By watching national network forensic crime shows, natch.

So there I am, sucking up microscopic forensic details on TV with the rest of the country, when *wham-o!*

It all happened so fast. The camera zoomed in closer than the world's best lover. A maggot writhed like a stripper from the dark cave of a deadly pale . . . but delicately shaped . . . nostril. With a tiny blue topaz stud.

The camera dollied back. *Hmm.* Not a bad-looking nostril at all. In fact, it's a dead ringer for mine. Tiny blue topaz stud and all. A very dead ringer. Literally.

I can feel my cold sweat. This is the same old nightmare: me flat on my back, unable to move, bad alien objects coming at me. Except I'm not dreaming, I'm watching network TV on a Thursday evening, like eighty million other people in America.

The object of the camera's affection is a body on the hot TV franchise show, *CSI Las Vegas V, Crime Scene Instincts*, what I nickname *Criminally Salacious Investigations*. Media is my business. I have a right to mock it. I am not in a mocking mood at the moment.

Who has tapped my very personal nightmares for network exposure? While my stomach starts to churn, the camera retracts farther.

Holy homicide! The turned-up nose *is* mine! And the chin, the neck, the collarbones, the discreet but obvious cleavage, the muscle-defined calves visible past Grisham V's burgeoning backside. . . .

Even the toenails are painted my color, Glitz Blitz Red.

I look down and wiggle my bare toes shimmering blood-bright in the living room lamplight. I'm alive but I'm alone, in all senses of the word.

Me with a body double? A doppelganger. A replica. A clone?

My heart was pounding as if I'd actually undergone a recent brush with scalpel and saw and had lived to tell about it. I'd never "felt" the presence of a missing birth twin, like you were supposed to. I'd never sensed an absent "half." Yet the detail that really unnerved me was the tiny blue topaz nose stud on the televised body. Hardly a genetic similarity.

Separated twins were supposed to be so alike that they often held the same jobs, married men who shared a profession, even dressed alike. Long distance. Without one knowing about the other. That small blue glint on the corpse's nose made me shiver. Facial resemblance might eerily echo some stranger's features. But the exact same impudent touch of nose jewelry?

No. Can't be. I'm an orphan so abandoned that I was named after the intersection where my infant self was found.

So who's been trespassing on my mysteriously anonymous gene pool?

I haven't taped the damn show, so I can't rerun my media centerfold moment. Who knew? I'm used to being on TV, but I've never acted, never aimed at a career as a corpse, and I've never been to Las Vegas.

My white Lhasa apso, Achilles, sensing agitation, came bouncing over to comfort me, his lovely floor-length hair shimmering in the bluish light of the television. I absently stroked his long silky ears.

Lhasas are often taken for largish lapdogs, but they've got terrier souls. Achilles is twenty pounds of Tibetan staple gun. I used to wonder why centuries ago the Dalai Lamas bred Lhasas as temple guard dogs . . . until I got Achilles as a puppy. He was a growling relentless rusher, that short toothy jaw snapping with playful nips. I'd push him back and he'd joyously charge me again. If an intruder ever fell down in a pack of these, it would be Piranha City. Flesh stripped from bone.

In fact, Achilles was named for his playful puppy habit of nipping at my heels wherever I went. And because he's my soft spot, my Achilles heel.

Yeah. I'm an orphan, I'm single. I love my dog.

And apparently I'm now anonymously famous. Or infamous.

CHAPTER THREE

Achilles' sturdy body next to mine radiated pure comfort as I impatiently waited for the *CSI Las Vegas* show to end. When the legally required credits ran, though, the local station cut them to the size of the fine print in a pre-nuptial contract. That made room for teaser images from the upcoming ten o'clock news. The information that this was "A Hector Nightwine Production" ran in letters two inches high, but I couldn't read a single name from the cast list. Not that a corpse usually gets a credit, not even on the reality TV funeral shows.

The local station, by the way, is my station, WTCH in Wichita, Kansas.

In fact, I had the weird experience of catching a flash of my face on the upcoming footage of the nightly news show and the onscreen line: DELILAH STREET, WTCH-TV PARANORMAL INVESTIGATIVE REPORTER. I'm used to that, but not after the shock of being personally dissected on primetime network TV.

My piece on the latest wrinkle on the local ritual mutilation and killing incident should run at least number three on the story roster tonight, right after the top two national stories.

I basked for a moment in the sheer joy of where and who I was. I had a great job and I was doing good work, important work. Woodward would have been proud of me but Bernstein probably would have wondered why I was wasting my talents on a Podunk town in the heartland.

Maybe that was because it *was* the heartland. My heart, my land. What a Brave New World lay out there after the Millennium Revelation of 2000! I'd been young enough to adapt fast, just a misplaced kid with an itch to become a reporter someday.

Of course some of the older folk couldn't accept witches, werewolves, and vampires as near neighbors, not after eating up scary tales about them all their lives. Kids, though, were rapt. After the Millennium Revelation, we learned these creatures—er, supernaturals—weren't necessarily evil, any more than humans were necessarily good. Serial killers, for instance, were pretty much a human phenomenon until recently.

Yet there were criminal elements among the newly outed supernatural population. When I graduated from J-school and got my first job at WTCH-TV, I was so hooked on these new but ancient resident species that I made them my beat.

I reported the crimes that occurred where the various breeds met and went wrong, fascinated by what twisted any creature to act outside the limits of its kind. I felt an unspoken kinship with the supernaturals. I'd been both outcast and—when I attracted attention for a too-good grade or even just the way I looked—preyed upon during my various institutional lives.

I couldn't wait to get out on my own. That's when my life would begin. And now the "beat" I'd built at WTCH, the sense of reporting what was really going on despite the community's tendency to bury bad news and anybody different in the back forty . . . well, I *thought* I was making a difference. For the public, for the people who watched my reports, for me, for the world in general. I guess you have to be young to believe so much in your own potency.

My piece running tonight focused on the crop circles that scribed ancient fertility symbols into the Kansas wheat fields. My thesis was that they weren't of alien, off-world manufacture, but an expression of the alien within our recently upended worldview and ourselves. Maybe they were a positive, attracting rain and sun. Earth symbols. I tried to open the viewers' minds. And my own.

A big personal problem I had with the Millennium Revelation was that the vampires it had shaken out of the topsoil were a pretty debased breed. Where was Count Dracula in white tie and tails when you needed him? The real vamps were no better than human wastrels, for the most part: druggies, partiers, and cheap criminals. Even the few who rose to white-collar jobs sported a sleazy rusty ring-around-the-collar from the one-nighters they pulled with doped-out prostitutes to get a little blood on the hoof.

And I took it personally. Let's just say that, as a pale-skinned young human female, I was always a top target for vampire lust and late-night snacking.

I tuned out the TV. I'd seen enough of my own news reports to forego another self-image fix. That vertical legless version of me, mike in hand, is old hat by now . . . unless I'm shown horizontal and naked, as on *CSI* just moments ago. I didn't have much time to brood on this weird coincidence. I had to stay up way past the news anyway. That's what happens when you date an anchorman.

I observed the opening "Eye on Kansas" news show hype with half an eye tonight. Rapid cuts between sweeping helicopter film of downtown Wichita. Yippee. Then Ted Brinkman, the anchorman, unleashed his studied baritone and the games began. His name was perfect for the job. He had the anchorman trifecta: razor-cut helmet of dark hair, flashing bleach-white teeth, and red power tie.

His slightly bloodshot eye-whites and the way his prominent canine teeth dented his lower lip at times was the just-right extra touch. Vampires were still a novelty on evening TV in Kansas.

Ted had to take injections so he could come in early enough to do the six o'clock show before the sun had set. He used a George Hamilton product that pumped melatonin into his skin, giving him that golden glow. The extra effort gave him a ratings edge. A lot of vampires were selling out their heritage to "blend in" nowadays, though not all of them were out of the closet, or the coffin.

Ted was coming over after the news to take me out to midnight supper. I insisted on all the old-fashioned time-consuming date moves because I was wary of vamps. Oh, not the literally oral sex thing. It was what women have had trouble with since Eve: the sincerity thing.

Whoever my parents, whatever my missing background, I was one thing for sure: what they call Black Irish. No fiery hair and freckles for me. My hair was drop-dead black, my eyes sky-blue, my skin wedding-invitation-white. I'd been vamp bait since I was twelve.

My natural pallor was catnip to them. That just-drained and ready-for-more look. I even shared their allergy to direct sunlight, though I could overcome mine with sunscreen. I cracked my first smile of the evening imagining Ted Brinkman slathered in sunscreen. All anchormen, vampires or not, are a bit too full of themselves.

So why even bother? Because I didn't have a life, at least a dating one. I kept hoping that someday I'd meet an exceptional vamp who grooved on my Ivory Snow skin and still treated me like a human being. Ironic goal, right?

I'd brooded myself through twenty minutes of droning stories and screaming ads, so Sheena Coleman was already doing her nightly bump-and-grind against the studio blue screen. Of course she had to compete with the weather maps the viewers really wanted to see.

Sheena was a weather witch. That meant she could control meteorological conditions to some degree, as well as report them. Actually, I found it admirable that she had a regular job. A lot of weather witches went into blackmail. You know, pay me or I drop a firestorm of hail on your harvest-ready crop. It was a crime to use weather witching for personal gain, but there were only so many government and corporate positions around for them. Sheena was tall, blond, and anorexic. She liked the limelight the way bolt lightning likes trees and power lines.

"There's a storm front moving across rural Sedgwick County," she explained, taloned fingers pointing to an orange crescent on the lurid green background. (I may be Irish but I don't like green; clashes with my baby blues.) "But it will take a quick swing north and miss the wheat fields." She gave her right hip a little bump and the crescent obediently moved over the blue of a water treatment plant.

Weather witches weren't all equally adept. It sucked a lot of their energy to produce major weather changes, so Sheena's little quasi-news/entertainment position was tailor-made.

"Guess it won't rain on Ted and me when we go out to dinner," I told Achilles, whose perky ears immediately took a dive.

Achilles didn't like Ted. I wasn't sure I did either, but every once in a while I had to take a stab at a social life.

So, I bustled around the dollhouse rooms of my small rented house. No apartments for me. I craved roots. I wanted a front door that opened on fresh air. A back stoop. A too-tiny kitchen with no garbage disposal. Achilles trailed me, a canine dust mop, sensing my excitement. Company coming.

Maybe it was time to give up the ghost. I'd always attracted a certain type of man. Well, *not* man. Ted had a great job for a vamp in the heartland. He was a pioneer for his, um, race. He was attractive, well educated, apparently long ago. He loved my looks, which was more than I did.

What was not to like?

Well, maybe that Vampire Lunge, for one thing. Vamps always made me feel like the smorgasbord at the local pancake house on Sunday morning.

I rushed into my bedroom to survey the clothes in the square old-fashioned closet. I'd been dithering about what to wear all evening; seeing myself totally unclothed on national TV hadn't helped.

I pulled out a seventies miniskirt dress. Weird era. The skirt barely covered my rear but the sleeves were choirgirl wrist-length and the top had a prim little mandarin collar that would convince any vamp to hold off on his neck lunge until the after-dinner mints. Of course tights were the required legwear for this truncated dress, and I had several pair as well as flat-heeled baby-doll shoes. All vintage. Born long before I had been. I loved that sense of connection to times past.

But I also felt like an overage baby doll. Not ready for prime time. As a dedicated reporter, yeah, I was ready for a jump to a major market. As vamp bait, I hoped I'd only get a wee midnight nibble. I needed . . . I don't know what I needed, except a little patience and a lot of love. Or maybe the opposite.

IF I WERE CINDERELLA I'd have lost a slipper by the time Ted finally showed up. He should have been here by 11:30, not after midnight.

I saw why he was late the minute I answered the door.

"You've been drinking."

"Just a mellow-outer after the show." He flashed the glass hip flask in his back pocket. Sterling silver was a no-no for vamps and werewolves, almost as bad as a sunburn. I doubted the "quick one" he'd stopped for had been alcohol. He knew I was not an easy bite.

He also pulled a bouquet from behind his back, white roses and gardenias bursting with heady scent. The gesture did sweep away my inbred suspicion. Growing up in an orphanage, even if it was called a "temporary group housing facility" for social services, will do that.

"Ted, these are gorgeous. Thank you."

"Gonna ask me in?"

"I forgot. Sure."

He couldn't cross thresholds without an okay. His eyes were only a little bloodshot. Could be the hot studio lights. Sure.

"I'll put these in water and then we can go."

This was starting to feel almost old-fashioned. Maybe Ted really was willing to put some effort into me, instead of offering the usual mesmerizing gaze and knee-jerk snap for the carotid artery.

I found a frosted crystal Victorian celery jar in the cupboard that made a perfect vase. No family heirlooms? Buy 'em at estate sales. Plus, since I'd earned full tuition to college but not a cent of spending money, I'd had to buy recycled to save every penny for so long that I came to love having . . . *saving* . . . the odds and ends of other people's family lives. These objects with their aura of someone else's history were adoptees, as I had never been.

I could visualize some Barbie-waisted corseted Victorian miss plunging this glorious bouquet of pure white dazzle and scent into this very celery jar as a makeshift vase . . .

"Ouch!"

Rose stems have thorns and one had torn a jagged slash on my forefinger. I automatically lifted it to my mouth. But Ted seized my finger with its Sleeping Beauty drop of welling blood and sucked like a leech. While I was trying to decide if this was deeply erotic, as the vamp tramps claimed, or just plain rude, the bouquet dropped to the carpet. Achilles came barking and running around our feet.

"Excuse me." I extracted my finger, which had painted Ted's lips a glossy girly red that was a bit of a turn-off, and bent to retrieve the flowers.

The enveloping tissue had fallen away. Something sharp and silver glittered among the green rose stems. I stood, bringing the phenomenon into the light. Not silver. Steel.

"You bastard."

Ted was too busy licking his lips to notice what I'd found. "What is it, Delilah? Don't tell me a little love-nip on the finger is too much? You must be frigid."

Achilles' barks and growls had turned into worrying Ted's ankles just in time. Ted did a two-step away from my dog, and me.

"X-acto knife razor blades," I said. "Duct-taped to the rose stems? You couldn't wait for a tender moment before fanging me? You couldn't so much as feed me dinner before tapping my veins? Frigid! I'll show you hot!"

I picked up the bouquet in its tissue paper and thrust the angle-cut rose stems at his chest. He shrieked and backed away. Rose stems are "woody," you know. And, by the way, never date a man who shrieks. Meanwhile, Achilles took a good Tibetan-staple-gun chomp out of his right ankle.

I backed off, laughing. "Not a man-bites-dog story, but a dog-bites-vamp story! I'm gonna call this in to the rival station, Ted. Oughta get a few chuckles."

"You are everything I've heard! Uppity. Frigid. Bitchy. I should have never given you a chance. If it weren't for your damn white skin, I wouldn't have."

"Date a Royal Dalton porcelain figurine next time, Ted! Probably lively enough for you," I yelled as he retreated through the door.

Damn white skin. That's the way I felt about it too.

Especially now that I'd seen a lancet pierce that skin on TV. Skin that had parted cleanly, bloodlessly. So my double was dead. Or had been filmed to look that way, more likely. People would kill to land the bit part of corpse on any *CSI* show in the country but I didn't think they'd literally die for it.

I locked the door behind Ted. My house was on the outskirts of town, a nineteen-twenties wood-frame bungalow. It felt like a phantom family home where an aproned grandma lurked just out of sight around the corner, baking blueberry muffins. Some days I could almost smell them.

Achilles quit barking and came twining around my ankles like a cat.

I shook my head, angry at myself. I'd put up with the Snow White thing since the orphanage. Even spray-on tans didn't help much. That crystal coffin in the woods was a real turn-on for the vamp set and every one of them I'd met had panted to picture me in it.

Now I'd seen myself laid out and dissected on TV. So I had a whole country full of eager watchers. *CSI* was still number one on the Nielsens, with spin-offs galore. Or gore. I bet my Dead Celebrity Q popularity number was sky high compared to my Q rating for being an ace investigative reporter for WTCH-TV. It's true. Some dead celebrities are more recognizable and popular than living ones. Lucy Ricardo over Madonna. John Wayne over Kevin Costner. Now dead Delilah Street over . . . live Delilah Street. Bummer.

That's when I realized that the worst day of my life had morphed into the worst night of my life. And here I thought my recently but not dearly departed suitor Undead Ted had won that title . . . cold. Worst Knight in Shining Fangs. Ever.

CHAPTER FOUR

I woke up at midnight, sitting upright in bed, wondering what my subconscious mind had heard.

The vampire's pale face hung over me like a diseased moon, so close that I was forced to fall back. He wasn't anything pretty from an old vampire movie, not a wistful Brad Pitt or even a ferociously life-hungry Tom Cruise. His dead white skin hosted a raging case of psoriasis and his oily dishwater-brown hair was long enough for its rat-tailed ends to twitch at my face and throat like barbs.

Suddenly I was up against a wall, pinned there by him. Vamps can do that, move faster than human perception. And he wasn't alone. He played lead bloodsucker with a backup trio, all as nauseating as their leader.

They were teen vamps who'd been bitten young. Someone had left them buried and forgotten a bit too long. That had made them ugly and mean.

Lead boy ran his fingernail down my cheek. It was ragged, with black oil and dirt obscuring any moon at the jagged tip. It was like being caressed by a jigsaw blade.

"Cool and white," he said. Then he said my name. "Delilah."

"Looks good in red, I bet," a backup boy cackled.

Suddenly I knew where I was, and it wasn't my bedroom on Moody Avenue.

I was back in the social services group home, and the boys were daylight vampires who were older, bigger, and way stronger than I. They knew just when to waylay me, when no one was around to stop them—except me, and I weighed all of ninety pounds at age twelve.

It was so clear. So real. It would be gang rape and then a group blood tasting. I'd be tainted two unrecoverable ways, even worse than I was now as an unwanted orphan.

I reached into my jeans pocket. *Jeans? I'd been accosted in bed. Since when was I wearing jeans?*

I was wearing jeans, and the pocket held a cheap plastic handle with a pointed steel blade dusted with diamonds. I'd been ready for this moment all my life and knew what to do.

I lifted my left hand, and then wound it tight in those repellent greasy strands of the lead vamp's hair.

The trio wolf-whistled. "Oh, she *likes* you, Hacker. Come on, Snow White; time to donate a little blood and a lot of booty."

My right hand snaked up to press the long-missing nail file I'd stolen from Miss Whitcomb, the supervisor, hard into the outer socket of Hacker's left eye.

Bleeding doesn't bother vamps. It can even be a turn-on. But the threat of having their eyes popped out "like a pair of pearls from an oyster shell," as I put it in my best Captain Jack Sparrow voice, did turn their dead-white complexions greener than crème de menthe.

They wouldn't have known what crème de menthe was, since they all had the reading level of a gerbil.

The quartet melted away as I sat up. In bed. I was sweating from my hair to my feet, and my right hand was coiled into such a tight fist that I turned on the bedside lamp to inspect the damage: half-moon fingernail indentations weeping blood.

I took a deep breath. In my own bed.

Alone.

Someone whimpered.

Achilles, looking worried, paced the floor beside my bed. Shorted-legged Lhasas aren't great jumpers. When I lifted him up beside me, he set about licking my face with a hot, loving tongue. He brought the warmth back into me and banished the dream. The nightmare. The trouble was, it was true to life.

My life. I'd been there, done that.

So much for the everyday adventures of an underage ward of the guardian state of Kansas after the Millennium Revelation.

I'D ALWAYS CONSIDERED MYSELF the orphan's orphan.

After all, no one had ever adopted me, or tried to. No one had fostered me. I just stayed at the Sedgwick County Home as kids younger and older came and went.

Maybe it was my funky name. Delilah Street. I'd supposedly been found there as an abandoned three-day-old infant, wrapped in one of those storm shelter Army-green blankets.

No dainty pastels for baby me.

But, see, there wasn't a Delilah Street in Wichita. Or Kansas. Or surrounding states. I'd looked. At least I hadn't been found on Lavender Lane. I'd have really developed a chip on my shoulder with that sappy name.

When Y2K and the Millennium Revelation came along, it was exciting that all the bogeymen were coming out of the closet and out from under the bed of night-time stories. Vampires and weres and ghouls, storybook stuff. I still wanted to read about *The Little Princess,* and Cinderella with those cool glass slippers, and Little Orphan Annie, who'd had a good dog and a sugar daddy, born before the age that recognized child molestation. Then, suddenly, the vamp boys came out of the woodwork and circled, flooding the social service agencies, as unclaimed as rabid dogs. Half-breeds, some of them. All predators. That's when they zeroed in on me.

Luckily, a couple years after the Millennium Revelation, some anonymous benefactor, likely a faceless charity, had sponsored my going to a girls' high school, and, later, to college. When I say sponsored, I mean paid the tuition. Period. Oh, sure, room and board at Our Lady of the Lake Convent School was covered, but nothing beyond that. College was coed and public. I earned some extra scholarship money and worked my way through it in the usual "fries with that?" student mode. No time for foolishness, including much dating.

I brooded about all this the rest of that long nonworking weekend. I'd trashed the roses and gardenias, but their sickly sweet odor lingered like the subtle breath of a funeral home.

Sometimes I had nightmares I didn't remember much of, almost alien abduction dreams. Compared to the remembered shards of my nightmares, a needle in the navel would have been child's play. I glimpsed something like a silver turkey baster and it was pushing between my legs. Made it hard to think of a penis as anything other than a blunt instrument after that. So maybe Undead Ted was right. I was frigid. Cold. In one sense, silver scared the hell out of me, yet called to me in all its more elegant forms.

Sometimes I thought I was a ghoul, gathering dead people's clothes and fragments of their lives from resale shops and estate sales. Compelled to buy weird Victorian sterling serving pieces at fire-sale prices; they were so tiny, so mysterious, so precious. A set of fairy-size forks for some forgotten kind of seafood appetizer. An opium pipe set into a lady's finger ring. Taxco Mexican jewelry with welts of bright blue glass dewing it.

I was born to be odd. Whenever I tried not to be, it went wrong. Like with Ted.

I moped through the weekend, sharing a sip of Bailey's Irish Cream with Achilles. He seemed downcast himself that idle Saturday. We sat together all afternoon watching old movies on cable TV, I stroking his long, soft hair.

Saturday night, he collapsed in front of his water dish, panting. I gathered him up, looking into licorice-black eyes that had dulled to the point of not recognizing me. After frantically riffling the Yellow Pages, I raced in my vintage Caddie for the nearest twenty-four-hour vet's offices. On the passenger side, Achilles lay inert. I stroked him the whole way, only one hand on the wheel, but he wasn't even responding to his name now.

The vet took him in with vague guesses and promises of intravenous fluids and constant care and a phone call if anything changed.

Sunday night I stood in a fluorescent light-glared room and they told me he was terminal.

"Never seen anything like it," the weary-faced vet said. "So fast. Blood poisoning."

I pictured small defensive teeth sunk into a bony undead ankle, and sobbed. Achilles lay dead to the world on a steel table, a beautiful dust mop of pale hair just barely breathing. My own breath came raggedly. Getting Achilles had been the first thing I'd done after leaving college and getting a job. He was the first and only creature to ever give me joy and affection. We'd been together for three years. I felt like I was strangling on poisoned cotton candy.

What did I want to do? they asked. Leave the body with them, like a *CSI* corpse? Or send it to Smokerise Farm for incineration? Rotting in a common grave, or reduced to ashes on my mantel?

What I wanted to do was leave with my dog.

Not . . . possible. I asked for a lock of his albino-white hair and opted for Smokerise Farm, where, I was assured, the ashes I received were guaranteed to be really his. I could select a suitable . . . vessel from a book of photographs. I chose one of an Asian shape, with a five-toed Imperial dragon on it. Achilles had been royalty.

Imagine, some people might pass off any old ashes on a bereaved companion.

Achilles was of a breed that had guarded Tibetan holy men for centuries. What if some of their masters' reincarnation mysticism had rubbed off on the dogs? Maybe I was just trying to dull the ache, but I somehow felt that Achilles and I would meet again some day. We might be in different forms, but we'd know each other.

Meanwhile, tomorrow was Monday, not Maybe. I had to go to work again. I felt like the walking dead. In fact, it would be a miracle if I didn't stake Undead Ted on the six o'clock news.

CHAPTER FIVE

I hadn't expected life at work to be pleasant after kicking out anchorman Ted, but it seemed he'd been busy over the weekend while I'd been losing my dog.

For one thing, when I entered the studio Undead Ted the Splitting Toad was canoodling with Sheena Coleman by the blue screen. For another, the news director, Fred Fogelmann, called me into his tiny windowless office for a little two-person conference.

"Sit down, Delilah. What's the matter?" He must have just noticed my maroon eye-circles (a problem with tissue-thin pale skin), so this conference was about something else. "You look like hell."

I tried to dredge up a patina of perky. Looking bad was a mortal sin in the TV biz.

He rolled right on before I could defend myself and my raccoon eyes. "Never mind, it doesn't matter."

That was even worse news, but I still couldn't gather any words or gestures to fight my way into a good mood.

"Er, there're some changes in the hopper." Fred was formerly a newspaper City Editor and he still talked like someone with a dwindling pint of rotgut whiskey in his bottom desk drawer.

"Ted's eager to get out on the streets." I bet. "To use his reporter skills again." Again? Really? As if he'd ever had them. "You've done a great job with the ritual crimes beat, but he'll be taking that over. And Sheena wants some street cred too. She'll be doing that 'pornanormal' spot you thought up. Fresh face, you know."

"You mean 'blond and anorexic'," I said, finally peeved enough to growl a little.

"Ann or Rex who?" He shrugged. What a with-it guy on women's issues!

I saw the strategy. Ted had grabbed the juicy beats I'd made mine. What's better to cover than sex and violence? Especially exotic sex and violence. Who did Ted think he was, his journalistic idol, sob-soul brother Geraldo Rivera? Really! Vampires and Geraldo are so over! And what did I get in exchange?

"I have something new for you," Fred said.

It was a good thing I was still feeling too down to pretend to be up, because his next words would have crashed me even if I'd won the lottery the night before.

"We've got a vital demographic that isn't being served and you're just the one to put them in the spotlight. I'm calling the feature 'Good Living After Death.' A lot of influential Baby Boomers underwrite those Sunset City retirement communities all over the country and they have a heck of a lot of interesting stories."

When you have to use "heck of a lot" as a news peg, you're in trouble.

"This old doll, for instance." He handed a black-and-white glamour photo from the Ice Age of film history across the desk. "Right here in Wichita at Sunset City. Quite a looker once. I bet she has tales to tell."

The name under the classic thirties' face with its arched penciled eyebrows made my pulse blip once: Caressa Teagarden, a major star who'd vanished from screen and media as thoroughly as Garbo, at about the same time. My love of vintage made me familiar with films and their stars from the silents to the sixties when the star system crumbled.

This would be a fun one-time change of pace, maybe, but a whole beat based on dredging up the almost dead? I knew what the problem was. The "whole group of senior citizens out there now" just won't die. Rumor had it that the North Koreans, banned from nuclear experiments, had gone to the cellular level, even getting into cloning. Through their various experiments, they'd invented a method of replacing death with a "twilight awake" state. A thing like that would rake in billions. Think Donald Trump paying to be preserved in amber and comb-over. Forever.

"It's set up for tomorrow," Fred said, totally co-opting me. "Slo-mo Eddie is the videographer. Cheer up, Del. A spin out to Sunset City should be real scenic. Some fresh air would put roses in your cheeks. You've been too deep into all that sicko murder stuff. You look like a zombie yourself. Do something to make the old dear happy. A little attention should do wonders for her latest face lift."

I sleepwalked out of there, living up to my new rep, Zombie Reporter. So that was my new beat, Death Warmed Over? Kinda like my career at the moment.

SLO-MO EDDIE was one of those lanky, laid-back guys, instead of hyper nutso like most videographers. Deadlines, dead bodies in rapid rotation, it can make you crazy. He chewed Butternut gum while I explained about tomorrow's assignment at Sunset City.

"What's the deal with this Sunset City dame?" Eddie asked. Videographers never paid any attention to the news, the culture, and the wider world. It was all *inside* the box with them. The camera box.

I explained. "If you have the money, you can retire in clover. Every resident gets the quarters from his or her favorite time of life. There are rumors that they live on only there, like a Virtual Reality personality."

Eddie shrugged. "Weird world."

"Yeah, the Retread Retreat. She probably won't look a day over this," I said, waving the photo.

"Sexy."

"That was then. We can't expect a woman living, er, residing, in a lakeside cottage at Sunset City to resemble any available photos of her salad days. She was a real star once, though, back in the days of the Silver Screen."

"So were we all, kiddo." Eddie snapped his gum and rolled his eyes back toward the TV studio. "Didya hear the latest on Undead Ted? He's had his incisors artificially lengthened. You know what they say about vamps: not enough fang, no wang."

Suddenly, I felt better.

Eddie loved gossip. Or maybe he just hated Ted. "I see Ready Teddy is getting into Witch Twitch. What a bimbo! So what's got you down?"

"It's personal."

"What? You got a life away from WTCH?"

AT HOME THAT NIGHT, I thought about Fast Eddie's mocking comment on having a life beyond WTCH. I stared into my faint reflection on the glass-topped coffee table. Achilles used to stretch out underneath it, dog under glass: safe, sleeping, and elegant in his wavy-haired, short-legged, sharp-toothed way.

The sight of myself on Dead TV still haunted me. I picked up my cell phone to dial one of my few female friends, a street-producer for *CSI Bismarck*.

"Hey! It's Del. Listen, Annie, I need a copy of the latest Vegas *CSI V* episode. Yeah, it was a live feed here in Wichita." Or a dead feed, to be precise. "No tapes available. I need the addresses of the producers and writers. Oh, just for a piece I'm working on. You know, always chasing the latest 'in' thing.

"You have a digital recording? Really? Fabulous! Sure. Just Fed Ex it. Overnight? Thanks, you're a doll."

Once I had the names and titles, my reporter self could call and find out what the hell was going on.

Figuring out what was going on in my dreams was another matter.

I didn't wake up the next morning with the usual nasty fragments floating around in my head. Instead, I had a vivid scene right out the *Wizard of Oz* movie.

I saw Achilles standing, wagging and waiting for me, on the yellow brick road. Only he was white instead of black like Toto, and the whole scene was black and white and gray, like the opening part of the film set in Kansas, not wildly Technicolor like the "merry old land of Oz" sections.

I looked down to sparkly sequined pumps on my feet. Black and to die for. Maybe I was going somewhere unexpected. Soon. But not into Dorothy's Oz. Someplace darker, a Wonderland all my own.

And Achilles was waiting for me somewhere out there.

CHAPTER SIX

"Can that piece." Fuck-up Freddy was standing by my desk at work, in blowsy mode with *The Front Page* shirtsleeves from the classic forties newspaper movie, a caricature in the flesh. The only thing missing was the green eyeshade and a garter on his flabby biceps.

"The old dame is dead," he said. "Pulled the plug on herself this morning. Cancelled the contract."

Oddly enough, I was sorry to hear that. "Maybe her death, the reason for it, is a story."

"Nah. The feature's name is 'Good Living After Death,' not 'Death After Death.' I need someone downtown to do a stand-up for a Cub Scout camp-out in the main park."

"That's about as exciting as filming an anthill."

"A good reporter can make a great story out of anything. Jeez, are you losing it, Street, or what?"

I DROVE HOME FROM THE STATION that night with a dopey new assignment sked riding shotgun on the passenger seat of the Caddy, just as Achilles' "documents" had accompanied me away from the vet's office.

It was beginning to feel like "loss" was my middle name. I had no other, anyway.

What more could go wrong?

I had not counted on the Revenge of the Weather Witch.

I had some trouble finding my bungalow on Moody Road. Because it wasn't there anymore.

I got out of the car, slammed the heavy door shut, and stared at the empty, aching socket of dirt where my house had been. All that was left was my refrigerator, lying on its massive metal side, looking like a heavy-metal porcupine.

I approached it over the lumpy ground strewn with toothpicks splintered from the wood and spine of my rental bungalow. It wasn't merely a rental. It was my first real home. It was a lost relative, and it was totally gone, sucked up into some passing tornado funnel.

Other houses of that era stood whole and sturdy on either side of it. My house was the only molar that had been pulled. Freak tornadoes, they were called. Unpredictable.

This one wasn't.

When you piss off a weather witch, she can make her wrath known.

My refrigerator lay there like a beached steel whale. Barnacled to its side was my metal clothes cabinet crammed with vintage duds and every last freaking piece of sterling silver I had ever collected at an estate or garage sale. Victorian fork tines bristled like WWII underwater mine prongs. Mexican jewelry draped the handles. Nineteen-twenties marcasite batted its steel eyelashes in the clear sunlight. The sky was blue, like my eyes; the clouds were white, like my skin. No black thunderclouds, like my wild Irish hair, appeared.

This was a very specific tornado.

At that moment a Fed Ex truck pulled up, white and gleaming in the sunlight. The tiny woman behind the wheel hopped down.

"Street residence?" she asked.

"What's left of it."

"Too bad! Was this house a tear-down?"

"Kinda."

"Sign here."

I did. She handed me a box stamped "Smokerise Farm" and a padded envelop large enough to hold a videotape and a newsy letter about Nightwine Productions from Annie in Bismarck.

I stood there, on the wind-blown prairie, contemplating my losses.

The fact was, my cup was overturned, but I wasn't. We were both half-full, and maybe the half-empty part wasn't worth keeping.

I had Achilles' ashes in a dragon vase and a lock of his hair in a silver Victorian locket. I had Dolly Parton, a running vintage car with 28,000 miles on it, mean-looking fins, and chrome bumper bullets the size of—Well, you know Dolly: talent, guts, and up-front plastic surgery. I had some money in the bank. I had a smattering of borrowed glitz and an empty refrigerator. And I had a shockingly large number of pretty, prickly Victorian sterling flatware sharp enough to function as martial arts throwing stars.

I was taking them all to Las Vegas, where they carved up way-too-familiar corpses on *CSI* and where a writer-producer named Hector Nightwine had a lot of explaining to do. Never trust a man with hyphenated job title. Or artificially extended fangs. Or both.

And I wasn't leaving Sin City until I knew . . . who I am. Or who I am not.

CHAPTER SEVEN

Dolly and I were stopped at a gas pump somewhere off of Interstate 70 in Colorado, where the whole world was trees and sun-sparkled creeks that shadowed the highway curves. The state also offered long, lonesome stretches with towns so sparse that a girl had to pee by a backcountry gravel roadside if she missed a freeway rest stop.

In the cities, you could get by driving all-electric or electric-gas hybrids, plug in at home and refuel at sleek, almost odorless ranks of compressed-gas dispensing stations. Vintage car enthusiasts operated all-gasoline throwbacks like Dolly for an extra fee or for free if you were poor enough. But out here in the boonies all you could get was pungent, pricey gasoline in old-fashioned pumps. You still couldn't beat fossil fuel for distance driving. And no farmer would run a hybrid tractor.

This shabby retro gas station (*Deliverance* West) had rest rooms, but I didn't like the look of the grinning yokels in the Ford 350 across the concrete island from me. Since I'd been on the road two days from Wichita I'd learned that guys with super-charged pickups were aggressive on the highway. On solid ground they were as untrustworthy as vamps with artificially extended fangs.

"Hey! We can help you with that great big hose, little lady."

That taunting, pseudo-friendly threat gave me the same cold internal paralysis I felt at the orphanage when the older boys cornered me in a deserted hallway: against the wall, on my own, needing to bluff and bully my way out of the trap. Sweat prickled my scalp and sopped my palms. Despite all the time I'd spent on a workout mat in college, learning self-defense, the instant purgative spasms of visceral fear never retreated one step.

And I couldn't either. Surprise was my shadow partner. So was bluff. I eyed them, then cocked the nozzle on the gas pump over my shoulder, like an Uzi.

"You've got it all wrong, boys. I'm not little. I'm not a lady. And the help you need with y*our* hoses is something you should consult a plastic surgeon about."

They took about ninety seconds to decipher my comment. By then I was topping off the tank and not concerned about milking every drop from the nozzle, despite the highway robbery price of gas. Just get me outa here, Exxon, with no untidy oil spills. Particularly mine.

The mountain men's bearded faces were finally falling as their grins grew feral.

"We seen ya on TV. Looked mighty good nekkid. Come on, Maggie doll, let us show you a real good time."

Nekkid? What lame dialogue! And who the heck was Maggie? Not me!

They were right about one thing. This little lady needed to hop into her driver's seat and hit all the door locks. But one man had vaulted around the pumps and was blocking the driver's side door. The other had penned me in at the car's rear.

One thing about growing up vamp bait in an orphanage where bullying is the house rule: you learn how to think on your feet if you don't want to be someone else's steak tartare.

I glanced at the combo pay-and-junk-food shack. Anybody remotely human inside had ducked out the back.

So I pulled the pump trigger and wasted ten bucks of Premium Unleaded dousing my helpful dudes from their shirtless overalls to their matching roadmaps of prison tattoos. My heart was pumping harder than the gas and my palms grew suddenly damp on the cool steel.

Bravado was one thing. These guys were brawny and stupid, a fatal combination.

"See this metal nozzle, fellas? I'm gonna turn it into a matchstick by striking it on the concrete in two seconds flat. You'll both look good as holiday sparklers. Give my regards to George M. Cohan."

They were so busy frowning at my mysterious vintage reference I thought their eyebrows would break their own noses. But their narrow eyes, light-colored and totally human, were still blinking with the dim primal urge to rape and pillage.

I sent the gas hose hissing at the guy by my left front fender, and when he naturally backed up, I leaped forward and swung the heavy Detroit-steel door hard into his torso.

His screaming *oooof* got me into the driver's seat. I hit the locks, turned the key, and reversed hard. The dangling hose I'd abandoned swung like a pendulum, its metal head striking sparks on the concrete island.

I backed the other guy off my rear bumper and gunned out of the station onto the access road, then onto the entry ramp, and floored it. It was oddly fitting that I aced an oncoming gasoline tanker into the right-hand freeway lane.

If Achilles had been with me in physical form, he would have taken those yahoos off at the knees. Now his ashes rode shotgun in the back seat, my ghostly talisman.

What was the matter with those warped bad ole boys? Calling me Maggie! Must have been serious Rod Stewart fans. Right. Of course the rocker was still at it, though, delivering greatest hits on stage. It wasn't clear if he was part clone, part hologram, all plastic surgery, or some entirely new hybrid of the Immortality Mob's busy marketing schemes.

My hands trembled on the pizza-size steering wheel but Dolly's alignment was rock steady. You could find these frozen-in-time steel cream puffs that'd been bought but lightly driven and stored in barns or garages for forty or fifty years at estate sales if you got lucky. Gas guzzlers, yeah, but horsepower enough to tow a Titan missile.

We sped at a sedate six miles over the speed limit toward Las Vegas. No motorcycle cop stops this ole girl. Who can you trust in this wicked world? No one.

Whenever I spotted a white Ford 350 in my rear-view mirror for the next one hundred miles, my hands went white-knuckled on the steering wheel. That attack had felt weirdly personal, and I didn't know those bozos from Adam or his firstborn.

Chapter Eight

My remaining possessions were in storage in Wichita, so I drove into Las Vegas with what was on my back and in the back of my car: laptop computer, my sterling silver collection courtesy of Frigidaire, Achilles' ashes. The trunk was large enough to hold a living room suite or about six dead bodies, so both my regular and vintage clothes had made the drive with me.

Luckily, the southern Las Vegas Strip fringes still support some low-end lodging. The Araby Motel decor was mock-1001 Nights and obviously functioned more as an oasis for quickies both paid and unpaid and had hourly rates as well as nightly, weekly and monthly. I took a room for a week. I'm usually an optimist. This was just a landing spot while I got the lay of the land.

Within forty-eight hours I discovered this glitzy adult entertainment theme park was seriously bipolar. Days were sun-baked and sweaty, but nights were dark and balmy under a blitz of dazzling light shows.

This was not Kansas anymore. Gone was the green and gold landscape surmounted by blazing blue sky. Instead, Las Vegas was the world's biggest velvet painting, all dark of night lit up by neon pinks, blues, yellows, greens, reds, and purples. Its daytime sunlit face seemed dull, a little sleazy, and oddly lifeless despite the crowds gushing like tides in and out of Strip hotel-casinos.

What had been Vegas landmarks at the turn of the Millennium—The New York, New York faux skyscraper silhouette, the half-size Eiffel Tower—were barely visible today. Even the concrete-needle condo towers that began sprouting in 2006 were mere dull gray exclamation points in a cityscape that sizzled, literally. The roar of the MGM Grand's golden gate-keeping lion and the Mirage's volcano were lost in the flame-throwing torrents that washed down and spouted up from the new generation hotel-casinos like the Gehenna and the Inferno, whose swooping architecture looked chillingly organic.

My target was not the Strip's new hellfire glory. The street map I'd bought at Sam's Town on the way in almost covered the chintzy bedspread of my Araby Motel room. Yes, a fold-out paper map. It provided the detailed overview I needed. The Araby still had rotary phones, a wireless connection was out of the realm of the possible.

Nightwine Productions took up a whole block of Sunset Road, opposite Sunset Park. Sunset Park . . . Sunset City. Maybe the word "sunset" was a good omen.

At least I was out of the Araby Motel's damp and tepid air-conditioning by four that afternoon, just when the afternoon sun was at its most blistering. The 60 SPF sunscreen lay on my skin like heavy cold cream. I'd tried calling Nightwine productions but had given up on explaining my mission after encountering an endless menu of options all inappropriate to talking to a human being. It was high time I was off to see the wizard in person.

Sunset Park boasted a lot of what Las Vegas has little of: trees shading a walkway meandering around a small, central lake. Plaques near the trees dedicated them to deceased loved ones. So Sunset Park was a memorial garden, if not an outright graveyard.

Farther back around the lake my shoes oozed into marshy ground sprouting grasses tall enough to mask hidden lurkers, or dead bodies. Walt Whitman had

called grass the "green hair of graves" and back here I
could believe it. This swamp-grass jungle you couldn't
see past, or be seen in, recalled the creepy reeds where
black-clad Victorian ghosts as solid as ebony tombstones
appeared in an old movie that had scared the heck out of
me. When I was a kid, those distant, formal, thoroughly
solid phantoms had terrified me more than all the gouts of
blood 'n' guts in teen slasher pics.

Now that chilling memory drove me back to the trees
dedicated to the dead, which seemed more normal.
From there I had a Realtor's eye-view of the Nightwine
headquarters on Sunset Road, a nice, noirish address
for a TV production company specializing in criminal
forensics. All it needed to be a Sunset Boulevard was a
nice, classic filmland murder.

More than a house or an office, it was a sprawling
walled estate occupying a full city block, not far from
Wayne Newton's spread, Shenandoah, on the same street.
Newton's place was unforgettable for the life-size 3-D
bronze sculpture of horses galloping out of the wall onto
a grassy corner area. (Newton was a noted horse rancher
as well as a headlining Vegas vocalist and had looked
preserved in something even before the Millennium
Revelation.)

I wondered what Hector Nightwine was as I studied the
façade of his encompassing, stay-out wall. Obviously a
man with a sense of humor, or hubris. The larger-than-life-
size sculpture galloping out of *his* wall was . . .were . . . the
Four Horsemen of the Apocalypse. You could almost
hear those armored, crushing steel steeds snorting. The
ghoulish berserker warriors on their backs representing
War, Famine, Pestilence, and Death bristled with enough
broad-axes, swords, and pikes to quell a riot.

I crossed the boulevard, darting between traffic, to eye
the scrolled-iron gate blocking the driveway. That's all

there was. No foot approach. I retreated back to the park to sit on a shaded bench and plan my attack on Nightwine's castle, obviously his home as well as his office.

I'd made sure to dress in my respectable investigative reporter gear: conservative blazer, blouse, and skirt. No checks or prints to give the camera's eye double vision. Everyone else around me was casually dressed in shorts and sandals and tees.

Except one.

I caught the gold glint of cufflinks on French cuffs. Custom-made silk-blend white shirt. Cream summer-weight wool-silk pants, knife-edge pressed, also expensive. A silk tie as smoothly blue as the cloudless sky, barely loosened at the collar. A suit jacket draped over the corner of a picnic table. Everything fit for a Fortune 500 executive in a boardroom, except the slim gold herringbone belt that curled around his narrow hips like a luxurious snake.

I took all this in within two seconds. Instant observation is a reporter's first line of offense. The expensive clothes played off a dark olive complexion too smooth to be a tan. His long-fingered hands incongruously held a small dead branch from one of the nearby trees, which he was showing to three young black children dressed in rainbow colors.

Their mother, thirtyish black velvet in Queen Latifah duds, relaxed at the concrete picnic table's other end, watching the man, and I could sure see why. His strong narrow Hispanic features had an aristocratic grace, as did the relaxed length of him.

It was easy to ogle him. All his attention was on the youngsters, who were jumping up and down around him, yelling "me first." That phrase had been so common at the orphanage it still put me off. I'd never crowded forward to beg for anything, even attention. They said I was distant,

a loner, but it got me through better than vying for beta
spots against the alpha toughs who ran the secret gangs
institutional life spawns.

A pig-tailed six-year-old girl in pink and lime-green
won the prize first: strutting over the grass, the Y-shaped
twig in her hands like bicycle handlebars, or as if she
were pushing an invisible lawn mower. Mr. White-collar
Coolio walked right behind, smiling and encouraging her,
the two older boys trailing them. Curiouser and curiouser.
I wished I had a videographer with me. They made a
pretty, contrasting picture: corporate Pied Piper leads
urban kids. Something resonated with me that made my
throat tighten. Prince Charming was focusing on the kids
with genuine interest and obvious enjoyment. When the
girl stopped to bound up and down in frustration, he bent
over her, put his fingertips just ahead of her beautiful dark
little hands on the sticks and they walked on together.

The girl squealed with joy and triumph as the bottom of
the Y-shaped twig jerked down at the grass. Oh. Dowsing
for water.

In Las Vegas? Except for cultivated water, like man-
made Lake Mead behind Hoover Dam, and this picture-
book lake, or sprinkler systems, it must all be desert under
the well-watered grass.

I watched the man waltz the two young boys around the
same territory, where each one "dowsed" successfully in
the same spot once he added his own touch to the process.
They were too young to realize they were all "discovering"
the same "well." Probably a buried sprinkler head.

The Millennium Revelation had indeed proved Hamlet
right that "there are more things in heaven and on earth
than are dreamed of"—including a large dose of Hell that
would have really bummed out the Melancholy Dane. But
some superstitious water dowsing wasn't among them.
We had weather witches in Kansas who could play a lot

of tricks with rain, wind, and fire, so why bother dowsing
for water? It was a pre-Millennium Revelation cheat and
outmoded anyway.

The guy, another under-thirty, surely, returned his
gullible little friends to a very grateful mama, plucked his
jacket off the picnic table, slung it over one shoulder, then
looked right at me.

The tables had turned so fast that I couldn't pretend to
be glancing away. And he was coming straight for me over
the grass on those braided leather Italian shoes anyway.

CHAPTER NINE

"You're a skeptic," he said.

"Um, yes. It's a fun game for the kids, but water dowsing is small stuff nowadays."

"Giving children attention and a sense of accomplishment isn't small stuff." His look was corrective and cool.

What an arrogant twit! Although I'd just been touched by his ease with the kids, it obviously didn't translate to adults.

"No," I answered, "but making them think they can find underground water with Witch-Hazel's twig is deceiving them to make yourself look good." I'd been deceived a lot in my childhood, and still resented it.

He lifted the twig, which I hadn't seen him holding at his side. It was slender and rough-barked.

"Mesquite?" I scoffed. "Doesn't it have to be willow?"

"Willow is traditional but not essential. I can dowse with anything that has three legs. A wood twig. A re-formed wire hanger. A midget with a hard-on."

My shock couldn't help coming out as a laugh. His mouth was unsmiling but his dark eyes glinted with humor and challenge. "Why don't you try it? You might have the gift."

"I doubt it. I don't have a gift for anything but my work."

He shrugged and held out the stupid stick.

I stood and took it. It'd been . . . oh, fifteen years since I'd touched a dead stick, probably to prod an icky bug out of my path.

"All right. What do I do? Walk around with the two branches in my hands and the third one pointed dead-ahead like—" Well, I wasn't going to say what it was pointed straight out like.

"Right."

Only then did I realize that he had no accent to go with the sleek Latin looks.

"Watch my purse," I ordered, and began circling aimlessly over the grass, "driving" a featherweight twig ahead of me. I went to where each child had jumped for joy, and then paused. "This is the place, isn't it? The sure-thing spot?"

He had perched on the picnic table to watch me. "That's the spot. You're an ace detective."

"I'm an investigator, but not that kind."

"Don't tell me: you investigate fraudulent phenomena."

"Sometimes. See? Nothing's here. Nothing's happened."

"That's because I'm not there."

I was thinking that might be a shame but it didn't prove anything.

He got up, draping his jacket over my purse so it wasn't thief-bait, and came up behind me. Then he put his arms around me, but not close, and touched both thumbs and forefingers to the twig in front of my curled fists. The touch brushed my knuckles, no heavier than a butterfly lighting on my skin.

The slim branches in my palms swiveled fast enough to give me an Indian burn. The third branch jerked down as if drawn by an invisible hand, one that could pull as hard as a Great Dane on a leash. It pointed straight down at the ground.

"*Ohmigod!*"

"You did feel that?" he asked.

"Oh, yeah." I had. Along with a peculiar sharpening of all my senses, particularly smell, like the sun-lit ironed odor of his shirt enveloping me, the damp mossy perfume of grass under my feet, a musky citrus odor of men's cologne at my back. My own slightly acrid sweat from the warm day.

I stepped away from him and his soft touch and scents. The powerful pull against the twig wilted in my hands.

"You found this spot before," I pointed out. "It does this sort of thing. Maybe the minerals in the ground are a certain blend here. Maybe there's iron in the fertilizer for the trees. Something chemical."

"So you do believe in chemistry?"

I didn't miss the double entrendre. My hard-nosed skepticism only amused him.

He was watching me with a faint smile, as benign as the one he'd shown the kids but more prickly, more prodding. I glimpsed the sliver of white teeth between his well-arched lips. Maybe he was a daylight vamp; some could "pass" as human if you didn't look too close, like Undead Ted. Vamps were always drawn to my Black Irish pallor and I hated that, like the girl in the old ballad who wanted to be loved for more than her yellow hair alone.

He glanced down at the grass. "You think this spot is a 'plant.' Tell you what. Take the twig somewhere else, wherever you want to go."

"What'll that prove?"

"I'll bring up the rear and try my talented touch every now and then."

"You seem pretty confident there'll be more 'water' around here. What's the source? The lake?"

"It began as a pond that overflowed a spring, but the water table dried up decades ago. It's all desert now, so the city manufactured this model."

"Including the Easter Island head on the islet in the center?"

"Yup. Grotesque, isn't it? Just one seems lonesome."

"So there are still remnants of the original spring under the land, you're telling me?"

He smiled mysteriously and shrugged again, his shoulders broad under the crisp-collared silken shirt, his hips narrow under that discreet snake of a gold belt that whispered "sexy" to my observer's eagle eye.

Maybe he wasn't a vamp. They couldn't keep their eyes off my neck and wrists, and he was totally focused on my eyes, on my mind. Which in a way was even scarier.

I grabbed the silly twig again, my palms still smarting from the first strike, and began weaving over the grass in an opposite direction. The late-day crowd was melting away. Distant reeds cast stilettos of shadow as the sun weltered red and swollen behind them.

I actually tried to clear my mind and believe that I could find water, that the stick would perform for me, for my touch alone. Say you believe in fairies and Tinker Bell, or Peter Pan, will live.

He followed me, but I felt nothing and the twig was unimpressed by my custody too. After a couple minutes he came up behind me, his fingers pausing on mine.

Not a bad feeling. Attractive guy, late twenties, no rings, successful professional and kind to kids, which was a huge plus in my rating system. Smelled good. Felt good. No evident fangs. Was this just a come-on scheme? my inner cynical reporter wondered. Was I falling for another load of—? Then his fingers moved past me to the wooden Y.

I gasped. *Bingo!* The branches in my hands pulled down harder than a twenty-mule team. My palms breathed fire as his fingertip touch became hands fully tightened over mine. We were being sucked into the ground by a hurricane-level force, my braced feet and his barely keeping us upright.

The day had gone dark, at first at the edges of my vision and now all the way to the center. Nothing to see but lightning flashing right around us.

"Hold on!" he shouted in my ear. Maybe he whispered and it only sounded like a shout to my instantly raw nerves. The words evaporated into a whirlwind. On either side of me his arms felt like muscle-roped iron, the only things holding me to this ground, this reality. This earth.

I grew clammy all over remembering my alien abduction dreams. This felt like the same endless, unanchored moment. I could feel my knuckles threatening to pop through my skin and my fingernails cutting into my palms, but I couldn't release the rods of acid fire between my hands.

And then a deep interior rush of indescribable pleasure swooped between my legs and up my center to some sweet spot that melded the physical and mental. The sensation swept mind and senses away into a secret sensual place that wasn't anywhere I recognized, not in my wildest dreams. Yet I was there. Light teased the darkness, flashing like a strobe on bare limbs. Male. Female. Albino snakes entwining in a black pit. It took me a moment to see four legs, four arms making the beast with two backs. Two sexes.

If these were ghosts, they were carnal ones. Sighs, guttural cries, fevered panting, moans, expressing either pleasure or pain, or both, entwined in some deadly dance of desire.

For I also heard grunts, screams, felt the thud of club on bone, the impact of hot metal on muscle and tissue. The albino snakes in my mind, at my fingertips, were now running red with blood. I was watching a savagely cut film, splicing love with death, desire with destruction. If this was death I witnessed, it was the death of a thousand blows and caresses and cuts and kisses.

Too much. More than I could withstand, a theme park ride into a horror movie. I wanted off. Out. Away. Out of the dream, the nightmare. I screamed into the violent darkness . . . and woke up silent, my head thrust back to howl but no sound coming out.

Ahead of me the setting sun was gilding the trees and the lake water. Ducks and geese and one toy sailboat skimmed the glassy surface, creating sandlike ripples. The Easter Island head shone like solid gold in front of its guardian palm fronds. Sunny afternoon had become twilight.

Was I alarmed, like I should have been? No. I lingered in a languid dreamy state, as if drugged. The afterglow of the light saber of sensation that had pierced my core reminded me of a divining rod finding and reaching its central element, the spot where earth met underworld, search met find, my spot, the mythical G-spot maybe.

The violence I'd glimpsed faded under that sense of fruition, of having finally made it to something untouched within myself.

Then I remembered that self, the one who wanted into Hector Nightwine's establishment so badly. The one who was now wrapped in a stranger's arms, my head leaning into his shoulder and chin, my body leaning back against something else. . . .

I spun around, away, so that we were facing each other.

The dowser was looking as dazed and embarrassed as I felt, thank God. His rich cocoa-colored skin had an ashy undertone. Tiny beads of sweat swept across his forehead, catching the twilight like a diadem.

He looked . . . dazzling. Like a fairyland lord come to take me away. From the electricity I'd felt between us, I was ready to go anywhere.

Girl, get over it! urged my inner best friend, Irma. She often came to me after nightmares. Sometimes she was an eighties housewife humorist like Erma Bombeck, but today she was a pert Shirley MacLaine French tart from a sixties film, *Irma la Douce*. Cable TV kept all the oldies but goodies alive. *He's a park pick-up. Cute, but what's with the magic water wand bit? Some sort of scam. Some pick-up shtick. Get your shit together.*

Irma was trying to shake me out of this bizarre state I was in. I felt like I'd been struck dumb by a lightning bolt of sex and death. And I felt another new overwhelming feeling. Satisfaction. Wow, this was weird.

Someone had to speak. Usually the girl was good at making awkward conversational transitions. Usually she felt that responsibility, anyway.

"Um," I heard myself say, "do you always go *up* when the dowsing rod goes *down*?"

What had I said? Irma? Was that you, you brassy flirt? Or was it the bolt of sheer sexual energy that had surged up from the ground to his dowsing rod and through my hands into his fingertips?

He stepped away and back. His dusky face reddened in the fading sunlight.

Even while I wanted to clap a hand over my suddenly sexy mouth, I realized that I liked that. His reticence. I wasn't normally this up-front. I didn't know what had gotten into me.

"It's getting late." He sounded as flustered as I did.

He reached into a pants pocket, but not for the car keys I expected. He reached in a thumb and pulled out a . . . golf ball marker.

Then he looked at the sunset, then east to a line of small trees, all neatly labeled with dead people's names, and finally past me to the Easter Island head.

He bent to impale the small object in the thick grass between us.

"What are you doing?"

"It's for my work."

"Then there really is water under this spot? I found it? Are you a landscape architect or something?"

He smiled, distracted. "You could call it that." Then he looked at me, hard, a question in his eyes. "Here's my business card, by the way."

In the descending dusk, I could barely read the embossed gold lettering on the heavy linen paper: RIC MONTOYA, CONSULTANT. An office address was followed by several phone numbers and an email address.

I walked away on shaky legs, planning to put the card in my purse on the deserted bench. *My purse!* Someone could have taken it while I was dallying with a dowser!

"Let me get that." He lifted his jacket from the picnic bench before I could. While I was checking my purse for signs of rifling, he pulled a small black object from his jacket side pocket. "Portable alarm. If anyone had moved my jacket it would have gone off. You haven't been robbed."

"Oh. What a relief! I'm new in town and all my ID, my credit card info, Social Security number—"

"It's okay." He rested a calming hand on my wrist, but I jerked away as if burned.

"Sorry," I said. "I'm getting a terrible headache. I guess I panicked."

"May I have your phone number, Miss—?" The sunset-gilded pen he produced like a magic wand shone, liquid lava in his dark hand, against his luminous white shirt cuff.

I seemed to be seeing everything in intensified colors, the sunset bathing us in an amber-orange glow, the grass darkening to emerald.

"Miss—?" he repeated.

Dummy. Speak!

"Street." I decided to skip the Delilah part. He looked like the kind of Latin lover who'd call you "Miss" while he was unzipping your skirt. A gigolo maybe. Was I thinking this because he was so attractive? "I never remember my own number," I said, stuttering a little. "Let me look at my phone . . ."

Girlfriend, get a hold of yourself, urged Irma. *He's probably straight both ways, gender and species, and you two have obviously got some heavy-metal chemistry going.*

I found the cell, punched "My phone #," and read it off, watching Ric Montoya, consultant (*on what?*), punch it into his own phone. Twilight had edged into dark by the time he escorted me to the curb and opened the door of my queen-size black Caddy with the red leather interior and white convertible top.

"A lot of car," he noted, surprised and intrigued by Dolly. What guy wouldn't be? "Should I follow you home?"

"No, I'm fine. It's just this sudden headache."

All I could see of him now was luminous splashes of white: that supernaturally white shirtfront, his flashing teeth and eyes. The lights inside my head were lurid red and green and blue.

"I'll call," were his last words.

Yeah. The elusive single male's familiar dating and mating call, cited in many animal behavior books.

And I'll see.

He will, girlfriend. I feel it in my bones.

Irma was playing Marie LaVeau now, the infamous New Orleans Voodoo priestess. That was the nice thing about having an inner girlfriend since before puberty; she could be multicultural.

I drove away with a pounding head, not even noticing where Ric Montoya had gone. But I had his number. Literally. Hooking up with a "just normal" guy would be great for a change.

Between the pulsing of every blood vessel in my head and trying to remember my way back to the Araby Motel in the dark, I didn't notice anything different about me until I felt a telltale warm trickle between my legs.

Shit! I was either having my period off-schedule, which would be weird because I'd been on the Pill forever to control killer cramps, or I was really, really into Ric Montoya. Or vice versa.

Or maybe both, if they didn't cancel each other out.

Oh, joy.

CHAPTER TEN

I woke up the next day and checked the Araby Motel's scratchy sheets first thing.

My panties had passed the period test last night. No blood. My dreams had been vaguely gory, sometimes a prelude to my periods, but the sheets passed too.

No "virginal" spot of blood, m'Lord. She is fit to marry a King. Of course she could just be pregnant . . .

I sighed, trying to come to grips with my sudden new Sunset Park side: sexy chick.

I'd always tried to act like a hip modern girl, especially once I'd got out into the working world, but sometimes I thought I was an oddball escapee from some forgotten fairy tale. I didn't remember a lot about my "wonder" years when things like hormones and periods and what guys might want appeared on the horizon.

Any shrink could tell you that never being adopted might lead to self-esteem issues. On top of that, my vamp-attracting coloring meant I'd had to stand up solo and secretly to the older bad boys who kept recycling back to the orphanage from foster home after foster home. All of them had long tails of initials in their case files, and half of them were OOW (out-of-wedlock) unwanted half-vampire spawn.

Every jaunt in and out of the institution just made them nastier.

Our Lady of the Lake convent school was a relief in getting away from the bad boys, being a girls' school, but the other students all had homes and families and their own venom-tongued ways of tormenting someone different.

By the time I hit college, working like a stevedore to earn living expenses, a social life was an afterthought. Somewhere, sometime after my institutional stays, I had the impression that I was no longer a virgin, in terms of not bleeding if you pricked me. Imagine how the fairy tale would have gone if Sleeping Beauty *couldn't* bleed? But I didn't remember when or how or who. Or what.

I also didn't remember a couple of heavy drinking college parties very well either. Maybe then. Whatever had happened, if it had, I came out of it with memory loss, nightmares, and such an aversion to vampire lunges and to lying on my back that the dentist had to work on me sitting up.

During my last year at the group home, my dreams of a humiliating and terrifying "alien abduction" pelvic exam began, mixed up with vamp boy attacks. That drove me in high school to the underground drug sellers for the "others." A lot of teen female werewolves had period difficulties during their "change," and I could get the Pill without a prescription or a pelvic, since many doctors still wouldn't treat supernaturals. No one ever questioned my supernatural credentials. They were selling meds like street drugs. Besides, who would want to masquerade as an outcast? All this shady rigmarole to get the Pill made me feel neurotic and squeamish and childish. From what I'd heard, women my age had abortions with less angst than I produced for a P.E.

So it wasn't that I didn't want male company or affection or that I didn't dream that someday my prince would come. It's that the dreams I remembered were always of a huge pale stingray hanging over me. I couldn't breathe . . . was I underwater? Being held underwater? *Being held down*? A lot of working women had that dream. The stingray's flaccid white wings were arched and veined like a bat's, and became a black shadow above me, diving down, smothering me.

So I had some sexual hang-ups. My mind veered away whenever my thoughts wandered too close to the mystery. But it wasn't rape. I'd never thought that was my problem. That nail file had done the job.

It was even harder to veer away from my old edgy emotions and fears now, after feeling that bolt of earthy energy from the ground under my feet, from the man behind me, whose hands in front of mine had tapped into all that subterranean sexuality.

Maybe my prince had come.

Literally.

So the good news at this point was that my sudden sogginess wasn't my usually predictable period after all. The bad news was that I'd never had much luck playing well with men and I might be heading for another major disappointment. At least my über-headache was gone and I didn't remember dreams of any kind from last night whatsoever. Round one to Ric Montoya. Too bad I didn't have time to moon over him a little.

I had a lot of other things to do, Hector Nightwine still looming number one on my A-list. I'd come back from the breakfast buffet at the Lotsa-Slotsa-Fun on this gentrification-doomed low-end part of the Strip when my phone rang at 11:00 AM on the dot.

My first phone call in Vegas! I let it ring two more times for sheer pleasure before I panicked and flipped it open. In the meantime I fantasized that Hector Nightwine's secretary . . . a male secretary named Niven . . . was on the line begging me to see his boss. *Hmmm*, my fantasies were definitely perking up.

"Hello."

"Good morning. It's Ric."

Number two. Not bad.

"Ye-es?" I'd never turned one word into two with that little purring note in my voice. *Get it together, girl!* Irma nagged me.

"I'm back in the park." *And* he gave great phone voice.

"Oh." Was it going to be *their* place?

"I wondered if you could come over before noon."

Hmm. Charming hot-dog-stand lunch in the park. Feeding bun breadcrumbs to the ducks. Settling down at "their" picnic table. Arranging something more formal. Dinner perhaps. Plus I could keep an eye on Hector's place and maybe figure out how to storm the palace somehow.

"Sure."

No, girlfriend! Hard to get.

Too late.

That is no way you play a hot guy, a fashion stud right out of GQ, *honey.*

I gagged my inner girlfriend. Sometimes she is way too shallow.

Ric seemed a serious guy underneath the high-end accessories. He obviously believed he could dowse for water, and . . . maybe he could. I have an open mind. But maybe I'd better consider wearing a Lite Days pad if we're rendezvousing in the park again. Those dowsing rod visions seemed to have touched something in me nothing, or no one, ever had before.

Still, visions of sedate sugarplums danced in my convent-bred head. A stroll, maybe an ice cream cone for dessert in the desert. Something sweet, mundane, and old-fashioned. Pure Kansas corn.

I PARKED DOLLY in a lot off Sunset Road and walked back to the area where I'd met Ric. It's a huge park, with tennis and golfing areas, but I kept bearing west until I spied

Kon Tiki (my nickname for Mr. Easter Island head). He got me near where I needed to be.

I stop, bemused. There is a dreamlike quality to the scene I walk into slowly. Time slows down like lazy molasses.

The park right here is teeming with busy men in suits and buff uniformed cops in buff-colored uniforms: Bermuda shorts and short-sleeved shirts that showcase tanned biceps and quads. The air buzzes with walkie-talkie communications. Chrome yellow CRIME SCENE: DO NOT CROSS tape wraps several of the dead-dedicated trees, cordoning off a pizza-pie-shaped slice of the open ground.

A chill runs up my spine when I triangulate between the reeds on the west, Kon Tiki's dour face on the lake's central island, and Sunset Road. This is "our" place and suddenly, this summer, it is verboten to anyone not among the city's law enforcement crowd.

"'Scuse me, miss." Officer Buff is looming beside me. "This area is off-limits to the public."

Luckily I'm stunned into silence long enough for an equally authoritative voice behind me to announce, "Miss Street is with me."

Ric Montoya is standing behind me. As has become usual for us. His designer sunglasses with their titanium frames only enhance his strong cheekbones, aristocratic nose, knife-edge jaw. He is still just as good-looking, just as professional, and he is eyeing me like I am a ten of clubs in a game of Twenty-One. Keep or fold?

"What's going on here?" I ask when Officer Buff has withdrawn in a state of high grouch. I know his type. Works out, hits the tanning beds, and thinks he's the cat's pajamas. Likes to pull over helpless women on a pretext, and if they're young and alone, screw them.

"Something I thought you should see," Ric says.

I eye the Crime Scene tape. I've been here before, at crime scenes in Kansas, with a camera crew. But not after melting down the previous evening on this very spot.

"I know it'll be hard." Ric is standing very close to me, face-to-face this time, his fingertips on my elbows. He has excellent fingertip technique no matter the occasion. "I know you saw something . . . awful. I felt that too. You need to see what's really there."

"I do?"

He leans away, stung. "No, you're right. *I* do. Maybe *we* do. I won't let go of you."

How many women have dreamed of hearing that from the right guy? But I know how he means it. Literally. He won't let go of me. We'll be linked. In touch. And he knows what this is about.

I nod. I'm a tough girl. I've seen dead people before.

Ric leads us to the tape, where we're questioned again. Ric flashes an ID. "The captain okayed it."

"You maybe. Her too?"

"A new associate, Miss Street."

The middle-aged officer is all on-duty starch. I could be a naked Madonna impersonator and he wouldn't blink an eye. "Go ahead."

We duck under the familiar yellow plastic ribbon, not attached to an old oak tree but to small pine and ash trees. Out-of-the-blue songs are running through my mind, the windmills in my mind. Interior distraction for what I might be seeing all too soon.

Ric leads me to where we stood together only last twilight. There is now an actual pit, larger than a bread box; say the size of a grave site, all the better to accommodate the CSI crew kneeling around the revealed centerpiece. This is a pair of interlocked skeletons lying in a tomb of desiccated limestone. A hard night's digging work. Someone really wanted them six feet under.

The skeletons seem blissful, even rapturous, unaware of their gruesome state, or even of when death came. Grinning skulls face each other in profile, all the teeth in place, as clean and even as pearl bangles. The spines and ribs are collapsed, but the arm bones intertwine, and the large leg bones tangle with each other forming a horizontal ladder. It's hard for a civilian like me to discern the finger and foot bones, but something about the pair's cuddling position, now eternal, screams young lovers.

When you're about to faint it's just like in those movie special-effects sequences. You stay fixed in place and the foreground is rushing away from your senses as if you were on a departing French super-train. *Zoom.*

Because I now find myself hit with a rerun of the exact visceral blend of high-impact sex and death I'd felt yesterday afternoon. These dry bones, so sedate now, are the writhing, naked, ultimately blood-soaked limbs of the coupling couple of my vision.

"Male and female," I mutter at Ric.

"Good. What else?"

"Passion and death."

"Is it ever different?"

I ignore his cynicism, too busy tapping my own.

"Murder."

His hands tighten on my upper arms.

I frown. "Old."

"Old? Who?"

"Old. Just old. Believe me, I know old!"

He stands behind me like a wall, his fingertips reading the tremors of my nerves and skin.

"Thanks," Ric says. "Don't say anything. The lead detective is coming. He'll be a pain. Let me answer."

"I speak for myself."

"When you know the ground."

"These are my . . . corpses."

"Mine too. *Shhh*. Delilah." He whispers in my ear. Touches it with the tip of his tongue.

Well, that worked. I am pretty much speechless. How did he know my first name? How did he know how to shut me up?

The plainclothes man swaggers over, dripping dislike. I can see why. He is short, squat, vampire-pale without any of the mystique that goes with a professional bloodsucker.

"If it ain't the Cadaver Kid again," he says to Ric. "I heard you were nosing around, Montoya." The voice is grating, egotistical, and, my very favorite thing to go after with a nail file, bullying.

"Detective Haskell." Ric's voice sounds icy but I can sense he is super hot under that cool white collar. I'm suddenly very attuned to what's under that cool white collar. "The captain likes me to eyeball these crime scenes. And I did call it in."

"You. Not your little casino luck-piece tootsie."

I stiffen as much as Ric had done on me yesterday. His hands clamp like handcuffs on my arms, a dislocated gag, but I get the message.

"Miss Street is a fellow professional," he says, smooth as variated tinted glass in a 24-carat gold-accented frame. "An associate."

"And what's your specialty, sister? Knee-work?"

I tear loose of Ric and round on the Lieutenant. He's middle-aged, middle-gutted, middling-haired; every position-loving, not-very-sharp man who likes to throw his considerable weight around instead of doing his job.

I draw on all the interviews I've done with women in law enforcement.

"Quantico didn't think so, Lieutenant, when I took their serial killer workshop with John Douglas. Granted this is all theoretical and speculative compared to what

you might dig up from beat work, but you have male/
female vics here, you have major trauma to the remaining
bones, which indicates an ultra-violent—and bizarrely
controlled—end. You have *coitus interruptus*, which
guarantees a textbook-sick perp, and you have very old
bones, which means a very . . . cold . . . case."

The guy stands paralyzed.

"Remind me," Ric murmurs in my same damn
oversensitive ear, "to forget about getting a pit bull."

"So you're FBI too," Detective Haskell says. "*Ex*-FBI
like our Meskin friend here?"

At first I don't get the word, "Meskin," but Ric's fingers
digging into my upper arms allow me to translate it, pronto.

"Right," I say. Claiming to be ex-FBI gives me much
more status than admitting to being a reporter. An ex-
reporter. "And I didn't quite get what you just said."

Haskell doesn't bother to translate. He just eyes Ric
with an ugly smile. "Our Cadaver Kid here is one lucky
bastard. Got a nose for dead bodies. Me, I think the whole
thing stinks. Maybe he's really working for the Christophe
syndicate or one of the other mob czars in town and just
knows where all the bodies are buried."

Before this confrontation can deteriorate any more, it's
interrupted by a cry from the gravesite.

"Most of the clothes are rotted to threads," a woman's
voice calls from the pit, "but we've found some surviving
artifacts."

She's right to call any finds "artifacts." This is almost
an archeological site. I recall glimpses of cast-off clothes
and am starting to date them. Quantico Girl? No. Retro
Girl. *Yes*.

A quart-size plastic bag holding a heavy load of large
silver dollar coins is passed up.

"Wanta bet there are thirty of them?" Ric murmurs in
my ear.

Then a sandwich baggie holding something small and black is also passed up to Officer Buff, but Haskell snags it. He stares at it, then eyes me with mean triumph.

"A gambling chip," he says. Tells me. "From the Inferno. So much for your 'old' theory, babe. So, Montoya. You came, you saw, you bombed. Get yourself and Quantico Girl outa here."

We retreat a few yards. Once we're alone, I fight not to double over and barf. Because I re-feel their pain, this live-dead couple. Interlocked bones, loved to death. I've seen them at their best and at their worst. Vics. I know the lingo, but it makes them into pawns, not people who lived and breathed and loved at one time.

I think about how everything I own could be pawned. Achilles' urn. My own soul.

Ric is shaking me loose of my flashback. "You'll have to tell me what you saw later."

He's frowning behind the sunglasses. They prevent sun damage and don't hurt his looks at all. Does every woman fixate on him like this, or just me? What is going on?

"He called you—" I start to say.

"He lives to offend. Anyway, it's true."

"Well, yeah, but . . . hey, what's really bothering you?"

"Besides you?" The easy humor is back. And then the frown. "The Inferno is the hottest hotel-casino in town for the Pseudo-Goth-Hypehead-Decadent set."

"And?"

"It opened three years ago."

"Oh."

"That's okay. Silver dollars haven't been used for gambling in this city since the price-run on silver in the seventies. It's up to the coroner's office to determine the time of death. Those bones looked well seasoned to me."

"It's not only that. I . . . saw . . . shards of their clothes, jewelry. Particularly hers. Strictly late forties or early fifties."

He's smiling down at me. "They teach you that at 'Quantico'?'"

"No, but they should have, if I'd been there. I *have* worked as an investigative TV reporter. I covered ritual murders, although in Kansas they were cattle mutilations, most often. Are you really ex-FBI?"

"Yeah. What about it?"

"You're the best freaking dressed Fed I've ever seen."

"Maybe that's why I'm 'ex.' Hey, I appreciate your coming over here. I wanted to establish that we have a right to be on this case. I didn't expect it, but you cooked Haskell's goose."

We? This case? Maybe. But I've got my own cases to solve, my own bones to pick.

Bone number one is not who Ric is, but what. We walk away from the crime scene for a heart to heart.

CHAPTER ELEVEN

"Now that we're alone, Ric, tell me what happened here. This murder scene is what the dowsing rod targeted last night, and I saw it. Only I saw that couple alive, and being killed. I've never had daylight nightmares before. You must have had something to do with it. You're a water witch, aren't you?"

Ric winced at my last phrase. "Water dowser. It's a respected . . . faculty among rural folk all over the world. I can do it a bit now, but it's not my particular gift. It's not any part of this Millennium Revelation upsurge in supernaturals and freaks at all. I'm not a freak. I'm not a witch or a wizard of anything. Just a guy with a quirky family gene."

"So what's your 'faculty,' if not finding water?"

He looked away, maybe appealing to the island god for inspiration so that I'd believe him.

"Most dowsers do find water. A very few find precious metals and stones. I'm unique, as far as I know. I see dead people. Underground. That's what I do. Know they're there."

"That's what you consult about?"

He nodded. "Law enforcement people are pig-headed and pride themselves on that. They just think I'm superbly educated and well-trained." He gave a self-effacing grin. "Which I was, no thanks to myself."

There was a story there, but I'd get it later. I can wait.

"A lot of them like to think I'm just lucky," he added. "I let them believe that I have a photographic memory for news stories. Most dead bodies in wrong places are MIAs. Someone's missing; somebody's reported something, if you look hard enough. Which I do. After the fact."

He met my eyes again. "You seem to have some folk faculty yourself."

"You didn't literally see them, the victims?"

"I don't see anything that specific. The dowsing rod draws me to the grave. I report it and the authorities always find a body. Or bodies. Sometimes they're more than human. Or less."

I shuddered. "Are you saying—?"

"Yeah. Human murder victims are the simplest. Sometimes the bodies are staked vamps, victims of vigilante attacks. Other things."

"In this case, you didn't sense the bodies' pre-death . . . agony? Their—" I didn't know how to put it.

"Their heat? Yeah. I got that this time, but only through your reaction." His bedroom eyes apparently couldn't resist giving me a visual pat down. "It adds a whole new dimension to my work, believe me."

I was blushing now, and on me, it always showed.

He managed to ignore that, at least. "This crime . . . feels . . . like revenge for infidelity. I've never picked that up before, never anything about means or motive. We make a hell of a combo, Delilah. I wasn't kidding about you being an associate."

Maybe. But he'd just seen me reacting to what I'd felt. He hadn't experienced it, not both the glory and the gory. I didn't like hanging out there on the naked edge like that, my emotions showing like a black lace slip under a white satin gown, literally in some strange guy's hands.

"I've got my own agenda here to take care of."

"I noticed. Now you know my secret. So what's eating you?"

I jerked my head toward Sunset Road. "I'd sure like to get an appointment with the man behind that wall but I can't even get past the driveway gate to the security call box inside."

Ric turned to eye the imposing property.

"There? Easy. I've been hanging in this park long enough to notice the pool service truck that coasts through those gates every day at four PM. If you can hitch your wagon to a chlorine machine, you're in."

"Thank you!"

My watch read 1:00 PM. I had time to plan.

Ric fingered my elbow-length mesh sleeves. Holding a dowsing rod like a psychic set of reins had given him a touch that could veer from sheer gossamer to a grip of iron. I'd felt that as intimately as I'd seen and experienced the dead couple's passion and death.

"I'll be in touch, Delilah. Okay?"

Oh, yeah, even though my knees were knocking about what that might mean.

Or maybe because they were.

Chapter Twelve

Three hours to kill.

Oops. That phrase had an ugly echo in Sunset Park now that I'd viewed the skeletons in the ground.

I wandered around, avoiding the crime scene I'd been banned from. I bought my own hot dog and drenched it in mustard that made my mouth pucker, avoiding onions for my possible interview later. I stared at the Four Horsemen of the Apocalypse across the street, meditating on Hector Nightwine and who, or what, he might be. Nice man, bogeyman, entrepreneur, thief?

At the lower end of the park, I spotted a dog run and stood watching from a distance, sawdust in my throat. I couldn't help being drawn there, thinking of Achilles. The signs advertised obedience trials at 5:00 PM every day. The word "obedience" made me smile through my tears. Achilles wasn't big on obedience but he was spot-on about everything I needed. Loyalty. Spirit. Elegance. Love.

My throat was clogging, caught in a vise. Here I was, a new woman in a new city, and my past still had me by the throat harder than any vampire.

LAS VEGAS SPCA the sign read. Women bustled around wire cages while I wandered among them, eavesdropping. What else is a reporter but a professional snoop? Just browsing.

"Gosh, I hope one of these guys goes soon," a petite redhead fretted as I passed. "The city shelter will have to kill any one that comes back today."

"Maybe we should put a sign out." The plump, gray-haired woman sounded bitterly passionate. "'Adopt me now or I die tomorrow.'"

"*Shhh!* Truth doesn't get good homes. People can't face that."

I'd seen death up close and personal at the park's other end. I couldn't face a return encounter here. So I hunted for an Achilles look-alike. Small, white, cute.

These were all big dogs. Crossbred. Unwanted.

One in particular hunched hopelessly in a big wire crate still way too small for it. It was a shaggy gray ghost of a dog, ten times Achilles' size, nothing cute and apartment-sized about it.

I approached the cage, then tapped the wires to see the most beautiful pale blue eyes ever, way better than my own, turn to me from a silver-and-cream furred face. A widow's peak of darker fur over those amazing eyes made them seem almost human.

"Too big," I heard the women whisper behind me. "What a shame."

Am I easy? Maybe. Or maybe I'm just ambitious.

"How big?" I turned to ask.

"A hundred and fifty pounds. He's definitely from the wolf-spitz family, but really big for the breed. Maybe a touch of Irish wolfhound or Alaskan malamute in him. The eyes are blue, but pale to gray in the right light. Random-breds are hard to tell sometimes, you know?"

No, I didn't know, except for the hole in my heart. I scanned the organization's single-spaced adoption papers. Eighty dollars, no other pets, a permanent address . . .

I copied Ric Montoya's street address in the appropriate blanks.

"Really? You want this guy? He's a monster dog. You'll need to exercise him daily."

"I run," I told them. "A lot."

So forty minutes later I walked out of the area with a huge gray dog wearing the black leather-and-steel two-inch-wide collar he came with, attached to a new limp nylon half-inch-wide leash, blue with white letters reading Nevada SPCA.

He will go where I lead, and that's to Sunset Road coming up on 4:00 PM.

"OKAY," I told him like he could get it. "I'm new here too. We've got to swing on a star and get into this place by hook or by crook. You ready?"

The pale blue eyes said yes.

We lurked outside in the juniper bushes until the pool service truck paused, then gunned past the electrically opened gate. We slipped in after the truck. I led. He followed. I held his leash. He already held my heart.

Can we really storm this castle? And, if so, who will care?

The truck chugged past the second round of gates, but I spotted the needed squawk box here. Also a camera eye. I'm attuned to recognizing cameras. I went on tiptoe to hit the lever and speak my piece into the impersonal infrared eye.

"Hi, Mister Nightwine. My name is Delilah Street. I'm a TV reporter from the heartland, and I've got a few questions about a dead body on a recent episode of *Las Vegas CSI V*."

I heard the echo of my own words. Recorded. Dismissed. No go.

Suddenly the box squawked back at me, sounding like a televangelist. Rotund. Ponderous. With great big bad hair.

"Miss Street. My deepest apologies for keeping you and your, er, associate, waiting. My man will be down post haste."

"Post haste," I told my new dog.

He tilted his huge head, then whimpered and strained at his leash, showing his teeth in a big grin. My God, he had a maw the size of a grizzly bear's! *Good dog*.

WHEN THE BUTLER APPEARED he was half what I dreamed him to be: natty, with an amiable, worry-corrugated forehead. A forty-something dude with a bit too much tummy and a smidge too little chin, but charming nonetheless. Not sexy, but certainly cute, especially with that pencil-thin mustache. I pictured Ric with same and was so *not* turned off that I banished that idea . . . post haste.

This butler guy wore a real monkey suit from a Fred Astaire movie, white tie and tails, and his skin matched the outfit to a T. It was paler than any vampire could manage on his darkest day. He was a literal symphony in living black-and-white.

"Please come in, Miss Street. And your little dog too." He gave—whoever—a welcoming but sardonic grimace. "However, I will keep custody of his, *hmmm* . . . leash, I suppose. Might as well put the Minotaur on a string. Gracious, he's ready to eat a grandmother—hopefully not mine—isn't he?"

Dog growled and showed his teeth. My, what *big teeth* he has!

"It's okay," I told butler dude.

Dog sat and lolled his tongue sideways out of his mouth. My, what a *huge tongue* he has!

The butler I wanted to believe was named "Niven" led me down acres of marble and tile-paved hallways to show me into a magnificent office where a magisterial man of size, dressed all in black, bearded and mustached, awaited me.

"I will take Mister, *ahem*, Dog to the kitchen for a soup-bone repast," the butler announced. "Don't worry, Miss. He'll be returned even fatter and happier than he left you."

Since Dog looked lean and hungry and still somewhat sad at the moment, I hoped so.

"Fine," I said.

"Thank you, Godfrey," said my host. "Do keep him out of the lamb for tonight's supper."

Dog immediately turned and dragged Godfrey out of sight. This did not bode well for the lamb.

We were alone now, and my heart was beating like one of the drums in Rod Stewart's "The Rhythm of My Heart." It wasn't reacting the erratic way Ric Montoya made it hiccup, but with the steady elevated rate I felt when I was hot after a story.

The magnificent office reminded me of Hearst Castle. I could barely absorb the details: enormously high coffered ceiling twinkling with gilt. Exquisitely carved wainscoting up to twelve feet, at least.

"Sit," Nightwine said before I could speak further. Did this feel like a dog-training class or what?

I sat, surprising myself. The rococo wooden chair would easily hold an archbishop. I felt like Alice in Wonderland. My feet didn't even touch the thick Turkey rug under my feet and I'm five-eight without heels.

"I must tell you, Miss . . . Street, you say?"

"I say and am."

"I must tell you, Miss Street, that I won't tolerate any of my copyrights being violated. Should you wish to make an issue of this, I will sue you to Kingdom Come. Which, the pundits tell us, will be sooner than we anticipate or like, given what disagreeable and unforeseen events happened at the recent Millennium. On the other hand, if you are reasonable and we can come to a civilized agreement, you will find me very amenable indeed to deal with."

That's when I realized that he took me for the double I saw playing the corpse on the *CSI* episode. That's when I also realized I had some decent pairs to play in my poker hand, primarily a deuce of queens: me and my double.

I mustered my forces to explain my mission. "I don't know what you think I'm here for, Mr. Nightwine—"

"A deal is a deal. You signed a contract. As you know, people clamor to play the corpses on my shows. Shopping mall auditions from here to Tokyo host hundreds and thousands of wannabe corpses. My show may pay the union minimum for a non-speaking extra, but the right corpse in the right episode can be in demand for speaking roles on other shows."

"I just had some questions."

"Speak to your agent. I can't recall if you had one or not."

I took a gamble. "No, it was just one of those mass open auditions."

Nightwine's bulk deflated a bit, as if he was a puffer fish relaxing.

"As you will recall from the contract, Nightwine Productions bought all rights to your likeness in this particular role."

"Do you mean naked? Or dead?"

"Both."

"Sort of puts some essential reins on my career."

"Of course we would give you a . . . dispensation, if a future role was not merely exploitive of your notoriety on my show."

"Notoriety?"

"I meant that as a compliment. It's much more difficult to portray a corpse than most people appreciate. That glassy morning-glory stare, that graveyard pallor, all natural to you, I see. Unfortunately the obsessive fans pick up on successful corpses and there's a black market in blue movies featuring my former players. I can't allow that. If that's what you're here to discuss—"

"Blue movies! No!"

"Delighted to find you the *lady*—" he caressed the word with a tongue that tied itself into a sensual knot of over-precise diction "—your appearance on my dissecting table indicated you were."

"*Your* dissecting table?"

"I oversee almost every autopsy on my shows. Attention to details is what has made them the most popular franchise in the world. We have more spin-off units than McDonalds."

Yuck!

"It's possible that I might find a use for you on a future show. Perhaps even a one-line part, if you wore a wig and contact lenses. Perhaps green."

"I hate green."

"Aqua? That would be a suitable compromise. I see you have added a creature to your entourage."

"An entourage of one."

"Well, I approve, although he is somewhat large and galumphing."

He could have been describing himself. I watched his beady dark eyes shift left and right. This was a man preparing to lie, or preparing to scam.

"My dear lady. I realize the compassion that spurred you to adopt such a beast—"

"You do? How?"

He shrugged great rounded shoulders as black and looming as mountains in a Chinese print. "Forgive me. My operations must be kept secret or I'd be ripped off. I have an extensive security camera system. I couldn't help seeing you in the park."

Voyeur! Did this creep see me dowsing with Ric? My pulse went stratospheric. I felt again the tempestuous emotions of the quick and the soon dead under the ground at my feet. And Ric's iron arms around me, his iron . . . never mind.

Nightwine nattered on. "The beast is huge and ungoverned yet might not be an impractical acquisition. However, where will you find rented quarters that will take him? Even apartments are supersonically priced around Las Vegas, and I'm afraid very few will accept dogs, especially a dog of size like yours. Believe me, I do feel for him. Perhaps I can help you."

"Why are you being so . . . hospitable?"

"You need a place to live where you can keep the dog."

"That's my problem."

"Yes, of course, but I do have a guesthouse on the premises. Completely separate entrance and egress, very charming, hot-and-cold running servants, laundry service, pool service."

"You propose that I rent from you?"

"You'll find me a very amiable landlord."

"No. I'll find my own quarters, thank you. I prefer my independence."

"Then our discussion is over, I fear."

"I don't know why you agreed to see me if you had so little to say."

"It's possible we could do business in future." Nightwine pursed his ruby lips. They were small and bee-stung and totally creepy. "Perhaps you may reconsider. In time. My door is always open."

"Are you kidding? You have one of the most air-tight security systems I've ever seen."

"Flattery is also always welcome." His large, cerebral brow frowned. "I do advise you to accept my offer."

Was I detecting a faint, sweaty blossom of guilt on that Olympian brow? But why?

"I don't need charity. Why would you offer it?"

Nightwine's stern face softened into a beaming smile.

"It was simply such a pleasure to *see* you again, my dear, even on my black-and-white security camera. And in the flesh, in living color, well, you are a symphony of pale peach and sky blue and with that very dramatic black hair. I was out of the country during your dissection and didn't view your segment until the show aired, and your . . . portrayal was quite, quite breathtakingly lovely."

He leaned forward to gaze at my bare legs as if they were basted with a golden almond-butterball glaze for Thanksgiving.

Ghoul!

GODFREY GAVE AN OLD WORLD BOW as he returned my new dog's scrawny temporary leash to my custody at the door when I left.

"Your associate was quite satisfied with the menu of our kitchens during your absence, Miss, but you'd do well to pause at an establishment dedicated to the canine palette and fashion wardrobe after you leave us. Might I recommend a stronger leash? Forged steel, perhaps. Twelve gauge. There is a Pet Palace about two miles from here."

I eyed the dog, who licked his chops, i.e., his huge white teeth, with his washcloth-sized tongue, much as Hector Nightwine had done while discussing my double's cameo appearance on an autopsy table.

"Thanks for the suggestion. Godfrey, is it?"

"Yes, Miss."

I gave him a high five that shocked the bejeesus out of him. "Thanks, my man. We'll be in touch again."

He shook his stinging white-gloved palm. "I sincerely hope not, but you are always welcome otherwise."

I doubted it. Hector had handed me the long goodbye, aka the brush-off.

But Godfrey was right. The new owner of a mondo big dog needed a mondo big grooming and containing set.

CHAPTER THIRTEEN

The dog leaped through the open window into Dolly's red-leather passenger seat as if claiming a cushy vintage doggie bed.

I'd planned to lower the pop-top for after-dark Las Vegas cruising, which it soon would be, so I unlatched the manual locks and hit the chrome control knob that had been futuristic in the fifties and Dolly was gettin' down.

The sense of freedom and safety the car gave me reminded me of my ignominious introduction to driving at fifteen-and-a-half. It also recalled Father Black. I tried not to think of him. Not that Father Black was a problem; no, the opposite. He was the priest who ministered at Our Lady of the Lake Convent, a slightly shy man in his late thirties with a kind, sometimes worried face. He'd been the only one to notice that I was nearing driving license age and had no one to teach me. So I learned to drive the aging stick shift Volvo the parish had bought him years before. We practiced in the school parking lot on weekends, and moved onto nearby country roads.

I never liked driving stick, but it was all I had and I got good enough to pass muster with it. The lessons ended on a humiliatingly sour note, though.

My dear bitchy classmates, all equipped with fathers and older brothers to teach them to drive their new Miatas and Beamers, started gossiping about Father Black and me. Sarah Anderson's mother, a hair-sprayed harridan in Prada pumps, stomped into the Mother Superior's office one day and said the lessons must stop because of the "scandal."

I was called in soon after, and all the swearing in the world that his instructions were purely fatherly weren't enough. I'm not sure Mother Superior bought Mrs. Anderson's line. Although she stopped the lessons, she said Mrs. Anderson had to chauffeur me to my driver's test and provide a car for me to take it in.

So I was delivered there in a (thank goodness) sporty six-speed manual Lexus that I then put through the paces. I'd vowed to pass the first time, come hell or high water. And I did. Father Black and I never communicated again, except for nods in the hall. He looked shy, worried, and now sad when I saw him. The woman's false charges had humiliated him as well as me, turning something rare and nice in my life, something fatherly, into something to be disowned.

Mother Superior told me later that the other girls had been jealous of me, but I couldn't see why they would be, when they had everything and I had nothing.

Anyway, as soon as I was on my own and could buy a car, I switched to automatic.

Dolly was such an extravagant find that she made me forget about my unhappy introduction to driving. She was bigger than a Lexus and way better looking than Mrs. Anderson. Her high horse-power chutzpah always lifted my spirits and that's what she did now.

Dog howled along with my chosen radio station, so I had to move it to *NPR*. Downer. Gas prices per gallon were rivaling the cost of Jimmy Choo shoes and the Supreme Court was all-boy again.

We stopped at a Peter Piper Pickle-Eater drive-through to load up on fast food. The shtick here was that everything came with pickles. Dog gobbled three Gargantua Burgers faster than I could order three more. He spit out the pickles even faster.

I sat and contemplated where the heck I could run and walk him so near the Strip. I'd have to buy a gimme cap and sneak him into my motel room as a guest. Hey, the rotating lady tenants brought in some real dogs of "clients." Why couldn't I have a genuine one? I'd paid for the week, after all.

THE SUN WAS LONG GONE by the time we hit the Pet Palace, a pseudo-Taj Mahal affair in a strip mall with the façade outlined in flamingo-pink neon that made Dog howl even louder.

"Shut up," I told him. "Rescues can't be choosers. You need a non-wussy leash. Don't worry. I'll make sure it's heavy metal."

I riffled through the papers I'd signed in Sunset Park in the parking lot's hot-pink glow. Rabies shot. Right. I'd take care of that in the next day or two. Swear to fix. Neuter. Important. I eyed my boy's silver-blue eyes. A quick nip and tuck. It would hurt me more than it would hurt him. What do dogs know?

I entered the Pet Palace's hyper-fluorescent lit interior and spent seventy-some dollars getting Dog-boy a stainless steel bowl set, several chew-bones the size of an Easter Island head, and a short leash with a chain big enough to serve as a watch-fob for King Kong. No dog bed was large enough for his big-boned frame. Why was there a rule that dogs had to sleep on tartan plaid? They weren't all Scottish. He'd just have to make do with the ratty rug at the Araby Motel. I had to deal with the scratchy sheets.

When I came out the parking lot was deserted for dinnertime down time. I'd put up the top and locked Godzilla of the North in the Caddy with the windows inched down all around.

He was staring soulfully at me, then perked his pointed ears, flaunted his grizzly-size teeth, and started leaping at the window.

Whoa! That's modern safety glass, Toto! Built to resist impact.

Maybe it was the sight of the Alcatraz-style chain in my hands.

Or maybe it was the jerk behind me who pulled me around to face him and three other guys. They were all so pasty-faced I took them for vamps. Then I noticed their sloping shoulders in plaid shirts and the plastic pocket protectors.

"It *is* her!" cried the one who'd laid hands on me. He had nails-chewed-to-the-quick hands. Nothing to worry about unless I was a manicurist.

I dropped my bags to the pavement with a steel rattle, gave Geek-boy an elbow in the stomach that cracked a couple of ribs, stomped his pal's foot in its shabby tennies, spun away from the third guy's grabbing hands and high-kicked his chin. I picked up Dog's chain leash and looped it around Bachelor Number Four's scrawny Adam's apple. Obviously this guy had not fallen far from the Tree and had been left for fertilizer by the snake.

It was a pleasure to see that my college martial arts training still gave me an instinctual edge.

Meanwhile Dog was howling up a storm.

No one came out to look or help, but the four guys were backing off, whimpering. I bent to retrieve my bags when I heard a nearing growl. I whirled on my attackers, who were crawling away even faster, pushing their plastic-framed glasses onto the bridges of their noses.

They weren't the problem, so then . . .

The growl grew multiple, mechanical, and closer.

Motorcycles churned into the parking lot, bumping up onto the sidewalks and converging on my disappointed suitors.

And on me, who happened to be still standing there.

"It's her!" I heard an adenoidal voice whine behind me. "Not us. *Get her! She's Maggie!* She's worth a bundle, dead or alive."

Motorcycle boots scraped asphalt as the dozen assembled Harleys paused to grumble like a minor volcano contemplating a major eruption.

These biker guys were way more threatening than the Geek Quartet. No helmets. Heads of unkempt hair as big as Afros melding into long sideburns into mustaches into mountain-man beards into industrial strength chest and arm hair under their leather vests into hairy knuckles on handlebars.

Their eyes gleamed yellow from out of the Sleeping Beauty's castle thicket of snarled hair, and their teeth gleamed yellow too. More like fangs. Parking lot lights glinted off the steel buckles and zippers and chains slathered stylishly over their leather pants and boots and, yeah, those muscle vests. They couldn't serve any purpose but bluff and glitter. At least these guys weren't tattooed from here to Kingdom Not-Come; not enough skin for the job, just those hairy ape acres . . . except they were from another animal family entirely.

Werewolves!

We didn't have those in Kansas. We didn't have much that was up-to-date in Kansas City. Or even Wichita.

Wait! The moon wasn't full. I looked up to make sure. While I was doing that three of them bounded off the leather seats of the Harleys and went to make Geek salad of the poor fools behind me. Their pathetic pig squeals propelled me onto the parking lot asphalt. I raced toward my car where Dog was going berserk hurling his handsome howling head at the windows.

Oh, my kingdom for a remote control for a '56 Cadillac! But I was It. My twelve-yard dash for the car made the motorcycles rev, swoop, and circle me. Not that I'd want Dog free to be jumped by these lethal cousins.

The leader was mounted again, his beard a wet tangle gouted with black blood and white spittle.

"You ride with me," he ordered, patting the long leather seat behind him.

Right. I didn't much like my chances with the Dirty Dozen, lupine division. I knew that once a woman is in an attacker's vehicle, her survival chances plummet to less than zero. I figured I'd be better off eaten or offed than driven away.

"I h-h-heard about h-h-her," one underling muttered through his fangs. All those overgrown teeth didn't do much for stage diction.

"She worth something? To who?"

"Aw, those porn movie and snuff film guys. Even some amateur freakos. Big-money collectors. Whole bunch of, you know, people with money."

I waited. Maybe rabbits had the best idea. Freeze, then run like hell. 'Course, they didn't survive too long and had to reproduce very soon and fast, at which I was lamentably behind.

The leader of the pack twisted his clawed, hairy hands . . . paws . . . on the Harley handlebars, revving his bike until it bucked to be off and running down something.

Like me.

I eyed my feet. I was wearing my meeting-Ric-in-the-park spike-heeled slides. Not great for rabbiting in. I wondered if my maybe-prince would eventually dowse my body up from some desert wasteland.

Meanwhile, Dog was trouncing the inside of my Caddy, to no avail.

"What's that racket?" Leader demanded of his minions.

"A domestic slave."

"Worthless. Balls of a wombat."

It seemed to me that Dog was getting really, really riled, but I'd locked him in and unless he could develop an opposable thumb, we were both sucked. Maybe the shelter would notice the nice stainless steel bowls and leash that came with him when they were called in to take charge of the dog at the murder scene in the morning. At least we'd had a good, greasy last meal together . . .

Leader was swaggering off his cycle to control or kill me, mincing a bit, because the two-footed strut just didn't go with his circus-dog-on-hind-legs act.

I waited until he was within three feet.

"You worth delaying my dinner for?" he was snarling when I kicked one rear foot out from under him, looped Dog's chain around his hairy neck and crossed my fists at his greasy, long-haired nape. Then I stomped his spine with my spike heel.

He howled his pain and anger, impressively, and the pack was circling for the kill—*me!*—roaring closer and closer.

I heard a crash of broken glass and glimpsed a huge shadow racing straight for the nearest Harley, which went down in a spark shower of chrome scratching pavement.

Dog took them out, Mohammed Ali at his prime on four feet, snapping jaws good for snapping necks, spinning out motorcycles like ducks getting dunked in a carnival game. One by one.

This supernatural quasi-human dogwatch crew was no match for a magnificent canine using all of his animal instincts unclouded by any other agenda than saving the human who'd saved his ass. Which was decidedly not wombat-balled. I resolved then and there to break the first rule of responsible animal ownership and not to "fix" him. Call it an emotional decision.

I figured that by now he kind of owned me.

CHAPTER FOURTEEN

T he cops came, when it was all over, in cars.
    Dog had taken off. The scarifying biker gang
had shriveled into a dazed clot of scraped, bleeding
werewolves. Apparently they'd managed to eat the Geeks,
for the only victim still left standing on the site was me.

I babbled a little about visiting the pet store and being
accosted when I came out. A woman officer took me into
the back of a cop car and got my very confused statement,
giving me a card for a place where I could get counseling
for victims.

I'd gotten enough counseling during my orphaned
childhood to give it myself, so smiled and stashed the
card, collected my goods, and accepted Officer Smith as
a ride-along while her partner brought up the rear.

"Kinda rough welcome to Las Vegas," she said as we
headed out, the wind whistling through Dolly's broken
window. *Where was I going to get a '56 Caddy Eldorado
Biarritz window replaced in Las Vegas?* Not even Irma had
an answer to that one. "Why're you staying at the Araby?"

"I can't afford much until I get a job."

"Get outa there as soon as you can. And collect that
dog you mentioned adopting from the shelter. If you'd
had one with you tonight, he might have scared off those
cheap punks. Maybe."

"Tomorrow," I said, glancing into the rearview mirror.
A gray lupine shadow was pacing Dolly and the squad
car. At thirty-five miles an hour. *That's my boy!*

"You're lucky, Miss. The Lunatics are a nasty gang. We've been trying to put them out of circulation for a long time. Apparently they got to fighting among themselves over you."

"Lucky," I repeated with a shudder. At least my new dog was off the hook.

The officer dropped me off at the Araby Motel and returned to the following squad car with extreme regret, but I swore that I'd have new quarters soon. Tomorrow. And I would. Dog was waiting at the door to my unit, eerily enough, part of the shadow cast by the one parking lot light that still worked in the entire complex.

As he stepped forward, I saw that his ruff was matted by werewolf saliva. I hoped his coat was thick enough to serve as insulation.

"It's a head-to-toe bite inspection for you, mister, in the morning, and a curry-combing with your brand-new brush. Then we're off to see the wizard again. I could use some serious backup for storming Castle Nightwine. Again."

He interrupted a frenzied licking of his messed up flank to growl amiably.

"I need a name for you." I ran my hand over his skull, down his neck, past the wide leather collar that was now dimpled with fang-marks.

His eyes shone in the one parking lot light, pale and luminous, like the moon. Not just blue, like mine, but with an overriding silver-sheen. Like moonshine.

"Quicksilver," I said.

He sat down, boxed at his nose with his paws and grinned up at me, his tongue hanging amiably through his very white fangs.

Quicksilver it was.

CHAPTER FIFTEEN

I was surprised the next morning when the outer gates at Castle Nightwine opened instantly for us and the squawk box recognized us. Apparently everybody knew our names at Hector's place. Kinda like on *Cheers*.

"Miss Street and Mr. Dog," came the cultivated voice over the microphone.

"Mr. *Quicksilver*, Godfrey. He has a name now."

"Very good. Proceed to the main door and do scrape your shoes and paws on the welcome mat."

Quicksilver had surprised me this morning with a natty coat under which not one half-were puncture or scratch lurked. Of course he'd kept me awake almost half the night with the sound of his relentless licking and grooming. Still, the results were worth it. He looked downright awesome now that his leather and silver collar had a Manhattan-tugboat-size chain for a leash.

We trotted up to the entry doors, which resembled the approach to a cathedral. Godfrey was his same dapper self, including the curled upper lip we knew and loved.

"Is the master in?" I asked, handing Quicksilver's heavy-duty leash into Godfrey's white-gloved hand.

"Mr. Nightwine is in," Godfrey said carefully. He eyed Quicksilver with a certain camaraderie. "As to who is the master—?"

Words I loved to hear. I'd thought I knew enough now to squeeze Nightwine by his carnivorous balls, and I would find out just how much shortly.

The study was the same scarlet lamp-lit retreat, a place of cigar smoke, aged brandy, and leather-bound books. Daylight never penetrated here. Maybe Nightwine was a vampire. The surname was highly suggestive and anyone could be undead these days. Nowadays, playing pin the fang on the vampire was a better—and scarier—social game than guessing gender preferences used to be.

"I thought you'd be back," Nightwine informed me in rotund syllables, like a judge. Or a parole officer.

"I thought you'd want that."

"Miss Street, is it? Really and truly?"

"Yes. It is." As much as a made-up name invented by a social agency could be real or true.

"You must understand that yesterday I thought you were using a pseudonym. I thought you might be a Lilith imposter playing some sort of con game."

"That's what Adam told Eve and look where it got him. Confining clothes and original sin. No fun fast."

Nightwine was silent. So I spoke again.

"So her name was Lilith. Wasn't Lilith the uppity woman Adam banished from Eden so Eve could get down with the snake and queer the whole deal? And then they both blamed Lilith?"

"That's ancient legend. I deal in the present and the future. The fact is, as I now see, you are a stranger to Vegas and to my production company. You must understand. We're talking copyrights here. I bought all rights to Lilith's likeness and its reproduction. I have the same deal with all my corpses, living or dead. Lilith was unexpectedly . . . unique. Superb. A horror director's dream. Alas, I've been given to understand she requested a genuine dissection."

"Genuine? You mean you actually kill people onscreen?"

"Certainly not, that would be murder! But some are freshly dead, yes. If they wish. We don't kill them, we don't assist them in any way, they do it themselves. In order for our agreement to be valid, they must use some means that doesn't leave disfiguring marks on the body."

"Suicides still have to be investigated, just like murders. And autopsies performed and . . . "

"Miss Street, as we have established, you are new to Las Vegas. You are also ignorant of its laws. Let us just say that certain statutes have been passed that allow for our use of such "talent," as we call performers in the entertainment industry, and that all investigatory and legal procedures are followed. The *order* of those procedures may simply differ from the order elsewhere. Las Vegas has always accommodated the entertainment industry, Miss Street. It is one reason Nightwine Productions are located here rather than Los Angeles."

Had I mentioned I wasn't in Kansas anymore? I wasn't even in Southern California's LaLa Land — and I thought that was as weird as a place could get.

"I think I understand, Mr. Nightwine. If your corpse is a real corpse, it is . . . ah . . . fresh and free of the . . . um . . . imperfections of death?"

"We prefer to 'dress' our own corpses."

"So the maggot in the nose was a director's touch?"

"Lilith made such a beautiful corpse that the director went light on the maggots, bloating, and rot. Etcetera. Do sit down. I realize our modus operandi is a shock. I'm sorry. Some people are *dying* for a taste of fame, even if it's posthumous."

I sat. "But . . . she wore my blue-topaz nose stud."

"And a dainty, poignant touch it was. Er, *is*, in your case. Like a tiny bejeweled tear. Exquisite." His beady black eyes actually weltered in some fluid as he eyed my nose and its little glint of bling.

"Well, Hector, I'm not dainty and bejeweled or crying, not to mention dead. I'm from Kansas and I'm somebody else than this Lilith entirely. I am not a posthumous person. Get it? I live, breathe, want answers."

"It just can't be. Not two of you in the world. So . . . telegenic. If you're not a sham, reneging on our deal, maybe you're Lilith herself. Maybe she made arrangements with a cheap reanimator."

"Cheap! I'm getting the impression that cheap is *your* style."

"You can't be real."

I'd felt that notion often enough in my dreams to feel my legs quiver a little. The reporter's credo: When in doubt, ask a hard question.

"Why not?"

"Well, we don't make mistakes. We offer untold opportunities to our non-extra performers. We *are* in high demand as a corpse factory. Our players are either alive mimicking death, or truly dead, and we keep scrupulous books on that, as the deceased often bequeath their royalties to loved ones. Lilith had no one to leave anything to."

"Right. Your corpses. Tell me about them—us, Hector."

"Ah, merely that we've found that the hyper-reality of modern media often requires real people for corpses. It saves dough and camera time to dissect them . . . dead. It's a last, spectacular way to make an impact as you, er, go."

"Nope. Dream on, Hector. I'm not reanimated."

"Ah. So. Then I would guess that you're an obsessed fan of the show. Perhaps you've undergone massive plastic surgery to become my Maggie."

"No scalpel has ever touched my lily-white skin."

Bad choice of image. I watched a soupçon of drool decorate his plump red lips.

"What can I say?" Hector tried next. "The corpse in question said her name was Lilith Quince and she swore she had no family."

"I don't either," I said. "That's why I want to find her."

"If she's really still alive, I do as well."

He'd knocked me speechless at last. What a cold-blooded—

"Her . . . and *your* Black Dahlia beauty," he went on, "has made Lilith the most beloved corpse on the series. The popularity spike is already awesome after only a couple weeks. DVDs are selling like crazy. I'm even licensing 'Maggie' dolls and other tie-in merchandise via China."

"Maggie wasn't her name," I said, confused.

Oh. I got it with a sinking stomach. The name memorialized the *maggot* emerging from poor Lilith's topaz-studded nostril. Hector Nightwine was one money-sucking ghoul! *Oops.* He might actually *be* one.

"I am so sorry, my dear. None of us anticipated her popularity. Please. You look even paler than usual. Have some wine, a bit of food, perhaps during an unreeling of a vintage film? I am quite the *cinéaste,* you know."

Maybe I know. Maybe I don't want to know. The plate of scones he passed over his desk looked . . . half-baked.

"No, thanks." Who knew where that stuff had been? "Cinéaste? That's a perversion I haven't heard of."

Hector sighed, a gesture that shook his brocade vest like a bowlful of eels.

"It's not a perversion. It means I am a gourmet of cinema. A devoted aficionado. One who appreciates the art of film on a deep and knowledgeable level."

I appreciated the art of film; my vintage mania meant spending way too much on classic film DVDs. His "appreciation" meant he produced a global television series that gloried in women's corpses literally littering the cutting room floor? I contemplated Lilith's likely fate—though Nightwine's initial suspicions about me being a reanimated version of a deal-breaker hinted she might *not* necessarily *be* dead—and mine. Funny, if I was so damn beautiful, why didn't anybody ever offer me a home? I picture me at age ten: pale, skinny, and mop-haired. You don't feel beautiful if nobody ever wants you. And then, all of a sudden, it looks like everybody wants you . . . dead. Vamps. TV producers. Nutso fans with a necrophiliac streak as wide as the Styx, the river that runs through Hell.

Nightwine still frowned into his scones, which made crunching sounds like bones as he nibbled away on them.

"Twin is out?" he asked.

"Possible but unlikely."

"I know! Clone?"

"In Kansas? We still use rainmakers. Besides, it would need to have been done in the twentieth century."

"Not too far back. Lilith wasn't a day over twenty-five." He blotted crumbs from his over-colored lips with a crochet-bordered linen handkerchief. His currant-black eyes twinkled with a sudden thought.

"I do, of course, have samples of Lilith's DNA. We don't want any hanky-panky as to the identity of our corpses," Hector conceded. "If yours matches hers, I suppose you'd be entitled to a small royalty."

"I don't want money."

"But you admit you're an orphan. She could have been lost kin."

"I don't want money from her . . . death."

He licked his tongue against his teeth. It was over-colored too, and moved like a sea slug.

"Don't be foolish, my pearl. You wouldn't believe the crazies in this town who would snatch you and dissect you on camera and then sell a tape of it, Maggie is that popular. I must protect my investment. And you might be of some use. You were an investigative reporter, I believe."

"You've been checking up on me."

"Yeth," he admitted with a lisp as he bit into a dark purple plum from his desktop bowl. Nightwine was always eating or drinking something. *Euww.*

"And then"—His glance was as encompassing and lewd as when he mentioned his beloved black-and-white movies—"I've had a chance since your last visit to scan all of my security tapes from Sunset Park the first day you visited. And the day after."

He paused as though to allow me time to tremble in my boots. Never gonna happen. It was too hot here for boots. I was wearing my forties purple platform sandals that made me six feet tall, for courage.

He reached out a plump forefinger and pushed the horns on the bronze sculpture of a bull on his desk.

I heard a mechanical whirring sound and turned as one section of paneled library shelves slid away to reveal a wall of television monitors. The central flat-screen one was huge, seven feet or so.

Nightwine lifted a remote control sporting about a hundred luminous buttons and pressed one. What was he doing, showing me a soap opera in progress?

Oh. It was Ric's face maybe two feet high and it was fine. He was making love to . . . my hair, and I was writhing into his body like a mink in heat as the image drew back at the clicking command of Nightwine's remote control.

The camera panned down to document our totally compromising positions and lingered suggestively on the operative prong of the dowsing rod shaking and dragging my hands as it plunged toward the ground. Who did this guy think he was? Alfred Hitchcock?

This wasn't just a security tape made by an automatic camera. Nightwine fancied himself a director. He'd taken control, captured every moment of the lost time when Ric and I had found the dead bodies and I'd channeled their last, lascivious, live moments.

I felt a flush sweep up from my chest over my cheekbones. God, we looked hot. Nightwine thought so too, or he'd have never stepped in to "direct" this routine surveillance moment personally. The original must have been an uninspiring long shot.

"This is when I realized that my Lilith," he said, "is worth far more alive. I could sell this . . . outtake . . . for hundreds of thousands."

"You're telling me that I'm a live dead sex symbol? You don't understand. That footage is not what it looks like."

"I do understand, Miss Street."

The remote chattered like a chicken. I was treated to a rapid run-through of the police scene the next day, the bodies in their excavated tomb, even me wandering over to the dog area to adopt Quicksilver.

"Perhaps you may be disinclined to believe it," Nightwine droned on in his prissy, pseudo-Brit diction, "but I actually am agoraphobic. I dread crowds and open spaces. I could use a . . . leg woman."

He leaned over his desk to eye my gams. I thought they were fairly okay too, hence my vintage shoe collection. Now I wished I'd worn leg warmers.

"You see, Miss Street, I am a victim of extreme success. I have so many spin-off franchised *CSI* shows that even an army of writers can't come up with sufficiently provocative scripts. So I mine the murders of yesteryear. Obscure ones, of course. Unsolved, as a matter of fact. You show more than a seasoned reporter's skills on my tapes. You have . . . something extra. And so does the most interesting Mr. Montoya. I agree that this cozy footage of you two is more than an idle turn-on for any passing voyeurs."

Ugh! Was he talking about himself? *Yes!!*

"I suspect that you are gifted as your equally attractive but lamentably absent 'sister' was not. You're a medium, my dear."

"Me? Ridiculous. I'm a reporter. I live and die by cold hard facts."

"I live and die by cold hard bodies. If you do indeed have a direct line to the dead, I want you to develop these skills. I want to know who those entwined corpses were. I want to know who killed them, and why. I want them to be the centerpiece of a *Las Vegas CSI* episode. I'll pay you well for any results you can . . . dig up. How you pay Mr. Montoya is your own business, but he is clearly an accessory before the fact."

I took a deep breath. So deep I felt a sharp pain in my side. Okay. I was alive. Unlike Lilith. Or unlike Lilith was presumed to be. I was also alive enough to really covet that footage of Ric and me, those close-ups of Ric's face while he held me. No one in memory had ever held me like that. No one had ever looked like that while holding me.

"I'll work for you," I said. Briskly. "I'll solve this case. And then I want those tapes. All the tapes of me and Ric, everything. No copies left."

"Not even one weensy one for my personal collection?"

"Not even one, Nightwine."

"You'll live on site?"

"Right."

How bad could it be? Besides, I could see that Lilith/me needed heavy security. And I didn't want Quicksilver exposed to any more werewolf gangs. He looked at me in a way no living thing ever had either. Except Achilles. I wasn't going to lose Quicksilver too, by God.

"All right." Hector punched another button on the remote. The wall of living images vanished again behind a gilded façade of book spines.

"There's more you need to know, Miss Street, more of the facts about underground life, and death, in Las Vegas

that bear upon your investigatory efforts," he told me.
"There's a thriving illegal traffic in the dead. Ask your
Mr. Montoya if you can keep your mouths off each other
long enough. Ah, I once was young myself, but it was
so long and thin ago. The dead and the undead are being
revived and employed: ghosts, zombies, vampires, and
who-knows-what other supernatural creatures. They are
being leased to the Vegas hospitality, entertainment, and
sex industries by a mysterious consortium that makes the
fictional and demonic Wolfram & Hart look angelic.

"I'm especially concerned about a related issue: some
of the resurrected dead have even been peeled off the
silver screen, the black-and-white movies whose images
were filmed on silver nitrate. Do you know what travesties
like this mean, Miss Street? They're taking Bogey out
of *Casablanca*, Bette Davis out of *Whatever Happened
to Baby Jane*, and selling their soul-less selves as cheap
tourist attractions. Some are even being prostituted."

I leaned back in my chair. "Godfrey?"

"Wonderful actor. Classic portrayal. Surely you
recognized him from *My Man Godfrey*? William Powell
in the title role. Nineteen thirty-six. Perhaps the greatest
screwball comedy ever made. A socialite played by
Carole Lombard picks up a Depression-era hobo during
a scavenger hunt. He becomes her family's servant, also
their therapist. He's really a wealthy man and, of course,
there's a romance. Powell was Dapper Personified in that
part. I am honored to have him running my household.
You would not believe what nasty, demeaning use such
a fine vintage performance could be put to in the local
brothels had I not snapped up Godfrey for my major
domo."

I gasped. Godfrey was already a pal and my inside
man at Castle Nightwine. He did not deserve servitude as
mâitre d' in a brothel!

"I see you feel a bit of my pain, Miss Street."

"How can someone rip off vintage film characters?"

"Ah. By exploiting a long-misused population among the dead. Can you guess?"

I couldn't and shook my head. This was a lot of reel life to absorb, especially when I still didn't fully trust the source.

"You see . . ." Nightwine said, leaning back almost half-horizontal in his reclining leather chair.

The extreme position made my nerve endings jump. I didn't like seeing even Nightwine in such a vulnerable position, although I understood it was calculated to earn my trust: harmless old grandfather leaning back to tell grandbaby a story.

"Zombies, my dear," he announced.

"Not my favorites."

"No one's favorites, or they wouldn't have been abused as slave labor for so many centuries in so many corners of the earth. They are the secret behind the construction of the pyramids, you know."

"The pharaohs used zombie labor?"

Hector nodded somberly. "That was in primitive times. Today the technique of overlaying a cinematic character on a zombie began forty years ago as part of an experimental 'black' project backed by a beloved kiddie animation movie company. Now it's a common, if concealed, reanimation project taken over by the immortality mob gone rogue. No one, nothing, is sacred or safe. Supernatural thugs of all descriptions harry anyone, including those who ask questions, as you have been doing."

"The immortality mobs?"

"That's what I call them. They came up in the usual mob businesses. Murder, Incorporated. Racketeering. Running supposedly-victimless crime kingdoms."

"You mean drugs, gambling, and sex for sale?"

"Exactly. But once the Millennium Revelation occurred, it literally opened up a whole new field for the mobsters: grave-robbing on a massive scale. Then they hijacked the film reanimation technology, cornered the market, and put their new slaves to all sorts of low uses for entertaining gullible tourists. Philistines!"

"Who are these mobs?"

"Their kingpins are hidden, naturally, but there are three major corporate forces in Las Vegas today. They're called the Triad. The Magus, Gehenna, and Megalith hotel-casino consortium, offensively adding up to a classic Las Vegas brand name, M-G-M. Then there's the Babel, Bedlam, and Brighton group known as the "killer *B*s. And the Thebes, Delphi, and Byzantium, the tri-cities. A new wild-card player is the Inferno, currently the hottest single hotel-casino on the Strip."

I was blinking by then because I was new in town. It was an international playground, and none of these names meant much to me. All we had in Kansas were a few Indian casinos and the occasional reanimated medicine man.

"Don't you worry, my dear. You need have nothing to do with these yobbos. All I have in mind for you is some genteel Nancy Drew, Brenda Starr level sleuthing and reporting."

Nancy Drew? Brenda Starr? Hector was from the Stone Age.

The Ice Age, my friend Irma's interior voice kicked in, *but humor the lascivious old slug. You'll be working again and maybe you'll learn more about Lovely Lost Lilith.*

Maybe? I damn well would.

CHAPTER SIXTEEN

"**W**ell?" Godfrey asked, sounding way too anxious for such a cool character in such formal clothes.

Quicksilver, on his chain, and I stood in the driveway, gazing on our new digs.

The place had a separate entry gate. Hector's joint loomed like Manderley behind it, grand but totally separate, a mountain behind a molehill. This was indeed a "cottage": one story, with a storybook roof of thick-piled green shingles that mimicked the thatch roofs of, say, the Shire. Or Forever England. Or Disneyland.

Rose bushes, climbing ivies, and tall spears of larkspur and hollyhock surrounded the stone walls, wafting an earthy, sweet scent a supermodel would have killed to call her own and bottle.

But it was all mine for a reasonable monthly rent. A half-circle of brick steps led up to the iron-hinged wood door. Mullioned windows peeked out from the riotous foliage.

"Well?" Godfrey asked again.

"I'll sure whistle while I work here," I said. This was my little lost Wichita house, only six times better. My throat swelled almost shut with emotion.

"Here is the key." Godfrey planted a credit-card-size oblong of plastic in my palm.

He chuckled at my expression. Nobody had ever much chuckled at me in my life, and I liked it.

"Master Nightwine is thoroughly high-tech," Godfrey went on. "He simply adores the illusion of low-tech. Hence my humble employment."

"There's nothing humble about you, Godfrey, but the manners."

"Precisely so, Miss."

He handed me a plain white card with seven numbers written on it, and then leaned close to whisper in my ear. That pencil-thin mustache tickled. Scratch getting one for Ric.

"This is the code that disables and reinstates Master Nightwine's surveillance cameras at this location. In case . . . Master Quicksilver is entertaining the ladies some night."

Quick whimpered and licked me anxiously on the wrist. I couldn't always read dog language, but apparently he didn't like being used as an excuse.

We all three knew who wanted to control whose privacy.

"Very good, Godfrey. You are the perfect man's man, and the even more perfect woman's man."

He bowed. "I should warn you that Master Nightwine's fascinations with all things vintage and filmic extends to the inanimate as well."

Darn it! Godfrey talked too much like a college professor sometimes. I tried to translate his message.

"You mean, he collects film *things* as well as people?"

"Exactly, Miss."

"You mean . . . *things* like my new residence?"

"Exactly, Miss. You are indeed quick-witted. I would refer you to a mid-nineteen-forties film featuring a fine actor-friend of mine named Robert Young. It was called *The Enchanted Cottage*."

"And just what was enchanted about it, Godfrey?"

"Oh, my. I may become . . . unmanned. It is an old-style romantic fantasy. Unabashedly sentimental."

"I've read a few romantic fantasies." And had never believed a one.

"Not of your era, Miss. A facially scared World War Two veteran, Robert, meets a young but plain woman played by Dorothy Maguire. Only inside the enchanted cottage can the beauty of the inner selves they see in each other shine through."

"A fantasy indeed."

"But most affecting."

"I'm no longer affected by fantasies, Godfrey."

"Very good, Miss. Master Quicksilver. I'll leave you two to get acquainted with your new residence."

After he'd gone, Quick and I eased on down the fieldstone walk to the door. The card slipped easily into the old-fashioned Alice-in-Wonderland keyhole. The round-topped door squeaked open on reassuringly old hinges.

We moved into a slate-floored entry hall. Cozy rooms opened off it to either side: a kitchen and dining room, a little laundry room with a big dog bed, a back stoop and a clothesline in the garden!

Also . . . I found an office off the kitchen and a media room off the parlor. A circular staircase led to a loftlike bedroom with a huge four-poster bed topped by a mountainous embroidered feather quilt and . . . a master bath with a triple mirror, double sinks, a huge walk-in closet, and a Jacuzzi.

Quick leaped atop the four-poster, deflating the quilt about three feet. Methought the dog bed in the laundry room would make a good footrest in the parlor.

After a half-hour of exploring, Quick and I retreated to the front parlor, where I'd installed the dragon urn of Achilles' ashes on the mantel. The place was thronged with window seats, so Quick stretched out full-length on one. I'd poured a glass of sherry from the quaint, mid-

nineteenth century bottle on the silver salver. Say that
three times fast: quaffing sherry from the silver salver.

I had one thing in common with Hector Nightwine,
odious as it was to contemplate. I too liked to combine
high and low tech. From this Stratfordian retreat of an Old
World cottage I would penetrate New World perfidies of
expendable media personalities, crime new and old under
the sun, the fate of lost body doubles, and the world wide
web of crime and extortion and immortality that made
modern Las Vegas all things extravagant and evil.

Quick barked, short and sharp.

I just nodded in reply.

CHAPTER SEVENTEEN

I REACHED RIC on his cell phone, his face tattooed into my memory from Nightwine's videos like my own personal R-rated image.

"Delilah," he said when he recognized my voice, as if he just liked saying my name.

I like hearing it, from him. Damn it, but Nightwine and his prying cameras had been right on: Ric and I had that certain something going.

"I need to see you," I said. Literal truth.

"Sunset Park? Hot dog stand."

"No. Someplace else." I didn't want us on camera anymore.

"New York, New York food court? Lunch?"

"Yeah. How will I recognize you?" My voice had taken on an alien, flirtatious tone. Ever since I'd tapped into the dead woman's pheromones I hadn't been myself. I liked some things about that, and hated some things. Rick was among the things I liked.

"I'll be the guy who wants to try dowsing indoors," he said.

WE SHARED A COZY CORNER at a plastic table in the urban New York City-themed food court with plastic chairs and food and knives and forks. Surrounded by faux brick walls with acres of iron fire-escape ladders, I told Ric about my strip mall attack the night before. I needed answers.

"So who were those matted men who tried to make hamburger patties of me?" I asked him. Maybe not so surprisingly, he knew.

"Nasty customers, a rogue gang of rabid half-werewolves. They'd been vampire-bitten in their human forms. It makes their own bites poisonous, even lethal, if you get enough, and they remain half-changed all the time. Not all the half-weres go rogue, but when they do you don't want to mess with them."

"Why aren't there billboards warning against them, like they used to do with AIDS?"

A few years after the Millennium Revelation, an inoculation had made AIDS and all sexual diseases history, at least in the Western world. It drove religious fundamentalists crazy to lose such a sure-fire deterrent to sex, and it made AIDS as legendary as the Black Plague.

"They're an animal form of AIDS, all right," Rick said, "but this is all top secret. It would kill the tourist business if it got out. The big hotels have security teams to take them out if they come too close, but the half-weres are cagey. They make lightning raids, usually at lower-end businesses, sometimes to steal. Sometimes to enlarge the pack."

"What do you mean 'enlarge the pack'?"

He leaned over the plastic table to brush my hair off my shoulders, just for the heck of it.

"Brides," he intoned like Bela Lugosi, following up by leaning way too close and kissing my neck. I laughed, but I didn't mind "necking" with a man who didn't need to tap my jugular like a keg at a frat party.

"Listen, Del." Ric's voice did a hot blowjob on my neck. "Werewolves run this town."

"You're kidding! These are the only ones I've ever seen."

"Because they're stuck in mid-change. Frustrates the hell out of them. Most of our regular werewolves are no worse than the mob bosses who founded Las Vegas in the forties."

I stared at him.

"Sure, those old mob guys were pretty bad, but they mostly killed each other. With bullets. Now that whole mob thing has gone corporate. With the Millennium Revelation it became obvious to some of us in law enforcement that werewolves had worked their way up the management ladder in Vegas. Figures. Unlike most supers, they only go feral three nights of the full moon a month, give or take a little waxing or waning. They pass as human and deal as humans most of the time, no more ruthless or crooked than the real thing."

"Amazing. In Kansas we only had the occasional were-cow."

This time *he* laughed. "I think that I shall never see, a were as weird as . . . *Elsie*?"

"So I'm from a farm state. I guess I'm just a hick."

He brushed his lips over my neck again, paused to suck a little. A little bit more. A lot.

"No hickeys," I told him. "I've had it with a lifetime of passes at my jugular vein. You swear you're not a vamp in disguise?"

"I'm not a vamp, in disguise or out. Look. You're an investigative reporter. You have a professional need to know these things. The moon will be full tomorrow night. You should see a cross-section of our werewolf population, not just the Wild Bunch."

"Yeah?"

"I'll take you there."

"I'm not sure I want to tangle with those things again."

"No, it's perfectly safe. Los Lobos. A salsa club. We'll go dancing. Werewolves love to dance."

"*Dancing?*"

"Yeah. Clubbing."

"Sorry, I'm Black Irish."

"Whatever that is, I'm more than okay with it."

"We Irish don't dance."

"You ever see any of the eighty-one touring companies of *River Dance*?"

"Yes."

"That's not dancing?" he asked.

"Only with our feet." I pushed my arms stiff against my sides, made a poker face, did one tiny jig step at the ankles under the table. God forbid anyone should see me cutting loose. "It's inbred. Sorry."

He didn't discourage easily but leaned closer, nibbling on my earlobe. All lips, no teeth. What a relief.

"That strait-laced Irish jig of yours is a cousin to the flamenco, one of the sexiest dances on earth. We Spanish can speak with our feet, as well."

"Salsa's like flamenco?"

"Nope. It's a lot easier . . . and looser."

"I can't see werewolves without going to a dance club?"

"It's the only place you can eyeball the full range of werewolves, the wonder of the change. Come on, it's a hot underground club and even a few gutsy tourists get there. Aren't you up to confronting what the Polyester Set is?"

That last dig did it.

He was still in sell mode. "The moon is just about to pop into full. I'll pick you up tomorrow night at nine."

"So late?"

"We want to be there at midnight, when the wolves run."

"Three hours to kill?"

"Los Lobos has knock-out margaritas, a mariachi band to die for, and killer appetizers."

I wasn't crazy about all those lethal figures of speech, but Ric was inviting me into an element of his culture, if not his world (I hoped). His equally inviting voice and eyes made it hard to say no. Someday soon maybe I wouldn't be able to say no to him about something way more serious.

THE NEXT DAY I hied to the Fashion Show Mall on the Strip and hinted to saleswomen older and bonier than I was where exactly I was bound. They winked and sold me a three-tiered indigo silk skirt with flounces at the bottom and a mesh camisole to match, plus a black lace mantilla for a shawl.

At home, I pulled my Wicked Witch of the West fifties plastic-and-rhinestone heels out of their box. Weird how everything vintage had survived the weather witch's insty tornado. Maybe old, pre-Millennium Revelation things didn't do post-Revelation hexes. The clear plastic heels twinkled with aqua rhinestones and the vamp (excuse the expression, it's a shoe thing) outlined my toes and instep with flamboyant rhinestone coronets.

Overdressed? Maybe. But then, could I really compete with Ric, who was a dandy sartorial blend of a young Tom Wolfe (ouch, wrong family name) and early Prince?

Before I left, I checked myself out in the full-length mirror at the end of the hall. The lighting here was dim, but the rhinestones on my shoes sparkled. I squinted. Wait! The rhinestones looked red, not blue. In fact, my whole figure looked angular and black and I had a green face and damned if I wasn't seeing the real Wicked Witch of the West from *The Wizard of Oz* wearing Dorothy's ruby slippers. Nightwine's "enchanted cottage" was getting to my imagination.

I stamped my foot in spunky Dorothy fashion. "Get out of my mirror, you mean old witch!"

The figure wavered as if under water and I saw it had been myself, the way you can look at something very familiar and see it completely differently. A red nightlight from down the hall must have reflected in the rhinestones on my shoes. The light was so low that my clothes had lost their color, that's why the nightlight. I shook off my sense of seeing someone else look back at me. I didn't want to start the evening spooked.

Plenty of time for that later, my pretty, Irma warned me with a sinister giggle borrowed pitch-perfect from the Wicked Witch of the West.

QUICKSILVER, IN THE BACKGROUND, was bewailing my abandonment at the quaint cottage that was Hector's guesthouse and my new digs. I stood on Sunset Road, waiting for Ric. I didn't want to introduce Ric and Quicksilver at the front door, which the dog guarded like the drawbridge to the Tower of London crown jewel collection. Not that I minded that after glimpsing Las Vegas after dark. The older Corvette that cozied up to the curb was low, sleek, and colored bronze. As in "bronze god," no doubt. Ric leaned over to open the passenger door.

I lowered myself into the leather seat and pulled the safety belt over my shoulder to snap it into the latch. We zoomed into the dark, up Highway 15 that paced the neon-lit Strip for a few miles. Then the car charged onto a rough-and-ready ribbon of unpaved road into the empty desert dark where the stars gathered into a mascara-thick layer of glitter. We were on an endless zigzag toward the Spring and Sheep Mountains. In the blue-tinted glass roof above me stars whizzed past like comets.

"Werewolves are ultra discreet," Ric told me, the dashboard lights playing laser tag with his clear-cut features. "They can afford to be, since, unlike vampires, they can pass as perfectly human most days of the month . . . if they're not raising obvious hell like your biker gang. Everyone overlooks it. Cops. Media. Tourists."

He went on, as if lecturing at some alternate world Quantico. "Some werewolves are almost like us, except for a little moon-madness once a month. Not too different from the female of our species."

He glanced at me sitting a little stiffly in a seat that was semi-reclined by design. "Nice shoes, by the way."

"Thanks. What am I going to see at Los Lobos?"

"Mostly traditional Hispanic werewolves. Not many gray timber wolves or white Arctic ones. Yellows and reds, in daily life everything from gang-bangers and taquiera owners to music idols. A mix. Werewolves come in all styles and flavors. Some are enforcers for the casino owners. Some *are* the owners. Some are wait staff. Some are your friendly neighborhood janitors and maids."

"And you?"

"I'm your friendly Latino ex-FBI guide. I don't belong anywhere, but I go everywhere. Okay?"

"Yeah. Lone wolf. I get it."

CHAPTER EIGHTEEN

I'd bought a doll-size purse on a long chain that I could wear while dancing, so the mall sales clerks had advised. It fit fine on the teeny table made for cocktails and appetizers.

The room, with a mirrored ball high above flashing laser lights, was dark and cavernous, divided down the middle at ceiling level by a Plexiglas sheet that reflected the mirrored ball. Below it, Us and Them mingled. Most looked like thee and me. But some of Them were scary, at least to someone who'd done the Asphalt Stomp with a full gang only a couple nights before.

Some were half-changelings on two feet with snouts and body hair disturbingly like fur but without the rabid expressions of the gang that had attacked me. Some were dressed. Some were undressed except for the rust and cream fur that reminded me that Quicksilver was silver and black and cream, and bigger, a seriously large-boned dog who could take out a gang of lean, agile werewolves. I was glad none of that bunch had managed to penetrate his thick fur, after what Ric had said about the half-weres' lethal bites.

Ric allowed me to savor one huge Midnight Margarita, moon-blue from Curaçao, before he coaxed and prodded me onto the dance floor. All around us human couples were swirling and twirling in the sexy Latin couples dance called salsa. Others not so human were bumping and grinding, doing the werewolf two-step.

"I can't dance," I told Ric again. *Don't ask me.*

But Ric was in his element, actually in his shirtsleeves, which played up his warm mahogany coloring. I was overdressed for a roomful of petite yet full-bodied Latina women slithering like snakes in their low-rise jeans and plunging, shrunken, midriff-baring tops. Ric was The Man in his white business shirt, high-end slacks, and brassy gold belt.

"It's just a three-step," he said. "Cha-cha-cha."

I mimicked his steps, looking down, trying to master the simple pattern as it shifted from forward to back and side to side.

I watched his feet, his legs, his hips. He had rhythm, that inborn Hispanic sway. All the men in the room, hairy or not, had it. Their moves were as macho as a matador's, sexy and sleek.

I was watching Ric's hips more than his feet.

One, two, three. *Oooh!* That ultra-slim gold belt was almost over the top, but it gleamed like the scales on a serpent in Eden.

He caught me moving to the motion of his hips, not his feet. He smiled with almost palpable pleasure, slid the belt out of his tailored pant loops even as we kept up with the steps and the music, and refastened its gold links around my hips.

Then he whispered: "As Jimmy Buffet says, 'I wanta see some movement below the waist out there.'"

"I don't have a waist." I sounded like a prig even to myself.

"Oh, yeah? Just watch." Rick grinned, hooked his thumbs in my skirt's elastic waistband and pulled down about three or four inches. I gasped as the cold metal of his belt hit my warm flesh. The skirt was barely riding on my hips, my navel was sucking air, and whistles echoed all around us. Wolf whistles, of course.

I could have died from embarrassment.

Other dancers were watching us out of the corner of their eyes. Some brown, Some black. Some lupine yellow. An awful lot of the chicks here sported pronounced widow's peaks.

Right. One, two, three, *gulp*.

My chilly Irish genes couldn't match their hot-blooded native grace. My two left feet could barely manage to keep from tangling with Ric's sure-footed moves.

"Pay attention, *paloma*," Ric advised. "All you need to do is change your weight from step to step and you'll be Jennifer Lopez. One-two-three."

"Fuck one-two-three! I don't ever balance on one foot. Someone . . . something might get me off-balance."

As *he* had, calling me by a Spanish name that sounded pretty and so natural. I'd made everybody call me the gender-neutral "Del" for so long that a three-syllable name seemed . . . way too intimate.

Ric gave up on trying to hold me in the usual my-left-hand-on-his-shoulder, my right hand a pump-handle-in-his-left-hand position. He pulled me aside, to the edges of the dance floor. Put my hands on his shirted shoulders, his warm palms on my hips, my air-chilled bare hips.

"Hit me. One-two-three."

I glanced at the Hispanic tootsies slinging hotsy-totsy hash from hip to hip all around me. They slithered like serpents, their pelvises jiggled like aspic, their legs strutted and three-stepped and they didn't even wear the sweet Wicked Witch of the West shoes I did.

Okay. One-two-three-*boom*. I watched Ric's eyes darken as my hips brushed his palms. Just barely. One-two-three-*boom*. Okay. He wanted it. He got it. My way. Just nearly there, but not quite. His pupils grew midnight-dark. He wasn't leading, I was. From the hip. From the heart. One-two-three. *Boom*.

The heat, the noise, the rhythm. It was getting to me. Moon madness. I let my hands slither down from his shoulders and undid the third button on his open shirt collar.

His eyebrow rose.

I swung my left hip hard into his right hand and undid another button.

Wolf whistles became a chorus, echoing around us from the hard wooden dance floor. *Olé*s echoed encouragingly. We were making a spectacle of ourselves, and I was now the main instigator. But the music was so engaging, so insistent.

On the next hip swing I undid another button. The skin beneath the shirt was as smooth and mocha-colored as a really great creamy latte and all this exercise was making me thirsty.

Ric suddenly swung me out, twirled my arms around myself and pulled me hard against him. My own crossed arms held me prisoner, pushing my back into his front, my cleavage into full focus as he looked down at me.

"The werewolves are dancing their paws off. Look."

Forced to take my eyes off him, off us, I saw that the Plexiglas flap had descended to the floor like a transparent iron curtain, dividing the dancers into Us and Them. Ric and I were on the tourist side. The transforming werewolves were circling madly in a salsa gone mad on the other side of the see-through barrier.

Some had already dropped to all fours, beautiful silver-tipped coats reflecting the rainbow shards cast by the mirrored ball, a kind of full moon, high above. The half-weres still danced a ragged form of salsa, their throats extended as they howled at each other and the unseen moon outside.

Camera flashes pinned them in a strobe-light landscape of alternating light and dark.

I turned my head, my face, into Ric's shoulder. We were molded against each other, like we'd been in Sunset Park when he, I . . . we had found the dead bodies. I felt again that unexpected, alien surge of long-dead desire, welling through me into Ric.

He remembered it too. He was murmuring into my hair, Spanish words that sounded like an incantation. Some I knew. *Linda*. Beautiful. *Querida*. Beloved. *Mi tigre hembra*. That last word was one for a Spanish dictionary. No one had ever . . .

My knees lost it first. I sagged against him.

Then he lost it.

Ric one-two-three'd me around a corner into the rest room hallway, pressed me against that wall, pushed a thigh between my legs until they were very happy, and kissed me into a paper doll.

My heart was beyond pounding, it was thrumming along with the salsa beat and the vibrating floor and walls, the werewolf howls. Rick's hands against the wall above my head put me in the close custody of his body. He lowered one hand to run a thumb over my sensitive inner lower lip, pulling a veil of saliva over it.

"You don't wear lipstick."

"With my coloring? I'd look like a clown on the Fourth of July."

"I can redden your lips." He ran his tongue over them and I felt the gesture everywhere. "*Via con mi?*" he asked.

Go with him? I understood that much Spanish.

"We're here to see the werewolves. Dance, wasn't it?" I asked.

"They are us. The car? We'll see 'em before we go-go."

Go-go-go! We didn't make it inside the car. Or just barely here. The full moon was a huge silver Spanish coin in the sky over Ric's shoulder when he bent me back like a ballroom dancer and pushed me against the still-warm windshield of his Corvette and went down on my bared navel.

I was so used to unwanted guys grabbing for my neck and breasts and crotch that this sensual assault on my middle felt like . . . something new, something delicious, something all fingertips and tongue, something passionate on the special, small scale, something really, really personal. His borrowed belt was nicely in the way so he had to fight it for possession, and it was as warm as melted gold now, more mine than his.

I plunged my fingers into his thick dark hair, watching his thumbs press into my not-model-concave belly. His tongue fought to penetrate my navel and bring me off with purely oral persuasion. I wanted to suck him into myself, here at this one point of contact.

His head lifted off me, like a dog's or a wolf's, alert, guarded, listening. "They're coming. We need to get safe. And then watch."

Inside the car, we huddled together as the great, galloping werewolves flowed past us until the small sports car shuddered on its suspension. I heard screams in the distance, amid the avalanche of howls. Human screams.

"Macho fools," Ric said. "They block the packs' runs, try to outdance them. They scrape their skin on the ground and bleed, but even the hungriest werewolves won't pause now to eat. They're heading for the great open wilderness of their ancestors to mate. The mountains and desert and hidden oases."

Wolfish faces flowed directly toward us and then around Ric's low-slung car, which still rocked and rolled at their passage. I loved their harvest-moon-yellow eyes, all Kansas wheat fields, and their silver-tipped fur, all Hollywood. The half-breeds came later, scary hunched loping half-blind mutilated creatures, hunting the moon and missing. I'd seen their more lethal like in the Pet Palace parking lot and shivered a little.

Ric held my hand, his eyes on me, not on the rushing hordes. "They were all as human as we are, once. The Millennium Revelation brought everything unhuman out."

"Not 'inhuman'?"

"Unhuman is different from what we mean by inhuman. It's not always degradation. It's just a difference. Like between man and woman."

I felt that last difference and the urges it engendered. Everything that night enhanced Ric's desire. He'd brought me here to seduce me with it all, the unreal, the hidden, the wolfish heart of Las Vegas. Of himself. And even, perhaps, of myself.

ALWAYS SENSIBLE TO A FAULT, I lashed myself into the seat belt before he took off from the parking lot. His arm reached over me, pressing against breast, belly, pelvis.

"The seat reclines."

In an instant, I was laid out almost horizontal.

On my back. Bound. Every nightmare revisited. I couldn't breathe, and reared up like a drowning person.

"*Whoa.* Del? What's wrong?'

"I . . . don't . . . do . . . horizontal."

The seatbelt whipped free at his touch and the seat snapped more upright again. "It's gone. We're out on the lonesome highway. No seatbelts required. Delilah?" His hand spread on my pelvis, warm and possessive. "I won't hurt you. Relax."

The low car thrummed along the concrete, vibrating like a blender until my bones sang with the motion. His hand moved on the stick shift, up, down, across, and I felt my body sway with the car, with his remote touches. I envied the glossy cue-ball head of the stick shift his touch. I wanted it.

His fingertips reached over to push the flimsy camisole up past my rib cage, to tease my skirt hem up to my hips. A luminous full moon rode in the dead center of the glass roof panel. Underneath me the steady thrum of horsepower vibrated my pelvis like a great cat's purr. Above me, a moon river of rushing werewolves seemed to meld with the ghostly clouds.

Ric's hand spread on my belly, caressing, claiming.

My primal fears wafted away into something I'd never felt except in Sunset Park. Primal desire. I was strangely out of it, dreamy. His fingers teased my skirt up over my bare hip, then caressed my breast under the camisole. Again I was lulled by that easy, fringe sort of lovemaking, what pleased him as he steered the car and trifled with my body swaying to the drone of the engine, the motion, the fondling.

He parked on Sunset Road and insisted on escorting me to my front door. I disabled Nightwine's security systems with my codes so we could amble inside hip to hip, our fingers entwined. The heavy sweet scent of flowers draped the cottage and the silent night seemed enchanted.

On the homey brick stoop Ric took me into the embrace of his smooth, expensive clothes to do the tongue tango again. We were pressed against the door, my hands stroking the muscles of his back through his silken shirt. They shifted while his hands tightened on the bare skin of my waist and hips.

Then Quicksilver, detecting a stranger's presence, leaped and scrabbled and howled on the other side of the door like a manic werewolf. Sure killed the mood.

"What do you keep in there, the Hound of the Baskervilles?" Ric asked.

"Not quite." I smiled mysteriously.

He unclasped and teased the gold belt off my hips, then threaded it back through the belt loops of his pants at such a slow sensual pace that I almost lost it again.

I watched him, loving this. I'd never had this. Being escorted home from a date by a man who'd disarranged my clothes and pushed into me from a dozen distracting directions.

Taken home to my own little cottage, where someone waited who cared but might ask awkward questions. Well, ask in a canine way.

I loved that Ric and I hadn't been to bed, stripped naked, that there was still so much more to discover about each other and our feelings, at our own tantalizing pace.

We arranged to rendezvous the next day. In Sunset Park, where he could meet Quicksilver on neutral ground. It seemed like the obvious next step. One-two-three, *bow-wow*.

CHAPTER NINETEEN

I will never understand dogs.

They see the returning master standing *right* in front of them *right* inside the front door and they still have to sniff your crotch to guarantee you're you.

Quicksilver was tall enough to make quick work of this ritual greeting but tonight he responded with a growl rather an eager leap to lick my face. I can't say I was all that fond of the face-lick anyway. He had a tongue the size of a Saks Fifth Avenue washcloth.

"*Back*, boy." I brushed past his second growl of parental distemper. It was kinda sweet that he cared about my dates, but a darn good thing I'd kept Ric out of sight and scent.

Quick's nails clicked over the wood floors to the kitchen, where I let him out the back door. The yard gnome, Woodrow, complained about picking up after Quick when I didn't manage a run in Sunset Park and do it myself. Tough. Growing things was his job and Quicksilver leavings made really potent fertilizer. Woodrow was, apparently, one of the perks of residing in the Enchanted Cottage of film fame.

But I was . . . what? Tired. In a way. And wired, in a way. I refilled Quick's water dish and leaned against the kitchen sink, daydreaming, until the dog's nails clattered on the stone back stoop and I let him back in.

To the background sound of the Loch Ness monster lapping at the giant stainless steel water bowl—another thing about dogs: they go out and *then* come in and drink up a storm—I ambled toward the bedroom. The fancy-framed full-length mirror at the end of the hall reflected all my bare-midriffed disheveled glory. I looked like a woman in a Calvin Klein perfume ad, hip, hot, and hungry.

I wasn't sure I felt the same way, but it was damn close. All so new, so alien to me.

I dropped my partying clothes over the chair and hesitated between the shower and the sheets. Nope. I didn't want to wash the night off just yet, so I slipped between the umpteenth-thread-count sheets and fell asleep before you could say "nightmare" and I could even think it.

Twittering birds announced the morning. The cottage always thronged with fragrant flora and noisy fauna, like a cartoon paradise.

I bounced out of bed humming "I Enjoy Being a Girl" from *Flower Drum Song*, took a long, hot shower, then donned sweatshirt and shorts to take Quicksilver for a gallop in the park.

Afterwards I had a quick, cold follow-up shower, gulped down some oatmeal and yogurt, and made a shopping list.

"You can come along, boy," I told an anxious Quick as I grabbed my denim hobo bag to leave, "but will have to guard the car. This is an indoor, girly expedition."

We both trotted outside. Although the cottage had a quaint carriage house that could function as a garage, I kept Dolly sitting under the carport. Sun was the only real enemy to an automobile finish in Las Vegas, just as it was for flesh-and-blood girls.

I stopped cold as I neared the car's side window. Quicksilver had turned it into a doggie door during the attack at the pet store lot. Now it was rolled up tight, perfectly whole and reflective. What kind of sneak thieves broke into your yard to replace an irreplaceable car window?

Quicksilver was dancing and panting at the passenger door, eager for a ride. I shrugged and went around to open the door and let him in. Yup. The window fit Dolly's massive frame perfectly. I shrugged and headed for the driver's seat.

In a minute, Dolly roared through the automatically opening gate onto Sunset Road. She loved Las Vegas as much as I did. No parallel parking slots except downtown. I headed for a big suburban mall. Lots to do before meeting Ric in the park. First a discount clothing store fringing the mall for, what else, clothing? My Kansas WTCH tailored suits and blazers looked like social-worker wear here in the casual West. And I bought a 30-inch, fine silver chain. I wore what I bought and bagged my old clothes as I went. It felt like I was changing skins, not styles.

Next, I wandered through the crystal and silver maze of the Saks Fifth Avenue cosmetics department. There was so much of this stuff, and my black eyelashes and eyebrows hadn't needed emphasis, not even for a TV camera. I'd had to wear the heavy masque-like foundation, though, to warm up my lily-white skin. Maybe that's why I avoided makeup off-camera. A woman behind one glittering counter with an awesomely flawless foundation job approached to ask if she could help me.

"Uh, yeah. I don't wear lipstick. It's too clownish for me."

"You're right. Your hair and eyes are so vivid. Have you tried lip gloss?"

"Just lip balm."

"Oh, there's lots more than that. With your black, white, and blue coloring you're one of the few that even orange would work on."

I made a face.

"You'll see," the salesclerk said, delving into the built-in drawers behind her.

And I did. It hadn't taken long after I smeared a sheeny sample across the back of my hand and remembered Ric's finger wetting my lips with my saliva. Three-two-one, lift-off! I left with three expensive little pots of tinted gloss named Orange Crush, Veiled Raspberry, and Goddess Gilt, for evening "sparkle."

I also left sold on a similar little product called Lip Venom.

According to the saleswoman, this spicy, tingly gloss "plumps the natural shape of the lips by increasing circulation with a blend of essential oils including cinnamon and ginger. Great for shiny, bee-stung lips." I bought the color called "Love in the Mist."

"And the tingle effect is catching," my saleswoman added with a wink.

I was feeling the tingling effect already, but left cosmetics and next applied myself to a mall bookstore. They had what I wanted, English-Spanish dictionaries, but not the exact type I needed. Then a thoroughly pierced teen clerk led me to the "slanguage" section where I found a tiny red leatherette-bound book titled *Street Speak in Spanish*.

If Ric's sexy murmurs included any dirty words I was going to know them. Already, just browsing, I'd learned that *hembra* meant "tigress." *Really?* Of course it could also mean "nut of a screw," which wasn't exactly complimentary. Or was it a different tense of *embragar*, which meant "to put in gear?" Ric had been doing a lot of *embragar* with both the Corvette and me last night.

Last stop was a shoe store, where I bought a pair of platform open-toed slides. I'd sometimes gotten a kick out of flaunting fire-engine red toenails while the videographers focused on my dead-serious face and stiff upper torso when I intoned my spiel for the camera. Maybe I'd always been a split personality.

Quicksilver was sitting by the car. I couldn't leave him locked inside and he liked playing guard dog.

Dolly approved of my new get-up. She was so anxious to get home her motor throbbed impatiently at the stoplights, which offered a low-rider next to us a chance to give a wolf whistle and shout a new phrase to look up. I wasn't sure if it was for Dolly or me, though. Besides, I was interested in impressing a high-rider.

"Who're you foolin', chica?" Irma's interior voice asked. *"You are goin' for forcin' that man into an insanity plea."* Maybe "Erma" was short for *hermana,* or "sister," in Spanish. Who knew I had so much Latin blood in me?

Quicksilver's nose inspected the crotch of my new jeans, but didn't seem to register that they were low-rise and nicely set off the thin silver chain around my bare hips. Or that the off-the-shoulder crop top was red and had ruffle-tiered sleeves like a flamenco dancer's skirt.

Okay, maybe this outfit was a little slutty. I couldn't help it. For the first time in my life I felt happy and strong at the same time and I wanted more of what made me feel that way. Who.

One-two-three, *arriba!*

CHAPTER TWENTY

Of course everybody eyed me when I walked Quicksilver from the parking lot to the dog area. They always looked at me when I walked Quicksilver, so I couldn't tell if my new outfit had any pulling power of its own. I left him with a shelter lady, who was only too pleased to entertain him for a while, and worked my way up the Trail of Dead People's Trees to the picnic table area where I'd first met Ric.

He was sitting on it, feet on the bench seat, white-shirted, facing Sunset, expecting me to be coming from Nightwine's estate. Maybe he was contemplating the Four Horsemen of the Apocalypse sculpture eternally charging out of the bland stucco wall.

"Hi."

He turned at my voice. Ric had that law enforcement professional face down cold: blank, noncommittal, and unflappable. The moment he saw me it melted, did a 180-turn, although I couldn't quite name his new expression, other than stunned.

He jumped down to the ground, met me coming toward him, still stunned. Now I knew how those night-time soap opera queens felt. He walked into me, or me into him, I don't know which. He hooked his fingers through my belt loops, brushed a kiss over my lips, cheek, neck, just under my ear.

I'd heard of skipping stones, not kisses.

"Delilah," he whispered. "*Muy tempestado*. A pity I have to go away soon."

"Away?"

"South of the border."

"Down Mexico way?"

"Yes, where exactly I can't say."

"For a long time?"

"It'll seem long now. Two or three weeks."

"But I wanted to find out about the dead couple. Nightwine will pay me for a solved case he can fictionalize on *CSI*. You have police access—"

"Not with Haskell on the case. Can't you use your reporter's wiles to check into it?"

"Librarians rarely need wiles and that's where I'd find information on missing persons from decades ago— newspaper archives."

"Good, a library is a fairly safe place." He grinned. "Then there's the angle of the Inferno gaming chip. And, if needed, I do have one police contact you might try: Captain Kennedy Malloy. See? Lots to keep you busy while I'm away. When I'm back, we'll go salsa dancing. The werewolves won't leave if they see you in this."

"It's not supposed to mean anything to the wolves."

"And that, *Querida*, means everything to me."

We'd billed and cooed as much as I felt comfortable doing in public. My Irish genes still had to be dragged kicking and screaming into the arena of open emotion.

I pushed off enough to capture Ric's eyes again. Seriously. "One thing. Does it bother you that our being so . . . *simpático* . . . started over a couple of dead bodies?"

"In Mexico, we celebrate the dead, we don't fear them."

"I know, 'Day of the Dead' and all that. But—" I lowered my eyes, not because I went for that flirtatious crap, but because I couldn't quite face some things. Like my own history. "I don't mean the impact of death. I mean the . . . sensuality that came with it. It's almost like it took us . . . me . . . over. I mean, I've never—"

"I know. But I've never either."

"*You've* never?"

"Not that intensely. I agree. We were borrowing from the dead. It was like their last bequest."

"Isn't that . . . creepy? Doesn't it bother you?"

He ran his hands down my midriff to my hips. "You bother me. That's the way it should be, *Querida*."

Okay, I liked it. I'd been asking for it, in the shy honest truth of that phrase, not as an accusation. I'd trusted Ric to know and appreciate the difference, and he did. It was always so touchy for women to be sexual without being misinterpreted. Maybe that's why I'd never wanted to do it before. Or maybe Ric was why I'd never been able to do it before.

Or maybe the dead bones, the skeletal lovers buried in the limestone crypt, had been waiting for a couple of fools with our particular weird talents and my dicey personal history to be infected with their own lethal passions.

Maybe we were doomed to the same fate.

If so, I could only hope we'd enjoy getting there half as much as they apparently had.

THE MAN-DOG INTRODUCTION was not as successful as the live-dead introduction in Sunset Park two days earlier.

When I escorted Ric to the dog area, Quicksilver's usual embarrassing crotch-sniff turned into a sudden snap. Ric's pelvis did an evasive maneuver as fast, skilled, and sexy as a matador's, but the fact remained that my dog had serious territorial issues.

"Bad boy!" the shelter lady and I shouted in unison. "*No!*"

Quicksilver sat down and commenced to lick his privates while casting resentful glances at all concerned.

The shelter lady and I giggled.

Ric was not amused.

———————————

"AT LEAST," he said, when he kissed me goodbye under Quicksilver's watchful ice-blue gaze, "I don't have to worry about your personal safety while I'm gone."

I was going to miss him. I forced myself not to look back as I led Quick back to Dolly at a trot, trying not to worry about Ric's personal safety on his vague quest south of the border. I didn't need to ask if it was risky; his tight-lipped dismissal of my questions said everything.

I latched Quick into his safety harness in the front passenger seat. We both knew that it would break away in a second if he wanted it to, but it was easier to look like I was following responsible pet ownership rules than to explain to traffic cops that he was more like a hyper-bright twelve-year-old than a dog. After he'd broken major automotive glass to roar to my rescue in the pet store parking lot I wasn't keen to tie him up.

"I'm going to be hitting the research trail," I told him as we pulled out of the park's lot.

"This town boasts two daily newspapers and a major university library. Somewhere in their records our dead folks must have left a trail."

Quick regarded me with such intelligent eyes that I wanted to put a pair of sunglasses over them so as not to give away his awesome IQ. While he was looking so Rhodes Scholarish, I added, "Ric is a great guy and I really, really like him, so you will not treat him like an appetizer tray, got it?"

Quicksilver growled softly and stared out the open side window, letting his tongue flap through his fangs so he looked like the usual idiot canine easy rider.

When your dog is better at undercover work than you are, you have a problem.

CHAPTER TWENTY-ONE

With Ric gone, I decided to devote myself to chaste, boring research.

Before I tried to dig up any news stories from the forties, I used the laptop (high/low tech again, my quaint cottage had a flawless and fast wireless connection) for online searches to background the Inferno Hotel and Casino. It was the hellcat's pajamas, all right.

After a brief flirtation with becoming a family entertainment destination in the early nineteen-nineties, Las Vegas embraced its old reputation as the Millennium arrived and did an about-face back to being the best that it could be, or in its case, the worst: Sin City.

The Inferno, only three years old but born to be a wild child, was the latest in knock-down, drag-out adult entertainment, cultivating a wicked reputation in an already wicked town. The Hades theme was wrapped around the house rock attraction, a group called the Seven Deadly Sins. I'd never heard of them, but we don't hear about a lot of things in Kansas, and feel the better for it.

I decided to check with Nightwine. He'd been digging up Las Vegas murders a lot longer than Ric and I had.

"You're looking delightful," Godfrey observed as he greeted me at the mansion's back door.

"How do you manage to cover every entrance to this maze of a place?"

"We CinSims are light on our feet," he said with a wink.

"Sin-sims?"

"Ah. You're new in town. That's what I am. 'CinSim' is short for Cinema Simulacrum."

"Godfrey, that's makes about as much sense as Pig Latin. Cinema I know. What's a *simulacrum*?"

"A delightful concept both medieval and modern. I'll let Mr. Nightwine explain this to you. It's a rather delicate topic for me to address."

I watched his gray ears (he was a walking symphony in tones of black, white, and all the shades in-between) tinge faintly darker. Red reads as black in black-and-white formats.

"Are we talking about something like the birds and the bees, Godfrey?"

"As it relates to my kind, yes, Miss. Now, let us repair to the master's quarters. I believe there has been sufficient time for him to have detected your arrival."

Nightwine and his spy cameras! I was sure we were bugged too, which may be why Godfrey had shut up about his exact, er, composition. He seemed totally physically present, just a bit monochromatic around the gills.

The double doors leading to Nightwine's office opened at our approach. The man seemed to have a remote control for everything, including his CinSims.

Godfrey paused at the threshold to announce me. "Miss Street, sir."

"Come in. Well, that is a fetching ensemble, despite being in the rough-and-ready mode favored by today's youth. Denim. Ugh. It should have stayed at Nîmes in France, but at least it seems to be shrinking nicely this century."

I'd forgotten that Nightwine was even more eager to ogle me than Ric, and wished I'd changed out of the low-rise jeans back into denim coveralls.

"I will reluctantly invite you to sit down."

I happily complied, since that put my bare midsection out of view behind the massive desktop.

"You noticed the gambling chip the police took from the grave across the street?" I asked.

"Of course. Most provocative. From the Inferno. My cameras also recorded the mass of old silver dollars. Thirty, I presume?"

I nodded.

"Something old, something new. Do tell me there was something blue, for then we would have a wedded couple."

In fact my vision had revealed that the dead woman had worn a blue dress when she was killed, although time and decomposition had destroyed any but a psychic shred of it.

Odd how fast I was accepting that I must be psychic. But then I'd accepted a mutual attraction with Ric lickety-split too. More had happened to me in Las Vegas in a few days than in a quarter century in Kansas. Call it the Dorothy Syndrome, only Las Vegas was my Oz, Quicksilver my Toto. So who was my wizard, or my wicked witch? Maybe Nightwine won the first part. He always looked like he had something worth hiding behind a curtain.

"I hear the Inferno has an evil reputation," I went on.

"You've been talking to government men again." Nightwine lifted his bushy eyebrows.

"Ex-government man, singular, like I'm an ex-reporter."

"The Cadaver Kid is almost as interesting to me as you. Together, you're irresistible. He's going away, to judge by that parting peck in the park. *Tsk*. So soon infatuation over inconvenient corpses turns into . . . old hat."

When I didn't answer he lifted one eyebrow even higher. "Or are you two cheating my cameras?"

"You and your voyeuristic toys are pathetic, Nightwine."

"Hector, please. So few know me well enough to insult me. It's a good idea to follow the Inferno connection, though. The operation is owned by a *muy misterioso* fellow named Christophe."

Hector's lapse into Spanish made me think he was still eavesdropping on Ric and me, but that name he mentioned rang a whole carillon of bells in my head. "Christophe is a French name."

"Christopher in French, in fact. It can serve either as a given name or a surname. This particular Christophe doesn't indicate which it is in his case. He's just 'Christophe' and quite the enigma. He appeared out of the blue, with money enough to erect a multi-billion-dollar mega-bed hotel and casino that is rumored to have even more spacious private club levels underground. The place is crawling with CinSims, and you know how I feel about their commercial use. He has been ruthless in their acquisition, and in offering the best odds in Vegas, which of course gives him droves of customers. The man is simply not greedy enough for this town. Very suspicious. Of course the Inferno offers every variation of vice, including some I'd not heard of before, which is impressive. Keep your eyes wide open when you visit. It should be an intriguing experience and I'd be interested in your opinion of the operation. Do be careful that you aren't kidnapped by a white slave ring, though."

I wasn't worried. My modest scouting expedition would never bring me into contact with Mr. Big, anyway.

"Could you fill me in more on CinSims?"

"It's short for Cinema Simulacrums, which won't mean anything unless you know what a simulacrum is. Do you?"

I happily pled ignorance and got the full lecture.

"In occult writings, the word *simulacrum* designates some object meant to represent a whole for magical purposes. In voodoo, a fingernail or a hair can represent the whole person it belongs to and is believed to trap part of that individual's essence. *Simulacra* like hair or fingernails can be inserted into a doll representing the person to cast spells upon."

"I've heard of voodoo dolls, but not that fancy name for the body parts used."

"Science fiction, of course, has eagerly embraced the concept of simulacra as artificial creatures intended to impersonate a human being. Although imperfect imitations, they're based on idealized forms of humans. The authors imagine that such creatures wish to become human or replace their human model. Hence such literary immortals as Pinocchio and Commander Data from *Star Trek*."

"I've heard of those guys too. But I thought Data was an android?"

"Time and usage have blurred the meaning of 'android,' but technically an android is an anthropomorphic robot—mechanical. Broadly defined, simulcra can be robotic, but in this context the term applies to a nonmechanical imitation."

"Right," I said, although as far as I knew he could be wrong.

"Then there is the simulacrum that is a copy of a copy, a thing so . . . dissipated . . . in relation to the original that it can stand on its own. Consider the cartoon character of Betty Boop."

"The baby-voiced twenties flapper with the huge eyes and the spit curls . . . boop-boop-a-doop?"

"The cartoon was based on a singer named Helen Kane, but Kane grabbed her share of glory by imitating another singer, Annette Hanshaw. Both Kane and Hanshaw are pop culture footnotes today, almost a hundred years later, but Betty Boop has become a commercial icon of the flapper and lives on in cheesy merchandise everywhere."

"You're saying the resurrection or animation, whatever you want to call it, of film images here in Las Vegas is that last type. They have a life that their originals never did."

"No one but I would say so, but, yes, I think they do, Miss Street, or could. A lot of soul went into creating those on-screen characters. Souls never die. No one knows precisely how CinSims are created—perhaps by pure science implemented by a touch of magic. The Millennium Revelation showed us that what scientists used to call superstition and magic do work in some cases. And if that is indeed provably true, the mob of immortality industries that have sprung up will never admit it, because it's a gold mine. Their process and products are trade secrets.

"It's nothing to me if a rich old fart decides to live on in one of the Sunset Cities as a well-preserved shadow of himself. I might try it myself some day. But the CinSims are far more than the crude animatrons of the late twentieth century! They are a synthesis of two delicate forms: film and the actor's art of breathing life into fictional characters. That's why I deplore their careless use to enrich greedy pockets. If you find anything to tie the Inferno and Christophe to the murder victims in the park, I will broadcast it to the world and bring the bastard down. And I will acquire his stable of CinSims with a view to freeing them, or at least employing them in manners to their liking."

Wow. Ric was out to break the zombie-slave trade. Nightwine wanted to liberate the CinSims. I was working with both of them. What did that make me? Supergirl?

I thanked Nightwine for his information and warning, and then was forced to give him a rear-view departure that produced a giant sigh. What an old lech! Luckily he seemed chained to his desk and his wall of audio-visual surveillance equipment.

Godfrey opened the doors and escorted me back downstairs, steering me into a . . . broom closet at the bottom.

"The master does not oversee scullery rooms," he said. "He has an aversion to objects of domestic drudgery."

I tried not to sneeze from scents of lemon oil and dust while Godfrey pressed a business card into my hand in the semi-dark.

"Since you will be snooping around the most dangerous hotel in Las Vegas, I suggest you go in the guise of a CinSymbiant."

"A silver-screen revenant like you?"

"No, no. Cinema *Symbiants* are perfectly human fans of CinSims like myself. They dress to imitate us, that being the sincerest form of flattery. This card is for Déjà-Vous, a vintage shop that accommodates CinSymbiants. There will be oodles of them at the Inferno, so you will fit right in and won't be molested. Christophe also owns Déjà-Vous. In addition, you should introduce yourself to my, er, cousin, who is quite a fixture at the hotel's main bar, the Inferno. You can't miss him. He's my spitting image."

"Godfrey! I can't ever imagine you spitting, not even in an image. You are not only a handsome devil, but you are a doll!" I squeezed his hand as I took the card for Déjà-Vous. His flesh was solid but on the chilly side. Oh, well, cold hands, warm heart. I wouldn't think about the zombie underpinnings. Zombies might be very decent folks.

We nipped back into the stairwell and into the brightly lit kitchen, where dinner aromas were already wafting about. I'd be eating a microwaved supper, then rushing over to Déjà-Vous off Charleston before it closed at 7:00 PM so I could turn myself into a walking silver screen escapee. What fun! I fully expected to have a hell of a time at the Inferno.

CHAPTER TWENTY-TWO

My own mother wouldn't have known me when I arrived at the Inferno at 9:00 PM.

Not that I'd ever had a mother to know me, or to not know me.

The hotel-casino was a bat-winged swoop of opaque black glass towering fifty stories or so. It was ringed with moats of fire and ice, with holographic figures writhing in them like the naked babes in the opening credits to an old James Bond movie. I always tried not to look at the naked and the dead if I didn't have to. Something about both states was unnerving.

I was fairly self-conscious when I turned Dolly over to the valet parking chap: he was a symphony of milk chocolate skin wearing a pleated white ancient Egyptian kilt, shoulder-spanning beaded collar, gilt sandals, and a jackal-head mask tricked up with really heavy eyeliner. At least he could remove *his* makeup with the flick of a wrist.

Who was I to snicker at the underdressed help?

The last I'd seen of myself in the Déjà-Vous mirror, my baby blues were hidden behind gray contact lenses. My hair and skin had been deemed black and white enough already for the silver screen. The dress du jour was a floor-length black velvet thirties gown with a giant pair of rhinestone clips on the shoulder. The severe neckline cut across my collarbones but draped well below my waist in backless splendor. I wore white satin pumps and

carried a silver fox stole that I was assured had died for
our sins eighty years ago, way before the animal rights
enlightenment, so why waste it? My hair had been drawn
back and coiled into a thick figure eight at the nape of my
neck, giving me a Spanish air that I sure wished Ric was
here to see. *Olé!*

Lots of lone women like me were ankling into the
Inferno in various cinematic get-ups swiped from the birth
of film around 1900 to fifties' science fiction thrillers. I'd
never been a groupie before. It was unnerving, since I
wasn't sure who or what we were being groupies of. Or
for.

My palms were a tad damp on the soft velvet bag that
matched the dress. The duds were due back at Déjà-
Vous in the morning, so I desperately didn't want to get
sweaty fingerprints on the vintage silk-velvet that went
for hundreds of dollars a yard now. That was the trouble:
I knew how rare and costly vintage clothing was, and
we all shouldn't be traipsing around in this stuff like
giggly prom queens . . . because my partners in crime
pouring into the Inferno were definitely gigglers from
ages eight to eighty-four. We fanned out through the icy,
air-conditioned casino that blasted screams and moans
and flares of fire as the slot machines swallowed bills and
spit out mostly sound and fury, not coins. Miniaturized
versions of the mirrored balls from Jazz Age ballrooms
floated above and around us like flocks of intrusive
heavy-metal bubbles.

The Inferno Bar seemed like a familiar refuge when
I first spotted its mirrored wall of endlessly reflected
liquor bottles. Then I noticed that the bar top was
polished exotic wood carved with exotic demonic
faces. It rested on a giant Plexiglas aquarium filled with
leaping flames and tiny capering devils. What were
these things? Fire lizards? Projections? Or slaves of the

décor? Some god-awful rock music was drilling through
the sound system, all wailing guitars, manic drums, and
tortured saxophones.

The sight of a dignified figure in a well-cut tuxedo
(with white skin, black hair and pencil-thin mustache)
was like glimpsing an angel on the threshold of hell. He
was holding forth between two barstools of red enameled
steel, a martini glass in one hand and a sterling silver
cigarette lighter in the other. (Gold, of course, would not
match the strict B/W dress code.)

"Hello, sir," I greeted him over the racket, "your cousin
Godfrey suggested I introduce myself to you."

"Ah." His eyes were slightly bleary. "How is old
Godfrey anyway? Still seeing that dippy socialite?"

"No, he's . . . employed now."

"Sorry to hear it. Work will be the death of the leisure
class. Martini, m'dear?"

"Not . . . yet. Godfrey said you could orient me to this
place."

"My bar is your bar, sweet lady. Have a seat."

"There aren't any free."

"Oh, so there aren't. A shame you shall have to balance
on those tricky little evening slippers. I suppose I'm
forgetting myself. I'm rather prone to that." He put down
the cigarette lighter after servicing ladies on bracketing
barstools. "Charles is the name."

"Nice to meet you, Charles."

"No. The *surname*. Charles. Nick Charles."

I got the vintage film reference right away. "Not the
famous detective from the pen of the man who created
Sam Spade? You solved the *Thin Man* case."

"Well, I and my wife Nora did. And Asta, our intrepid
wire-haired terrier. And a few bottles of Gilbey's. Have
you ever heard of an intrepid wire-haired terrier?"

"No, only of an intrepid Lhasa apso."

"Don't know that breed. Sounds rather Shangri-La, something chichi the ladies always go for."

"As a matter of fact, the breed was sacred to the Dalai Lamas and forbidden to leave Tibet, but an Englishwoman smuggled out a breeding pair decades ago."

"Ah. The English make the best spies. Look so harmless, don't you know? 'A breeding pair.' I'm always in favor of procreation, so long as it doesn't result in children."

"This was puppies."

"Noted. What do you wish to know?

"What is this noise?"

"I quite agree." Nick Charles took a long swallow of his martini. "I prefer Paul Whiteman. That 'noise,' I fear, is at the behest of our host and my estimable employer."

"Our host?"

"Christophe, of course. Showy fellow, but low-brow. I imagine the man never owned a monkey suit." He spread his arms to display his handsome tuxedo. "After six there is nothing else I'd rather be seen in, except a bathtub full of gin."

"Godfrey said you could show me around the Inferno. The less public areas."

"I'm supposed to anchor the bar, but I might be able to slip away for some detecting work. Even better, I have a reliable chum who might be up to an easy break-and-enter job."

He gave me a friendly and totally gin-disabled lascivious once-over. "Poor fellow. He is always overlooked and eager for recognition. Speaking of which—" Nick Charles ran his glance over the line of female CinSymbiants lining the bar. "Where's Nora? Nora should be here. She always sees to me and my martinis."

Several slinky dames in gowns like mine presented unlit cigarettes, many in holders. Nick Charles dutifully lit them in turn, if a bit shakily.

Where *was* Nora Charles? That woman was the pepper to his salt, Myrna Loy to William Powell, his sophisticated wife. But now William Powell was a split–screen personality: Godfrey at Nightwine's place, the Good Time Charles, Nicky Charles, at the Inferno. And no one had thought to give either Powell CinSim the women made for them in the movies: Carole Lombard and Myrna Loy.

I felt a chill of apprehension and indignation. Nightwine was right. The CinSims shouldn't be up for sale, ripped from their film environments and partners, doled out among Las Vegas hotel-casinos and clubs as enslaved attractions, without free will or a say in their own usage.

Before I could launch into a barside invective about that I noticed that Nicky Charles had ebbed away down the polished if perverse wood.

"I've been waiting for you," a velvet basso voice said behind me, close enough to send a subtle vibration from my ear down to the soles of my dancing slippers. It was a stage voice, all timbre and open throat and intimate inference.

At least he hadn't added the hokey "all my life."

I turned around to eyeball him and then I wasn't sure he had a life.

He was as white as a corpse . . . whiter. He had white-as-marble clothing, skin, hair. He seemed as tall as the white cliffs of Dover and I was wearing high heels. The only thing dark on him was the rimless sunglasses that obscured his eyes.

"Dance?" he asked. "The floor is solid black walnut and very smooth." When I looked around to see some couples in motion around us, I was in sudden motion too, my white-gloved right hand in the custody of his left, my feet forced to retreat to a rhythmic advance.

No. The eyes behind the glasses wouldn't be white. They'd be pink. Mr. Foxy Fox Trot wasn't the walking dead (maybe). He was an albino.

"I don't usually do the senior shuffle," he murmured into the coils of my fancy bun, behind my left ear, "but I had to get my hands on that magnificent back."

And he was doing just that, getting his dead-white hand on my naked back as we danced. His temperature felt neither hot nor cold, but lukewarm. His oddly callused fingertips (maybe horny in both senses of the word) played my spine from nape to bottom curve like a musical instrument.

There was nothing vintage about this dude, except maybe glam rock 'n' roll from the seventies. His white hair, shoulder-blade-brushing long, looked spun-glass soft. Spun fiberglass had been called "angel hair" when it decked fifties Christmas tree angels until recognized as a health hazard and taken off the market This image fit a guy wearing such opposite attire as a loose white poet's shirt that would have done Byron proud and supernaturally tight white leather pants that a young Mick Jagger would have killed to have six pair of in bad-boy black. The obsidian sunglasses added a Blues Brothers note and hid any creepy rabbit-pink eyes.

"And by whom do I have the honor of being fondled on the dance floor?" I inquired in Jane Austen diction.

"Gives great grammar too," he said. "Call me Snow, sweeting." His accent was part Brit, part indefinable European. "I'm the lead singer for Seven Deadly Sins." He gestured at an empty stage visible over a mob of bobbing heads between the bar and the distance stage.

"And which deadly sin are you?" I asked politely.

"Oh, all of them right now, I imagine," he purred. That baritone voice could indeed purr. "Pure Lust and Gluttony at this moment, can't you tell? I'll be mortal Envy if I learn you're taken, then Anger. When I get you into my bed I'll be Sloth incarnate, because we won't leave it for a month. I'll be sheer Greed for you the entire time."

This was flirting in hyper drive. Flirting was against my religion, but I realized that I could now get all the wrong frissons in all the right places since Ric and I had literally connected over the dead bodies in the park, not to mention certain dances with werewolves. As for dancing with Snow, his commanding lead made my two left feet into twinkle toes. But this guy was so over-the-top sexy and amusing that I couldn't take his line personally. A slinky Nora Charles gown had been inciting men on and off the silver screen for decades. Not to mention that I was getting the best back massage of my life. Well, the *only* back massage of my life.

What was it with men in Las Vegas? First Ric, then Nightwine, now this. Snow's fingers made a sensual glissando return trip up my spine to my nape, then began pulling out the industrial-strength bobby pins that held my chignon in place. My hair, like the walls of Jericho, came tumbling down.

"You're ruining the CinSymbiant illusion," I pointed out.

"Illusions are for small-time players. Reality rocks. What's your name?"

He gently tugged down my hair. What a cinematic game this was! I knew he'd really get off on it, so I spoke slowly through a Mona Lisa smile, like Lauren Bacall taunting Bogie with her "put your lips together and blow" how-to-whistle line in *To Have and Have Not,* a bit of dialogue supposedly written by either Hemingway or Faulkner. Who knew what those old lit guys could get up to?

"De-*lie*-lah."

"Ah, De-lie-lah." My dopey name sounded delicious in his hybrid accent. He was pulling my hair and head even farther back, almost like a vampire—a rather bloodless one—baring a throat. But a throat wasn't his thing at the moment.

"Instead of lusting to cut my hair," he said, "I suggest that you grow yours."

He released it and finger-walked down my spine again until his hand slipped under the draped velvet curtain of the gown. "When we make love under a curtain of black and white locks it will look very sexy in the Venetian glass mirror over the bed."

Okay, he was hinting he wasn't a vampire with that mirror reference, but he sure was a sensualist in my book. I stared into the disconcerting rimless black sunglasses. What's a pseudo-film goddess to do with a line like that?

"You might want to rethink that mirror, Snow. With me, I mean. I have a way with mirrors." I was bluffing, but my close recent encounter with the witch in the cottage mirror had made me cocky.

Maybe I wasn't just a medium, but a *silver* medium. I seemed to be sensitive to anything made of silver . . . a silver-screen movie strip, mirror backing, sterling jewelry . . . now, mirror-shade sunglasses.

Snow lifted one almost-invisible white eyebrow above the right dark sunglass lens as his hand polished my shoulder blades with my own loosened curls.

"A way with mirrors? Should be interesting. Gotta run, Delilah. I'll see you in your dreams if not in my mirror."

He left as swiftly as he had appeared. The air around us had been electric, charged, sometimes hot, sometimes cold, and always just right, like Baby Bear's bed was for Goldilocks. Except I was closer to Snow White and bears could eat up a girl abandoned in the woods as easily as they could gobble porridge.

CHAPTER TWENTY-THREE

After Snow left, it was as if an invisible bubble around us had burst. The crowd tightened around me, buzzing as lights bathed the stage. All the nearby women eyed me, their expressions drenched in envy.

Looks can't kill . . . yet. So I held back and stood apart as the women surged forward to watch the Seven Deadly Sins strut onstage to screams, whistles, and applause.

The woman in shreds of glittering crimson costume that bared almost everything could only be Lust. Another woman in equally skimpy lurid poison-green was obviously Envy. The rest were guys in stock rock uniforms: tight black leather pants and tarted up jackets, vests, and shirts. Gluttony must be Mr. Patchwork Velvet Vest in vegetable shades of greens, orange, and yellow. Sloth sported drapey silver-gray jersey slathered with white rhinestones. Anger's black leather biker jacket was inset with blood-red lightning bolts. Greed's outfit was the color of money, a forest-like mélange of green, amber, and rust with an overall glitter of gold and silver.

The Sins began playing. Gluttony's insistent initial percussive beat gave way to Anger's rumbling bass guitar. Sloth's rhythm guitar amplified the low vibration until a raw, repeating riff from Greed on lead guitar seized the stage. Then Lust and Envy joined in with a harmonic chorus of mock-orgasmic "oo-oos."

The audience's screams greeted a gorgeous life-size dragon (assuming dragons were the size of a killer whale) as it descended from the high above-stage flies, snorting clouds of smoke and fire from its two heads. I recalled from my Our Lady of the Lake religion classes that Revelations portrayed the Devil as a dragon.

The pale glittering figure on this dragon's back slid down one formidable scowling, bestial head to bound to the stage. The crowd went wilder.

Snow was Pride, of course, the only missing Deadly Sin.

His costume, bejeweled white from shoulder to white patent-leather boot-top, evoked Elvis. The whipping mane of white hair recalled blues-man Edgar Winter, but the total effect was pure blazing fallen archangel, Lucifer in the Sky with Diamonds.

Whew. I found it all so obvious . . . yet completely fabulous erotic-rock theater. The memory of Snow's far more understated dalliance with me only intrigued me more. Why hadn't the rabid fans swarmed us? Was he somehow invisible to them? I bent to reclaim my fallen hairpins before they were trampled flat. A woman nearby bent to help. We rose together.

"Can I keep one?" the woman pled.

I summed up her pleasantly plump face and the embroidered velvet shawl that camouflaged middle-aged spread. She'd obviously stayed behind to assist me.

"Why?"

She leaned up to whisper hotly in my ear. "He touched it." Her warm, worshiping gaze flicked to the curls I was twisting back into a chignon and pinning into place. He'd touched them too.

"Listen," I told her. "My name's Delilah. I cut people's hair, not the other way around. So forget it. No locks for the lovelorn here."

"I'd pay . . . five hundred."

"He's just a stage performer. It's all glitter and illusion. Who is he anyway?"

"Cocaine's been the Seven Deadly Sins' lead singer for ten years, but he's so much *more*. He owns this hotel-casino and hot properties like it all over the world. They're the only places SDS performs anymore."

She had leaned so close that her breath and words blended in my ear.

"The online chat groups say his mouth is hotter than brimstone and they call him Ice Prick, though no one knows from personal experience. The tabloids claim he's an albino vamp. He denies it violently, but I saw him looking at your throat. Let him have it, honey. It'd be heaven."

This was way more than I wanted to know. If I'd read this description in a personals ad, I'd react with a shudder rather than a frisson, given my personal history. What creeped me out most was the frigid prick part, not the vamp suspicions. Accused witches in medieval times had claimed the Devil had an icy penis. Now I knew the reason for the nickname, Snow. It was all sex, drugs, and rock and roll. With the supernatural follies mixed in until *un*done.

A vampire bite isn't fatal, everybody knew that now, unless the parties wanted it to be. Some vamp tramps ached to become vamps themselves, despite the inconveniences, and that took an exchange of all bodily fluids. Some longed to be drained to death. Maybe it personalized the slitting-one's-wrists in the bathtub form of suicide.

For me, I'd not yet found a way into workable ordinary human sex. Now that I'd connected with Ric, I didn't need to take the obscenic route. But I'd sure enjoyed our little tango duel. Hell, I was only human, even if Snow wasn't. I knew enough to know what I really wanted and needed: a little love and support. Hard to come by, but I'd glimpsed it now, in two forms, man and dog. I was one lucky girl since arriving in Las Vegas. All I had to do was stay alive to enjoy it.

I peeled the groupie's avid hand off my wrist before the woman tried to skin my back for a trophy–Hector had been right that ghoulie groupies would tear apart the objects of their obsessions—and gave the mock-blind man in the bright lights a last glance. The music was raw, rhythmic, but I didn't need to listen.

Nick Charles waited for me beside the Inferno Bar, his comforting, smartly sloshed, dapper self, a spare martini in hand just for me.

"Thanks, Nicky. I needed this."

"Everyone does but they don't know it yet." He reeled only slightly as he picked up his own almost empty glass. His martini glasses were always almost empty.

I leaned against the bar to sip gin and vermouth like the lady Myrna Loy's Nora Charles always was, wishing I had my own Asta on a leash at my feet. Poor little Achilles. Sudden tears stung my eyes like undiluted gin. The unconditional love of a dog is impossible to replace, even with another dog as awesome as Quicksilver.

"I'm glad—" Nicky leaned groupie close on a soft scent of vermouth. After all, we *were* married for the evening, "—we met up. Word around the watering hole here is that the Inferno is the hub of all the straight and kinked crime in Las Vegas. That chap onstage in the shiny pajamas is rumored to be the headman of the mob that runs this place. Hard to believe his act. What is his problem?"

I took his arm with a smile. Sexy *no*w translated way different from when he'd been the sex kitten's pajamas back in the day.

"Another one for the road?" Even as Nicky spoke he nodded at the bartender. "The traffic on the Strip could kill a sober pedestrian."

I laughed and hitched my skirt and myself onto a bar stool to eye the bartender. "I'll have an Albino Vampire."

His congenial face went as white as mine was naturally.
All along the bar, chitchat stopped. Glasses ceased
clinking. Other bartenders froze in the act of pouring
scotch, gin, vodka, wine, beer. Obviously, Christophe's
staff knew the boss hated that rumor.

"What's . . . in it?" My bartender sounded like he was
being invisibly throttled.

Behind me Cocaine—Snow must be a, *hmm*, pet
name–was pouring out a great rock ballad about Lady
Velvet. I could feel his sunglasses zeroing in on my
bare, defenseless, and still so well pampered back, and
proceeded to ad lib a recipe. "A jigger of white Crème de
Cocoa, a jigger of vanilla Stoly, a jigger of Lady Godiva
white chocolate liqueur topped with a swirl of Chambord
raspberry liquor the color of blood, in a martini glass."

Nick Charles regarded me with awed approval and
a gentle palm clapping. The bartender shortly after
presented me with a dazzling white dessert of a drink
tricked out with a hint of hot pink. The boys and girls at
the bar gasped as one.

Nick and I chimed rims, then I swiveled to face the stage.

Cocaine/Snow still had the spotlight but the sunglasses
might be looking anywhere.

I lofted my glass in a farewell toast.

Snow lashed his spun-glass angel hair around like a
white Persian cat-o'-nine-tails and ended the song with
long, wailing banshee of a guitar chord.

I'd have liked to think the final flourish was just for me,
but then so did every woman present, and most of them were
storming the mosh pit, clawing each other for the honor of
being one of the women Snow bent down to kiss.

Ridiculous. I turned to Nicky. "Time to rock 'n' roll."

"Could you say that in English, please?"

"Time to do a do-si-do around the executive offices
here. Are you and your friend in Security game?"

Chapter Twenty-Four

Before you could say "illegal entry," I had another uninvited hand on my bare back, this one clammy. I turned around to see . . . nothing. I felt another brush.

"Cut that out!"

I still saw nothing.

"Ah, lady, give a guy a break. It's pretty lonesome walking in my shoes," said a street-weary voice.

I glanced down. The plush blood-red carpeting that paved the casino area we were walking through was registering the imprint of a pair of size twelves, but that was the only sign that a fresh CinSim who was about as sexy as a cantaloupe was following me.

"Nicky!"

He was bringing up the rear, and I was beginning to wish it was *my* rear.

"Claude gets a bit carried away," Nicky said. "He's been invisible for almost eighty years. He hasn't had much chance to make a . . . *hic* . . . pass at anything more than a visiting breeze."

My knowledge of vintage film was finally paying off. As I recalled, H.G. Wells's *Invisible Man*, played by Claude Rains in the classic film, was a scientist who found that his secret formula for invisibility turned him into an insane killer.

Just who I'd want feeling up my spine. Science gone wrong was always turning people into monsters in the movies from the nineteen-thirties to the fifties. I sure as heck didn't need one of them guarding my back.

"*Shhh!*" Nicky leaned against a wall. "This is the entrance to Christophe's office. Only Claude can disable the security cameras."

"Why?" I asked.

"Because I'm invisible, silly," Claude said with a parting pinch to my butt.

"Watch that! Vintage velvet fingerprints, you know."

"So I see." Claude chortled like a lovesick seal, but I felt the air rush of him passing me to slip through the office door.

"Do we really need that creep?" I asked Nicky.

"He's just misunderstood."

"He pinched me!"

"Believe me, I would myself if I didn't think Nora was out there somewhere, waiting for my personal attention in that area."

"I'm sorry, Nicky. It must be terrible being separated like this."

"At least Godfrey manages to come in now and again when his boss releases him for an errand."

"Releases?'"

"We're tied to our environments. We'd melt like the Wicked Witch of the West if we wandered off without permission and suitable . . . adjustments. Has to be that way. Couldn't have valuable investments like us two-stepping down the Strip to the next hotel."

"That's outrageous!"

"It's better than being trapped onscreen saying the same lines over and over the rest of our, er, lives. However, I do relish a return to my detecting days. What are we looking for?"

"I don't know. A reason why an Inferno gambling chip that's no more than three years old would show up in an eighty-year-old mob burial site."

"How do you know it's a mob burial site?"

"It's on present-day public land that was raw desert decades ago. And inside was a dead couple. In evening dress. Coupling. Shot *and* stabbed to death."

"*Flagrante delicto,* right?"

"Is that a dessert?"

"No, my dear, it's a refined way of saying they were caught in the act and nailed for nailing. That does indeed have an old-time mob feel to it. Gangsters' molls were major players in early Las Vegas."

"I was thinking more Romeo and Juliet. They seemed young."

"The bones?"

No, the vibes, but I couldn't admit my occult visions, not even to a walking illusion.

"Aha!" Meanwhile, the Invisible Man was having a field day rooting through a sleek white Louis XV desk in front of an audio-visual equipment wall that made Nightwine's look like a Tinker Toy.

"Is this what you wanted, lady fair?" Claude asked with demented courtesy.

On the desk's glass surface a series of sketches spun to catch my eye. I rushed over. At first I took the drawings for coin designs, but then realized that they were sketches for the Inferno casino chips.

I'd never gotten a good look at the one Detective Haskell's CSI team had unearthed and bagged. Now I was looking at the drawings of its prototype, of several prototypes. Curiouser and curiouser. The styles were a parade of decades, from the forties to the teens of our own century, and they all bore the unmistakable mark of that Art Deco master, Erté. Who'd lived into his nineties, but had been dead these, um, thirty–some years. Maybe.

I sat in one of the white leather and steel chairs before the desk, flipping through a cavalcade of designs. It was like ogling Cadillac dream cars from the forties to my

Dolly in the mid-fifties to the post-2000 all-electric and hybrid models of the present day. It was like viewing the private commissions of a dead artist.

"I really need to see the version of the chip Haskell's got in his evidence baggie," I murmured, knowing I had about as much chance of that as flying.

Someone answered my request, though, with a deep, throaty growl.

I looked over my shoulder.

Oh. A huge white tiger sat between the door and me. I felt the air-rush of the Invisible Man living up to his name as he whooshed right out of the room. The longer tufts of hair at the tiger's cheeks . . . jowls . . . trembled in the *vroom* of Claude's unseen departure. The Fuller-brush stiff whiskers twitched, but the jungle-green eyes remained focused only on mine.

Nicky edged away from the desk. "I need another martini."

I eyed the tiger. "I don't think it does room service."

So there we were: me on the chair, Nicky against the wall, and the tiger between the door and us. I continued to study the sketches, there being nothing else to do. Maybe a dozen different designs, from the female nude holding up a bubble to the silhouette of a spike-spired castle to the open-jawed, fang-toothed maw that could have been a striking serpent, or snake, or tiger.

"What d'you wanta bet the fangs are the current chip design," I said. Nicky didn't venture an opinion.

I looked up. The tiger was still doing guard duty, but its gaze was focused behind me.

I looked across the desk's sleek surface and, sure enough, the tufted white patent-leather executive throne was occupied. Must be a back entrance to this office.

"Imagine seeing you here," Snow said.

"Yeah. I feel the same way. Déjà vu to you too."

Still the same? Not quite. He was wearing a silky white satin jogging suit and his hair ended in damp rat-tails. He was fresh from the shower after the long, hot shower of adulation in the mosh pit.

"You are the elusive Christophe, I presume."

"Not so elusive. You, however, appear to have slippery talents. Those sketches are unsigned, of course, but are still valuable."

"Especially since the artist was dead for the later dates on these drawings."

"Death," Snow mused, "the artist's last, best agent. Value skyrockets post-mortem. You were planning to steal and sell these?"

"No." I tossed them back on the desktop. "Just to admire them. I don't believe in ripping off the dead."

He pushed the black sunglass lenses tight against the bridge of his nose. "Death. So hard to tell what it is nowadays. Take Nicky here, for instance."

"Sorry, boss." Nick stepped away from the wall, empty martini glass in hand. "I was looking for an open bar."

"Better skedaddle back to the Inferno bar, my friend. You know they always serve your brand."

Nicky glanced at me, the tiger, Snow. "Miss, I don't fancy leaving you here."

"I can take care of myself, and several others. Cheers, Nicky. Keep that new cocktail on the menu for me."

The tiger growled. Snow frowned. Nicky left.

"Leave us," Snow told the tiger.

It didn't move, its gaze sharper than a mine-cut emerald while it watched me.

"Now," Snow said.

I turned to him in surprise. The command had been harsh, but who could read those mirror-shade eyes? When I turned back, the tiger was gone.

"So," he said. "What do you want?"

It was a global question, but I managed to concentrate on the immediate. "I want to know when the Inferno chose its chip design, and what that was."

His pale hands fanned the white drawing paper like cards in a deck. His fingernails, I noticed, had no moons at top or bottom, but were the uniform dead white French manicure nail-tips.

"You were right. The fangs, of course. Why did you want to know? So badly. "

"I investigate these things."

"The icons I choose for my hotel?"

"You're really Christophe?"

"Among other things."

"And I don't want to know *that* badly."

"No, not itinerant young ladies who show up at dangerous places in backless gowns."

He smiled as he dealt the sketches like a hand in a game of cards. It was hard to see him smile; the lips were so pale against that whitewashed skin and shark-strong teeth. His canines were slightly elongated, no more than I'd seen on some perfectly normal humans.

"The Inferno," he said, "has always been a dream, or a nightmare, in men's eyes. Trying to date it or its artifacts is like trying to pin down sand. Take these drawings, study them. They are all dust in the wind."

I stood. "No thanks. I've seen what I needed to. They imply the Inferno isn't the brand-new concept it pretends to be. That somebody has been waiting and planned to spring it on the Strip for a long time. And now here *you* are."

I'd hoped my hint that I suspected he himself went "way back" like the chip designs would get a response, but I was disappointed. Snow remained enigmatic, saying nothing.

No tiger still stood behind me, though, when I turned to leave. I paused.

"What?" he asked.

"I don't want to give you my back."

"It's a little late, don't you think?"

"Never too late."

I started to turn, then whipped around to look back. He was gone, the chair empty, the precious drawings still lying there to be studied. Never trust a deal that came so easily. The Devil was good at those.

I walked out, heaving a huge mental sigh of relief, wondering what Ric Montoya and Hector Nightwine and my own investigative reporter's instincts had gotten this Kansas orphan into. Nothing I couldn't handle. I hoped.

CHAPTER TWENTY-FIVE

I dropped the CinSymbiant clothes back at Déjà-Vous the next morning. They rented or sold their wares and offered me the gown and clips for $600 but I settled for the gray contact lenses for $30. I'd enjoyed wearing undercover eyes and might want to use them in the future. Like a lot of people with vivid blue eyes, I was tired of being remembered only for that.

I did have to pay for the three missing hairpins I'd let the Cocaine groupie have. A buck-forty. I should have charged her the going rate for a Cocaine memento. Might have been able to afford the gown then.

It also turned out that the "owner" had ordered that I be given a twenty percent "handling discount" on the entire package. Cute. Call him Cocaine, Christophe, or Snow, this guy didn't miss a trick.

I hopped into Dolly with a high heart, my laptop in the passenger seat. Quicksilver was not institutionally welcome and I was visiting the Nevada Historical Society library to look up missing–person candidates for the lovers buried in Sunset Park. I'd even called the police captain Ric counted as a source, Kennedy Malloy.

I almost swallowed my wisdom teeth when an alto woman's voice answered to the name. She did tell me, reluctantly, the mint year of the silver dollars found at the site, 1921. Still in circulation in the seventies. I couldn't tell if her reluctance was the usual police reticence, or if she was as startled as I was to suddenly find Ric a bridge to a strange woman.

When I thought about it, it figured that his inside man at the Las Vegas Metropolitan Police would be a woman. What woman wouldn't want to tell Ric anything he'd want to know? Maybe I was prejudiced. As I drove I replayed our meeting. Had we been hit with some love potion that had been trapped with the dead lovers all these decades? Everyone liked to think romance was magic, a form of mysterious chemistry, but what if it was something catching, like the plague?

I was glad to be heading for a place where I'd always been able to keep my feet on the ground and my head in the here and now: a library.

A quick online search revealed the Clark County Library had the *Las Vegas Evening Review Journal* from 1930 through 1958—when it had long been just the *LV Review Journal*—on microfilm. I explained "no dogs in the library" to Quick and soon had Dolly aimed toward the University of Nevada Las Vegas. The Clark County Library was only a block or so from campus on E. Flamingo Road.

Once there I settled in, grateful modern microfilm was nothing like those old reels of white-on-black filmstrips people had to reel past at seasick speeds years before, If I found anything of interest, I could simply print out a facsimile for a small fee.

My only distraction: the ads for what were now vintage clothes . . . oh my! Cheap as Saturday night sin. If only time travel was a post-Millennium Revelation option!

WHEN I GOT HOME, I noticed a scent of lemon oil and Mr. Clean. Someone had been tidying the premises. Quick was out. That wasn't unusual.

During our first night in the cottage, he'd pawed open the French lever on one of the living room windows. I didn't know he'd been gone until he jumped back in that way when I was making breakfast. I tried tying the window lever shut, but he used another one. The next night I tied them all shut . . . and he untied one with his teeth. This was not a dog that would sleep by a cold fake fireplace all night.

So I now left the window over the laundry table open and Quick spent his nights doing whatever really big dogs do. I couldn't blame him for not wanting to be cooped up. I just hoped he didn't get hurt. Even Superdog could run into trouble.

I put down my photocopies and headed along the hall to the bedroom to change into something comfy, like T-shirt and shorts. My image in the mirror at the hall's always-dusky end made me pause. Last night when I'd come in, it seemed as if I had glimpsed someone else in that mirror, a different girl in a different vintage dress.

Then my double vision had cleared and I saw it was me, only I had blue eyes in that reflection, not gray, despite the color-dampening contact lenses. Weird. But the hall was ill lit with a single overhead fixture, and I'd been drinking, not to mention scared and stressed. Now, in daylight, I just looked like me, only more casually dressed in slacks and a knit top. I'd barely changed before the doorbell rang with an old-fashioned melodic chime.

When I rushed to open it, I found a little green man standing on my stoop. No, he didn't have the big black bug-eyes of an extra-terrestrial. He just looked like an impish offspring of the Jolly Green Giant of TV commercial fame. The silver sandals he wore did nothing for his hairy hammertoes.

No *ho-ho-ho* from him. "Sign here, lady." As he handed me a computerized device I noticed a green delivery truck outside the open gate. The print on the side read MERCURY EXPRESS. HOMEGROWN DELIVERY SERVICE.

The plain white box was big, flat, and light, but way too deep to be pizza, unless it was a triple deep-dish Chicago style one. Besides, it was only faintly warm from the summer's day and the sun-heated back of a metal truck.

I gave the green guy a three-dollar tip and got a nasty look in return. "I should get hazardous duty pay for delivering to Nightwine's place, lady."

Twinkletoes stalked away, chiming. I hadn't noticed the bells on the toe sandal straps before. Only in Las Vegas, where every service person wore bizarre themed costumes. It had been a costume, hadn't it?

I was chuckling to myself when I laid the box on the dining table and pulled off the annoying invisible tape at the sides. I heard the encouraging crinkle of tissue paper.

This was beginning to look like a present. Had Ric —?

Okay, my mind was jogging on only one track lately.

Oh. *No!* It was the gown, and clips, from Déjà-Vous. A sheet of white vellum written on in thick dark burgundy ink read: "With my deepest compliments and self-interest. Snow."

Amid the folds of black velvet coiled a slender lock of white hair, maybe nine inches long. Then I noticed a P.S. under the note's signature: "If I give you a piece of my power, maybe you won't feel compelled to cut it off, cut it all off, my modern-day Delilah."

I could practically hear him purring those words. Ridiculous. I couldn't, wouldn't accept anything from him, and had, in fact, refused to accept the "handling discount" even though the clerk had whined about making out a new receipt. You might have thought the guy feared his far-distant boss.

I was more angry than annoyed now. The soft lock of hair reminded me, so painfully, of my Achilles that it brought tears to my eyes. I couldn't resist the temptation of recapturing the lost sensation of petting my lost Achilles, of reaching out to touch the long, pale hair.

The damned thing . . . moved, faster than I could see. Like a serpent it coiled around my right wrist, then

tightened into something hard and silver and familiar.
One-half of a handcuff.

Gooseflesh ran up my right arm along with an interior
shiver that made me shudder. As soon as I'd registered
the lock's silken circling of my wrist I'd felt it harden
into cold metal.

The doorbell rang again.

Honestly! Couldn't anyone just leave me alone today?

I stomped to the door in my bare feet and pulled it
violently open.

The man on the stoop looked familiar, but totally human
at least. Well, sort of. I placed him: the police guy from the
Sunset Park crime scene. That bigoted Detective Haskell.
How had he gotten in here without going past the security
system and Godfrey? Obviously, the delivery service had
been passed through security, because it was a previous
visitor, given the crack the guy made about Nightwine's tips.

"Yes?" I asked. "You want?"

He walked in like he owned the place and planned to
rent it to someone else.

"You. Downtown."

"Me? There must be some mistake."

"Yeah. Yours. This isn't an invitation." He grabbed my
arm.

I pulled away.

He jerked it back so hard I grunted protest.

The sound of a motorcycle revving its engine distracted
us both.

We had not heard an engine. It was the deep sustained
growl of a hundred-and-fifty-pound dog, like something
you might encounter in a tiger cage. Quicksilver was
standing in the hallway arch, moving forward.

"*Jesus!*" Haskell didn't drop my arm. He drew his
semiautomatic from a rear paddle holster with the other
hand and pointed it at Quicksilver.

"No!" I twisted myself between Haskell and Quicksilver. No more dogs died on my watch, in my own place. "Don't shoot. Quicksilver, *no!* Sit."

Haskell unleashed his own version of a growl. "Get that animal locked out of my sight or he's chopped liver."

Quicksilver was strong, big, and fast, but I wasn't going to risk him against a hail of bullets, and I was sure Haskell was the type to overkill.

"Back, boy!" I didn't have a good place to pen him up, so I pushed him into the kitchen, and then shut the pantry door on him. "Stay!"

When I turned, Haskell was right behind me, stuffing the gun down the front of his pants as proud and pleased as if it was something else.

My heart was still pounding from the sudden threat to Quicksilver, but I found my calm, cool TV reporter voice. "What's this about, Detective?"

"Dead freak at the Inferno and you're all over the security tapes mixing it up with her in fancy dress. Very fancy dress." He eyed me slowly, as if I was a naked centerfold.

"If you want to talk to me about it—"

"Talk, nothing. I want your fingerprints. Your DNA." He swaggered closer on each sentence.

Quicksilver's claws were bounding against the shut door. It wouldn't hold him forever. I had to get out of here before then. Cooperation, capitulation, was the best move for both of us.

"I'm onto you," Haskell said, getting literally in my face. "You're not ex-FBI, lady. You're nothing more than a suspect, a damn likely one. You have the right to remain silent. You have the right to an—" He stopped to stare at my wrist. "You're already wearing what's left of one set of handcuffs you've escaped?"

"It's a fashion statement," I snarled. *Damn Snow for making me look like an escaped felon!*

My show of resistance gave Haskell the spur he needed.

"You'll be making a statement, all right." Haskell spun me around to snap both my wrists behind my back into the real thing. "You damn Goth punks with your fake prison tattoos and your heavy-metal jewelry. Think you can sneer at the police. Think again."

He pushed me face-first against the nearest wall. I avoided a broken nose only be turning my head fast.

My heart was pounding so hard I could hardly hear anything over it. No wonder. First there'd been the threat to Quicksilver, now the swift administration of my favorite phobia: bound and in the hands of bullies. I didn't know what had happened long ago to kick it off, but this scene was much too close to that for continuing sanity.

I had to calm down and think.

Meanwhile, the bastard was indicating that I should spread my legs by nudging my inner thighs with the muzzle of his semiautomatic, simultaneously patting me down and feeling me up fore and aft.

Rage and fear mixed into a potent stew inside my chest, but my head kept fighting for control. He was police. He could maul me but he couldn't really hurt me.

"You white-trash bitches," he was muttering. "Always bad-mouthing white guys and you turn around hot to be Meskin meat. All that good white skin wasted as black boys' and bite boys' meat." He pulled my hair, hard, back to examine both sides of my neck as if I were a horse for sale. "No freaking bite boy nibbles. Wrists clean, but . . . oh, too bad, somebody's been bruisin' 'em."

Yeah! Him!

"Bet you've done this bit before, babe, and liked it."

He jerked on my handcuffs. I bit my lip to silence a cry. Evidence of fear and pain only encouraged sadists like

Haskell. "Maybe you give out from the femoral arteries. That it? You a thigh baby?"

A deep voice tolled like a basso bell in my mind. *You have a witness.*

Haskell's head jerked up, as if he had heard it too. "Is there someone here?"

I could hear a faint throb of fear. Like all bullies, he feared someone bigger. And, yes, of course! *I did have a witness!*

"Nightwine," I called to the ceiling, remembering his security fetish. "*Do something!*" Just because his security cameras were rolling 24/7 didn't mean he was actually watching my particular episode of VPV*: Vegas Police Violence* at this moment. What could he do? Or Godfrey for that matter? Other than "witness."

The gun barrel left my thighs as Haskell stepped back to point it due north.

"You got an accomplice up there? In the attic? This is only a one-story place. Answer, bitch!"

"Nobody else is here, but this cottage stands on Hector Nightwine's property. He produces all the *CSI* shows."

He grabbed and pulled my hair again. "You think I care who you service?"

"He's my boss and a very paranoid man. The whole estate is covered with security devices. You're on *Candid Camera*, Detective Haskell."

"I don't believe you," Haskell said.

But he was nervous now and backed away from me. "Crazy too. Talking to the ceiling. You're making it way too easy. First I got you on impersonating an officer, and now the biggie, Murder One. Bet Cadaver Boy will be real upset about this. Too bad."

He grabbed my handcuffs and used them to pull, push, and half-drag me out of the cottage. How'd he get in here, anyway?

I saw his car parked on the street. He'd scaled the wall, so he must have disabled a section of the alarm wiring. Even better: Nightwine had him filmed violating personal property without a warrant outside as well as in, like the L.A. police getting into O.J. Simpson's Brentwood property after finding his estranged wife dead elsewhere. Johnnie Cochran could make quite a case of this. Too bad he was dead. Then again . . .

Haskell slammed me into the back seat of his unmarked car, not bothering to push my head down so it didn't bang the doorframe. I managed to duck, having seen enough crime shows on TV and enough live arrests in Wichita to know the drill.

I fell sideways on a seat that smelled of sweat, vomit, and strawberry car freshener. I almost added to the vomit and was half-sorry I didn't, although I wouldn't want Haskell to know what he'd done to my nervous system.

I managed to work myself upright, despite the bruising handcuffs. I had excellent lower body strength from self-defense workouts. Too bad it hadn't paid to use them.

He drove me down the Strip, a slow, public route that allowed people to gawk at me when the car paused at the interminable stoplights. I'd known cops. I'd worked with them. Most of them were good, dedicated people. But when one went bad, he went very bad indeed.

At the cross street of Paradise, I spotted Quicksilver weaving in and out of the colorful trail of tourists on the sidewalks like a shaggy, ghostly greyhound.

The pantry door would have to be completely replaced by the resident brownies, but I didn't mind. It was good to know he was nearby and keeping it as discreet as an animal his size could.

Good dog.

CHAPTER TWENTY-SIX

"**D**owntown" was more than a figure of speech in Las Vegas. The main police department offices were there, near the Fremont Hotel, but homicide, aka crimes against persons, had long since gotten its own building in the Sin City That Never Sleeps.

Haskell left me handcuffed to a small, scarred table in a miserable cubicle of a room with soundproof tile on the ceiling. (I wasn't about to yell to *that* eye-in-the sky ceiling for help, anyway.) In front of me was a table bearing nothing but one empty ashtray stinking of tar and nicotine. I was sitting in a chair so plastic and imbued with sweat, fear, and other less mentionable bodily fluids that it made my skin crawl.

I really needed to go to the bathroom but knew that if I asked anyone he'd make sure I didn't. I'd covered crime stories. I knew how cops made suspects squirm by any means. So I was guilty of . . . what? Back exposure with intent to seduce? It actually crossed my mind to wonder if Snow would bail me out. It was probably his set-up anyway. His note had implied that I had power of a sort. Too bad nobody had clued me in on exactly what it was.

"Miss . . . Street?" The woman who poked her head in the door was blonde but hard-edged. Maybe five years older than I was. Carried her shoulders like she worked out and had mojo authority. Was a pretty cool chick, really. Ric's captain friend. Oh, shit.

I nodded.

"I'm going to have to testify to your phone call proving prior interest in the Inferno, from witnessing the Sunset Park crime scene."

"Be my guest."

"Being a hard-ass won't help you."

"Funny. I thought telling the truth might."

"Haskell says before this came up you impersonated an officer on that crime scene."

"I implied, he inferred. He was being sexist."

Blondie's poker face didn't move. She faced sexist every day.

"And racist," I added.

A little of the ice broke. She really did like Ric.

"Haskell has issues," she conceded. Malloy started to leave, then hesitated. "You might want to reconsider saying anything."

I nodded. Message received. My truth could be my fall. I felt a shiver of silver moving along my arm to my hand. A white flash settled around my neck on a chain. *Won't you wear my ring.* No!

Haskell poked his red, hypertensive face into the room. "Guess what. Guess you do have a man upstairs. Your 'lawyer' is here."

All right! My lawyer. Pretty fast service from someone. *Hmm.*

"I hope you haven't cuffed her," I heard an authoritative voice say in the hall. A boldly black-and-white CinSim rolled into the room, maybe 270 pounds of designer suit. He had a baritone deep enough to take out the Three Tenors. Cool enough to chill dry ice.

"My name is Mason," he said. "Perry Mason."

Not Johnnie Cochran, but not bad.

Nightwine must have caught up with the tape pretty damn quick after we left. Who else would send Perry Mason, for God's sake?

I sat up straight in my scuzzy jailhouse chair. I couldn't wait for my next line. "My name is Street. Delilah Street."

He took the chair across from me like a pope deigning to sit on a toadstool. "What a coincidence. My personal assistant's name is Street. Della Street. May I call you—?"

"Delilah."

He looked uneasy for the first time "Delilah. I like it. Now, Delilah Street, how do we get you out of this mess?"

"I thought that was your job."

"Here, yes. The convincing explanations later are up to you, young lady."

The Snow groupie had been found dead in a Dumpster at the hotel's rear the morning after my jaunt to the Inferno. She'd been strangled. Her image flashed into my mind's eye, a harmless-looking middle-aged woman, really, except for the fanatic's mania in her eyes and voice.

The hotel security cameras had recorded everything, including shots of this very woman looking green when Snow had come on to me. Cameras had also recorded our fight over the hairpins later and my obvious rebuff. The police theory was she'd come after a lock of my hair later and I'd killed her. Groupies could be annoying, but the police scenario did presume a certain element of self-defense on my part.

Perry had picked up on that immediately, ace attorney that he was in book and on film. When he drove me home in his black fifties Caddy convertible that felt like Dolly's love match, I told him I'd finished my evening at the Inferno breaking and entering the executive offices. He frowned impressively.

"Pleading innocence by virtue of being occupied in another crime is not a viable defense. Miss, er, *Delilah* Street. Also, from your own testimony, you left the office in plenty of time to commit mayhem elsewhere."

"Didn't the hotel cameras capture the body being Dumpstered?"

"A good question. No. A black batlike shape covered the lens for several minutes that early morning."

"Should they be looking for a vampire?"

"Perhaps. The neck was not marked by a ligature, or tooth marks, it was mauled. It would be impossible to tell if a vampire bite was involved. You, of course, are not a vampire?"

I showed my pearly whites, blunt and even. "Not to my knowledge. In fact, I have a deep aversion to vampires."

"Doesn't everyone?"

"Not vamp tramps and Snow groupies."

"You think this woman could have had an opportunity to approach this 'Snow' person after you left his office, and he killed her?"

Was Snow a killer? I didn't know. What did I know . . . ?

"The woman was demented," I said. "All those Snow fans are. You should see them claw each other in the mosh pit to be one of the so-called lucky few he bends down to kiss."

"On the mouth?"

"*Yeah!*"

I recalled how Snow rose after each extended smooch and placed his palm on the latest conquest's forehead like a televangelist to push her back into the crowd. How the woman fell, senseless, into a buoying mass of her sister fanatics. And then disappeared beneath the swell of clamoring wannabe recipients of what they called the Brimstone Kiss.

"Those mosh-pit women clot like those spawning fish called grunion," I said. "Someone could disappear in their midst and never been seen again until—"

"The Dumpster."

"Exactly."

"I've seen the security film the police confiscated," Perry said. "You don't look dressed to kill."

"What?"

"The woman was strangled. It took force. The killer would have been marked, or disarranged. The police haven't gotten a warrant for your rented clothes, but Della tells me that Déjà-Vous says that you have them."

"You want them?"

"I have access to private labs. Better we know any damaging evidence first."

"Be my guest." I brought him inside and gave him the big white box when we got to my cottage. A silver bracelet slid down my wrist with the gesture of surrender, a bangle of pink cubic zirconias. Snow was so predictably partial to pink. Until now, I'd had no idea he could add jewels to my silver gewgaws. Hmm.

"Meanwhile," Perry said before leaving, "don't speak to the press. Call me if the police approach you for any reason. And let my office do the investigating."

I nodded twice, but sat the fence on the third condition.

"Don't worry about a thing, Delilah. From what you've told me that detective is the one in trouble."

There was one thing I wasn't going to tell Perry Mason or anyone else, because it might make me very unconvincing: that I'd glimpsed an apparition of a woman in my hallway mirror the night before the little green delivery elf and Detective Haskell had barged into my cottage this morning. But the more I thought about it, the more I recalled about that apparition of a woman. Woman? She had been a girl and she'd worn blue velvet with a sweetheart neckline. At least the bodice was blue velvet. The long skirt and short petal-shaped sleeves were blue taffeta. Definitely a late-forties get-up.

Her hair had been light brown, pulled up and puffed out at the sides to resemble the the sixteenth century heart-shaped headdress seen in portraits of Mary Queen of Scots. She'd been as doomed as that beheaded queen of Scotland, but she was a child of the 1940s, every detail

screamed that. She was the dead body from Sunset Park,
sure as God made little green cacti, and she was dressed
exactly as I'd known she had been clothed.

How did I know this? I'd sensed some of it the day
when Ric and I had met and melded dowsing for the
dead . . . with mental medium tricks . . . with passion by
proxy.

Yet it shook me all over again, to see her standing in
my hall mirror. Details I'd sensed when Ric and I found
her—wrist corsage, sterling silver heart locket at her
throat, beseeching baby eyes, everything—had reassem-
bled whole in my own hallway. Had even *replaced* my
own reflection. She couldn't have been more than seventeen and was about to be mowed down like Bambi's
mother.

Somehow, I understood she came here because her spirit
knew I was trying to identify her, but the vivid memory
of an apparition wasn't evidence I could use with others,
except Ric. I felt angry and helpless. And I knew from her
lost, plaintive eyes that she had just felt helpless, which
made me even angrier.

So. What solid facts did I have? I had the information I'd
copied off the microfilm reader, and I had the testimony
of the ghost in my mirror, mute for the moment, but
plenty eloquent anyway. I was free to keep investigating
for now. My lawyer (I did kinda like that term) had said
the police evidence against me was only circumstantial,
but a black hair had been found on one of the three Déjà-
Vous hairpins and I knew DNA testing would prove it
was mine, although it would take time.

Thank God.

Perry Mason took the dress box. I thanked him profusely
for all his help and eyed Quicksilver, hanging back by
the oleander bushes bordering the estate fence. He'd been
keeping up with a lot of Detroit steel today.

I pushed the code to open the gate for Mr. Mason to drive out. As soon as his car's shark-sharp tail fins had vanished, Quick was at my side, slurping my hands and growling in alternate rhythm.

"I know. Our hands and paws were tied, boy, but it's over."

I had a brain-splitting migraine, my wrists and shoulders were sore, and my soul was soiled.

Otherwise, I'd come out of the ordeal pretty well.

When we walked back into the cottage, Godfrey was waiting. He must have used the rear kitchen door.

"Welcome back, Miss. Mr. Nightwine has ordered dinner in for you. Not to worry, it's from the Bellagio. Medallions of beef for you and a fine steak, very rare, for Master Quicksilver, as well as a soup bone from the Paris hotel. My master also left this written message and bade me not to keep you from your recuperation."

Godfrey refused to stay for thanks, but bowed his way out immediately.

Quicksilver sat salivating over his napkin-covered silver tray, so I wafted off the linen and let him have at it in the kitchen.

Godfrey had left the other tray, bearing a single white rose in a sterling silver vase, on the breakfast table. The mellow Las Vegas dusk was tinting my window rose-gold. I pulled a damask napkin off a nouvelle cuisine feast of tender beef and garlic mashed potatoes to die for and chocolate mousse, but read the note before I ate.

My Dear Miss Street,
Godfrey has left, along with these culinary offerings, a tape of the recent events in the cottage I have allowed you to use. A copy of said scene rests in my private safe. Any trace of these events has been erased from the streaming tape in my central

*security system. No one will ever see or know of these
distressing events save you or I. I am only keeping
a record for prosecution purposes, should the need
arise and should you wish to pursue such a course.*

I am most *distressed that the authorities in any
form should violate my property and your rights in
this brutish fashion. All of my resources are at your
command should you decide to proceed against this
creature in any manner.*

Your devoted servant,
Hector Nightwine

Okay. I sniffled a little with my dinner, which was
superb and didn't move unless I did it.

CHAPTER TWENTY-SEVEN

I woke up in the middle of the night, a teasing trickle of ice water cascading over my breasts. The invading cold made me sit upright, clutching for the ebbing neckline of the old-fashioned brushed-cotton nightgown that I'd found in the closet, now far enough off my shoulders to suit a Gothic heroine.

Then I understood what was happening. A couple dozen alien, icy metal snakes were writhing over my collarbones, nipping at my breasts with needle-sharp fangs! I switched on the bedside lamp and jumped out of bed, hoping to escape the nasty feeling. I only agitated the metal-scaled serpents into a faster, colder dance over my flesh.

The mirror above the dresser flashed back a chorus-girl sparkle. I was wearing a glittering rhinestone Egyptian-type collar from the base of my throat and down my cleavage, writhing serpent-chains that ended with arrowhead-shaped heads with vampire-sharp fangs.

Snow! Sending his costume jewelry flunkies to belly dance on my bod when I was out cold. What a bastard! He made Haskell seem like a small-time gnat. He made Hector Night-wine look like a slightly kinked teenager by comparison.

I lifted the cold, dead writhing lengths off of my living flesh. Necklaces this flashy were for sale in every Las Vegas hotel glitz shop, but none so carefully wrought. What was happening here?

The answer hit me with a sharp new chill: Snow was thinking about me. The shape-changing jewelry echoed his thoughts, desires. He was reminding me of the leash he had put on me, the soft loop of his albino hair that had become metal . . . had now become chains of rhinestones. Except . . . I lifted the stones to the mirror to study their electric sparkle. These were *diamonds*. Holy Hell!

I sat up in bed, my arms clasped around my knees. I was wearing a gently used granny gown and probably a hundred-some carats of supernaturally lustful diamonds.

As I breathed in and out, trying for calm, the necklace shrank into a modest silver circlet. Maybe Snow hadn't expected me to sense his midnight invasion. Maybe he hadn't expected calm. Maybe he hadn't expected me to come calling on him the first thing the next morning.

I sure hoped so, because I would, and then there'd be Hell to pay.

WHEN I HIT THE INFERNO I went straight for my inside man, Nicky.

It was only 10:00 AM. I expected a headliner like Snow to be zonked out somewhere decadent with a bevy of groupies until late afternoon. I even expected Nick Charles to be off someplace where CinSims kick back when off-screen.

No. Nick was at the bar, as debonair as ever, still dressed in a formal black-and-white tux.

"My dear girl," he said, rising like a robot to the occasion of my striding in on a rush of fury. "You're looking quite . . . flushed. Did you win at the slots?"

The blackboard above Nicky's amiable, sloshed face snared my attention. In pink neon chalk, it announced: HOUSE SPECIALTY: ALBINO VAMPIRES.

"That's highway robbery!" I said.

"Noooo." Nicky focused carefully on where I was looking. "It's not a Highway Robbery; that's made with rum. *That* is the hot new *house* drink. The boss ordered

me to forsake my martinis for it. Didn't you already order
one the other night?"

"Order it? I invented it!" While I tapped my fingernails
on the heavily varnished bar I noticed that I was wearing
a half-handcuff bracelet again.

Bastard! Lech by remote fondling! Thief!

I felt a presence behind me and turned. Snow, of course,
long white hair, night-black sunglasses, white silk tee,
slacks, and jacket. The man must bathe in bleach!

"That's my drink," I opened.

"If you order it."

"I made it *to* order, right here. Just the other night. I
named it."

"Catchy title. You used my ingredients, my bartender."

"It's still mine."

"My version is slightly different. That's all it takes for
legal ownership. Try one."

He snapped his fingers. I again noticed bloodless, mani-
cured nails as slick and opaque as white gloss-enamel paint.

A martini glass as albino as my concoction of the other
night was soon wafted down in front of me, exact to the
topping-off drizzle of raspberry liqueur. Also wafted
down was the bill: twelve-fifty.

"Highway robbery," I repeated, for the record.

"You need to taste it to be sure."

I did, recognizing my own yummy ingredients. Nothing
added, nothing subtracted.

"*My* recipe."

"You haven't finished it."

What? He wanted to get me drunk? I tilted the wide
glass lip to mine and chug-a-lugged a lot of heavy-proof
liquor. I was so mad I knew my system would burn it up
and spit out very sober nails.

Something soft and sweet bobbed against my teeth.
Something from the bottom of the glass. I slurped stinging

vodka and sweet liqueurs until I saw bottom. Oh. A drunken maraschino cherry, skewered by an arrow of white chocolate. Sweet, plump, succulent. Nice touch. I left it.

"The cherry," Snow said, "is a tribute to your bartender expertise and your undercover skills. Otherwise, nothing personal."

I knew an insult when I heard it. Also, a reference to my quasi-state of virtue, that even I didn't know for sure. "I want to talk to you. In private."

"My office?"

"No tigers."

"No invisible allies."

I stood and let him precede me through the crowded casino to the place we'd last negotiated.

When we were alone in the office, I looked around, tapping my toes. No tigers.

As he went around the desk, I held out my half-handcuffed right wrist. "I don't appreciate this."

"Why not?"

"I took it to a jewelry shop before I came here. Nothing will take it off. Not a jeweler's diamond-toothed saw, not a pinpoint acetylene torch. I want out of it."

"Why do you think I can help you with that?"

"It's your sick toy!"

"How so?"

"*Your* hair?"

"And how did my hair become your hair *shirt*?"

"I—" Time to own up. "I touched it."

"Why? Because it was mine and you couldn't resist?"

What ego! Pride incarnate of course.

"Because it was white and long like the coat of my dead dog."

"Which you loved."

"A dog that had *earned* my love. Brave. Protective. True."

"Hardly like me, of course. So you claimed the lock of my hair because it reminded you of a dead dog. I can't say I'm flattered."

"You should be! Achilles was worth six of you. He got blood poisoning from biting a vampire ten times his size. You tackle anything like that lately? No, you pick on passing strangers. Achilles didn't need to harass hapless women with bewitched hairs."

"Yet the echo of his hair bewitched you. Just that. Nothing to do with me."

"Nothing to do with you. Look. I'm the last woman in the world who'd ever be in your fan club. I think you're despicable, the way you encourage your worshipping fans, poor, deluded creatures. It's immoral to kiss them into insensibility so they become mindless zombies. It'd be normal if you'd screw them, but, no, you keep them lost in permanent unfulfilled infatuation. I've seen them wandering around the Inferno, drinking, gambling mindlessly. Maybe doing drugs. That's a shitty way of drumming up loyal customers, Snow. I've even been suspected of killing one of them because she fixated on me after you mauled me in the Inferno Bar."

He leaned back in his white leather executive chair, balancing a black Mont Blanc pen on his pallid fingertips. "You weren't exactly stopping me."

"I took you for an amusing freak," I said, very deliberately.

I couldn't see any expression behind the dark glasses but his fingertips pressed so hard on the pen that I actually saw them grow whiter, or maybe they looked that way because a blush of pale pink blood showed through his skin above the pressure points.

Interesting. He had a circulatory system. That was a big argument in academic circles: did vampires have circulatory systems? Sure they drank blood, but since they were dead, they didn't have a heartbeat or a pulse. Given their rep as hot-blooded lovers as well as big drinkers, how the hell did they get it up without a pulse or heart beat? Assumption was only available to a few select saints, and they all skedaddled for heaven, not vampire games. Vamp tramps, totally hooked on the blood-sucker-as-Don-Juan mythology, would never tell. They were mesmerized by the vamp powers, and any tales they lived to tell were big on ecstasy and vague on details.

"I took *you*," he said finally, "for an amusing fool."

I'd been called worse. "I want this *off*!"

"Can't do it. It has a mind of its own, in case you hadn't noticed."

"It's your familiar."

"Now I'm a witch as well as a freak?"

"Or a warlock."

"You don't know what I am."

He had me there.

"But you'd love to find out." He leaned forward as I leaned away. "You can't resist finding out, can you, Delilah? Your whole life has been about finding out . . . about other people, not yourself. You don't have a life."

I understood that calling him a freak had brought this challenge and I was momentarily ashamed. A reporter gets used to feeling like an advocate of the downtrodden. Snow? Downtrodden? What about my manacled wrist?

Even as I thought that, Snow said, sympathetically, "It could be worse."

In demonstration, my solo handcuff linked to one that appeared on my left wrist.

Snow grinned and picked up the pen again with unbound hands. "Is your cuff half-empty, or half full?"

This kind of confinement ramped up my horizontal binding phobia, which Haskell had done nothing to help. I was stuffing panic down as fast as it raced up my esophagus to my throat, keeping cool.

One cuff immediately snapped open and my left wrist dropped free.

Snow spoke seriously. "The police didn't need to cuff you merely to bring you in for questioning."

I hated that he guessed, or knew, about my humiliating arrest. "This police detective named Haskell did," I said. "He's a bully and bigot."

"What's to be bigoted about you? Unless someone discriminates against annoying snoops."

"It was about the company I keep."

He digested that for a few seconds. "I still haven't made my point." He nodded at the half-handcuff. "It could be worse."

The cuff thinned and wrapped itself around my wrist like a serpent, spilling chains over the top of my hands and ringing one finger.

I'd seen some heavy metal bands. I knew this arrangement of chain-linked wrist bangle and ring was called a "slave bracelet."

"I'm a mammal person," I said, "I don't agree."

"Or even worse," Snow said.

I felt the icy swift shiver of the silver snake move up my arm and down my torso under my clothes, settling in a broad cold swath around my pelvis and streaking between my legs to harden into shape with a metal snick like a lock turning.

It felt like a chain-mail bikini bottom, not that I'd ever had a personal acquaintance with one. Haskell and his rough handcuffing were forgotten in the face of a medieval device turned bondage accessory: a freaking chastity belt. It recalled my recent nightmare. Fear became fury, then fear again.

"Obviously, it's not *my* familiar," Snow said, yawning.

Liar! He loved hiding behind his sunglasses and manipulating me into cheesy bondage gear that made me feel naked in front of him, physically and mentally. Stooping to calling him a freak hadn't helped.

"Still," he added, "it's a good thing that coveting is a commandment and not a Deadly Sin."

Before I could react or speak, the silver snake slid away again, ice water on the move, back to my wrist. Oh. It had morphed into a bracelet dripping charms: a circle of adorable Achilles faces, long-haired, hidden-eyed, sagacious.

"An admirable breed." Snow dropped the pen to the desktop like a small bomb. "I've always been partial to Lhasas myself."

I was still fighting not to blush at the unexpectedly warm sensations the adventurous example of "could be worse" had caused. Snow was interested in me, in teasing me? Sexually? Didn't he have enough groupies? I eyed the lovely Achilles bracelet and melted a little. Why did I suddenly feel in the wrong for descending to name-calling? That didn't stop a retort.

"I've got more to worry about than your migrating familiar or my hijacked drink recipe. My freedom is on the line."

He nodded. "Mine as well. Do your job, Delilah. That's the fastest route to the freedom you crave. And maybe mine."

I didn't know what he meant, didn't want to know. I did know it was a good exit line, so I took it.

CHAPTER TWENTY-NINE

Nowadays a whole encyclopedia could occupy a disk the size of my little fingernail, and here I sat again in the Clark County Library looking at late twentieth-century microfilm of mid-twentieth century personalities and events.

But that's when Las Vegas was founded, in the post-World War II world of exploding prosperity and post-Prohibition mob expansion. I found it sad that banning liquor had spurred a drunken binge of organized crime in all areas of vice: gambling, prostitution, and racketeering. And the baby-booming Las Vegas founded by visionary psychopath Bugsy Siegel was at the heart of it all, where mobster and middle class met, each legitimizing the other.

Of course, like all visionaries, Bugsy had been punished for it: he had been found dead in 1947 of several bullets to the head at the age of forty-one. The thirties and forties and fifties were the era of drive-by shootings on an epic scale, like the St. Valentine's Day massacre. So they'd shot up Bugsy's pretty-boy face through his living room window.

I unreeled the early history of Las Vegas. First came the El Rancho Grande and the Last Frontier. The 1948 founding of Bugsy's beloved Flamingo Hotel was the turning point. The first hotel-casinos were small, upgraded motels three hundred miles from Los Angeles and an endless drive from the rest of the country, but they were an adventure destination for those lost souls in search of glamour. Only a few years later a successful animator named Walt Disney would create an adventure destination for the whole family called Disneyland.

Bugsyland had always been an adult playground, saturated with sex, booze, and gambling. And it had been worth fighting over.

I vaguely knew that the East Coast Italian Mob of Mobs, the Jewish mob (from whence Benjamin aka Bugsy Siegel), and other mobs, chiefly Chicago, which was Irish, met, maneuvered, kissed Judas cheeks and rubbed out each other in Las Vegas.

But I'd never heard of the French mobs until now. The Italian-Irish-Jewish mob triad made sense. All resulted from the massive influx of European immigrants through the Golden Door mentioned in the poem beneath the Statue of Liberty. The French had given the U.S. that Amazonian artwork and its defining image—not masses of refugees. Why would a French mob, small and superior, figure in the founding of Las Vegas?

So little was said of it that I had to literally read between the lines of microfilm. The word "Inferno" in one article riveted my attention, though. "Monsieur Reynard, chevalier of France, has announced his plans to build a lavish hotel-casino called the Inferno, complete with Folies Bergère-style bare-breasted chorines, along the highway already occupied by El Rancho Vegas, the Last Frontier, and the late Bugsy Siegel's Flamingo hotel-casinos. French investment would indeed add luster to the thriving desert strip of nightclubs. Some have compared the future Inferno to Montmartre's Moulin Rouge in Paris."

I got it. The naughty French had invented the can-can and the topless chorus girl at the Moulin Rouge in the late nineteenth and early twentieth century. Why wouldn't they exhibit an interest in such a wide-open site of American adult entertainment as early Las Vegas? Even today, Nevada was the only state in the Union to legalize houses of prostitution.

But a French mob? It defied imagination. Weren't the French far too refined to resort to machine guns and blood and guts . . . ? Well, yes, except during their own late-eighteenth century bloodbath of a Revolution. American gangsters had come up with the Tommy gun, the Thompson sub-machine gun. The French had come up with a really big butcher's cleaver, the guillotine, a hundred-and-fifty-years earlier. French. *Christophe.* Could it be — ? I finally found Reynard's first name. Christophe. And Reynard, if I remembered my convent-school French, meant "fox."

So why was there no further reference to the Inferno for seventy-some years?

A few more turns of the microfilm reel made all that clear.

The Jeanne d'Arc Day massacre.

St. Joan had been the French peasant girl who'd led the French king's forces against the invading English in the fourteenth century, a peasant girl turned God's own general, then martyr and saint. She'd been bound and burned at the stake as witch. Historically, the French had it in for werewolves. It was the English who burned witches — and Joan — at the stake, not the French. Centuries later, the French delegation to Las Vegas was found massacred on May 30, 1946 — the day Jeanne d'Arc died in 1431 and, after she was *finally* canonized in 1920 as a Catholic saint, her feast day — literally torn apart on the site of Sunset Park. I needed to find out much more about this little-known fact of the city's history.

Much as I hated to, I had to defer to Hector Nightwine's encyclopedic knowledge of Las Vegas and its history. When I got back to my Enchanted Cottage, I was forced to make an appointment through Godfrey. Dinner was decreed.

Given my suspicions about Nightwine's menu—the man had a ghoulish interest in murder, death, decomposition, and dissection, but then, so did a huge proportion of the American reading and viewing public—I agreed with a sigh. I would take the diet books' advice and eat "healthily" before dining out.

Something told me to dress for dinner. I riffled my vintage clothes rack and found an early fifties cocktail dress. Its black satin portrait neckline filled with a pricey rhinestone Weiss necklace from the same era as soon as I shimmied myself into its tight sheath skirt. I topped it off the look with a close-fitting black velvet cocktail hat that ended with a pompon of shiny blue-black cock feathers at my right temple. Just right for a human sacrifice. Black satin wrist-length gloves sported a rhinestone button at each wrist, and a three-inch wide rhinestone bracelet from my collection complemented the Snow necklace.

Man, I would accept this Weiss necklace if offered, even from Snow. It would bring at least six hundred dollars on eBay. Too bad Snow's decorative devices kept morphing and never added to my permanent collection. I guess Snow was like that, raining, freezing, and melting on my parade, all the time.

Godfrey welcomed me at the manse's front door.

"Very chic," he said, eyeing my get-up. "A bit past my heyday, but otherwise quite appealing. Somehow the fifties are so depressingly dedicated to . . . corsets."

Godfrey's era was the no-underwear-to-speak-of thirties of bathtub gin and speak-easies, but corsets would appeal to the expansively overflowing Nightwine, for sure.

It struck me that a freelance investigative reporter had to be a woman of many faces. And figures.

The Nightwine dining room rivaled Hearst Castle for expansiveness, with only us two at opposite ends of the endless table. The soup course was a beef consommé that didn't look yucky or make me think of yak blood, so I tried it.

"Now," Nightwine said, "what do you need to know?"

"Nothing much. Only who founded Las Vegas."

"Who? Or. . . what?"

"I like that 'or what'? Intriguing, to say the least."

He sank back into his own bulk, happy to be speaking and not moving, except for his right, fork-filled hand.

"The vampires," he said, "never had a chance."

"Not *my* impression of vampires."

"Poor creatures. It's a matter of time zones."

"Pacific Coast time is hard on vampires?"

"I'm speaking of more personal time zones," Nightwine said. "Werewolves by nature are 24/7 creatures. The vamps are handicapped by their daily twelve hours of sleep during daylight hours. When it came to days of the month, werewolves could do 26/31 without losing half of every twenty-four hours to casket time. That's why werewolves are still a force in this town and vampires are on Skid Row."

"Christophe?"

"You think he's a vampire, my dear?" Hector smacked his lips. "Very tasty."

"Christophe?" I asked, amazed. Hector hadn't yet shown any sexual preference besides dead or alive, and edible. Come to think of it, vampires might fit his double bill to a T as in, yes, Tasty.

Hector regarded me soulfully. He dabbed his beard and mustache with his napkin as if mourning any tidbits that had escaped his voracious maw.

"I was praising the oxblood soup you seem to be enjoying as well."

Oxblood soup! I pushed away the shallow dish, trying to be a polite guest and not gag. "I don't do raw."

"*Tsk*. You'll miss out on many delicacies."

"You can have my share." I decided to stick to salad for the rest of the meal. "So you're saying werewolves are still a power in Las Vegas? That's not common knowledge, and the only werewolves I've seen so far are those wretched half-weres and some pretty ordinary folks who like to dance and have a good time, then go for a four-footed midnight ramble in the mountains. If they run down anything and eat it, they aren't any worse than two-legged hunters and probably need the calories more."

"The half-weres you've seen are veterans of the Las Vegas Werewolf-Vampire War back in the forties and fifties of the last century. It's not in the history books, of course. Only the mob was here and they were the third leg on that triangular struggle. Some of the werewolves suffered vampire bites during the hostilities and found themselves frozen in a half-changed state. They also got the vamps' immortality but were shunned by the pure werewolves. So today they are about as low as most of the remaining vampires on the Vegas totem pole. No. Your Christophe is not a player from the old days, if he is a vampire. Why do you think so?"

"The so-called career as a rock star suits the vamp lifestyle. He's pale as death but as arrogant as all get-out. And he hypnotizes his slavish groupies and turns them into mindless zombies. He's got more brides than the social register."

"Do I detect a soupçon of jealousy?"

"No!" But I felt a bit hypocritical saying this while basking in the glitter of Snow's vintage necklace. "From what you've said, if he is a vampire, he's challenging the social and business order that's been mainstream in Vegas for almost seven decades."

"Do you think he could?"

"Sure. He'd have the nerve. Whether he'd last. . . ."

"My conclusion exactly."

"Meanwhile, I'm more worried about whether I'll last. You know that the Las Vegas Metropolitan police consider me a suspect for the murder of one of Christophe's groupies. I can't solve the murders at the park across the way if I'm being held for Murder One myself. I appreciate your . . . producing . . . Perry Mason to spring me from custody, but I'm hoping I won't need a trial lawyer."

"Can't your FBI friend help you?"

"*Ex*-FBI. Besides, he's out of the country. I want to plough ahead on your assignment before Detective Haskell has me sent to the penitentiary."

"Haskell!" Hector grew so agitated he pushed away his blood-soup bowl. "That bastard has done everything possible to interfere with my true-crime investigations. I think he's on somebody's payroll."

I'd never seen Hector Nightwine lose his Rhino of the Jungle cool before.

"So where do I go to get to the bottom of these forties murders?"

"The werewolf-run Triad is the Magus-Gehenna-Megalith."

"No. I don't want to find the anointed kingpins. I want the malcontents. Where are the vampires who lost the Werewolf-Vampire war? You can't kill 'em, after all. They have to be somewhere."

"I told you. They were driven out."

"They just left Las Vegas?"

He shrugged those massive shoulders. "Oh, there's one old wreck of a hotel they'd tried to make the flagship of their Triad. It's deserted now. Steve Wynn is rumored to be interested in buying the property. Oddly enough, a deal has never gone through for all these years."

When it came to vampires, I didn't believe in "oddly enough."

"Abandoned hotels just sit here for years in Las Vegas?"

Hector shrugged and leaned back while the salad course was placed in front of him.

I could swear that some of the black olive slices were moving. Wriggling, sort of. That didn't stop Nightwine from holding forth.

"In 1967 Elvis Presley married Priscilla Beaulieu at the Aladdin Hotel. By nineteen seventy-four, Elvis was dead. By nineteen eighty-five the Aladdin was a dying hulk. By two thousand, it had been bought, razed, and resurrected, if a bit shakily. By 2007, it was revamped as Planet Hollywood."

"You're saying the vamps—"

"In this case it is just an expression. Although, given the blood-sucking done in Hollywood. . . Las Vegas is about nothing if it is not about decay and resurrection."

Speaking of which, my own plate of greens had been placed before me. From his position by the sideboard, Godfrey winked. My salad appeared to host no black olives, moving or not.

"No doubt," Nightwine said, his fork chasing down an escaping olive, "the property is tied up for eternity. One thing the vampires are masters at: they know how to protect what's theirs in legal perpetuity."

Which meant they never gave up.

Neither did I. "I need to talk to someone who was around at the time of the Werewolf-Vampire Wars."

"You and sixteen hundred tabloid reporters."

"I work for you, Hector. It would pay you to help me out more than some scummy scandal-seeker."

"My dear Delilah! You have just put us on first-name terms. I'm so . . . flattered. If you're not going to eat your blanched maggots, do let Godfrey bring the plate to me."

And here I took them for sliced almonds!

Hector munched disgustingly, then spoke again, with his mouth full. "You do realize, my dear, what anyone who had been around then and was still surviving would be?"

"An old vampire?"

"Vilma Brazil," he mumbled between maggots.

"*She* is the old vampire?"

"More like the old vamp. A B-movie actress from the forties, when the difference between a mistress and a whore was as thin as cigarette paper. Alas, she is still legitimately alive, more's the pity. She wrangles CinSim wardrobes at the Twin Peaks. You'll not want the management to know what you're up to, but give her an ear and a few twenty-dollar bills and you'll hear plenty."

"Great." I stood.

"You're not staying for the main course? It's fit for a king."

"I eat like a bird."

Especially after dining with Hector Nightwine! He had a real future as a diet guru, through aversion training.

If I hurried, I might catch Vilma Brazil at the Twin Peaks.

CHAPTER THIRTY

Dolly purred like a puma when I revved her out of the cottage's carriage house and through the gate onto Sunset Road.

I think she approved that my get-up matched her DOB: Date of Birth to us crime reporters.

I'd freshened up at the cottage, putting in my gray contact lenses and running black lipstick over my original red. Moving among CinSymbiants and CinSims as either of them was a great disguise in Las Vegas. The hall mirror insisted on imprinting on my eyes as true blue, but my purse mirror told me I was passing as cinematic gray.

I left Dolly to the tender mercies of a parking valet who resembled a young Arnold Schwarzenegger and clattered solo into the Twin Peaks on my fifties spike heels. Where was Perry Mason when you needed him?

Where fashion made forties women look statuesque and stern and seriously sexy in a dominatrix way, fifties women had looked fussy and frivolous and French maidish in a Trixie way. That look suited me fine right now. Nothing like being underestimated for collecting lots of information.

The Twin Peaks had a CinSim transvestite revue. Now that'll blow your mind. Velma, I discovered, was wardrobe mistress. I found her backstage sewing chorines of indeterminate gender into torn costumes and gluing marabou feathers back onto pasties and posing pouches. Good thing I was a hardened reporter.

"Vilma Brazil?"

"Yes, dahlink?"

She looked ninety the way it would look on silicone and bleach, kind of like your brain on speed: scrambled. But beneath the drawn-on eyebrows reaching for the sky and the frizzled platinum curls, her eyes were blackberry-bright and nicely avaricious.

I sat on a plain wooden chair in front of a mirror dusted with powder and glitter. Funny, my CinSymbiant-gray contacts never registered in a mirror. I faced my blue-eyed self and then forgot about it.

"If you have a tip for me," I told Vilma, "I have a few tips for you." I let the corner of a twenty-dollar bill play Peeping Tom out of my evening purse. Luckily, legal tender doesn't change much through the decades.

The twenty disappeared down her cavernous cleavage. One thing will never let a girl down: silicone.

"Whatcha wanna know, baby doll?"

"I need to speak to a vampire."

"Are you press, that it? You want, like, an interview?"

"I am press, and, yes, I want an interview, but not with just any vampire."

"Honey, any vamp is hard to come by in Vegas nowadays."

"I need to speak with a vampire of the old school. One who was here during the Werewolf-Vampire Wars."

"*Shhh!*" She looked around, as if even the wig stands had ears.

Well, the Big Bad Wolf from Little Miss Riding Hood had had great big ears. And eyes. And teeth. One wondered what else big he had.

"That's so dangerous, dahlink," she whispered to me. "If the *WW*s don't devour you for it, the *V*s would drink you dry."

"Then there are still . . . *V*s in Vegas?"

"Just a bloody few. All the Old Ones left; only a few young hotheads stayed behind."

"How young?"

"Pre-Millennium Revelation, but only by a few decades."

"All I need is one that witnessed the wars."

"There *is* only one of that vintage and he's kept under wraps so deep you could wear them on an Arctic expedition."

He. The oldest living, sort of, relic of the wars. He'd be at least a hundred-something, young in vampire years. A kid in their terms.

"Where can I find him? How can I, um, interview him?"

Velma's blood-shot old eyes were focusing hard on the poker hand of twenty-dollar bills that fanned through my fingers.

"There's a way you might do it, but the odds of you getting out of there undead are pretty low."

"Money talks, Velma honey. Now you talk to me."

So she did.

CHAPTER THIRTY-ONE

Déjà-Vous outfitted me again and Dolly got me to the rambling wreck that was left of the 1001 Arabian Knights Hotel and Casino. Or so the mostly shot-out neon sign said. The name made me think of a cultural blend of Sinbad the Sailor and King Arthur's Round Table, but people were a lot less politically correct in the mid-twentieth century. The place sat on the bitter south end of the Strip below all the new high-flying hotels, where even the Johnny-come-lately hotels had not yet hung out their neon shingles.

It was true vampire time now, the dark of night lit by street lamps. Blowing sand beat a tattoo on the deserted hotel's shabby fifties-Moderne sign out front, still advertising STEVE LAWRENCE AND EDIE GORME.

Right. *Steve and Edie who?*

This property was clearly condemned. The windows were boarded over and the entrance was marked: DANGER. ACCESS FORBIDDEN. Not to mention the forbidding razor-wire-topped cyclone fence surrounding everything.

I parked Dolly across the Strip at our old home away from home, the Araby Motel. Having lived briefly at the Araby Motel, I'd soon found a low-profile parking space for Dolly behind a Dumpster under a broken parking lot light. No reason *she* needed to associate with that broken-down dump. The Arabian Knights, not the Araby Motel. Maybe that was how the motel had been named, after its big brother.

I felt conspicuous as I crossed the wide street, but nothing much was happening down here. The sun had taken a dive behind the Western mountains. One of those faint twinkles in the foothills was Los Lobos. In an earthy flashback, Ric was sensuously edging my skirt waistband down past my belly button in some instant rewind in the sky and from the scrapbook of my memory.

Meanwhile, I was edging my laced-up oxfords, virginal white, over the glass-strewn sand that surrounded the Arabian Knights. The outfit from Déjà-Vous was as authentic as it was ridiculous. The clerk, a pimply-faced punk, had winked, clicked his tongue, and noted that this getup was hot stuff among the geriatric set.

Right. White hose, white garter belt, and white cotton, waist-high, full-coverage panties—ick! I'd read that Elvis had gotten off on those but he was *soooo* over. My get-up was fifties kitsch, not to mention the dead-white uniform and the kinky little black bag.

But a reporter on the trail will suffer anything for a prime interview and Vilma had promised that I'd meet a mondo-big player from the vampire side of the WW-V wars if I played it right.

A mini-tape recorder was stashed under one the ridiculous steel garters . . . those things left welts on my thighs! Water-weight again. I had tucked a tiny notepad and pencil up my tight, short white sleeve. The whole outfit was undersized, with the blouse buttons straining to display my cleavage, but I'd been assured this was the exact right costume from the exact right film of the period.

The lobby was empty, dusty, and moth-eaten.

A shred of desert wind shuffled all the litter around. Gaming tables tilted on three-legged stands. Playing cards with their numbers sand-tattooed off laid false trails through the endless rooms.

I found a bank of elevators. Even back in the forties, Las Vegas hotels aimed at height. This one was only ten stories, but it had been a Tower of Babel in its time.

Litter snaked across the marble floors. I jumped, imagining rat claws.

What I saw was even worse: a trio of shambling figures in the long black coats of always-cold junkies. They slunk along the outer walls like mongrel dogs, cowed but ready to attack in a pack at any sign of weakness.

Their eye whites and fangs glittered in slivers of light from the streetlamps. One limped. Another gnawed compulsively on his own filthy knuckles. The third edged nearer.

I retreated to the elevator bank and paced along the closed doors, pushing dead buttons and wishing for a nail file. *Let me in, let me in*! My disguise would earn me a pass from the chief resident vamp, Vilma had assured me, but she hadn't mentioned the homeless, hungry vamps on the chief's perimeter.

They were coming closer, forming into a gang of three. One brushed its long, filthy nails at my arm. Undead Ted looked like the prince of vampires compared to these vagrants.

Above one set of elevator doors the floor number ten lit up.

I can't explain how spooky that was. One floor on one elevator. I'd been told something was here. Apparently, something had noticed that I was here and that I wasn't going away.

The light descended slowly on the dusty gilt monitor. I pressed my back to those elevator doors and reached into the black bag, which made my circling vamps pause. Did I carry a wooden stake in my little black bag? Didn't I wish! Above me the numbers lit up in turn: Eight. Five. Three. Two. One.

A *ting* like a microwave finished cooking hit my ears. Any sound but wind here was shocking. The doors did what elevator doors are supposed to. Open.

My heart beat me half senseless. This was what I wanted, but it was totally spooky.

I backed inside and pressed the top button. Ten. The penthouse. That's where the story was. The vampire trio had decided to get bold just as the elevator doors snapped shut. One pinned a narrow finger in the closing crack, leaving a shriek behind as the car shot upward. A convex mirror in a corner of the elevator ceiling made me look like Jessica Rabbit, all mammary glands, all the time, in the distorted reflection.

The car zoomed upward with surprising, twenty-first century speed.

WHEN THE ELEVATOR DOOR opened at the top, a weary man in a gray flannel suit was waiting for me.

He eyed me up and down with contempt and resignation.

"He's waiting for you. You'll have to pass through security. Let me see that bag."

I handed it over, feeling like any cowed modern airport traveler.

Wow. Inside was a stethoscope. A packet of hypodermic needles. A bottle of alcohol and lots of cotton balls. Latex gloves. And an instant camera. Weird.

"This way, Miss." He returned the bag to me unrifled.

The guy showed me through a plain brown door. The moment it shut I regretted being here in the worst way. The room was a giant shower stall, all white tiles and fluorescent lights. No windows, no obvious doors. I was totally trapped.

The lights went nova. A deep male robotic voice instructed me to turn with my arms extended. I quavered about the presence of my blouse-sleeve notebook, but didn't set off any alarms.

A section of tiled wall opened and I was in another chamber where a moving spray misted me from stem to stern. The odor was evergreen and eucalyptus and I had a sense of being scanned, as if by X-rays.

The next room was steam-filled and almost wilted my starched uniform.

I passed into yet another chamber, dim-lit after the glaring inspection room, and managed to rub my thighs together to activate the tape recorder.

"Nurse Wretched," a voice declared from an overhead PA system. I'd given my name as "Ratched." "This is your patient."

The dim lights came up.

I was not alone. Really not alone. A half dozen clones of me—busty young women in tight white uniforms— flocked around a hospital bed accessorized with trees of IVs and other high-intensity medical paraphernalia.

The object of their attention lay sprawled on the sheets before me, Las Vegas's oldest living vampire, a scrawny, filth-brown man with nails the length of an abused pony's hooves and hair long and unkempt enough to make a supermodel's career.

My heart, and gut, sank.

I'd fought my way into this?

The rasp of heavy breathing magnified by machines surrounded me. My sister nurses grinned to show their sharp canine teeth. The breath sounds? Mine. I was the only breathing being in this place and I was being monitored as if *I* were the sick person.

"You're here to h-h-help me?" the skeletal figure on the bed wheezed.

I grabbed the stethoscope, finally understanding what a forgotten nest of undead this place was, my knees shaking.

"Breathe," I said, placing the silver circle on that hollow, filthy chest.

"You must be kidding."

"No. I can . . . read your state of health through this instrument."

The wild-animal glittering eyes focused on me. "And . . . my state is—?"

"Vigorous." I snapped the bag shut, determined to bluff my way through this. I actually believed it and he so needed to hear it.

The balloon-bosomed nurses arrayed themselves around him like chorus girls. He was used to flunkies, but was essentially a never-satisfied man.

I played doctor, rather than nurse, because only an authority figure could get anything out of this lecherous geezer. "I believe that unresolved issues from your past are hurting your recovery now. Why did the vampires lose the war?"

Even I sensed the instant suspension of all sensory devices: the security, the girls' phony solicitousness.

"Not lost," he huffed, clutching his bony chest.

I immediately applied the silver stethoscope head to it again. My medium. Silver. Even when it was chrome.

"Cold," he complained, writhing with the satisfaction of feeling something, anything. The surrounding nurses showed their fangs and backed off. Those shrunken gums grinned up at me, the teeth brown and sharp, like rusty razors.

"I can make you a star," he promised.

IF THERE'S ONE THING some men like better than gratuitous sex, it's telling war stories.

I lounged alone on the hospital bed with my host while his rakelike fingernails unthinkingly caressed the tape recorder lump on my thigh, taking it for some sort of vibrator, no doubt.

The creepy girl vamps hugged the room's walls, waiting
for the old guy to fall asleep. Then they'd storm me for
a group bite. I wasn't as worried about them as the lean
and hungry vamps on the street level. Besides, I bet it was
hard to catch the old guy asleep. As long as I kept him
talking about his glory days of yesteryear, I was okay.

"So you're the sole survivor," I encouraged him,
forcing my nurse-white false fingernails (thank God I
could ditch them afterwards) through his kinky, gray,
snarled locks. Snow's hair was sable-soft but right now
his metal familiar had shrunk to a cheesy ankle bracelet
with a dangling (two guesses what parts were dangling)
Playboy Bunny charm. I was not here to think about
Snow, but the old guy might give away something about
him before I left.

"Sole survivor." He relished the words the way
Nightwine savored mobile olive slices. "The sole survivor
to stay on, despite all the mob action, even if I had to
play dead to do it. See, my empire was going south. My
lieutenants were using the fact that I like my privacy to
take over. The Big Boys from the East Coast and Chicago
outfits had brought me in to clean up the Alakhazam
Hotel operation, but my own staff was conspiring to take
over my Las Vegas interests. The only option was to let
someone they couldn't buy or bully take over for me."

I got it. "You made an alliance with the vampires."

"Yeah. Good businessmen. Went for the jugular, like I did.
Immortality would allow me to pursue my first loves, flight
and females. I loved engineering things that people believed
couldn't be done. Nice undergarment you're wearing, by
the way. I invented that fashion-forward look."

I stared at him the way he was staring at my conical
brassiere.

"What?" he demanded defensively. "I read Victoria's
Secret catalogues. Better class of model in them than

in *Playboy* these days. That Hugh Hefner was just a
wannabe me."

Actually, Howard Hughes, or what was left of him, had
a point.

And then he stuck that point, a curling, yellowed
fingernail, down my open blouse front while I pretended
to wriggle away in delight rather than disgust.

"You're quite the aerodynamic genius, in the air and in
the sack," I cooed. "So who did the deed? Who bit you
over to the Dark Side?"

"I'd only let a woman. No guy was sucking on anything
of mine. She was a beauty. Dark-haired like you. Built.
Lips red as roses. I was going to make her a star."

Wow, was that a tired line! I glanced at the hovering nurses,
who were clearly slavering over my virgin neck, wrists, and
femoral arteries. All brunet. Crimson-lipped, white-toothed.
All right out of a Hammer film from the sixties. *Vampire
High. Rocky Transylvanian Horror Show Mountain High.*
I'd fit right in if I didn't figure out an escape ploy.

I'd read up on Howard Hughes during my research.
He wasn't in on the founding of Las Vegas, but came
along shortly after. And he had indeed been asked by the
mob to clean up the situation at the hotel. His playboy
days were fading then, and he probably was tending
toward the obsessive-compulsive disorders and paranoia
that ended with him holing up in a string of hotels he
owned, possessed of a germ mania but in a skeletal,
filthy, unkempt state himself, with long tangled locks and
mandarin fingernails like claws.

His reported death and burial in the seventies and the
location and state of his huge assets and will remained
lucrative tabloid paper mysteries for years. He could darn
well be exactly what he seemed to be: a madman who
had made a deal with the undead. The ramifications were
mind-boggling.

Meanwhile, I needed to know more.

"Oh, Vampy Boy." I let a false fingernail coil in his iron-gray chest hair. Singular, as in one hair. "Tell me who bit you into eternity? I need a role model."

The cunning eyes in their corroded setting squinted at me. "Looked a lot like you. A Black Dahlia. Dark devilish hair, heavenly blue eyes, wanton red lips. Vida was her name."

Vida. Spanish for "life." She couldn't possibly be—? No. But she could still be . . . alive, so to speak.

He went on reminiscing. "She worked for the werewolves, but her heart had turned vampire. Liked the kick of giving blood along with her body. I suggested they turn her all the way just for me, so I could pick who'd suck me into immortality."

The selfish bastard!

"Where is she now?" *Poor undead woman!*

He shrugged. "She had issues. Left for California with some master vamp. Some Podunk town in Orange County, when I could have made her a star here. So. Now I am vampire. Now you will stop asking questions and become my bride. I need another one."

"I don't date older men." But I *was* wearing all white . . . even my undies.

A scrawny but powerful arm captured the back of my neck and drew me toward those neglected-knife-drawer teeth.

Around me I felt the busty nurse vampires closing in. Once he got the first bite, they would get seconds. Pickings were lean around here. Sharp nails dug into my nape, Nosferatu on the march.

The nurses were swarming my limbs, pinning down my arms and legs for their master.

I was immobile, helpless, out of options.

Then I felt that familiar, loathed cold shiver streaking up my ankle to my garter belt past my industrial-strength push-up, push-out bra to my neck.

Vampire Empire-builder chomped down hard on the wide silver dog collar suddenly circling my neck. Several rotting teeth shattered to the gum line as he screamed with pain and frustration.

I started kicking and flailing in all directions. The shocked nurses froze, and then zeroed in on the blood pooling at their master's bleeding gums. Periodontal disease is such a golden opportunity for the blood-based set, and there is no loyalty among bloodsuckers.

I rolled off the bed, scrambled to my feet, and dashed back the way I had come, the heel of my hand knocking Gray-suited Man against the white tile walls. In the hall I skipped the elevators and ran clattering down the fire stairs.

DOWN THE LAST TURN I ran into a free-range vampire coming up, unable to wait anymore.

I grabbed the iron railing and kicked hard at his chest, sending him tumbling down like a die cube on a table.

I clattered after him. These sturdy lace-up oxfords were the next best thing to butt-kicking boots. Maybe nurses needed that edge.

He fell into his two buddies, who kicked him aside to come for me. By then I had gravity on my side again, and momentum. I barreled into them, using my elbows, the strongest joint in the human body, ramming into ribs, collarbones, noses. Ordinarily vampires could take all I had to give and break me like a shoetree.

But these guys were so hungry they ignored my defenses and came snapping at my carotid arteries, one on each side. They hadn't seen my silver dog collar in the dark. Between the mythic power of silver and the stubborn nature of Snow's familiar to bend or break to any power, they gashed their mouths into bleeding rivers. I kicked them aside, onto their fallen comrade. Last I glimpsed they were snapping reflexively at each other.

I kept running.

The night was dark and the traffic was nil, but Dolly was waiting in the Araby Motel lot across the street, her headlights on and her engine racing like a Stephen King car.

I made for her and then eyed the dude waiting in the passenger seat. Dude? Dog. Quicksilver sat there panting, his tongue almost touching his gray chest hairs.

I never wanted to think about a gray chest hair again.

But the poor dog had run his pads off to find Dolly, and me, just in time. Now that we were reunited, he went pushing out the passenger door to down some poor wino who had happened along.

Wait! Another wino was grinning vacantly at my window. Thank God I'd left the top up.

Not a wino. A half-were. I opened the heavy door hard into its torso and came out, wishing for a silver bullet. I guess I had one. Quicksilver leapt the broad Caddy hood in one bound and landed claws down on the flattened half-were, tearing out its throat with one shake of his mighty head and jaws.

I fell back into the driver's seat, while Quicksilver snarled and ran down two of three more escaping shadows. All half-weres.

I knew he'd taken out the half-were motorcycle gang at the pet store parking lot, but I hadn't seen the carnage up close, in living color. A rich river of blood was oozing toward Dolly's left front tire.

Quick was plenty busy doing things I didn't want to see, although I couldn't help hearing them. I turned on the ignition and eased Dolly back out of the blood flow. The dog was part wolfhound. What part of that didn't I get? He was born to hunt and kill wolves. To protect flocks. And to him, I was flock. I was lucky to have him. Half-weres were predator scum, not even "unhuman," as Ric put it. I just didn't like to see where those teeth had been.

I had a chance to think while Quicksilver finished doing his business. Expecting a quick exit tonight, I'd left Dolly unlocked with the keys in the glove compartment. Now they were dangling from the ignition. Quicksilver and his clever paws and teeth? Dolly herself? Snow's pretty damn good remote manipulation of silver skills? My life-saving dog collar was now a charm bracelet loaded with tiny vintage Cadillacs.

So, I wondered, was this little mobile accessory of mine the Mark of the Devil, or a protective talisman? And was Snow evil incarnate, or maybe something more interesting? Hair, after all, is a literal "lock" and is associated with my namesake.

Who knew, who cared? Maybe Snow knew and I cared, but right now all I wanted was to get the hell out of here.

Quicksilver hopped into the passenger seat and I leaned far over to pull the wide door shut. I revved that Caddy engine and we blasted out onto the Strip, heading for the bright lights of Las Vegas Central due north.

CHAPTER THIRTY-TWO

R ic called me as soon as he got back the next day.
   "Man, what a mess."

"Where were you?"

"I could use a night at Los Lobos. You ready to rock 'n' roll?"

Hearing the soul-deep weariness in his voice, I decided that mentioning my petty personal problems was minor. I could have pointed out that the exertion of dancing wasn't the best medicine for a burned-out traveler, but I was too selfish.

"Salsa," I corrected, "but it's not the full moon quite yet."

"We'll make it so."

"Yes, sir, Captain Picard."

"Where are the hot-mama low-rider jeans?" Ric asked when he picked me up outside Hector's estate. I respected his decision not to confront Quicksilver on his own turf yet.

I fluffed my turquoise silk skirt in the car. "I felt festive."

My fluffing gesture had made my silver bracelet jingle jangle like spurs.

"Nice bracelet. Navaho work, isn't it?"

"Um—" I glanced down to find that the bauble had gone Native American and added turquoise stones to match my dancing skirt. "Yeah, I guess."

"You didn't know when you bought it?"

"I found lots of old silver jewelry at estate sales in Kansas."

I told myself that I hadn't actually lied to Ric; I just hadn't hit him in the face with Snow's nasty little permanent present. Still, I felt queasy about dodging the truth with him, and changed the subject pronto.

"The turquoise doesn't quite match the rhinestones on my shoes."

He eyed and recognized the vintage plastic heels from our last, and first, date. "Those your lucky dancing shoes, *chica*? Or mine?"

That was another subject I didn't want to delve into, what could happen between us tonight. Haskell's ugly innuendos had tainted the growing ease of my relationship with Ric.

"So what happened where you were?" I asked. "Or can't I know?"

"Juarez."

I eyed his taut-jawed profile against the passing headlights, wondering if Captain Malloy had ever had this view.

"Oh. The thousands of factory girl murders that have been going on for decades. It must have been awful." I could say that with feeling, having been haunted recently by my own youthful innocent, Jeanie with the light brown hair.

His lips tightened, if that was possible. "I've been on it since I joined the FBI, fresh out of Quantico a few years ago. That's when they started calling me the Cadaver Kid. Sometimes I find the fresh dead. You would swear life had just kissed their cheeks goodbye. There's something . . . sweet about that. It's good to settle their families' anxieties and get police evidence, but many of them don't make it from the coroner's facility to a funeral home."

"Why not?"

"Hijacked," he said tersely. "Their bodies have hardly deteriorated. If they're raised as zombies, they have most of their faculties and such fresh, young corpses are in high demand as CinSim material."

"Ghastly! Can't anyone stop it?"

"Nobody's stopped Juarez," he said. "It often suits the powerful to use tragedies to enrich themselves."

After a moment he spoke again. "Sometimes I find the long-dead. They are only dry bones, fragile as precious parchment. I feel like an archeologist, privileged to reveal them. Then there are the savagely murdered ones. They still fester in the earth like plague victims. Bruised, bleeding. All those young, helpless girls. It was like being clawed at by . . ."

Groupies? I almost said. "Why were you there? Isn't it dangerous?"

"Damn right. The drug lords and traffickers in human and unhuman labor run the city with huge gangs. Police chiefs don't last twenty-four hours before being gunned down, and U.S. border forces and drug and immigration agents are often assassinated or caught, tortured, and killed within a day of entering the city."

"Ric!"

"That's why they want me there. I can blend in better than an Anglo agent and there's always my sterling track record at finding corpses. This time I found a DEA agent they'd done a torture voodoo act on. The body had to be brought up in pieces. At least the CinSim runners won't get him."

"Oh, my God! I'm glad I didn't know where you were and what you were doing. It's a wonder you don't have post-traumatic shock syndrome."

Ric shook his head as if dislodging memories of carnage.

"I need to be there. A lot of bodies have needed finding over the years. Some serial killers are working there, and the usual gangs of smugglers, thieves, and rapists. Nobody really cares about the deaths of these young women except their families. The Anglos who run the border factories like the cheap labor and provide buses that are about as secure as a sieve. The workers often have to stay overtime and miss the bus schedule. Their long hours send them home on foot after dark and Mexican culture doesn't give much respect to women out after dark. They're picked off by the border predators so fast that a girl can be seen leaving the factory one night and sleep in a shallow grave by the next morning."

"All human predators?"

"No." He was silent for a while. "Vampires and werewolves too. And then there's the regional boogeyman, the *chupacabra.*"

"Chupacabra?"

"A blood-sucking goat-killer. It's been described as everything from a small half-alien, half-dinosaur tailless vampire with quills running down its back to a pantherlike creature with a long snaky tongue to a hopping animal that leaves a trail of sulfuric stench. Some claim they're alien 'pets' or cloning experiments gone wrong. The UFO nuts call such creatures Anomalous Biological Entities, aka ABEs."

I had a shuddersome memory of the trio of dead cows near Wichita. That half-dinosaur tail reminded me of the huge reptilian track I'd found there.

"Have you ever seen such a thing out on the desert?" I asked.

He paused for a minute or more. "Maybe. I've seen a lot of bizarre things out in the desert. *Chupacabra*s? Rogue humans and unhumans are scarier, and human predators are worst of all, because they have no need to kill to live."

"You found more victims this trip?" Personally, I meant. These weren't numbers, statistics; these were lost bodies and souls he dowsed for.

"Twelve, some as young as fourteen. The oldest was twenty-two. They'll be identified and catalogued and buried again in the desert, with only a crude headstone. It's beginning to feel sadistic to dig them up, but the authorities keep hoping each new death will nail some single maniac killer who can die for the sins of all the opportunistic rapists who fill the border cities."

We were out of the city now and driving on the dark, almost deserted highway toward the distant faint twinkles of mountain habitations. We were silent for a while, lulled by the empty dark and the roar of the Vette's engine.

"It must . . . take something out of you to find all these bodies," I said finally.

"It always has." His glance slid toward me and darted back to the empty highway.

He was trying to decide whether to tell me something. Usually I wanted to know everything. Relentless reporter, that's me. Nothing I can't take. No knowledge too devastating. Now I didn't know about taking on whatever Ric was holding back. I sensed still-raw wounds underneath that smooth, defensive exterior. I didn't know if I was one of them. Or could be.

He decided to let me in a little more. "I've always maintained a certain control, a certain distance, when I work. Ric Montoya, human cadaver dog. Ever since . . . Sunset Park, I don't have that distance. I don't just find them and deal with the dead. I *feel* them now. They expect something of me I've never had to give, like they're reaching out of the earth to grab me with their living-dead hands, their living-dead minds, their living-dead emotions and needs. It's . . . exhausting."

"And my fault?"

He wouldn't look at me. "I'm a dowser. You're something else. A conduit. A medium. I don't know what you are and I doubt you do either. It's not your fault, but I can't just dowse any more. Thanks to you, I'm a tuning fork. I vibrate to their presence as if they were alive and I were dead, a mere medium to be activated. I feel their pain, their undone deeds, and their broken hearts. It's too much."

What could I answer? He was right that I didn't know anything when it came to these matters. So I asked.

"When you dowse for the dead now, do you feel the same electricity we generated in Sunset Park together?"

"No. That's ours. And theirs, the dead couple's. Oh, I've sensed lust and greed in these sex killings, but nothing as positive as that."

"It *was* positive, for us, then, wasn't it? I've never felt anything like that, over a grave or anywhere, with anyone." I put my hand on his on the steering wheel. "Ric. I missed you."

He turned to see me, really see me, and his mouth melted.

"Oh, Del. Delilah. Take me away. Take me away tonight."

I saw the despair in his dark eyes and nodded. I knew a prime assignment when I heard it, and I wanted this one very, very much. The tension between us had changed from our own professional problems into an unspoken need to shake ourselves loose of them.

Ric was shimmering and glinting in his soft, expensive clothes, which I now recognized as a defensive barrier against the death he wrested daily from the brutal earth.

I felt quite the glamour girl, all soft and silken folds and uncertain emotions. He read me like a book, dowsed me, and understood what I offered, wanted what I was willing to give. Only I didn't really know what that really was. So I also felt nervous, as usual.

The Los Lobos parking lot looked mundane, filled with cars not quite old enough to be interesting. Ric's was low, sleek, sexy, a quick getaway. Another barrier against death.

This time the place looked under-patronized. I noticed the frayed edges of the country-music posters on the walls and saw the gouges in the wood plank floor.

I ordered an Albino Vampire to my specs, watching the waitress scribble down the directions. Ric ordered the same, cocking a dark eyebrow at me.

"That's a pretty potent cocktail. You trying to get me drunk, Q*uerida*?

"Not until we get home, *hombre*."

"*Su casa or mi casa*?"

"Do you have *uno perro*?"

"No. No dog. Do you have *uno* Spanish dictionary?"

"*Sí.*"

Trumpets and mariachis hailed us to the dance floor.

I was beginning to get the rhythm. One-two-three. *Oomph*. I didn't care this time what the onlookers would think. I was desperate to distract Ric from the awful job he'd had to do. Werewolves did the two-step, but so did my disordered emotions, wanting to soothe him, envelop him, ease him, please him, and end the angst.

When he jerked my elastic waistband down over my hips, below my navel, I put my hands on his shoulders. One-two-three, seduce. He buried his face in my neck and shoulder, pushed my torso into his. I so wanted this man to find salvation in me, or that elusive state that haunted Edgar Allan Poe kept searching for, surcease. Was this sex? Or something else?

Right now I was haunted by something that ate at my stomach and burned in my throat. I had to tell Ric, warn him. He needed to understand that I might be even more . . . touchy . . . now.

"Ric, this wasn't anything like what you experienced in Mexico, but while you were gone—"

"What happened?" His profile had grown sharp before his face turned to me. He'd interrogated hundreds of suspects. He knew when they were aching to conceal something.

"Haskell happened."

"That pig. How? Why?"

"When I was investigating the Inferno I ran into one of the Seven Deadly Sins' lead singer's groupies."

"Cocaine. Yeah, I've heard of him. A very bad player."

"His groupies are crazy. This one and I had a brief encounter."

"You into girls, *chica*?"

"Not that kind." I slapped his shoulder playfully.

Making a joke of my story was a calming technique. Ric could sense the tension in my back muscles. I could feel his hands smoothing them even as we danced.

"Short story: this Cocaine character was out pressing the groupie flesh in person and stopped to play with my hair in passing. The video cameras recorded this one woman trying to get a lock of my hair afterward as a souvenir. That creeped me out, so I told her back off. She turned up dead the next morning in the hotel Dumpster. Haskell came to my cottage and arrested me."

"For what?"

"For questioning."

"Arrested? Just for questioning? That's not procedure. Oh. You don't mean handcuffs?"

He had stopped dancing so we just stood there while other couples flashed their moves around us. We stood motionless, in each other's arms, so close our breaths fell into comforting sync. It was getting harder to pretend I'd shrugged off an ugly and traumatic moment.

I just nodded. "I knew a very personal pat-down wasn't procedure."

"How personal?"

"For the barrel of his gun, very."

Ric dropped my hands, a good thing because his had become very hard fists. He muttered some Spanish curses too low and too fast for me and my handy little *Street Spanish* book to translate.

"Hector's security system got the incident on tape," I told Ric, wanting to defuse him. "Haskell's screwed."

"Jesus! You were *taped* being manhandled?"

"Hector's destroyed every security tape but a copy he gave me, to use if I want to bring charges. Or destroy. I'm only mentioning that I might be a little . . . twitchy about being touched right now."

"*Querida.*" Ric pulled me closer, put his forehead to mine. We began swaying to a slow dance, a slow-motion floating island amid a stream of frenetic salsa-dancing couples.

"Forget that. Forget Haskell. You're with me now. I'll make it better."

"It just might have triggered my old phobia. I might not be . . . what you expect or want. Too much trouble."

"You're trouble, all right. The kind that makes *me* very twitchy. Let's get out of here. I know just the place to soothe all your cares and woes."

"Really? Where?"

"My place."

We left before the werewolves had really begun to dance, but it wasn't a full-moon night anyway.

Ric opened the Corvette's passenger door. The car was a low-riding hammock with rocket power. The seat was already half-reclined by design, but at least he didn't bother snapping the seat belt for me. Not being belted in didn't worry me. Ric drove as if he was one with the car, fast and powerful, outrunning everything . . . Juarez, Haskell, my old nagging fears.

The low car thrummed along the asphalt as it wove its way out of the mountains, clinging to every curve with a dreamy sense of déjà vu. Again the powerful engine vibrations massaged my spine. Again Ric's hand moved on the stick shift, up, down, across, and I felt my body sway with the motion. After a while, all my cares and woes had been outrun. I was only here, only now, only with him.

He seemed to sense my evolution from edgy fear to edgy interest.

No full moon flirted with us through the Vette's blue-tinted glass roof. No werewolves haunted the hills as they ran through the freedom of their change.

It was just us and the night, and this time he wasn't taking me to be dropped off primly at my cottage door.

This time he was taking me home with him.

CHAPTER THIRTY-THREE

Ric's car stopped, purring. The end of motion disoriented me. Ric opened the car door, pulling me up and out. My ankles wobbled as my hands returned to his shoulders, his to my hips. We had cruised past a gated entry and were in a newer housing development, nice but not palatial. He waltz-walked me inside, past a courtyard where wind chimes and a huge central fountain made aural love to each other.

Inside the house was dark, quiet. It wasn't that large, but everything about it felt chosen, sensual, perfect. A huge stainless steel refrigerator purred against one wall. Faint light glinted off dark granite countertops and other stainless steel appliances. Ric paused at a long kitchen island, where he caressed the granite, black with glittering silver and blue veins, like precious ores. "It's called blue pearl. You. Me. Here."

"Horizontal," I protested. Besides, it looked like a sacrificial altar.

We were in another room where I heard water flowing, clinking like tiny coins in fountains. It was cool there, humming with an air-conditioned serenity. Ric sat me down on the hard edge of an interior fountain. He slipped off my Cinderella slippers, set my feet in cool water. I hadn't known my dancing-princess soles were burning until then. My soul, burning. His fingertips dribbled fountain water on my chest, which he licked off until his mouth had pushed my neckline down. My nipples blossomed in his mouth and exploded at the touch of his teeth.

He pulled me up and onward, pushing me down on a velvet sofa to put my shoes back on. Why? He was taking me apart and putting me back together, and all the while the dark, soft sound of his unseen rooms ate away at my composure.

Bedroom. Music. It was a smart house. Sound had followed us through, tinkling, glittering, humming. Celtic? Spanish? New Age? All of the above.

I noticed a low bed on a pedestal, satin sheets. Mirrors.

"Is this a vampire's lair?" I joked, afraid of the way everything about him was pushing into me. Claustrophobic again, in my own body and not remembering why.

He danced me into another room, pushed a light switch, flooding us as if we were in a photo studio.

The master bathroom. I saw a blue pearl granite hot tub sunken in a rim of unlit candles. Mirrored doors, windows, a big mirror over the double sinks.

"See my reflection?" he asked. "Do I look like vampire to you?"

He looked like dark hands moving over my pale skin, a lowered angled face making love to this woman in the mirror, my double with her clothes half off and still hidden, still private.

He finger-walked my skirt up to my hips. In the mirror. His feet pushed my shoes apart, spread my legs like a cop doing a very personal arrest. A shattering memory of Haskell drowned in a sudden liquid shot of desire. Ric wasn't, never would be, Haskell, and I was finally able to make distinctions between my fears and my desires.

"Glad you wore those hot mama shoes again," Ric said. "Make you just the right height for me."

I was pretty *non compos mentis* by then, but I liked being just right for him and I knew what he meant. We'd been brushing against each other all night, hip to hip, so I just purred a little.

"This is the way we stood in the park. You remember? In daylight. This is what you ambushed me into wanting, into feeling, into wanting to do with you. It was just the usual water-witching demonstration, except you were so soft, so moist, so cool, an oasis of flesh. I owe you an orgasm."

So I'd felt more than a hard-on back then. I leaned my head back on his left shoulder, watching his hands on me, playing at the extremities of our mirror image, not quite revealing myself to me, or to him. I saw faint auras, mine ice-blue, his hot and yellow. They melded to make green and purple where they touched.

"Nice cologne." I inhaled deeply. I'd first scented it in the park when all my senses had sharpened. "What's it called?"

"Night," he murmured into my hair.

"Is that with a *K*?"

"No. I'm definitely not that noble."

Below the line of the mirror, his fingers slipped into me, toying with my inner silk, a movement so easy, so natural. An action only in the mirror, where neither of us could see while his fingers delved where we both could only feel. His left forefinger reached up to tease the spaghetti straps off each of my shoulders in turn, using just his nail. That roving fingernail edged my camisole neckline down in eighth inches until only the swollen precipices of my nipples held up the soft fabric.

"You like to tease yourself," I managed to say.

"You too."

"I teased you?"

"You didn't know it but what do you think it was like, this strange lush woman in my arms in a public park, writhing against me in broad daylight?"

"It was night to me. All dark, all dancing in the dark."

Even as my insides heated to the boiling point, a small cold voice I'd always had in my head, along with Irma, uncoiled. *You're ruined. You can't escape the past you don't know.* And I remembered every nerve-wracking, uncertain, humiliating failure of my so-called life. The Reporter stirred, came forward, said objectively . . .

"Forty percent of women are non-orgasmic."

And, as far as I could remember, which wasn't much, I was personally batting zero percent in my personal life when corpses and ex-FBI guys who could dowse for the dead weren't involved. There were no dead bodies here now.

Ric looked so good in the mirror as he made love to me, his dark lashes sexy shadows on high cheekbones. His fingers pulled out of me. Warned maybe. They lifted before me in the mirror, slick and shiny. He brought them up to my face and painted my lips with their transitory glisten. I inhaled his fingertips, pulled them into the hot cavern of my mouth.

"I live in Las Vegas," he breathed in my ear. "I don't believe in odds. My whole life has been bucking the odds."

He pushed my skirt up in back, pushed me over until my hands under his grasped the smooth gilded faucets. We were dowsing for the depths within ourselves. I heard the hiss of a zipper, the notched touch of metal teeth, felt the brush of silken linen, then pure soft silk, and velvet flesh stretched taut to push home into me.

"In the park," he was saying, "the wand had never driven so hard and strong and deep for the ground, but it was driving somewhere else, too. Not just down and back, as we passed over it, and as the rod will do. It ached to enter you. I couldn't blame it. I felt that urge too, but I couldn't let that raw wood violate you. It took all my strength to control it. To keep it away. To keep you untouched. To keep you to myself."

I felt an irresistible object pushing into the most wounded part of me, a no man's land of mystery and perhaps even hysteria, on the soft friction of velvet against silk. Velvet had nap. Silk would give first, as scissors cut paper.

"I hurt," I said. But it wasn't his impending presence; it was as if a rubber band had shrunk between my legs.

"That's good, Delilah," he murmured, "and I can make it hurt more and less and better."

I glanced up at Ric in the mirror. His face was cast down to watch my body, his hands moving on me but not further invading me until I said so. Somehow that reflected face seemed a truer window than any I'd ever looked through or into for a long, long time. I believed what he said, that the tightening lovely ache inside me, at my innermost gateway, would evaporate with his entry.

"Yes," I said, loving how he waited until my last *ssss* had faded into a sigh before he did more.

He was murmuring musical, sexy Latin words now. Their sibilant alien sound pierced me to the bone. The swollen ache became an eruption as he rocked into me. Suddenly my interior was a vast tense, spreading plain. The outer limits of my senses stretched, screamed their joy at being explored. Something was gathering, on the high plain fringes, something cataclysmic, storm-laden.

"Let it go," Ric urged in English. "Let yourself go."

I was running with the wolves. Werewolves. Whole-weres. Running like quicksilver or my Quicksilver, under the moonlight, my body a bright full moon aching for observation of its wonders.

I threw back my head, let the earth's silver dowsing rod delve me like a dream lover, and howled my freedom to the star-sprinkled skies.

MY FACE WAS TURNED into Ric's shoulder again. We were upright, I pressed against him, he against me, still joined.

What if you didn't know anything about yourself? Not really.

Like most people, I'd grown a protective shell, only mine was thicker than most. Hard as nails. The phrase meant the metal nails that won't bend under the hardest hammering, but I always thought of women's fingernails when I heard it: that odd growing part of us that is such slight protection, brittle enough to break at one wrong glancing word or gesture; tough enough, if we're driven enough or desperate enough, to wound.

Oh, some of us flaunt our fingernails, paint thin clear enamel carapaces over them, sometimes tinted as pink as rare meat, sometimes bold and red as a stoplight, sometimes glittery like jewelry. But they are still a fragile element of our bodies, no matter how thick the shell over the exposed nerves and thin-skinned flesh beneath, and pulling them out was an ancient form of torture.

My nail polish was neutral and effacing, but as impervious as shellac.

The Wichita, Kansas, TV studio had the usual food room: sink, microwave, dishes, silverware, vending machines. Although the on-camera women were supposed to be uniformly slender, the support staff brought homemade pastries and desserts. We gathered around the treats to nibble or gorge, depending on our metabolisms and moods of the moment.

One time a woman had exclaimed that some hit of whipped-cream, chocolate-laden sugar was "better than sex." A quick poll named the top better-than-sex dessert: carrot cake. A lone vote for banana cream pie won a lusty group laugh, and the woman who craved those huge trans-fatty glazed donuts was told with giggles and knowing titters that she could combine the two. I'd laughed knowingly too, although I only got the reference now. My own fave had been lost in the hullabaloo: gourmet coffee and chocolate.

Now I knew that little office coffee klatch conversation for an exchange so shallow that even Irma at her ditziest was light years away from explaining the enormous risk and reward of having sex.

The wellsprings of trust involved dazzled me. The emotional liberation of feeling trust on such an intimate level left me with a peace and gratitude for being alive I'd never imagined. All the happy TV commercial couples, the hyper-passionate romance-novel couples, had seemed part of some elaborate play everybody else liked to pretend they were now starring in. What I felt here and now was real. Was it love? That fast and easily? I didn't know. I'd just have to trust that, whatever it was, it was right for us both. That, beyond the first-time mechanics and even though he whispered—warning, apologizing— that I'd be . . . tender, *delicado* . . . the next day, as long as I felt this inner conviction, I'd never be sorry. Trust. It meant that Rick would not hurt me, and if he ever did, I knew the pain would be mortal.

That's how I felt as I beached myself on Ric, feeling his body as a solid breathing wall behind me. His fingers were caressing my inner outer edges. A wall. A wave.

His shirt collar was still open. In the mirror I glimpsed a shadow, blue-black, the only dark place on him besides his hair and eyelashes. My open mouth swiveled to that sole entry to him.

He was still inside me, against me, behind and in front, fingers and one long, hard thick finger, so I felt deliciously surrounded. I let myself sag against him, held up by his invasive prongs like a paper doll on pushpins.

The shadow at his throat, his collarbone, teased my eyes.

My head lolled on his shoulder. "What's this?"

His face was close, focused down on me, eyes slit. I touched his skin under the slightly open collar.

"What do you think you feel, what do you see?" he asked.

I brushed his collar aside. Frowned. "You're . . . wounded."

He made a humming sound like a purring cat. My fingers pressed against the shadow. Puffy flesh, darkening as I touched it.

"Ric! Did . . . I do that?"

"Yeah. When you zoned out over the dead zone in the park. You . . . spasmed. All over. I felt every tremor. Then you turned your head into my neck and shoulder. And bit. You did that."

I stared at his bruised skin just peeking beyond the white starched corner of his shirt.

"I bit you?"

"Yeah."

"No! I'm not a vampire! I hate those bloodsuckers. I'd never do that."

He touched my lips, pushed his forefinger onto the ticklish top of my mouth until I panted with a strange sort of lassitude.

"Maybe you're a werewolf. I don't care. It's okay. It's a totally human thing, called a love bite, a passion mark, a hickey."

What was I?

"A DELICIOUSLY PASSIONATE WOMAN," he told me in the kitchen, where he applied an ice pack and antibiotic ointment to his neck on my insistence.

What I regarded as a scary untreated wound he seemed to consider a sensual trophy. Weird. But what did I know about any of this?

"But I need a little R&R until our next round. Waiting makes all the difference," he added, his eyes hot-fudge warm.

Not me! I resisted, not insisted. I feared, not dared. I was a . . . nice person.

Not hot.

Ric came close again, pulled me hip to hip. "We could . . . share a shower. A bed. Sleep. Or we could do what I really, really want to do."

"And that is?"

"I want to drive . . . you . . . home again."

Oh. The very thought of that low, leather-lined car with major vibrating road feel undid me. Ric's hands on the stick shift. Right. Drive me home. The reins were back in his hands. Drive me.

By now the semireclining passenger seat, sans seatbelt, would have been tolerable, but Ric didn't lower it. Instead, he pulled me down sideways once we were on the road, across the central compartment, my head pillowed on his iron-muscled thigh that any woman would have killed to have.

I was strangely out of it, dreamy. His fingers teased my skirt up over my bare hip, and then caressed my uppermost breast under the camisole. Again I was lulled by that easy, fringes sort of lovemaking, what pleased him as he steered the car and trifled with my body swaying to the drone of the engine, the motion, the fondling.

We made the same dreamy approach to my cottage door; only Ric stopped us at the bottom of the shallow steps to the front door.

"I hate to say this, believe me, but I've got to leave town again."

I didn't will it, but my fingers curled hard into his jacket lapels.

"Just a quick trip to D.C. to report on the Juarez situation. I'll be back in a couple of days."

"What'll I do for a couple of days?"

"Keep checking out the Sunset Park killings. That ought to keep you in the libraries and out of trouble. Besides, you'll be tender."

"So you want me on the shelf while you're gone?"

"I want you somewhere safe, Del, and thinking about when I come back."

"You got it," I said. Promised. I ran my hands along the smooth, silken edges of his lapels.

I was so besotted at that instant that I wanted to make love to his clothes, but I stopped myself from asking that he leave me the jacket. Now I understood why the public high school girls had coveted and worn their boyfriends' letter jackets. Or leather jackets, depending on what crowd they ran with. I had been so retarded! But Ric was catching me up fast. Hickeys. Letter jackets. Lust.

Chapter Thirty-Four

Quicksilver had given me the doggie third degree when I returned from my rendezvous with Ric. He'd not only sniffed my crotch and growled, but he sniffed my discarded clothes and growled even more. Then he curled up in the corner of my bedroom and regarded me accusingly while I began preparing for bed. At least I was home alone. Sort of.

That intent pale-blue gaze was enough to make me take my underwear off behind the closed bathroom door. *Jeez!* I escape having overprotective parents to answer to by being born an orphan and then I get a dog that thinks he's a *duenna,* which means chaperone in Spanish.

All I, or anybody reasonable, would say about a twenty-four-year-old fallen woman was . . . *high time, honey!* as Irma put it.

The shower water reminded me of the many fountains in Ric's house. I adjusted the temperature until it fell like flowing warm satin on my body. I really wouldn't have felt comfortable sleeping in Ric's bed yet. One stage at a time. I donned my long granny nightgown and slunk back into the bedroom in the dark, easing under the covers.

I heard a long, disappointed, canine sigh from the corner. I'd call Quicksilver a bluestocking, except that he didn't wear any.

MORNING WAS THE USUAL BRIGHT AND SUNNY. I decided to take Quick for a nice long run in the park to make up for my absence last night, and the absence of my supposed innocence, which his wolfhound nose could apparently detect.

Halfway through it, I let Quick off the leash to run far and wide, and sat out the rest of the marathon on a bench.

"*Tender?*" Irma asked me. "*¡Ai, carumba, chica!*"

Ric had warned me, but tender was a way too nice word for it. I was as sore as hell. On the other hand, the abiding discomfort reminded me of the excellent adventure we'd shared last night. I couldn't wait to do it again, probably much sooner than advisable, like today.

I must have been giving off super-satisfied pheromones because two strange guys immediately plopped down on the bench on either side of me.

They wore those bright-colored knit golf shirts with the itty-bitty alligator embroidered on the chest, one pink, one green, and plaid pants to match. Serious muscles filled out the Florida duds on all fronts. Their faces were hawk-nosed and bleak-eyed.

"Our employer wants to see you," Mr. Flamingo Pink said.

"Here I am."

"On his turf."

Oops. "Turf" was not a respectable corporate byword unless it was part of a Surf and Turf lobster and rib eye dinner at the local Stake and Ale.

"I can't right now. I'm walking my dog."

"You're not walking and I don't see a dog," Mr. Chartreuse answered. "Let's go, doll."

Each had taken me politely but firmly by the elbow. Together they lifted me almost off the ground. I spotted a white van idling by the curb.

Elbows, as I may have mentioned before, are the strongest offensive part of the human body. I was about to smash mine into colorful kidneys on either side and sprint to freedom.

Then the name on the side of the van registered.

Who sends a *labeled* van to kidnap an unwilling woman? The Magnus-Gehenna-Megalith Hotel and Casino Consortium, that's who.

"It's to your advantage," Flamingo Pink growled. "The head man is interested in you. You know how rare that is?"

Yeah, very rare, which was probably just the way he wanted me cooked, the freaking werewolf.

"He wishes to talk to you about a job," Mr. Chartreuse chimed in.

With these guys, "a job" was probably dangerous, illegal, and maybe even fattening. But I'd been itching to get on the inside of the M-G-M operation. *Voilà!* as Christophe might say, if he was really French.

"Okay. But I, ah, I can't just leave my dog alone here in the park."

"God," Flamingo said to Chartreuse. "These dames today and their little purse pooches. Who do they think they all are, Paris Hilton?"

"All right," Chartreuse said, "but it had better be house-broken."

Quicksilver chose that minute to come barreling back toward me, fangs bared.

The men jumped back, leaving me free.

"We can't take that thing." Flamingo sounded afraid of more than Quicksilver.

"It's Team Malamute or nothing," I said.

Their brows wrinkled until their hairlines lowered a full inch. I think I got their problem. The M-G-M was a were-run operation and Quicksilver was half wolfhound.

"Sit," I told Quick, who promptly obeyed. "He's really well-behaved."

"Yeah, right."

"It's both of us, or I do my tae kwan do routine and he eats you."

My introduction to werewolves at Los Lobos had made me regard them, perhaps foolishly, as just another breed of dog with alpha and beta modes bred into the bone. If they had the upper fang, they'd bite. If they were the slightest bit conflicted, they'd cave and wait for their master's voice.

"Well, we could always use him out at Starlight Lodge," Chartreuse said, snickering uneasily.

"At the lodge, right. Can always use an extra canine there."

With a mutual, rather mysterious shrug, Flamingo and Chartreuse caved.

They weren't in full werewolf power and the boss wanted to see me. Presumably he could stomach seeing Quicksilver too. At least for a while.

CHAPTER THIRTY-FIVE

A panel van has a way of feeling like a jailhouse wagon. I felt a lot of regretful heebie-jeebies as Quicksilver and I were carted off as willing passengers. We could take these guys, I was sure of it, but once we were in the hotel-casino, the odds would tip decidedly in the goons' favor. And there were people who would miss us, pronto, but not Ric, who was out of town again. Better not to waste a minute.

"Who is the boss?" I asked.

The watermelon pair snorted in tandem, rather doglike.

"Mister Cicero is the boss of bosses. His consortium controls six top Las Vegas venues." Flamingo lit up a stogie. Its foul smoke floated back into the second tier of seats and nearly choked me.

Six. Then he was a silent partner in three no one knew about.

"It's a big compliment Mister Cicero has even noticed the likes of you," Chartreuse said, snapping the rubber band on his wrist. Apparently he was trying to stop smoking, which was futile with a partner who was a walking pink chimney.

I coughed discreetly. "I just want to know how to properly address him."

"'Mister Cicero, sir' should do it." Chartreuse was sounding choked now too.

"You should be better dressed," Flamingo said. "Mister

Cicero likes his people to look sharp."

If the golfing outfits were part of that corporate directive, I'd prefer to remain a Raggedy Ann in workout clothes.

The van sped toward the huge, lurking bulk of the Gehenna, which had a fiery moat filled with holograms of mythological monsters (at least I hoped they were holograms), then buzzed around the impressive entry lanes and porte cochère to the rear.

Quicksilver and I were ushered inside into a locked, solid stainless steel, private elevator and shot upward a zillion floors. Flamingo and Chartreuse stared blankly at the floor indicator, their hands folded discreetly over their colorful crotches. Perhaps that was where they carried their hidden artillery.

The elevator doors opened on a corridor carpeted in black plush. Everything here was hushed, muting even Quicksilver's clicking claws. We reached a door of embossed metal, which opened when our escorts hummed a certain melody into a voice-pad. Actually, it was more of an *a capella* howl.

The hair, such scanty stuff as it was, stood up on the back of my neck. Quicksilver's thick-furred hackles went haystack high, but he managed to quiet his built-in urge to bay and bark warning. What had I gotten us into? Whatever it was, I hoped it proved useful as well as scary.

I wouldn't find out a damn thing about the powers that be, and were, in Las Vegas sitting in Sunset Park nursing my newfound sexual itch. This was where I wanted to be. At the center of the hidden action, learning things, no matter the cost.

The office beyond the door was palatial, carpeted in mossy, dark emerald-green shag and paneled in black-stained pine. It felt like being in a night-time forest glade and was lit by etched globe lamps that mimicked dozens of full moons.

Quicksilver whimpered, feeling the ancient spell of dark forest and moonlight. I felt it too. Something Druid-like.

A huge redwood desk sat under a chandelier of milk-glass moons, the wood grain gleaming like watered silk under the overhead lights.

A man walked from the room's shadows to sit in the thorny embrace of a deer-antler chair behind the slab of desk. He wasn't very tall, but he was barrel-chested and pewter-haired, wearing a gray sharkskin suit that gleamed like a hematite gemstone. His mouth was wide, his eyes were Jack Daniel's-gold, and his nose was long and sharp, as were his ears. Both sported tufts of black hair.

Oh, Grandpa, what big eyes, ears, nose, and teeth you have! Can I sell you this Ronco rotating hair-removal device . . . ?

Quicksilver leaned his shoulder against my hip as we stood side by side, his own long canine nose pushing into the palm of my hand. It was dry and hot, and I could feel him panting slightly.

"Sit," Mr. Cicero said. So I sank into the black leather club chair in front of the desk, pulling Quick against its side. "Lights out," he ordered his staff.

Behind the casino boss, in the impenetrable dark, a screen lit up. I watched silent footage of myself at the Inferno, with Snow and Nick Charles.

"You have impressive resources," I said when the screen went blank and the many-mooned chandelier lit up again. How had he stolen security tapes from the Inferno?

"And you have an impressive fan base, Miss Maggie."

I didn't bother to correct him. I didn't want my real name issuing from those thin lips and through those sharp white teeth.

"I'm looking to raise the gate on my headlining show," he added. "Your presence could accomplish that."

"Show? I'm not an actress."

"Your appearance on *CSI V* makes that clear. However, you have unwittingly become a major media personality."

"Dead!"

"Exactly. I propose to add you to my headlining magic show."

"As what? A corpse?"

"Why not? It would be a huge draw and we can certainly play off of that, but I propose a climactic resurrection. Everybody loves a comeback. It would pay very well. I can make you a star."

You and Howard "Yellow Fang" Hughes! Irma hissed inside my brain.

"I'm not a professional performer," I pointed out.

"What about your classy performance as a CinSymbiant at the Inferno? And you weren't even paid for it. Obviously, Christophe is negotiating for your services. I have simply one-upped him, my rival hotel owner. You have the look of the moment, my dear Miss . . . Street, is it? That last name must go."

"Christophe? You think he wants me for his stage show? He was just hitting on me."

Cicero snickered and his flunkies, especially Flamingo Pink and Watermelon Green, snuffled and snickered too, in their cowed, canine way.

"Christophe doesn't 'hit on' humans, sweet cheeks," Cicero said.

Then what had he been doing? Or . . . what was I, really?

"I can double whatever he offered," Cicero added. "And, I can let you *live*. That's worth a bundle, don't you think?"

I was having a hard time thinking. "Christophe has his Seven Deadly Sins onstage. Why would he want to hire me? I can't think of an eighth sin I could be."

"Annoyance?"

"Surely that's not . . . deadly."

"I'm beginning to think so," Cicero said. "You will be my Maggie, a *CSI* body extraordinaire. I'll put your name up in neon."

"Hector Nightwine owns the Maggie franchise."

That ought to kill that idea, Irma cheered me on.

"You will be called Margie, then." Mr. Cicereau said. "Or Magpie. Something close, but not too close. The lawyers will be debating that intellectual property issue until the Second Coming, if you believe in such things."

I certainly didn't believe that there was anything "intellectual" about the property he was appropriating, but I only said, "The Millennium was certainly predictable, but we didn't get a Second Coming out of it."

Meanwhile, I'd been reading the papers on his desk upside down. Investigative reporters get good at that fast.

I was surprised to see his name spelled out on a letter. It sounded ancient Roman or Italian, but it was spelled "Cicereau." Of course! England had never had a big werewolf issue, because it was an island and the wolves never got there. The werewolf was a creature of the forests in what became Germany and France. I'd done an online search on werewolves after my first time at Los Lobos.

All the medieval werewolf trials had been held in France, where maidens and murderers were sacrificed to the river Seine to placate a dragon-gargoyle. Right now I felt much more like a sacrificial maiden than a murderer, but who said you couldn't be both, especially in your own defense?

"I have a first-rate magician," Cicereau was saying. "You will be an additional assistant in a special, headline cameo. Sexy costumes, some of the usual tricks— vanishing, sawn-up, then, presto, no costume—a tasteful nude profile in the mist, perhaps as a sacrificial victim, then a dramatic death and resurrection."

"I know nothing about magic." But I marveled at how Cicereau had read my mind about the sacrificial part.

"Fortunately, my house magician does. Perhaps a bit too much."

Cicereau flashed emerald cufflinks set in drug-lord chunky gold as he shuffled papers on his desk, hiding the letter, reminding me of Ric's way smoother fashion sense. "You need only provide your very recognizable physical presence and follow his commands. A couple days' rehearsal should do it."

"I don't play well with others."

"Neither do I. This is not an option, Miss Street. Either play nicely with me, or I'll have you torn apart and tossed to Detective Haskell."

Quicksilver stood, legs braced, growling.

"There is wolf in that dog," the boss man said, careful not to move.

"I know."

"He makes a dangerous pet for a human."

"That's why he's a partner."

Cicereau's yellow eyes flashed with both approval and unleashed hunger. "Perhaps Madrigal can find a place for him in the act. If not, I expect you to control him."

"As much as you control me."

"And I will, because the life of everything you value . . . this dog, that man"—he didn't say who, but I saw he had learned about my doings here in Las Vegas, inside out—"will depend upon you becoming a prime attraction at my hotel. Don't forget all the roaming Maggie freaks out there. I can give you top-level protection."

I took a deep breath. And here I thought Snow was controlling! Even now I felt his chill bracelet coiling up my arm like a platinum snake, growing fangs that sank lightly into my forearm. A warning, or a sign of solidarity?

That was the trouble with unhuman allies; they were so damned hard to read.

And who, or what, was this Madrigal, besides sure to be seriously unhappy about having an unwilling rank amateur thrust into his headlining stage show?

CHAPTER THIRTY-SIX

The really bad part about becoming part of Team Gehenna (an ancient name for Hell, don't you know?) was that once inside the massive structure, like Dorothy in Oz I wasn't sure of ever going home again.

One of Cicereau's lieutenants took Quick and me into custody. For a flying monkey he was pretty chunky-hunky. I'd noticed him blending into the black pine of the office walls. He had a pronounced widow's peak in a thicket of dark hair streaked with silver. He wore a black suit, gray shirt, and red tie like a gout of designer-silk blood. He was young despite the silver streaks, but easy to sum up. Hard body, hard mind, hard heart. Cicereau had called him Sansouci. In French the phrase meant "without care."

It didn't fit him. Everything about him screamed extreme control, including his icy manner as he escorted Quicksilver and me a few floors down in the silver bullet elevator. I smelled an astringent cologne in the elevator's austere close quarters. Aquavit on ice. *Essence du* hit man.

With all the warmth of a vampire undertaker, Sansouci showed Quicksilver and me to our new home, suite, home.

It was ultra luxurious: two huge bedrooms and several living areas. We were given a pass card to the hotel running track, gym, spa, and exercise rooms. We would be under constant surveillance, Sansouci informed us, even when

I walked the dog on the rooftop swath of grass. And, by the way, the drop to the Strip below was forty stories and traffic was always heavy.

I didn't mind slamming the door shut on his straight, impervious back, which stayed there, facing out into the hall like a guard.

Exploring the suite, I found a refrigerator stuffed with rabbit food veggies and fish. Message sent. This was *me*. I doubted the Gehenna gang went much for broccoli or even rabbits when on their monthly wolfish runs through the desert. That was *them*.

My bedroom closet held a tracksuit, running shoes, pajamas, slippers and nothing else. Meanwhile, my heart and brain were revving on hyper drive, worrying about Godfrey and Nightwine missing us, worrying about where I'd allowed Quicksilver and me to be taken . . . and taken prisoner.

The reporter in me realized that I had a unique undercover position to exploit until I learned what I needed to know. Like all undercover assignments, this one was uncertain and scary. I had been ordered, immediately, to visit the magician called Madrigal's far more palatial suite two floors above. Of course Quicksilver would accompany me.

Mr. Big may have been my assigned boss, but I was curious to see how his headliner would like being saddled with a *CSI V* corpse and a gigantic wolfhound.

Clad in my same Sunset Park terrycloth shorts and top, Quicksilver and I passed the suite door and the waiting Sansouci to return to the elevator. Once inside, we all three faced forward and stared mutely at the floor indicator.

Oddly, Sansouci remained inside when the elevator doors opened. Quick and I were on our own with the magician. His suite was dead ahead, the door surface crossed with glittering gold wands.

I rang the doorbell. Yeah, penthouse suites at the Gehenna had doorbells. Hell didn't let just anybody in.

I wasn't sure if "Madrigal" or "Mad Max" answered.

Whichever, he was tall, broad, and bronze-skinned, with sea-green eyes and golden-brown dreadlocks. He wore a sleeveless tee that showed off elaborate bicep tattoos and martial arts pants. I couldn't help noticing that his pecs were so developed that his nipples stood at permanent and distracting attention. I felt small and pale and stupid and very unwanted, which wasn't a new feeling for me since kidhood, even though I'd outgrown the small part.

"What is this?" Madrigal's deep basso held the charmed singsong accent of the Caribbean islands, soft and welcoming where his physical appearance, however melting pot hot, was rigid and off-putting. "Little Orphan Annie and her dog, Sandy?"

"Mr. Cicereau wants me to use the name Margie."

"Yeah. I got my marching orders, and I saw that particular *CSI V* episode. What do you do besides sneeze maggots?"

I couldn't help wincing on behalf of my maybe-baby sister, Lilith. "It was a job. Apparently I made a good impression in it."

"Nudity and gore work rating wonders. A magician's assistant, on the other hand, works hard. She has to be smart, strong, and supple."

"I can do that."

"And the dog?"

"Smart, strong, and fanged."

He sighed hard enough to distract me, then stepped back from the door to let us in. "My act doesn't need some T and A ratings upswing."

T and A meant tits and ass, and I sure didn't like being reduced to that formula. "I haven't seen it, but I don't doubt it."

"Then why are you here?"

"I wasn't asked."

His hands knotted in front of him. Then he looked at me for the first time and flicked his bronze eyelashes upward.

Observed, of course.

"Where do we rehearse? I asked, thinking that might be private.

He shook his head slightly. "On stage, during the day. We'll have lots of time," he said, bitterly.

I recognized what he really meant. *Later, we'll have time to really talk.* He seemed to be as monitored as I was but maybe he'd learned a way around it. A magician would.

I didn't want to believe that this he-man magician had been as easily corralled as I had, because, if so, then my particular goose was royally cooked and garlanded with cranberry sauce as runny and, like Snow White's lips, as red as blood.

CHAPTER THIRTY-SEVEN

Rehearsals began that very day. A leotard and tights, rose pink, had appeared in my closet. From noon to 4 PM Madrigal and I worked out.

"You're too tall, too heavy, too busty, too clumsy," Madrigal said when he saw me clothed in neck-to-ankle Spandex that made me feel way too naked.

We weren't alone during this embarrassing summation. A tiny doll of a girl in a white outfit like mine hung back in the wings, watching us.

"Syl," Madrigal called with an extravagant bow and arm gesture. She came running onstage as lightly as a forever pre-pubescent ballerina. Her hair was Swedish white-blond and her skin had the sugary glow of a pastel gumdrop in blended Easter candy colors, lavender, white, yellow, pink. She was the born sugarplum fairy.

For the next hour I watched her curl into a box that seemed no more than a square foot in dimension and squeeze into six-inch false backs behind deceptive magical cabinets. Syl was triple-jointed, fairy-like, and astounding. She not only collapsed every joint in her body, she coiled into herself like a Slinky. She was also mute, I finally figured out. And her full name paid tribute to her physical plasticity: Sylphia. Emphasis on the *PHEE* as in a form of Sofia. Which meant wisdom in the ancient world. Or maybe the *phee* in her name was for *fey*.

Whatever, I watched them work together in awe and shame.

Lilith and I were an insulting replacement for Sylphia's abilities and artistry, bit players who should have stayed on the bottom fifth of the Screen Actors Guild membership list. But here we were with our shiny cheap media magic and had to perform.

That first afternoon Madrigal taught me to curl into a fetal bundle as small as my stiff and medium-boned frame could manage, but when I had to do it in a lady-sawed-in half box, I freaked from the dark confinement.

Sylphia fluttered to my side, tiny hands soothing my shaking shoulders. Her face was a mime's mask of heart-felt sympathy. I looked into her pale almond eyes and wondered, was she an enforced worker here too? Was Madrigal?

He unpeeled her from me with gentle fingers, then un-pretzeled me not quite so gently.

Madrigal seemed major upset. With me, with the situation. I couldn't blame him. Nobody professional wanted an amateur for a partner. We split for the dressing rooms. I tried not to watch Syl shed her leotard and tights like a paper cocoon. Mine were sweaty and seemed glued to my tense, damp skin.

A knock on the door revealed Madrigal, already changed into thick green terrycloth, the house robe.

Syl's thin eyelashes fluttered distress as he beckoned me out, silently.

He was our fearless leader. I followed.

He walked me into his private dressing room and then the shower, turned on the water, and tested it on his wrist as if warming milk for a baby. Then he pulled the opaque glass door shut as water pattered inside. He stripped off my leotard and tights with one long gesture, not bothering to watch as I hopped, naked, to free my bare feet from the snarl of Spandex. He dropped his terrycloth robe, yanked open the door on a cloud of steam, and stepped in with me before I could register anything but a wall of caramel-colored skin. Luckily, the shower was so frothy neither of us could see much but hot mist. Nor could anybody else, even a spy camera.

"They can't hear us in here," Madrigal murmured in my ear, his hand on my elbow.

I flailed a bit, still freaked by our sudden nude tête-à-tête.

"This is the only way. The werewolves revere human mating rituals. They only mate once a month in furred form. Naked human lust 24/7 inspires them. They'll assume our presumed union will guarantee your continuing cooperation."

Oh.

Madrigal pulled me more closely under the shower's hot tropical rain. He also pulled me closer against him. I didn't want to think how nice all this wet heat and slippery skin felt after the frigid uncertainty of being snatched from the Las Vegas streets and forced to turn myself into a human Windsor knot.

"I hear your name is Maggie," he said.

"*Lilah,*" I corrected. I was starting to split personalities, not wanting to pass as my maybe-sister, not willing to be fully answerable as myself.

"You're too solid for this profession," he said, "but Cicereau only expects me to make a show of you, not a true performer. Neither of us deserves to be a pawn in the were-packs' game."

He was pretty, oh, solid himself.

Gad! I'd put myself in a position where my new sensual self was bereft and alone. Who wouldn't welcome an ally in this situation? Who human? So what was Madrigal? Better question, who was I? Was it normal to be a little edgy yet excited when suddenly naked with an attractive stranger in a tropical steam bath of a shower? Pardon me for not knowing. They didn't teach us anything about this at Our Lady of the Lake Convent School. In fact, I couldn't remember much that they *had* taught us at OLLCS. While I was dithering, my trip back down Amnesia Lane pretty much killed any knee-jerk libido I had left.

What remained were the usual mysteries and insecurities, hints and allegations. Sure, my background was weird and isolated, but I'd managed to pass as a smart, savvy cookie since college. Trouble was, I had no idea what "normal" was. I did realize that I had pretty much shut down any sexual outreach or input after whatever bad had happened, whenever and wherever that was.

In the real, working world, I'd learned to look good for the camera and pass unmolested through all inter-sexual social situations. My aloofness only made me more attractive, more of a "challenge," to the wrong guys. I'd never met any right guys until Ric. And now—hot dog!— every guy, except goons, hitmen, and werewolf CEOs, seemed sort of right if I didn't get too picky or wigged out.

While I was doing all this useless navel-gazing, I suddenly saw that I really *was* seeing my own navel through the mists of steam. And a lot of naked and tattooed Madrigal standing behind me.

I put out my palm until it hit a barrier and married with its own image. The surface I touched was cool, smooth, and solid glass. Mirror. So why was it cold when the shower stall and steam were so overheated?

I had stepped close enough that there wasn't much mist veiling me anymore. I ran my palm down over my reflected image in a hopeless gesture of self-defense.

A modesty veil of steam welled up like a geyser from the floor, obscuring me to my neck. The nuns would be as proud as if I'd publicly disavowed patent leather shoes.

"Did you do that?" Madrigal asked.

"Do it? No, I just thought—"

"Thought what?"

"That . . . that I was a little overexposed for conspiring under the guise of coed showering."

He stepped closer, behind me.

Oh, no. I apparently was now sensitized to rear approaches.

His arms reached out of my shoulder-high mist to place both his palms on the mirror.

"Touch it again," he said.

Well, um, "it" was one of those sneaky indefinite pronouns and my mind was no longer the lofty, pristine summit of rational thought it had been.

"The mirror," he added more softly, his voice thrumming at the top of my head. There was just enough purr in it to tell me that he grasped, and was male enough to enjoy, my confusion.

Damn! I would become the coolest chick this world had ever seen someday. Meanwhile . . . I did as he suggested.

And then I saw what he had seen, which wasn't just me naked, but which was the mirror, *softening, blurring* under my hands. As if I could sink into it.

My palms were tingling way more than any other part of me, which was an improvement, in my estimation. I felt icy electrical static nips at the very heart of them, where headline and heartline and lifeline met and crossed. This was the hollow center of my hands, which I could never flatten to any surface. This was . . . the navel of my hands, as I had one at the center of my body.

I'd never felt anything in these zones before, but now they were almost alive. My hands pushed into the silver graven image of themselves and it was as if I were touching a second self lurking just beyond my sight.

Madrigal's hands commandeered my shoulders.

"Lilah. Come back."

I didn't want to. I was enthralled by Mirrorland. I could sense others moving out there, even picture myself out there.

Madrigal pulled my shoulders back until I was pressed against his hot, wet body, so physical, so crude compared to the call of Mirrorland, of those insubstantial, shifting things in the mist.

He wrenched himself and me away from the mirror to face the mechanics of the shower, the steamed-over glass door, barely visible and a poor excuse for the magical looking-glass door I'd just opened in the mirror, and the glitzy, gleaming overdone gold shower head and controls.

He'd wrenched me away from all that by pressing me against all of him. Was that my choice? The power of magic and the mind? Or the power of desire and the body?

If so, I never wanted to make that choice.

"Relax, I won't crowd you, here or onstage."

Madrigal's grip loosened. I sensed his mind backing off slightly, the usual singsong sensuality in the words, yet our closeness had turned comrade-like. Even as I breathed a sigh of relief, I wondered what he really wanted. I wondered what I really wanted of him and if I could betray him if I had to.

"I have friends who'll be looking for me," I warned.

"So did I."

Not good.

"We'll have to work up a routine for them," he said.

"I want out. Can't you tell? I'm claustrophobic and I have major issues about being bound in that damn horizontal corpse position from *CSI*."

"That industrial-strength familiar of yours might be a key."

I tried to feel the silver upon my body: the thin, hip-slung chain I wore under everything, a talisman of Ric and his . . . I guess it was love. I wanted to believe it was love. And where was Snow's hair shirt, as he had called it? I couldn't feel it, hadn't thought of it, felt it, since being abducted.

"My familiar?" I asked, playing for time to think. He surprised me.

"The were-hunter. Don't think they don't know what he really is. They must know they can't have you without suffering its presence. They must want you very badly."

Oh. Quicksilver. *Were-hunter*. Sounds serious. *Good dog!*

"Not as badly as I want them," I answered.

"You think you're a hunter too?"

"I am. A hunter of the truth."

He laughed, hard. Okay, that was a pretentious line but we crusading journalists get a little over-intense at times. I told him what I had used to be, not that long ago.

"Investigative reporter? I wish you could do an exposé on this operation."

"Sylphia. You two can't leave?" I asked.

"It's not that simple. We could maybe. Each in our own way, but we'd have to forsake the other. She's not the only one to consider."

I nodded, although he couldn't see the gesture. "You're lucky to have such solidarity."

"And cursed."

"I'm neither lucky nor cursed. Help me get out of here when I need to go, and I'll do my best to come back for you and Sylphia."

"All you have going for you is that were-hunter."

And I didn't know what the hell a were-hunter was, except the obvious. I had a deep-down feeling that Quicksilver was way more than anyone might take him for, even the werewolf mob. Even me.

"What are we working on tomorrow?" I asked.

"The mirrors."

"Mirrors?"

"Everything magic is mirrors."

"That's where you could really teach me something. I may be too tall, too heavy, too busty, too clumsy, but I think you're right. I might have a way with mirrors."

I felt his large hard hands on my ribcage, his thumbs softly brushing the roots of my breasts until I shivered.

"I was speaking of the attributes of a stage magician's assistant. I wasn't speaking of my own personal preferences."

Okay. His unbreakable bond to Sylphia wasn't sexual or romantic. That realization made me uneasy but I liked him even the better for it. And what had he meant by a "stage magician" as opposed to . . . some other kind? Like the real thing?

"We have to let them believe we have mated." He Frenched me in the shower, tasting fluoridation and my fear long enough so that I knew he liked it. Liked what? The water, the fear, the sweet sensuality, the danger of our hidden alliance? Who knew?

"Use my robe when you leave. Cicereau and his were-goons don't deserve a thrill."

He left me there, wet and steamy. I grabbed the fallen terrycloth robe as soon as I stuck a toe out of that shower. Then I checked for the silver familiar.

It was again a charm bracelet—did that mean that it would work like a literal charm? This time it was a jangling collection of sterling silver keys, with one lock among them all: a wolf's head, its open fangs the aperture that all or any of those keys would slam home to.

Snow had spoken. Or I liked to think he had. The keys to everything I sought were here. Okay. That gave me an agenda. An investigative reporter always liked that.

CHAPTER THIRTY-EIGHT

Syl descended from the dark of the theater flies on a thread of unseen spider-silk.

I watched her, overwhelmed.

Madrigal's huge hands were on my waist, but his eyes were on Syl.

"Exquisite," he said.

"What is she?"

"I don't know. Fey. Fairy. Far too good for the Gehenna."

"How did you two—?"

"Familiar." His hands slid away from my waist. "Damn!"

I felt his anguish as if it was my own, but it was a formally expressed anguish.

"Our alliance was our doom, yes?" he said. "She was far better than I had earned at that point. I supposedly 'saved' her from indenture to the Dread Queen, but I was indentured myself, although I didn't know it then." He shrugged away his frustration. "My 'act' depended upon her."

"Dread Queen? Are we in *Alice in Wonderland*, or what?"

"Wonderland." He gave a weary little snort. "Don't worry your little head about it. They're my look-out, and you do need to look out. They're not really mortal, but you sense that."

I watched. Watched Syl swaying slowly from the upper dark to the spotlit ground. I was sure that she did it for him.

And then I spied her twin still high above us.

A twin!

She was as petite and perfect as her double, the dark sister with her hair loops of shiny licorice, her skin a glittering dark-neon pattern of turquoise, purple, fuchsia, emerald. She oozed downward on a bungee cord to her lighter sister . . . twirling, spinning, suppleness personified.

I watched as they met in the middle some forty feet above the stage floor and twined into a lover's knot of sisterhood.

"And now, introducing me," I said. Sardonically.

I saw that we'd all been impressed into service on the stage. Impressed into exploitation, like the CinSims. Only here, with this established triumvirate, I was the odd woman out.

I sighed and dropped my eyes from the fey creatures twining down toward Madrigal and me. Quicksilver was sitting in the empty aisle, looking like he only needed a cigar in his mouth to masquerade as a Broadway angel.

"PHASIA," Madrigal told me that evening in the shower in answer to my soggy questions. "Sylphia's . . . sister, I suppose. Even I don't know. They're why Cicereau keeps me alive and working. The pack ran me down on the streets of Las Vegas when I had a contract at a smaller hotel. Their fangs notched me, their saliva filled my veins." He guided my fingers to the tattoos on his left forearm. I felt a Braille pattern of fang scars underneath the camouflaging ink.

"How? For how long?"

"First Bite," he said. "It makes you their servant, but not a supernatural. How long? Sixty years. So far."

My heart began to beat faster for a reason other than the hot, steaming water. I grasped Madrigal's tattooed upper arms. They seemed the epitome of strength. Why couldn't he use it? "You look thirty years old. You've been in Las Vegas that long?"

"Thirty years is a heartbeat for my kind, but any burr under any kind's skin is eternity."

For some reason I was not eager to probe exactly what he and his assistants were. Also, like most reporters, when I was hot after a certain story, it would take a world war to distract me.

"Then you know about the Werewolf-Vampire war?"

"Know about? I'm a prisoner of it. And my wards with me."

"Wards?" For a moment I thought he meant magical guards, like talismans.

"Sylphia and Phasia. I brought them into servitude with me."

His wards, as those to *be* guarded.

"You'd be gone from here if you could leave them," I said.

"Yes, but I never will do that to them."

"And me?"

"I want you gone. You upset the balance. You make it even more unlikely that I'll be able to free all three of us. Cicereau's stake in us is stronger because of you."

"So I'm both savior and anchor?"

"More anchor."

"I know I'm useless in the act, on stage. It's not me."

"That wasn't you on the *CSI* episode?"

"No."

Madrigal didn't seem surprised, but thoughtful. "Then perhaps Cicereau has finally miscalculated."

"Does it matter? I'm still here, a prisoner expected to reprise a role I never had, never would consent to."

"What did you mean, you might have a way with mirrors?"

"I see things in them other people don't."

"That's a very minor talent."

"Have I ever claimed to be a useful magician's assistant?"

"Cicereau expects your dazzling stage debut by tomorrow night."

"Then we dazzle, but meanwhile, how can I move around this hotel, unseen?"

"With Sylphia, but you would have to trust her webs."

"She's as trapped as anyone here. How can she be untrustworthy?"

"Her webs are part plain spit and part fairy dust. Her nature is predatory, to bind and devour, despite her deceptively dainty look. I care for her, but I can't control her. If you partner with her, you risk your life."

"*This* is your familiar?"

"A familiar should be both sheath and weapon, wall and goad. Were they not dangerous, they would not be useful."

"Swell." But his words kind of defined the role of Snow in my life, didn't they? "She was kind to me."

"She has a heart and a mind, only her nature is always . . . uncertain. And she is very jealous of me."

"These shower 'conference calls' of ours?"

"Have made her suspicious and bitter. A familiar is a jealous god."

Didn't I know it?

CHAPTER THIRTY-NINE

I was used to being a failure, but I wasn't used to failing at a job.

After Madrigal's last Margie-less show was over and the myriad stagehands had left, I crept back to the theater and climbed the black iron ladder against the outer brick wall high into the flies.

Above me the deadened lights—as shuttered and heavy-lidded as a hooker with industrial strength mascara—could cast no cold, critical eye on my feeble maneuverings on the wires and lines that stretched down to the stage.

I just wanted to rehearse on my own, discover what I could—and couldn't—do in this new arena I'd never chosen.

I grasped one of the bungee cord lines, wrapped it around my wrist as Madrigal had instructed, and . . . jumped. Flew like Peter Pan. Dive-bombed. Let myself out on a string of elastic until I thought I would crash and burn, then let myself be snapped back to the top of the building, waiting for my skull to shatter bricks.

I was a human yo-yo. I never hit sidewalk or sky, but boomeranged back and away from disaster at the very instant of impact.

I finally clung to one of the high perches where the performers rested before the next death-defying plunge. Scared, exhilarated, and beginning to get the rhythm of fall and rebound, of being a human Slinky. Also of trusting the equipment, the instructor. *Wait!* Wasn't this all a metaphor, maybe, for human relationships?

Madrigal would not let me crash and burn. His masters didn't want that. He wouldn't tolerate it, no matter how bound he had been. I crouched, panting alone in the dark, watching the one bare light bulb left burning below, an ancient theatrical custom called the "ghost light."

I guess I was beginning to know a few things about ghosts. And light. And myself.

The impact came out of nowhere like a clock's narrow metal pendulum swinging into me: unannounced, sudden, slicing.

I was off my safe perch, spinning into empty air, grabbing for any stopgap.

I caught a hanging bungee cord. It burned the skin from my palms before allowing me to rebound, then bounce down and up, and finally dangle forty feet above the stage floor. Low enough to see salvation. High enough to die.

I tried to decipher what had happened.

I was alone. I was working the ropes and bungee cords. I was making progress! I had been . . . seen. Watched. Sabotaged. Torpedoed.

I looked down. None of Cicereau's very earth-bound werewolves were prowling. Even Quicksilver had been left cooped up in our quarters. Dumb me, thinking I was a solo act.

So I looked up.

I spotted two gleaming figures, lithe and alien.

One came plunging down at me, spewing loops of lucent fibers like strings of pearls.

The other came sweeping across my lifeline, living tendrils from her head whipping around my bungee cord and severing it.

I had no choice but to grab a viscous rope of . . . spider web.

Ooh. Sticky. Stretchy. The black stage floor was rising like a solid wave, ready to crack my skull. The brain inside that skull understood that Madrigal's familiars were strenuously objecting to my new alliance with him.

Familiar. I didn't spin spider silk from my . . . well, let's not think what. I didn't have snaky Medusa locks to use as hangman's nooses.

I knew something they didn't know. I had a familiar of an albino.

I felt a strong silver tug. I was instantly wearing a strongman's belt, an all metal-mesh waist-cincher draped with chains on silver rings. The chains whipped out to loop around Phasia's snaky tendrils and pulled her down, down, down.

I heard a strangled screech.

I was too busy rebounding up to the ceiling to much notice.

Sylphia, she of the temporarily tender heart, was scurrying, all four limbs working in mirrored tandem, so they were eight, up the farthest reaches of her glittering web.

I floated like a butterfly, I stung like a bee. My silver chains sliced through her web like a buzz-saw through butter.

Once again I found a tiny perch high above everything and clung there.

Sylphia and Phasia surged upward at me, possessive female venom on the move. They were tiny, super-strong blends of will and tenacity and pathetic need. Madrigal was their god, but he was not their species, as I was not.

For the first time, I understood the driving frustration of the vampires at Howard Hughes' hospital bachelor pad who had striven to claim me, in vain. (Excuse the expression.) These creatures and I were not compatible, and Madrigal wasn't compatible either with his lethal, ladylike familiars, but they were locked into an uneasy trio.

What, or who, was I compatible with? Ric. Ric. I
wanted to think just Ric.

But also, a little. . . with Madrigal, or these spider/snake
harpies would have never tried to destroy me.

And . . . maybe, on a very bad day, Snow.

Shit.

But I had to use what tools I had.

I sent out my own built-in tendrils (although they were
actually add-ons) and after ten frantic minutes of old-time
herding and roping I had both familiars trussed up under
the ceiling in cocoons of silver chains, silk, and snaky hair.
They were bundled up like spider food, but they reminded
me of naughty Victorian girl-children: pretty, dainty, and
malevolent, like the illustration of the "The Girl Who Trod
on a Loaf" in a Hans Christian Andersen fairy tale, who
had ended up chained down in Hell covered with spiders
and snakes and other creepy-crawlies, oh my.

I left the Slime Twins to work their way out of their
own webs and mine. The silver chains broke off my belt
and kept them in tight custody while I slipped down.

Before I left, I asked Sylphia to meet me in the theater
after the final rehearsal the next day. I had to use what
tools I had, even if they venomously hated me.

QUICKSILVER SAT BY MY SIDE in the theater's empty seating
area when Sylphia came spinning down from the flies, a
fugitive pale glitter against the dark. Theater houses are
always dark, even in the daytime, lacking any light but
that provided by spotlights.

I knew and had recently felt Sylphia's compassion.
It was running short now that Madrigal and I had been
forced to confer daily in pseudo-sexual situations. I
doubted that there was any likelihood of consummation
between them, only a deathless bond that had no natural
way, like sex, of expressing itself.

I patted Quicksilver's head as Sylphia landed on the neighboring seat, playing the butterfly rather than the bee at the moment.

"You said you needed me." Her tone was childishly arrogant.

"I need your help, so I can leave."

"Leave?"

I nodded. "I don't belong here. I don't want to be here, which I think you can understand. There are those who miss me."

"Those?"

"A boss. A lover."

"Tell me about your lover." She posed on her heels atop a seatback, the piquant face avid.

I glanced at Quicksilver. "Not in front of the dog."

"Why?"

"He's very possessive."

"Why?"

"He's my . . . guardian."

She digested that. "Phasia says if I help you that you'll be gone."

"I'd like to think so."

"And your familiar?"

"Gone with me. I'd never leave him behind."

I saw her rainbow eyes flash at my last sentence. She was powerful, fey, unhuman . . . and so humanly insecure. For a moment I wondered if she could free them all, all three, in an instant, but didn't, because it kept Madrigal hers. That wasn't love, but she wasn't my species either.

"We will need Phasia," she said at last.

I nodded.

"She is even more dangerous than I am."

I nodded.

"I like your . . . dog, is it?"

That was the best she could do.

"He likes me too."

That threat was the best I could do.

No way could Quicksilver follow the paths these two fey creatures could carve for me. I was on my own with alien female rivals whose only reward would be my absence, by hook or by crook. But first was another rehearsal day, a final preparation for our debut, reluctant as it was for me. I would rather die than mimic it on the Gehenna's gigantic stage.

"I'VE THOUGHT ABOUT YOUR ACT," Madrigal said. "It must reprise the *CSI* appearance and surpass it. The core of it is the ten-second camera pan of you naked on an autopsy table."

"One thing. That wasn't me and I wouldn't have done it."

"Right. It was your . . . double. To save that lost sister of yours, would you have done it?"

Well, what was she to me, or vice versa? Strangers. Still, if I could have done that nude bit part and saved her to be found and met by me today . . . but no way would an Our Lady of the Lake Convent School student have done that. Yet, if I was sure it would save her? Lilith? If she was some severed part of me I needed to find and unite with—?

After all, Hector had me on plenty of tape already. A lot of my barriers had been crashing down lately, publicly and privately. Why stop now when it really mattered?

SO THERE WE WERE, on stage for a preview for the hotel's management guys and their wives and girlfriends. My stomach was a storm of nausea and tumult.

"Sylphia!" Madrigal looked and called into the dark above us.

She came twining down on a thread, a thread that unwound into a rainbow of colors . . . aqua, lime, lilac, pink, and yellow.

Each of those colors wove around me, creating shining silk gowns tighter than cocoons, covering and revealing at the same time. I was a moving rainbow of scintillating, titillating fabric and was slowly being levitated horizontal until I floated under Madrigal's hands, sensing the glittering rainbow mummy wraps that bound me.

His hands paused above my center, my navel, and I wafted upwards, stiff as a board, and felt the iridescent bindings peel away, leaving me . . . naked. The moment was beyond traumatic, but before my stomach could rebel and heave out its contents, Phasia appeared above me. She twined her strong, sinuous muscles around me, a living rope of exotic tinsel. She imprisoned me and clothed me with her thick, dry, scaled length. Her heavy bonds made a bikini over my hips, a bandeau bra over my breasts, a collar around my throat and a turban on my head.

Horizontal. Bound by pulsing serpentine muscles. A nightmare!

I prepared to shriek, drawing whatever shallow breath I could.

Madrigal bent over me, his face as frozen as a dream lover's. His lips parted as they reached my mouth. They touched mine. I opened for him. He withdrew.

Magic. A glittering red rhinestoned apple was in his mouth, taken from mine, shimmering, bejeweled, saliva-slick, and sensual.

I heard the audience of a couple dozen gasp. I felt their attention shift from me to Madrigal, to the shining forms of Sylphia and Phasia as they wrapped and trapped him 'round and 'round in their spidery, serpentine webs. I thought he deserved better, but that was not what this show was about.

This act was all about the webs of power and submission, not about me. I was utterly forgotten at my most revealing moment, ceding the spotlight to Madrigal and his slinky, shimmering familiars and damn glad of it.

That's Kansas for you.

The werewolf management was on their—for the moment, human—feet, applauding. Drinking, making merry. Good. Hopefully, they'd be out cold when I came calling later tonight.

CHAPTER FORTY

Madrigal stood behind me, his fingertips on my shoulders.

We were alone on stage and faced the mirrored back wall of his favorite place-switching cabinet.

Our images were reflected, but mine was hazy, shimmering at the edges with a halo of aura. My eyes in the mirror were not so much blue as transparent. The entire surface had a blue cast.

Madrigal extended his spread fingers to it. They touched the surface, the way kids play at making "spider" in the looking glass.

"Do you notice anything?" he asked.

"You could play concert piano with that finger spread?"

"Thanks. I like steel drums. Look at the reflection."

I did, frowning. I prided myself on being observant, but this was like a trick picture puzzle. There was the mirror with its weird blue cast, there was us looking as we usually did. I wasn't about to say we made a handsome couple, although we did. I was way too aware of Sylphia and Phasia hanging in the flies overhead, quite literally. Maybe asleep in their spidery, serpentine nests. Maybe not.

When did arachnid and reptile familiars sleep? Not often.

"Front-surface glass," Madrigal said finally, answering his own question. "There's not that eighth-inch gap, that discrepancy between the real object and the reflected one that gives away that it's just a reflection. It's useful for kaleidoscopes. I'm the only magician in Las Vegas to use it."

I placed my spread fingers on the glass. He was right. I was touching fingerprint to fingerprint, with no break in image.

"Why use it?" I asked. "Audiences never see or suspect the mirrors are there if the illusion works, and no one in the audience ever gets close enough to study the reflection."

"Not inside the cabinets, no. But I know the difference, as do my assistants. I want my illusions to be as perfect as possible."

"Great, but—"

"I'm telling you that this is a custom-made and rather rare mirror. If you do have any 'way' with mirrors, maybe you can find a new way with *this* mirror."

Oh. I put my other hand on the mirror and stepped closer. My eyes looked über-blue in the mirror's twilight indigo color. It reminded me of a vintage Evening in Paris perfume bottle. It made inky blue-black highlights shimmer in the hair of my reflection and gave my dead-white skin the faint azure glow of skim milk.

I didn't feel that I was gazing at my double, Lilith, but at a more translucent image of myself. Like the thin skin that can form over sitting milk.

Translucent. Light drawing through, not *at*. I pushed my fingertips hard against the cold glass surface and felt it warm as they sank into it. I felt them dent it, as they would living flesh.

I took a deep breath and plunged my right hand through, jangling charm bracelet of keys and all. It disappeared, and my flesh sprouted goose bumps from my right forearm to all over my body.

Madrigal's fingers lifted from my shoulders. "You feel as cold as dry ice."

Dry ice. A mere mist. Chill and foggy, often used as a stage trick.

"I'm going in," I said.

"Wait! I don't know what's going on here. What's on the other side?"

"Maybe freedom." What did I have to loose, except maybe my skin peeling off in an acid bath?

I walked into my own image, which was not totally my own image, into the sheer frigid stream of wintry breath beyond the blue horizon.

My blood thickened and pooled into sludge in my veins. My heart stopped, like a clock paused between *tick* and *tock*. I had a split second to regret Quicksilver. Ric. My lost Lilith. That was about it. A pathetic litany of a life. Maybe Nightwine on a good tick-tock.

Me! Alive and ticking.

I was walking down a long corridor of blue ice, like the inside of a diamond. I saw forms entombed there. Human. Half-human. Not human at all. I faintly recognized some from my unremembered past. Kids. Teachers. Nuns. A ghost of Lilith seemed to stalk me through the tunnel, its image impressed briefly over every semi-familiar face I glimpsed.

Finally I walked into a dead-end of cold metal reflections, surrounded by myself in every direction. This was nightmare, not release!

Then I knew exactly where I was, and my pulse began to thaw from a ponderous, sleepwalking rate to high excitement.

The stainless steel elevator! I was alone inside it and it was moving, swift and silent as a mercury current. The doors opened soon after, splitting my image, easy as axle grease, through them. I felt like Moses walking through the Red Sea, only I was parting liquid walls of frozen water. I passed through, into a dark, dimly glimpsed passage: the hall leading to Cicereau's office.

I felt invisible. I'd moved into the ghost of my previous reflection in that elevator. Was there some simulacrum of myself still in Cicereau's office? What had been reflective there? No mirror. A mob boss doesn't like to look himself in the eye. The walls had been dead black. The carpet equally absorbent and dark. The desktop had gleamed, but it was warm and bloody, not cool and blue.

Ah. A slab of horizontal mirror behind the wet bar counter. And there had been a vintage mercury glass ice bucket, too. A lovely, rotund, convex gleam of reflection, backed by a mirror, grabbing the shape of every body in the room into a bent version of themselves, including me. Great camouflage in case I was caught.

Bless you, booze brother, for the traditional bar decor! But for you I wouldn't be able to break into this room.

I found myself crouching on the black marble wet-bar top in front of the ice bucket.

The marble was gravesite cold and I was warm, living, whole. I scrambled down to the deep green carpeting, studying the scene.

The office was empty at this hour past midnight. Cicereau was probably rambling through his gambling hell or toasting high rollers in forty-thousand-dollar-a-night four-thousand-square-foot suites.

The flat computer screen was framed in silver, a wireless ebony keyboard and mouse lay before it. Evidently even guys with large canines liked Bluetooth.

My face reflected in the slumbering dark screen until I rolled my fingertips over the mouse ball. *Hmm.* Reminded me a little of the head on Ric's stick shift. *On the car*, my friend Irma piped in. *Don't mess up your first disembodied breaking and entering with distraction.*

I'd never broken and entered anything before, and I certainly didn't feel disembodied. I was here. In person. Okay. Now I felt grounded.

I felt free, in control of the surroundings and myself. Was I really . . . a physical being? I felt everything I touched. I felt *here*. So what had I left behind? An image of me? A ghost? Lilith?

No time for an identity crisis. I sat in Cicereau's big leather chair and clicked and rocked and rolled through his personal computer files. Where to look? The business stuff had to be hidden behind high security passwords. But I wasn't an IRS man or a Fed after his current crimes. I wanted to know about his past. Where? *My Documents. Photo Album.*

And there they were. The grandkids. They unmistakably *were* grandkids, lapfuls of wedge-faced wolfling kits, looking as human as all get-out. Grinning with missing teeth. Wonder when the fangs came in? Kindergarten? Fourth grade had always been a challenging time. Maybe then. First shape-change? Maybe at puberty when all that embarrassingly private body hair begins growing. Hey, a furry face is a way to escape zits for a while.

And Cicereau was beaming in all the pictures, wearing that barrel-chested suit coat, looking rapacious in a purely corporate way. Cicereau in all the pictures, grinning behind the wee ones' parents. Looking not a week older than he had in his office a day ago.

And Cicereau finally pictured wearing a fedora in black-and-white images, grinning toothily next to heavyset guys in wide-lapelled pin-stripped suits. Gangsters. Wise guys. And then Cicereau wearing a vintage tuxedo, like my pal Nicky, with a benign just-family grin on his pack-Family face. No silver hair, no beer belly, a sleek, slim fortyish father standing next to his achingly slight, sweet Cinderella of a daughter who was elfin where he was earthy, shy where he was sly, dewy where he was already looking dissolute.

Two things were clear: Cicereau had found an immortality potion that didn't make him into a half-were.

And I had found . . . *her*.

The girl in the blue dress buried in Sunset Park's sand and stone. *Her.* The girl with a heart full of first love and a body primed with unleashed feral passion. *Her.* Born to be wild.

Her. Doomed to be slaughtered.

Her. One of Ric's Sunset Park dead bodies. The long-dead girl I had channeled through the medium of Ric's dowsing rod. In a way, she was my older, younger, more sensual self.

Cicereau's *daughter*.

CHAPTER FORTY-ONE

While I stared at the happy black-and-white family photo on the computer screen, awash in puzzlement and naked envy, I heard a clunking sound somewhere out there.

Pipes maybe? The massive air conditioning system in these mega-hotels coughing? *No!* The private elevator doors opening.

I stood, clicking out of Cicereau's Photo Album as fast as I could while checking the room for hiding places. I doubted I could manage any mirror tricks on such notice. I was too new at it. Besides, Madrigal had probably helped me out on the other end.

Here, I was on my own.

So, what's new, Kansas pussycat?

I eyed the moony globes of the lighting fixtures. The last thing Cicereau and his staff needed to know was how I'd managed to break in here. *I mustn't get caught.* I grabbed a stapler from the desk and rushed to the door.

I couldn't hear any oncoming footsteps because of the thick carpets but I sure sensed incoming unfriendly fire. I dialed the light control to dark and with one whack the heavy metal stapler slammed the shattered plastic control to the carpeting.

The room went dark. Thudding feet were coming toward me at a dead run. One pair. One man. I had to knock him unconscious before he saw me.

I made sure to stand far enough back that the opening door wouldn't nail me. I still clutched the stapler. In a locked-down position it made as good a blackjack as anything.

It was against my nature to sandbag some unsuspecting henchman who was just doing his job, but I'd have to steel myself to do it. And hit hard enough to knock him out. I put myself back in my self-defense class mode; first, scream like a girl; then, fight like a guy. Actually, the first scream needed to be the deepest, most manly voice I could manage, shouting "*No!*"

Mike Wu had insisted that we all have an inner toddler with a visceral tendency to obey that parental shout, even serial killers.

Trouble was, I didn't want Cicereau and minions to even know my sex. The stapler across a skull was going to have to shout "no!" for me.

I waited, trying to keep my breathing from gushing like a geyser in the silent room.

Someone slammed the door flat against the wall and immediately shut it. Good thinking. He knew that one piece of wall was vacant and took it himself. And now he had me trapped.

I heard him move across the shut door, blocking it for good measure. And then I heard a lock snap. Just one of those cheesy set-into-the-doorknob switches, but it'd be hard to find and release quickly in the dark.

I had to take him down.

Right now his hand was brushing the wall on the right side of the closed door, looking for the light control dial.

The patting motions found the empty plate, and paused.

I couldn't help nodding, although no one could see me in the dark. Right. No light.

Except I saw two faint gleams turn on. About two inches apart. Yellow-green. Funky chartreuse, actually.

Shoot! This was some kind of super and he knew how to make those little lights of his shine. His eyes. Wow.

Maybe six feet off the ground. I was five-eight in my magic show workout ballet flats. It was going to be tough to get high enough to hit his head.

On the positive side, those reflective irises told me whether he was facing fore or aft.

So . . . just how much did they see in the dark?

I crouched low, hearing him move toward the desk.

The computer chimed as he turned it on. The screen would add some ambient light to the room. Can't have that. I stood and hurled the stapler at the sound.

The display screen slid across the desk and shattered to the floor.

There also went my only weapon.

I'd slid back to the door during the crash and turned the knob button sideways. That was the "open" position, wasn't it? I'd seen these locks a thousand times on rest room doors.

The chartreuse eyes moved up from the level of bending over the laptop to full height again.

They came slamming toward the door just as I sidled away.

He thumped to a full stop against the wood. If I'd still been standing there, I'd have been caught, and semi-crushed too.

Maybe I should give up now, while I still had an intact skeleton. What would Cicereau do to me, really? I was his prize performer.

I'd only been snooping in his private office, digging up the dirt on his long-dead daughter. Maybe he'd thank me. Maybe he didn't know what had happened to her. *Maybe I could hallucinate in the dark*. There weren't any photos of her on his trophy wall. No, he himself had wanted her dead and buried for some reason. Ric and I had unearthed her, against all their hopes and plans, promising to make her loss and death into a *cause célèbre* again.

While I calculated this and that, the eerie green eyes
lunged at exactly where I was standing.

I stepped one giant step away, soundlessly, the carpet
muffling my movement.

Green Eyes cursed. It was a growled word, untranslatable,
the werewolf equivalent of "fuck" probably.

I so wished for Quicksilver, but this had been a solo
expedition. It would have to be a solo escape.

I fumbled behind me and found one of those vintage
cigarette stands, the metal equivalent of a birdbath
pedestal. I lifted it in both hands and swung it in a wide,
blind swath.

It connected with flesh and bone, hard enough that even
I winced.

I heard my victim, my stalker, hit the door and slide
down it, half-dazed to go by the muffled growls.

I was blocked from the door. My only exit would have
to be reflective.

The slab of mirror that reflected the bottles and glasses
awaited me, but I needed a door out of darkness and into
infinity and a light that would put the mirror into play.

Cigar aficionado Cicereau's office was filled with
tabletop lighters. It would be sweet to use the fat-cat
werewolf's affectations to escape his security guy.

I fumbled on the bar top until I felt a lighter embedded
in a marble miniature of the Gehenna and cocked and
depressed the mechanism. Dozens of tiny flames reflected
in the glassware, the silver ice bucket, the mirror behind
them all.

I saw myself, a crouched pale figure. I saw Green Eyes
behind me, the hit man called Sansouci, rising dazed
against the solid wood door. I embraced my own reflection
and went oozing through the melting mirror-glass,
Madrigal's voice in my ears, calling. "Come back."

CHAPTER FORTY-TWO

I moved as I always did, because I chose to, beyond the mirror backing of the wet bar. It was still like breaking through a sheet of ice as gossamer as a dragonfly's wing.

Dragonfly like, I darted along silver tunnels. I traversed aluminum air-conditioning ducts, into a chill headwind. I must have been crawling, because the ducts were too square to allow for an upright human to pass, but it felt like swimming, as if I were moving through half-set Jell-O.

I broke through a thin blue skin and was suddenly facing myself.

Neither one of us was wearing a thing, except for the cellophane afterbirth coating of the front-surface mirror.

I was back on stage and not happy.

Then I noticed that my double didn't wear a familiar form . . . and felt my living silver talisman weaving itself into the hair at the back of my neck, out of sight, but not out of mind. Creepy. Still, I appreciated its loyalty and discretion.

"This is insane," I told Madrigal. "I can't do this."

"No." He embarrassed me further by walking around me and my twin in a figure eight pattern, summing us up fore and aft.

A terrycloth robe dropped on me from above. I looked up. Sylphia was hanging sullenly from a silver thread, playing chaperone.

While I shrugged into the heavy material, Madrigal studied my mirror image.

"It's not Lilith," I said.

"No. And it's not you either. It's your reflection in the mirror."

"Reflections don't peel off into their own personas."

"You already have one double whose existence you never suspected. Maybe this explains Lilith."

"She was real enough to fool a camera and crew and a director."

Madrigal lifted one of my reflection's hands. It was limp, lifeless. "Only a reflection, as I told you. Without my magic, she wouldn't even stand up."

"*Your* magic?"

His attention was all on . . . Del 2.0. "*Umhmm.* I do have some that isn't bound."

"Then maybe you did all of this. It isn't my 'way with mirrors' at all."

I did so not want it to be me. I didn't believe in this shit.

"Maybe." Madrigal turned so fast his dreadlocks whipped his own cheeks. "It's time for you to leave."

"I think so too."

I had a lead to pursue in the real world . . . a real, weird, solid lead!

Cicereau's *daughter* was the dead body.

If the Sunset Park deaths went back to the Werewolf-Vampire War in the forties, my romantic Romeo and Juliet idea was much more likely. The thirty pieces of silver in the grave represented betrayal, and what could those young lovers have betrayed but "both their houses?" House Werewolf and House Vampire. If only the vampire swain would appear in my magic mirror at the cottage to confirm my theory! But the girl had seemed to imprint on me. I wondered if the guy had imprinted on Ric somehow. Certainly their passion had affected us both. Me, mostly. Ric, I could tell, was not sexually retarded in the slightest. *It's not fair,* Irma grumbled, *the guy always had the edge!*

If I could prove all this, Nightwine would have a terrific supernatural cold case to present on *CSI V.* I'd have solved my first Las Vegas mystery and would have a real income again, and Ric would . . . well, he'd have the satisfaction of knowing who his dowsing rod had dug up. And maybe he'd also have some useful incriminating information on one of Vegas's biggest crime bosses.

While I was daydreaming, Sylphia and Phasia spun down to the stage floor on their eerie bodily-fluids-made rope.

Madrigal turned to me. "Get dressed in what you wore here and get the dog."

I nodded to the stage wings. "I don't need to get Quicksilver."

He was waiting just out of the audience sight lines, a happy doggie smile on his face to see me back in this location.

"Here are her clothes." Sylphia threw the jogging shirt, shorts, and shoes at me.

Wow. Everybody wanted me out of the Gehenna but Cesar Cicereau.

I joined Quick in the wings to don the clothes, sitting on the cold stage floor to pull on my socks and shoes. A cold silver circle under one sock told me where the token was now, an almost reassuring normality. What I wouldn't give to leave this creepy magic show and return to creepy Nightwine Manor and Sunset Park!

I finished tying the shoelaces and then eyed the pallid naked image of myself a bit nervously. She stood beside the prop cabinets, inert as a mannequin. I hated leaving that behind, this shadow of myself. It was like letting a voodoo priestess have a hank of your hair and an envelope full of fingernail clippings and then slip off to Hell with them. Beside me, Quick growled agreement.

Madrigal came over to us, squatted, and addressed us both. "This is the one opportunity for you to escape with no one the wiser. I can animate your reflection enough to fool an audience. This spares you unwanted exposure, Del, gives Cicereau what he thinks he wants, and gives me the time to plan my . . . our . . . own escape."

"But . . . who or what are you?"

The murky green eyes drew close to my own.

"A magician who doesn't need to waste time answering your questions. The route out of here will be hard. You and the dog must rely on Sylphia and Phasia, as against your natures as that is."

Quicksilver's hackles rose at the news of our partners in flight. "It's the only way," Madrigal said. He slapped his awesome thighs. "I don't want you two cluttering up my stage and agenda any longer."

Why not? I was used to being unwanted.

OUR ESCAPE HATCH was exactly that: a hatch in the stage wall, about the size of an oven door. It was fine for Phasia and Sylphia, and even me, but it was a tight squeeze for Quicksilver, even if he belly-crawled.

I didn't like to see a proud dog like Quicksilver crawl, not to mention the tight corners he'd have to turn in the building's extensive mechanical ducts. We would be doing the equivalent of navigating a great pyramid's narrow alleyways between secret chambers.

"Can't you just sneak us out through the hotel's public areas?"

"Of course I can," Madrigal said, "My tricks of legerdemain could even keep you out of plain view most of the time. But Las Vegas hotel-casinos have the most advanced, pervasive surveillance system in the world. Your passage will look strange enough to betray me if Cicereau's technicians should happen to spot it in a random check.

"You will not appear to be gone, thanks to your mirror-silver substitute. Your furred familiar has always kept out of their sight. If they ask later, I can always say that the dog ran away. They never liked his presence anyway."

Quicksilver growled at this, whether from contemplating the hatch we were clearly about to vanish into, or recognizing Madrigal's slight.

"Okay," I said. On second thought, I wanted Quick with me when my life was in Phasia's and Sylphia's tiny cross-species hands.

Madrigal pounded the rusted-in handle open. Phasia and Sylphia were glow-worms slithering into the opening's black vacant mouth. I wriggled in next, regretting that my warm-weather jogging clothes left my knees and elbows exposed to scrape metal.

Quicksilver took a last deep inhalation of my scent (*embarrassing!*) and we disappeared, head and tail, from the stage area and Madrigal's little world.

The mechanical ducts were surprisingly spacious, perfectly suited to hands and knees work. I suppose the extensive air-conditioning systems such huge buildings required needed frequent tending.

Great. So now I could fret about crawling right into the face of some workman. I could hear mechanical groans, wheezes, and pings all around us, as if we were in a haunted house.

Phasia and Sylphia stopped frequently as the hidden network of ducts intersected. It was truly freaky to see Phasia extend her long thin tongue to "sniff" the air for human traces. She could have had a fine future in X-rated movies. Not that Sylphia was any slouch.

She spit out web and dropped over black edges on a viscous thread, returning to nod and lead us forward again.

Of course, Quick's long curved nails made a constant rat-scratching sound, which echoed until our party sounded like an advancing army of rodents the size of Godzilla. Luckily, as we progressed, the clack and clatter and groan and sputter of so many mechanical systems functioning overpowered any sound one of us could make.

Our progress stopped when I ran into Phasia and Quick into me because Sylphia had frozen. With our silence, we heard a strident cacophony like eighteen million machines being tortured by ghosts.

Phasia's snaky tendrils twined around my neck and head and her sickeningly supple tongue tasted my ear. I heard hissing vibrations rather than speech. "The central chamber for all the operating systems. Your last stage of the journey will bypass this, but you must go on alone."

Red working lights illuminated the area and my eyes slowly adjusted enough to see the door to another hatch.

"You can take this route to the outside," Sylphia said.

"Is it safe?" I asked.

"Safe enough for your breeds."

And if we went tumbling down into the maw of a furnace, say, or a garbage compactor, who would ever know what had happened to us?

I eyed the round metal hatch uneasily. "How do I get it open?"

Phasia's Victorian doll's face registered contempt. Then her flowing curls became writhing serpents that fanned out around the round door, fastened on, and twisted.

There yawned another black hole to nothing, but I was growing pretty tired of our escort service.

I shrugged and eyed Quick. He looked like a dog that was more than ready for "walkies."

I put my legs through the hole and pushed off with my hands, Alice down the rabbit hole. There was no lost kitten ahead of me but a big, bruising dog was hard behind me. We whirled away, riders on a water-park slide that wasn't wet or in a water park.

Curiouser and curiouser.

We landed together in a cloud, a cloud that smelled of powder, and detergent, and perfume, and sweat, and precious bodily fluids. If I smelled all this, I could imagine what a wall of pungent and confusing scents was hitting Quick's super-sensitive nose.

I actually stifled a squeal as we plummeted to a stop. It had been rather fun. Then I blinked at the artificial daylight that was pressing down on me like a migraine headache.

It took a few minutes for my eyes to adjust and determine where we were.

We were in a giant Dumpster-sized bin at the back of the Gehenna, surrounded by towels and bed linens. We'd left the sinister hotel that had held us prisoner by . . . a laundry chute.

Actually, struggling out of all that smothering fabric and heaving ourselves over the giant bin's edge onto the inner service courtyard's asphalt surface was the hardest part of our journey out of the hotel.

Quicksilver and I finally stood on the Strip sidewalk, buffeted by packs of tourists pushing trails up and down the famous street.

Against the horizon of neon lights, the Gehenna's signage stood out. Live and in person! it trumpeted. Margie, as You've Only Glimpsed Her: Nude and Dead. Again.

And here I'd taken Nightwine for a necrophiliac creep. That was before I'd met Cesar Cicereau, mob boss and hotelier . . . and father of one of the dead bodies in Sunset Park.

So who was the guy whose grave sweet Jean from my cottage mirror had shared? Who was the man to whom she had given her girlish heart and body? I kinda wondered that about myself too.

Who had made her own father want her dead?

And who had made it possible for werewolves to live on like vampires, eternally?

Ric knew a lot about werewolves and maybe vampires, and maybe more about me than I felt comfortable with. That could be because I wanted someone to know it for the first time in my life. Even though there was a lot about Ric I didn't know, and might never know.

Oh, well. Hell! Yeah, literally.

Chapter Forty-Three

Quicksilver and I hoofed it back to our Sunset Road home, footsore but happy to be together and free. I patted his head as I punched in the code that would open the gates to our cottage.

"They didn't much like you at the Gehenna, but I sure was glad you were there."

He made excited whining sounds that meant: *let me in and at my food bowl, Mama!*

Inside I found the cottage rooms neat, cool, empty, and peaceful.

Only the blinking red light on the cottage's non-vintage answering machine intruded on the homecoming mood.

First I filled Quick's water and food bowls.

Then I gobbled some cherries and grapes from the refrigerator and poured myself a gleaming goblet of Merlot. I've never been a wine snob and Hannibal Lector can keep his "nice Chianti" for the liver-eating among us, which were unfortunately too populous lately, post Millennium Revelation.

Then, ever the reporter, I skimmed the Las Vegas papers that had piled up and found a second front-section story that made me raise my eyebrows and then some.

Last . . . I listened to my messages.

First.

"My God! Del! Where are you? I'm frantic. Your cell is on voice mail. All I get here is an answering machine . . ."

Ric's voice. I replayed the message. *Would I like to be a spider-sylph with him in my web!* Truthfully, the sound of his voice snapped me the last bit out of a very bad dream.

I redialed instantly and got his cell phone.

"Del! You're back. What the hell happened? I've been frantic—"

Hey, I liked somebody being frantic about me, especially twice.

"I'm okay. It's been . . . surreal. Can we meet? Talk about it? I've drummed up some good leads."

"Leads? Do you have any idea? I need to see you."

"Right. I have lots of new info."

"Screw the info. I need to see you. See that you're all right."

"Where? When?"

"Now. Um, I don't know. Where do you want to be seen?"

"With you."

There was a long pause. "I know you've been through something. I don't know what. What will make it better?"

"You."

An even longer pause.

"How?"

"Just get over here."

"Your dog on the premises?"

"Yes, but he'll be off for a run by the time you get here. He's ready for one."

RIC ARRIVED only ten minutes after Quicksilver left.

I let him in, kissed him with fresh layer of Lip Venom on, and then settled him down with his own glass of Merlot. Between my tingling lip gloss and the wine, he was licking his chops like Quicksilver enjoying a steak.

"You're going to make me an addict of a girly beauty product," he said. "So where have you been?"

"And where have *you* been? But me first."

"Suits me, believe it."

I told him about my abduction and brief magical stage career at the Gehenna. I didn't mention my new mirror-melting facilities.

"I'm not surprised," Ric said after a couple steadying sips of wine. "You did the right thing. Undercover credo: don't struggle when you're outmanned, pretend to go along, and then get the hell out. Plus, you've identified one of the corpses in Sunset Park. Good job."

I loved it when Ric treated me as an investigative equal. I'd been kidnapped by a couple of incompetent wise guys. It had been more freaky than threatening, and I had gotten myself free, with more knowledge than we'd had before. Of course, I didn't mention the mirror or the "girl I'd left behind . . ."

"So I come home to a pile of newspapers," I went on.

"I subscribe too."

"Then you must have read this little article."

I knew the small-type headline by heart: CITY DETECTIVE ATTACKED IN SINKHOLE. I watched his face as he saw it: total LE (law enforcement) non-reaction. That's when I knew.

"What's the Sinkhole, Ric?"

"Badder than bad. More north than North Las Vegas. Actually, its location seems to . . . . move. You don't want to go there, even if you can find it. It's where the worst predatory unhumans hang out, the penny-ante, low-brow loser unhumans, I should say."

"Kind of a Brigadoon for hell-raiser set. Why do you think Detective Haskell was there?"

"Probably had a snitch in the area. Haskell is pretty penny-ante and low-brow himself."

"True."

I got up, collected Ric's wine glass, and refilled it. Mine too. When I brought his glass back, I brushed knuckles with him.

He flinched. Not much. Just enough.

I sat down opposite him. "The newspaper says that Haskell was attacked and beaten. Pretty badly."

"Couldn't have happened to a nastier guy."

"He's in the hospital, Ric. The story says he was mutilated. In a very sensitive area. Chewed."

Ric put down the wine glass. He stood up. A good offense is the best defense. "What? You think I'm a freaking werewolf?"

"I can see your bruised and cut knuckles from here. I think you should tell me what you did."

"Am I asking you the gory details of your sojourn at the Gehenna? I'm sure there are some."

"A few. Nothing serious. What did you do to Haskell?"

"First I got seriously mad. No one mauls you but me."

"I'm so flattered."

"So I faked a snitch appointment and went down to the Sinkhole at night and beat the hell out of him. It was a fair fight. If he'd had any balls he could have beat the hell out of me."

"Apparently he doesn't have much for balls now."

"That wasn't me. I left him unconscious and got out of there. He didn't even see what hit him, didn't know who I was. Something else must have got to him after I left."

"You don't sound sorry."

"Are you?"

"*We* might be. He's still alive. He must have you on his list of possibles."

"No, I tell you. I dressed for the neighborhood. *You* wouldn't have recognized me. He didn't see anything coming but my fists. I suppose you're pissed because I went out and avenged your honor. You're liberated and you wanted to do it yourself."

"I'm liberated," I agreed, "and I want . . . you."

He actually waited for the rest of my sentence. "I want you *to* . . . ."

Here's the thing. Sure, I wanted to solve the crime, get the better of Nightwine's pride and money, establish myself as a player in Las Vegas, get the hot story, save that poor dead girl's soul maybe, but mostly I wanted Ric.

"I want a date. Formal."

"Easy." He sounded relieved. The little woman just wanted a formal night out, a date. "Where? When?"

"Some hotel. Some restaurant. You know Las Vegas, but maybe you don't know me. You pick. The place, the time, the action."

I almost heard his breath stop.

I'd been putting my faith in him and I didn't really know a thing about him, except he was as good as I was about maintaining secrets. Seeing Madrigal and his mysterious assistants had made me unhappy with the status quo with Ric. This wasn't going to work unless I got behind those very attractive barriers he erected. Why did he never shed his clothes? Why did he like to control my vertical and horizontal so much?

Yeah, I had phobias to overcome. But so did he.

This had to be an equal deal. I was willing to play a little strip poker if I got a little strip poker back in return. So. My challenge. Me. Stripped. And his play. Next.

CHAPTER FORTY-FOUR

Ric stood up, clearly confused. Intrigued. Hot. Cold. Wary.

"You're not mad that I took out Haskell?"

"You're not mad that I crashed the Gehenna? Good. Now we only need to find out who the dead guy in Sunset Park was. But before that, there's something I want more."

I leaned into Ric, running his silk-wool blend jacket lapels through my hands. I'd learned that he liked that once-removed form of intimacy. I wanted, as I'd just thought, more.

"Your clothes always feel so good," I said. Then . . . "I'd love to slow-dance naked in your arms."

I felt him catch his breath, then think about it. We'd been intimate, but this was intimate on my terms, not his.

"Sounds like a plan," he said carefully, as if not believing his luck.

My own breath stopped. I'd wondered about his reticence. His privacy. What it hid. I didn't just want me naked with him. I wanted him naked with me. I wanted to tease him past his shelters, his borders. We were both experts at emotional poker playing. Sometimes you have to raise the stakes to see the other player's cards.

His eyes were all pupil, dark, half-satisfied already. "One condition."

"Only one?"

"You wear something that makes getting you out of it interesting."

I thought. Nodded. "So where in Las Vegas can we do this naked tango?"

Ric had taught me to be a tad exhibitionistic lately, but Los Lobos was out. Maybe in his mysterious, dark, glittering house of mirrors . . .

"*Your* naked dance. First drinks and dinner. Then we cha-cha. A big Las Vegas evening out. Leave it all up to me. I'll pick you up tomorrow at . . . seven."

"Isn't that a little late?"

"It's going to be a long, late night."

His words resonated in my throbbing heart, pulses, and especially elsewhere.

"Long?" I repeated.

"Naked," he echoed.

We nodded, agreeing and excited by it.

TALK ABOUT TWENTY-FOUR HOURS of sheer anticipation. Ric wouldn't pick someplace . . . public. Would he? Then again, he liked to show me off. I preened a little at the thought of his Latino possessiveness, a trait someone like me, always listed on the orphanage records as unwanted, unspoken for, would treasure. My wounds, his wounds, our aphrodisiac.

He called my cell phone that afternoon. "Drinks at the Palms' Ghost Bar, dinner at the Paris restaurant in the Eiffel Tower."

"Those are primo venues. How did you–?"

"No questions. This is just a friendly dress code alert."
"Expensive too. And neither of those places have dancing."

"Nor nudity."

I could tell my crazy impulse had really turned him on. Me too.

I ransacked my closet, looking for the perfect gown to get out of. Who was I? A stripper? Yeah. Something spectacular. Something . . . very frustrating. My fingers hesitated over the black velvet thirties Nora Charles gown. Perry Mason had returned it with a disturbing message: no DNA on it other than mine. Not even Snow's? What was he, invisible? In that case, Claude should have left a traceable memoir of his playful butt pinch. Time to figure that out later.

The gown? No. Too Snow. I didn't like to mix my . . . encounters.

At last my fingers slid along the slippery surface of one of my oldest vintage gowns. Made to order for my *querido amigo*. I smiled wickedly. *Yes*.

I wore a long, black velvet thirties cloak when Ric called at my door.

"That's it? That's all?"

I shrugged and slipped out the door before Quicksilver could get a piece of my cloak or of Ric. The cloak had an ivory satin lining that almost caught in the door of the Corvette as Ric ushered me in.

Ric was wearing an off-white blazer that looked as smooth as clotted cream over an ice-blue silk shirt carelessly open at the neck. His trousers were black wool-silk with a formal satin stripe up the side. Las Vegas dressy casual.

We skipped the line of gaggling tourists in front of the elevator to the Palms Hotel's Ghost Bar, the city's hottest destination, and fifty-five stories up. No shorts, no hats, no tennis shoes, no baggy or torn jeans allowed. Dressy sandals permitted, no flip-flops.

The Ghost Bar. I knew I'd be uneasy there. My kind of medium had not been defined yet when this place had been created. Sitting in this nineteen-sixties meld of blue and green furniture against silver and ice-white, I let my cloak fall back to swathe the chair behind me and studied the holographic photos of motion picture stars on the wall.

I knew Ric was studying my pale satin gown, all buttoned up to the neck in back and down to my wrist, thinking of my all too solid flesh beneath it. Nothing intrigues like extreme modesty.

I inspected the ghostly faces on the wall. The images blurred as you moved past them. They simulated life. Only, I *felt* them. Even the animate silver necklace around my neck thickened with my second-hand emotions and tightened into a dog collar under the pale satin.

I sensed their unspoken anxiety at being reduced to dead icons and instantly knew the weaknesses their fame had hidden. *Watch me, love me, pick me!* Hadn't I felt that all in the orphanage, on my own lonely stage? And I hadn't I also found fulfillment in front of a camera? Playing a persona, a crusading journalist in my case.

I felt their pain. Idolized. Commercialized. So much more than mere image.

Clark Gable. Carole Lombard. Mae West. Gary Cooper . . . Cary Grant. Irene Dunne. Joan Crawford. Bette Davis. Katharine Hepburn. John Wayne . . . Tyrone Power. All dead and harried. All silver screen stars. Some had lived into Technicolor days before fading into forgotten idols. All had made their marks in silver nitrate in shimmering black and white. Glowing. Vibrant. Powerful.

That was their heyday. I felt it in my soul. But it wasn't gone. Their images began to move in the hokey holograms. Some of them had been lovers, I sensed. Some of them had even been Howard Hughes's lovers! They were much better off captured in this holographic Hall of Fame, not preserved as Hughes was, old and at his worst, still trying to hang on to his money and power no matter the cost, to himself or anyone else.

No, these kings and queens of old-time Hollywood were best viewed through a Vaseline-coated camera lens of memory. They sensed that I was simpatico, sensed my admiration, my emotional guardianship. *Delilah*, they sighed. *You see us. You love us. You will preserve us.*

How?

Ric touched my hand. The music had a relentless, funky beat. Pre-orgasmic. "This place speaks to you."

Right. Shut it up!

"*You* speak to me," I said.

He was . . . the Sheik of Araby . . . Rudolph Valentino . . . Ricardo Montalban . . . Ricky Martin . . . my Latin lover. He pulled me up from the cocktail table and led me onto the glass-floored balcony at the Ghost Bar lounge with its fifty-some-floor drop to the Nude Bar far below. People were swimming nude below, and even at this impossible distance I must have felt exposed.

"I don't notice any lingerie impressions under this gown," Ric murmured in my right ear.

"It would ruin the lines." I struggled to keep my composure as the migrating silver familiar became a thong panty, delicate but way too intimate and . . . *cold!*

He looked down those tens of floors. "So the people looking up from the Nude Bar far below—?"

"—would see France if they had fantastic vision." *And no silver thong in the way*, Irma added impishly.

"Not as fantastic as my imagination," Ric said. "You ready for . . . dinner?"

"Sounds like a plan."

THE PARIS RESTAURANT was only a third of the way up the Eiffel Tower but the view of the Strip and its lights was fabulous.

We were shown to the primo table, at the exact right angle of the restaurant overlooking the Bellagio's dancing fountain light show. The dinner had a dozen courses, small and exquisite.

Each approach of the head waiter and underlings, each sweep of new people being seated, gazing at us as they passed and were ushered to a lesser table, wondering how we rated the primo spot, locked us into public behavior that only intensified our hidden private agenda: calculated seduction.

When dessert was finished, I passed on the after-dinner coffee. While Ric sipped his, I slipped the rhinestoned lipstick case holding the small bottle of Lip Venom from my purse and brushed it carefully over my lips. It was almond-colored and super-shiny, like my gown.

Ric's eyes, coffee dark, devoured my every gesture. I was becoming quite the femme fatale where he was concerned, but this femme had butterflies as well as fine food in her stomach.

"Something new?" he asked, eyeing the gown.

"This *is* a wedding gown."

"I can see the something blue," he said, gazing into my eyes. "What's old and borrowed?"

"The gown is old."

"I guess I'll have to find something that you can borrow."

"I can think of something of yours I'd like to borrow already."

AFTER OUR HIGHLY VISIBLE DINNER on the Strip, Ric drove me onto the highway and its river of headlights. We headed north of the city until it became dark and deserted. No one was going this far. I'd never gone this far. We turned onto a narrow straight road like the one to Los Lobos, except there were no mountains. We were deep into the desert itself. The car stopped on this path to nowhere. Ric opened my car door. I unclasped the cloak. He escorted me out, eying the modest front of my ivory satin gown in the moonlight.

He lifted my left arm, studied the twelve satin buttons closing the sleeve from wrist to elbow.

"I've decided tonight that you're a really promising sadist, my darling Delilah."

I lifted an eyebrow.

"I'm even more afraid that I like being your masochist," he conceded.

Well, that revved my engines! Ric mine, to do with what I pleased. What pleased me, pleased him. And vice versa.

He rested my hand on his shoulder and began undoing the buttons along my left arm.

It had taken me forty minutes to do the sleeve buttons and the back of the gown except for six inches between my shoulder blades. For that stretch I'd needed the kitchen witch. She had cackled over every button and had made me describe Ric in lewd, loving detail. Poor thing had been dead for several centuries and was now a domestic drudge. A little vicarious kick seemed the least I could do for her.

When the sleeve was undone, Ric did the Latin lover bit and kissed my knuckles, my wrist and my arm up to the elbow. Then he relinquished that arm and lifted my right hand to his shoulder. I managed to brush my knuckles across his lips before he started to undo that sleeve.

"What is this thing, really?" he asked.

"Gown from the thirties."

"They did hand-sewing as late as that?"

"Oh, yeah. That's about all. The depths of the Depression. This wedding dress was rather . . . cheap at the time, really."

"Not my depression. Wedding dress. Well. We'll have to make this like the first time."

"It isn't."

"No reason it can't feel that way."

He began undoing the buttons on my other arm, painstakingly working the nooses of twined ivory thread off every stubborn satin-covered button, patient as a spider, as wired as a rodeo bull, his control building his excitement, as it built mine.

As my skin grew supersensitively charged with sexual electricity, I could no longer feel the location of my former silver thong. I fretted about where and how it might show up during this unveiling. Not to worry. The thought is mother to the act. I felt a fleeting shiver down one leg and under the arch of my right foot, almost making me giggle, a mood-destroying itch if ever there was. Something icy thin curled around my big toe. I was now the possessor of a terribly discreet toe ring, and free to let every other inch of my body luxuriate in Ric's slow, elaborate love-making.

He repeated the Continental kisses from my hand to my elbow and braced both of my arms on his shoulders. Then spoke.

"Now. . . . for the fucking forty-eight buttons from your hot naked little ass to the sweet, soft virginal nape of your neck."

"You counted them. I'm flattered."

"Several times, like counting the number of beads on a rosary. You sure know how to get to a Catholic boy."

"I didn't go to Our Lady of the Lake convent school for nothing, but it was an all-girls institution and we wore navy and green uniforms. The only time we had a chance to dress up was when a senior girl got to wear her sister's wedding dress to crown the statue of the Virgin Mary with flowers for the May procession. I, of course, wasn't a candidate for Virgin crowning."

"And you had no sister to loan you a wedding gown anyway."

I hesitated. Was I an only child? Then what or who was Lilith? I hadn't told Ric about that part of my mission and now seemed a little late.

She who hesitates is lost.

Ric's fingers moved adroitly between the cheeks of my butt. "I'm going to take you apart from the bottom up, and then from the top down. Any objections?"

"Only if they turn you on."

"We don't need that, do we?"

I shook my head, leaning against him as his fingers began the long, delicious, interminable climb up my spine. His hands slipped inside of the satin gown as he opened it inch by inch, and my hips soon were pressed to the hard vertical divining rod of his erection.

An almost full moon was rising over his shoulder, showering us with warm white light.

"This satin matches the color of your skin," he said into my ear, my neck. "It's a real rush." He kissed me for the first time, and jerked back.

"Wow, that stuff is still like an electric shock."

"Lip Venom is guaranteed to please."

"Painted hussy. Then bite me again, baby."

We kissed while Ric wrangled slippery satin buttons through loops of twined thread. It would be tricky work even for a lady's maid.

The cool desert air ran up my spine along with the motions of his fingers and knuckles. I got really hot goose bumps. Ric finally undid the top button at my nape and pulled down the open gown in one sudden sweep, satin spiraling away into sand. I had what I had wanted, my naked body encompassed by his clothed one. It was the ultimate form of trust and a lot of other, less abstract needs and wants and emotions.

"You are so bold and beautiful," he said, his hands soft as silk against my bare skin. He pushed me away, looked at me. I'd seen lust a few times, but never such shattering love.

From far away I heard the music of an iPod in the car playing dance music, slow dance music. He pressed me to him, started those liquid Latin motions that were all hip and heart, his hands moving over my bare torso, molding me to his soft, expensive clothes.

They were his shelter, those clothes, their softness. I knew now that he'd felt a lot that had been hot, harsh, cold, and brutal. My body tried to soothe all that away. I was living satin in his arms, and the roughness I felt—of buttons, a cold gold belt, zipper, trouser welt—it roused and hardened me to meet him as an equal.

We stopped moving, stopped dancing. In the hills and mountains I heard wolves howling for home. We both wanted that.

I stepped away from him and felt the desert wind chill every inch of my naked skin. He stopped moving. Bereft. Out of control. Feeling the cold night wind, not for the first time.

I put a finger to his throat. "You. *Señor*. I want you up against the car. I'm going to open you up from here . . ." I pressed my nail against his throat and ran my finger down the buttons of his shirt, past his guardian gold belt and down the swollen welt of his zipper to where it ended between his legs. "To there. Any objections?"

"God, no."

I started at the bottom, as he had, caressing the weight, the length, pushing aside the soft expensive clothes, baring a few vertical inches of his torso, running my hands and mouth over what I exposed

He shivered. I shivered. Alone in the night. Outside ourselves. Beside ourselves. Inside ourselves.

We clung together. Slow dancing. Nothing to say. A bond forged stronger than stainless steel. Secret.

THE CAR'S LONG LOW HOOD vibrated as the engine idled in the night. Ric had turned it on, turned on the car stereo to some music that pumped iron. When he began to lower me to the car's warm hard steel hood, I clutched at his upper arms, his clenched muscles suspending me above the abyss in my own mind.

All motion stopped. "Can you lie back for me, my Delilah?"

Never could. Never had. Helpless. Pinned on a slab of something hard and inanimate, my feet barely touching the ground, my torso a target for a vicious game of darts. Having to submit. To lose. To lose everything. Everyone. Even Ric, maybe? Even now. The living nightmares crowded at the edges of the star-spangled night sky. *Never! Never again!*

"Maybe," I said, because it was Ric asking.

Like the road not taken, asking made all the difference.

I FELT THE STRONG ARM and shoulder muscles that had wrestled the mysterious forces of the underground since boyhood holding me suspended over the car, over the edge as if I could hang like that forever in his arms, on my particular edge. It was my decision. My call.

This evening had touched so many sore spots on my soul. I never remembered anyone dressing or undressing me or even doing my hair. I'd always done it all myself, somehow, from the earliest age, at least in memory. That memory held no shred of someone giving a final pat to my coat buttons or my braids. No one crooning a lullaby, no one calling me a pet name, except when I was almost adult and cheerfully blue-collar waitresses or salesclerks would call me "hon" or "dearie." I was supposed find this condescending, but I didn't. I enjoyed it. Pathetic, right?

So Ric's playing undo-the-buttons with me and his verbal, murmuring ways during lovemaking undid me. I would do almost anything for him. Maybe even this.

Is that what love was, pushing yourself beyond your most ingrained outer limits? I'd got what I had wanted.

A narrow door of flesh to his innermost dark continent. Now he wanted, needed, my complicity. Small price to pay for a possible paradise.

I nodded and was lowered slowly onto the warm hood. It was like lying on the back of a purring hot steel tiger. Rick pressed down on top of me, the narrow warm slit of skin I'd unveiled feeling firm and smooth against my naked body. My hands could still cling to the strong, soft fabric of his jacket sleeves, cling and clench and hold on.

Meanwhile, he was murmuring his pleasure, solely in Spanish now. Every word was preceded by the possessive "my."

Mi belleza . . .

And I knew that the center of him was reaching for the center of me, dowsing, stiffening, plunging . . . I braced myself for this truly terrifying act, this terrible centerpiece of my nightmares.

Mi tigre hembra . . .

And I felt, beyond my fear, a stirring of excitement, a wanting to be found, discovered, to have that divine divining rod taking my measure, the measure of his tigress.

Mi oasis

And his shelter.

Mi agua

And I was his water.

Mi sangre

And his blood.

Mi virgen

And he was the first man to breach me, outside of my nightmares, before, and now in the very imitation of my worst nightmare.

And it was done.

My fists caught his arms and pulled him closer, farther in, nearer. I was so relieved I had to bite my lip. I almost laughed out loud with relief. He was so much *smaller* than my nightmare metal rapist, but of course you couldn't laugh. You couldn't tell a man that. He was still plenty large enough that I could tell I'd be *muy delicado* later.

But now I let the surge of pleasure take me and wrapped my legs around his hips and rocked in the thrilling lullaby of his hot Spanish blood and sweet Spanish words.

Mi desposada! he cried as my insides started quaking with satisfaction and we shuddered together, and I could scream this time, long and hard, as the killing pleasure took me.

Mi desposada. I'd have to look that one up. . .

"Are you all right?" he asked finally in English.

Given that I was laughing and crying and almost swooning, I could understand the question.

But I could only nod.

He was still holding me and still talking softly, more to himself them me, but the words were music to my soul, even in English.

"I love you so much, Del. You can't know what this moment means to me. Here. Now. I've been born again. I could die making love to you. But I never want to die so I can make love to you forever."

I was too blown away to answer, or even to say: make up your mind.

I just clung to him, not believing I'd just cleared such a horrible personal block. Every word Ric said, in English or in Spanish, eased a senseless fear and a vague, terrifying memory. But I couldn't speak of my feelings. What I felt was beyond words.

"I suppose," he said finally, "I'll have to get you back into that dress with every last button done."

"You can skip a few now," I said, kissing him on the throat while I began closing him back into his clothes, "but not very many."

CHAPTER FORTY-FIVE

I woke up in my cottage bed, alone, thinking of Ric.

Desposada meant "bride." I'd greedily clawed through my Spanish dictionary for the word as soon as we'd kissed a lingering goodbye at the door and I'd gone inside. Quicksilver was sniffing and sulking, but I ignored him for the first time in our association to find that word and hold it to me.

Not that I wanted to get married or to "trap" a man or anything formal. To be wanted that much was the thing, after being unwanted for so long and pretending not to care. He'd had me on "Hello, this is my dowsing rod," but now I felt totally unhad, if that makes sense.

Still, I saw myself clinging to my dictionary and my word, pretty pathetic, pretty teenage.

On cooler reflection, I was still in the dark about Ric.

I'd taken the biggest risk of my life and for it I'd gotten an important step in my personal redemption, but only a slim bit of insight into Ric's complex soul. Finally I'd met someone who was more mysterious than I was. Someone who was also able to bring me deeper into myself than I'd ever allowed.

Was it love, or addiction, or an adrenaline high? Or an undercover operator using me?

Last night on the long ride home Ric had listened to my tale of long-lived werewolf casino bosses and lost dead daughters.

"We need to know who the man with her in the grave was. That's the key," he said.

I couldn't stop recalling our last moments on the car's hood. How he'd spun so that I was on top of him. No sense of binding, just Ric serving as my bed, his eyes and lips heavy and satisfied, content, liking my weight on his chest and hips, my fingers toying with his hair and lips.

I liked everything about him. Wasn't that a warning signal? I'd never had a decent connection with anyone male before.

"*Querida*," he'd said. "Don't run away on me now."

I'd run away before. From the orphanage. The convent school. I thought no one knew but me. Ric was The Man. Police. The FBI. He'd be able to check up on those things. Me. My history. He'd be able to manipulate me. My history.

He manipulated my hair as it fell over my shoulders onto his chest. My lips as they went dry and vacant, wondering what to say next.

"We have to find out who the man was," he repeated.

"The boy."

"Why do you say that?"

"They were just kids."

"She was immortal werewolf spawn."

"Not her fault! Or her choice. She was her father's daughter, and I wouldn't care to be in her shoes."

"Shoes. Tell me again what shoes she wore?"

"Platform heels. Satin. Navy satin. Made her taller. Older, she thought. She wanted to be older, so no one could control her."

"She's way older now." Ric frowned. "Do you think her father could have had her killed?"

"Her father?"

"You saw him."

"Yes."

"Why?"

"The pack is everything. With eternal life, family is less. He could sire more cubs. More beta bitches and more alpha bastards."

Ric ran his hands over my back and butt. "Del. I know he's despicable. He also uses the CinSims like toilet paper and Mexican zombies as cheap labor. He may even be behind that stuff in Juarez. That's why I want to bring him down so badly. Help me."

Wow. Even I knew how seductive it was to have a man asking, "Help me."

I lifted myself away. "How will we find out about her guy?"

"Detective work," he said, sitting up and making extreme love to my bare shoulder. "Delilah. We'll never be free to live our own lives until we solve this murder."

I made that "we'll" into an "I" in my mind. Where could I find out about this dead, forgotten guy? Somewhere in Las Vegas.

Ric would be looking.

So would I.

I just wished I could fully trust him enough to tell him all the other aspects of my search. About my strange facilities and Lilith. Yet, despite my complete unveiling and satisfaction tonight, I'd still only literally unzipped a tiny sliver of Ric's soul. That wasn't enough.

I'd been born suspicious, raised alien and alone, and suspicious I would live . . . or die.

Chapter Forty-Six

I went back to Vilma Brazil.

I sure as heck wasn't going back to Howard Hughes, or what was left of him.

It was 4:00 PM and she was knocking back a Bacardi Breezer in the dressing room.

"Hey, kid! You made it out in one pretty unslavered-over piece. How is old Howie? He was really hot for me once, you know. He was gonna make me a star."

"He was gonna make any girl a star. He's living dead in Las Vegas and glad of it. What can I say?"

Vilma shook her peroxided fright wig. "He used to be quite the dude. Slicked-back black hair. Pencil-thin mustache. But he was always a tad strange. Hey, so was I."

"Weren't we all?"

"She was a werewolf princess, you said."

I nodded at Vilma's conclusion. The girl in that photograph, the girl in the mirror, had been just that: young, innocent, tender, and supernaturally gifted. Her daddy's pride and joy. And his biggest disappointment in her choice of mates. She had been playing Juliet to some unknown teen vampire's Romeo.

Neither of their houses would have permitted such a union, or could have permitted them to live after making such a union. Add a little Othello and Desdemona to the mix. Murderous possessiveness. By fathers of their children, by clans of their very different lifeblood.

"Who was the head of the vampire syndicate back in the forties when Las Vegas was busy being born and mortal mob bosses thought they'd rule the roost?" I asked Vilma.

"Only one, not heard of since. He was going to build the most stupendous hotel-casino in Las Vegas before the vampires lost the war. He was going to call it—"

"The Inferno." I knew the answer as I said it. The Inferno had fallen only to rise like a phoenix eighty years later. How much time was that to a vampire? The blink of an undead eye.

Vilma lifted a drawn-on eyebrow almost to her thinning hairline in recognition of my lucky strike.

"Yeah. I remember now. He was going to name it the Styx or something hellish. The vampire crew was from the house of . . . it's been so long. House of Wrathescu. The vampire king was Wilhelm XII. He has not been heard of since but may only taking a vampire nap, as we humans would reckon it."

"He was Juliet's dream lover?"

"He was no one's dream unless you wanted a nightmare. You've seen what form of eternal life Howard won. No, this Wilhelm was old and corrupt. Not the stuff of films or Goth girls' romantic dreams. But I recall that he had a son of the spirit, one bright and blazing comet that he had bitten into the clan. A toothsome young vampire."

"His name?"

"Something vaguely and tantalizingly Christian. A prince among vampires. Foreign, from the land where werewolves were put to torture and the test as nowhere else. Kind of funny that a vampire-werewolf romance would end the Werewolf-Vampire War here in Vegas. I don't know the details. Howard would."

My fingernails were biting into my palms until my blood and dread seemed to well up together to my brain.

"And the name of this vampire prince?"

"Christopher," Vilma said. "I heard talk about that. Some humans considered the name part blasphemy, part undead hubris. Christopher is the saint said to have carried the Christ child safely across a river. The vampire named Christopher was said to carry away Christian maidens. No girl or woman, it is said, could resist him. So you get the poor little rich werewolf girl and her bitter end. Yet you say a vampire died beside her? Can't believe that would be our pretty boy."

Dead bodies were dead bodies. Even supers, when killed by the proper means, dissolved into mere bones and dust like mortals. Who knew for sure just what these two dead lovers had been? Who knew who or what *they would have become* had they not been killed?

Maybe whoever had killed them had known, or guessed.

CHAPTER FORTY-SEVEN

I left Vilma with more questions than answers.

Chief among them was: who and what was Christophe?

The name was suspiciously akin to Christopher, but Christophe felt a lot older to me, as old as the serpent in the garden. And maybe the serpent had been a better catch for a woman like Eve than one lousy apple.

Maybe Christophe-Cocaine-Snow was the key to the mystery of Sunset Park. Maybe he was the key to the history of vampires and werewolves in Las Vegas.

Maybe he was the key to my own role in all these events, past and present.

Inquiring reporters want to know.

I remembered the Cocaine groupie I was suspected of killing. She'd mentioned online discussion groups where my accessory-buddy was known as the Ice Prick, possessed of a potent Brimstone Kiss.

Maybe I should do a little online cruising.

I headed home to the Castle Nightwine cottage, where my laptop worked without a hard-wire connection, thanks to whatever resident unseen elves or brownies of the Internet hung around the place.

Quicksilver arrived home just after I did, bouncing through his ajar window like a huge, furry beach ball. He was glad to see me. Why did I think I'd been under his distant scrutiny on my jaunt to the Twin Peaks?

Because I was becoming the belle of unseen surveillance here in Las Vegas.

First, there were Nightwine's local security cameras and Cicereau's stolen videos of me at the Inferno, not to mention Snow's access to all of the Inferno pics. Then there was Quicksilver's literal tailing of my movements, which I welcomed. And there was Snow's possible remote viewing via the silver shape-shifting familiar attached to my epidermis.

And then there was Ric, who so far seemed to rely on just background checks and calling to ask where I was and where I was going to be when. Yay, Ric! He was a bit over-zealous, but at least just simply human. So far. The line between protective and possessive with all these . . . er, entities, was razor-edge thin.

I got online and Groggled the Seven Deadly Sins and Cocaine. Six hundred thousand entries came up. I Groggled "brimstone kiss" and got a million. (Groggle billed itself as "the drinking person's search engine" and seized fewer copyrights than its more famous predecessor.)

Okay.

There were a ton of Web sites with names like cocainefreaks.com, sevendivinesins.com, and brimstonesluts.com.

That "sluts" group looked promising.

I avoided logging in or signing up, but was still able to peek in on a few discussion chains, message boards, and forums. The subject called "orgasmicidyll" caught my eye, now that I knew the feeling.

"Omigod!" began one gushing entry. "I got it. The Kiss. After the January 16th show. First, the Scarf. Like hot freezing acid around my neck. The Kiss was Cold, then Hot, then Searing! I am so totaled! It is better than a jackrabbit vibrator and it lasts, oh, soooo loooong. I live for the next one, if I can be the first and only femme to get a second shot at Sweet Oblivion. Cocaine's got to slip up sometime, and I pray that it's with me."

What the heck was a jackrabbit vibrator? I personally did not expect much from a jackrabbit except long furry ears.

I might, now that I'd been in Las Vegas, expect something
from . . . a tiger. Or a lion . . . or an alpha wolf . . . or the
right unrotted vampire . . . or an FBI guy. But not from
a rabbit of any sexual persuasion whatsoever. Might as
well get it on with a rat! But then a lot of women later
concluded that they had.

But these Cocaine-aholics were unabashed addicts.

I read a few more entries, trying not to heave at the idol-
izing prose. "Exquisite. Indescribable. White Lightning.
Albino e-XXX-tasy. I'd never had any patience with
teases of either gender and Cocaine sure had these poor
twits on the ropes.

"The Holy Day," one demented kissee wrote, "was my
Independence Day, July 4. I was right in the middle of the
mosh pit line. His scarf felt like a falling feather from an
archangel's wing and then came the Brimstone Kiss, all
pulsing volcanic fury like the Devil's own fiery breath. It
seemed to go on forever and I never wanted it to end."

Well, it had, honey. *Get over it,* Irma seconded me.

All of the groupies used cutesy login names: Cherry
Tomato, Hasbeenhad, Candycaine, Powdered Sugar,
Kissycat.

I glanced at the signature for the woman who thought
being enslaved by a Brimstone Kiss was her Independence
Day.

Lilith.

Hey, someone on this list might already have used
Delilah even. Both were classical Old Testament names,
classical lady vamp names. Didn't mean that I was *that*
Delilah. Or that this Lilith was. . . my Lilith.

Still, my look-alike Lilith had been working in Vegas.
She'd had the opportunity to see the Seven Deadly
Sins, even to get caught up in mosh pit gropings. No! I
couldn't imagine my look-alike clawing in a mosh pit for
a melodramatic smooch from a self-important . . . freak.

I hated to think so anyway, but I couldn't know for sure. Then something prodded my memory that made my blood chill and set like strawberry Jell-O in all my veins.

"I've been waiting for you," had been Snow's opening line when he came up behind me at the Inferno Bar the first time I'd encountered him.

I'd taken it for a corny pickup line. Now I knew that Snow was a lot of things, most of them scary or despicable, but he wasn't corny.

He'd mistaken me for Lilith.

And had covered his error so fast and smoothly that I'd never tumbled to it.

"*Oooh,*" warned Irma. "*That is one major bad boy! He might have killed Lilith. He had her snowed, for sure. Better stay out of his contrail.*"

True, but the answers I wanted might lie there too.

I definitely had to consider Snow as the revived Christopher, or a progenitor or descendent thereof. Certainly, he was the force behind the resurgent Inferno, which was a gauntlet thrown down before the werewolf lords who had run Las Vegas since vanquishing or bonding with the human mobsters here in the late forties and fifties.

The only vampire trace that had existed since then was Howard Hughes' investment in the decrepit hotel at the south end of the Strip. So Christophe had come out of nowhere a few years ago, fronting his rock band, collecting his groupies, and bringing the dead and buried concept of the Inferno up from the ashes.

No wonder Cicereau was worried.

So was I.

And there was only one place where I could go to find out the truth and set my worries to rest. And I'd better go undercover.

CHAPTER FORTY-EIGHT

Night found me back at the Inferno, dressed so no one I knew could spot me, hopefully. And I meant No One. Especially not Snow.

I didn't go to Déjà-Vous. The boss man knew everything that happened there.

Estate sales for older folks often sold funky wigs as well as potty chairs, useful for Halloween. So tonight I wore a glossy head of synthetic cinnamon-colored locks, straight and shoulder-length. I'd rustled up some stretchy double-knit nineteen-sixties slacks and a glittery tube-top, and then added gray-tinted heart-shaped sunglasses to subdue the color of my eyes.

I avoided the Inferno Bar and my pal Nicky to cross the dance floor toward the concert stage. I waved my ticket and struggled forward an hour before the show to stand packed with the other Snow groupies in the mosh pit.

The stage was six feet above the seats. Watching the stage from up front was a literal pain in the neck, but the groupies around me were percolating like happy little coffee beans, wired and jumping up and down to survey the bare stage and the instrument layout, to glimpse a roadie moving a mike or placing a water bottle. A lot of them were done up like Goth girls. Purple-and-black witchy wigs, tats, chains, leather, sunglasses rendered them unforgettable, but anonymous. Whatever their fashion statement, all the women sighed and swooned at anything alive on that stage, no matter the gender.

Everything was a buildup to the entrance of the Seven Deadly Sins and its lead singer.

"My girlfriend's made it," a wild-eyed blonde next to me said to no one in particular.

"With Cocaine?" a woman behind me gurgled.

"She got the Kiss."

"Ohmigod! When?"

"Two years ago. After the *Live Again!* concert. She's in the downtown club. I've been coming for three months straight now but I've never gotten close enough to the stage to see more than his hair."

I was impressed. "You must have moved to Las Vegas."

I was met by a circle of shocked gazes.

"Oh, yeah," an older woman said. "We all do. You're not a confirmed Cocaine fan unless you move here to see every one of his performances."

"But your jobs—?"

"They have McDonalds everywhere, honey."

"Don't tell me *you* didn't move here for him?" another one demanded.

"Well, I did move here—"

I was about to say for other reasons, but these crazed women had no other reasons. If they had known the silver "love beads" around my vintage sixties neck came from the hair of the love object himself they would have torn me apart for souvenirs.

I wanted to feel superior to these obsessed groupies but I was beginning to wonder if maybe there wasn't something wrong with me to be immune to their idol. Well, mostly immune. And there *was* something wrong with me. I'd always suspected it and now was coming to admit it. Part of that something was good and strong, and part of it maybe was not very good, and also strong.

Even with the armor of my reporter's cynicism, even with having seen and spoken to—been touched by—Snow up close and personal, I was beginning to feel the fever. The jittery, longing, excited group mania. My feet should have been hurting from standing on carpeted concrete for so long, but I was hopping from burning sole to sole like the rest of them—young, old, and in-between—hopping and hoping and shivering with belly-deep excitement.

"It's him!"

"He always comes on last, idiot! That's only the guy who puts all the different guitars in place."

"The tabloids say he's screwing Lust."

"No, she's boffing some record mogul."

"She's *craaaaazy*!" wailed a fan.

"If it's anybody in the band, it's Envy. All that evil green costuming."

"That why *you're* wearing poison green tonight?"

I had to fight to keep in the frontlines, which I needed to do to be seen as a major Cocaine freak. Personally, I'd never gotten the point in writhing around for the attention of some unreachable star. I thought briefly of Ric, who was plenty sexy without having to sell it, and was squeezed back a whole row in position when I didn't concentrate on keeping my hard-won place, so I had to elbow forward again.

These fevered close quarters were forging a mob. When the band members strode on stage one by one, everybody jumped up to see them. I found myself pushed forward into the second row. Oh, good. We'd be able to see their feet *and* feel their sweat.

Then the fireworks started. I saw the giant dragon heads descending. Wasn't that in Revelations? The Devil coming down as the Dragon? Snow the Devil? Somehow I didn't think so. Or maybe so. As he slid down the head of one of the dragon's two heads to the stage in his patented entrance, I felt my silver beads elongate into a long strand, circle my throat once like a choker, then dangle into a long loop down between my breasts to my belly button. Every bead was as cold as ice. Or sleet. Or Snow.

The distraction allowed the surging groupies to push me another three rows back. *Damn it!* This groupie routine required the chutzpah and concentration of being in an estate sale line.

I wormed my way forward as the instruments warmed up to ear-splitting level. I was back in row two, where I wanted to be: too far to be swept up in Snow's Brimstone Kiss, right in the middle of the action to register on the minds of the Cocaine groupies, to be seen as one of them. To join their club and pick their brains. What was left of them.

The music revved up. It was overwhelming down here in the mosh pit. My bones vibrated to the beat. Every time some nice hefty middle-aged lady tried to squeeze me out of my row I pushed back, with interest.

Time ceased. It was all deep bass vibrations and amped-up raw rock music. Snow looked cool in his open Byron shirt and seam-splittingly tight white leather pants. I had to admit he was a riveting performer, his voice hard-driving sandpaper on the hard rock stuff, then slow, low, and sincere on the ballads. Right. That's when the women switched from screaming that drowned out even their idol's voice to moaning and swooning.

It was a long two-hour set. For me. During the intermission, the women babbled all around me, their milling tension holding me upright when I was about ready to sit down on the cold concrete to rest my bones and eardrums. Except I'd have been stomped.

The second set went much faster, Lust and Envy bracketing Snow with their colorful writhing forms. By then I didn't envy them their proximity to the kingpin and I was as incapable of feeling lust as a loaf of Italian bread.

After the encore, I was embraced by the hysteria and a wave of screaming and pushing women as Snow bent to the mosh pit to sweep up a few lucky fans for the Brimstone Kiss. Didn't that name imply the Devil? Wickedness sells. Or pseudo-wickedness.

I fought to keep my second tier position and actually glimpsed the idol up close. He wore numerous white silk scarves around his neck, the better to snare the chosen groupie. One swooped up the woman in the poison green outfit. The scarf lingered behind, the only material token of her Brimstone moment.

Everyone around me was surging forward. The mob was literally pushing me up, like a buoying wave. My God, I was next in line! A loop of silk chiffon snared my neck. I was pushed up, up toward Snow's ice-god face and hair. *No!* I was here to infiltrate the fans, not ace them out. I grabbed the sides of the scarf, feeling a cold slither as the silver necklace became a wrist to elbow bracelet on my right arm. I stared into a tiny reflection of myself on curved black mirror shades. I felt my mind, my essence yearning toward my medium, silvered glass.

The scarf slithered around my neck, ebbed away. I fell back hard, aware of glittering black sunglasses looking elsewhere. Another woman was lofted on the wave of raving humanity and claimed a kiss from those frost-white lips. She shrieked in bereavement as he moved on.

"Oh, you poor thing!!!" A woman was weeping and embracing me. "You almost made it. It's so tragic. So close."

Right. I almost made it. An excellent position for me in the Cocaine groupie world. Almost favored. And in. In like . . . Lilith?

CHAPTER FORTY-NINE

The winners clung together, weeping, unable to leave the foot of the deserted stage.

The losers ebbed away to the Inferno Bar, or to the gaming tables and the rest rooms, where they probably surveyed their tragic, bereft faces in the mirror and gave them soul kisses.

Horse hockey! I caught up with the crew that had made for the Inferno Bar.

". . . hung like a horse," one of the losers was saying.

Ludicrous. I was an objective reporter. You can't, uh, snow me. Hung like a hunky mortal man, if I had to make a guesstimate. That I could was a bit annoying.

"My God, that scarf! I'd give anything to have it around my neck. I bet it feels just like his hair."

One of the true believers focused on me, stroking my wig in a creepy way. "You felt it. The scarf. What was it like?"

I wanted to say "China-silk import chiffon, really cheap."

I said, "Like air, clouds, steam heat."

Man, this was easy; I had them swooning on their bar stools. I ordered an Albino Vampire to up the ante. They hadn't realized that option existed, so I was swarmed.

"It's a house drink," I said, "really smooth and creamy."

It hurt not to claim credit as I watched the cash register *ca-ching* at a rapid rate as Albino Vampires were served all around.

A hard-faced brunette wiggled onto the bar stool beside me after pushing off a blitzed blonde to make room for herself. "You're new in town."

"Right."

"Do you know about the Club?"

Yeah. You put it on your steering wheel to keep creeps from stealing your car. "Club?"

She leaned way nearer than I needed. There were vampires, and there were vamps. "Club AV/DC."

Okay. I wasn't born yesterday even if I was from Kansas. AC/DC meant alternating current or alternative lifestyle. The latter meaning was a code word for folks who swung both ways. Bisexuals. Also nowadays, bi-humans or unhumans. Different strokes for different folks, and *very* different folks, but this gender preference stuff had all gotten a lot more complicated after the Millennium Revelation.

AV/DC, on the other hand, might mean Albino Vampire/Doting Cows.

The brunette pressed a card into my sweaty palm. "We meet every night. Have a few drinks. Dance. Watch Cocaine impersonators. You might like the scene."

No, I needed to *research* the scene. "Thanks! Impersonators?" Her breath riffled the phony hair around my neck. "You won't need to lose out on any Brimstone Kisses there."

My blood, predictably, ran cold. Was she was hinting that an illegal vampire club had attached itself to a star? Snow.

Is that what had made Lilith a shadow in my mirror?

NATURALLY I SHOWED UP AT A GATHERING the next night in a one-story shop near downtown that had obviously gone belly up. Times were tough even in Las Vegas. This felt a lot like going to an AA meeting, not that Alcoholics

Anonymous had ever been my thing. I'd covered the organization as a reporter. I found the religious bent hokey but it had worked for a lot of people, including the TV station owner. The news biz still ran on eighty-proof for blood.

The Cocaine Club occupied an end spot in the usual one-story strip shopping centers that dominate Las Vegas off the Strip with a Capital S.

I brought a covered casserole, as requested, even though I had to buy it at Albertson's deli and heat it in the cottage microwave, then transport it in a padded aluminum wrapping. Anything to look properly domestic while getting my . . . rocks didn't quite apply to girls . . . hormones off. I set the casserole, Velveeta and macaroni, down beside the huge aluminum coffee urn. Like that was the only drug here. Yeah. You could smell Albino leather here like perfumed pheromones.

The women—and the attendees all were women; apparently the Brimstone Kiss didn't do cross-gender— had that frantically worn look of desperate housewives. They were the same personally enterprising women who had made romance cover model Fabio a household name for a brief shining moment thirty years ago. Given the usual male incapacity for dealing with women beyond sex, generation, and child support, I could get these babes' fantasies.

On the other hand, despite my early childhood experiences, I was beginning to think I really liked most men: Ric . . . my male guard dog, Quicksilver . . . maybe even, on a particularly generous day, my unAmerican Idol Snow . . . and could cut them some serious slack under the right circumstances.

"You have a Web site?" I asked the aggressive chick whose shoulders would rival a defensive lineman's. It had been listed on the card: brimstonesluts.com.

"Definitely. It's an online world. I hear you almost got the Kiss last night."

"Yeah. So close." My fingernails tapped the table as I poured steaming amber liquid into my Styrofoam cup. The cup was white, but beyond that it was nothing the real Snow would touch on a bet.

"That's okay, honey. There are more of us than them." Her consoling hand-clutch almost stapled my knuckles together, thanks to her painted claws.

"What exactly does a Brimstone Kiss do?"

"Take you to paradise."

"What kind of paradise?" I was not the type to take even a free pass to heaven. One never knew what one was getting.

"I don't know! The recipients are all too incoherent to say. Pleasure Central, I guess. And nobody comes back down to write memoirs."

Hearsay. I was all for nirvana, but I had to have a free sample first.

I left the group meeting with a lot of questions.

Most of them were for Snow, if he would answer. Or if I could make him.

CHAPTER FIFTY

I was beginning to pick up a pattern.
Then. Now.

Christopher. Christophe. Krzysztof, maybe. Who knows what other variations?

My charm bracelet had changed into a silver circle of lips. Cold silver lips.

I suppose Snow knew where I was going around Las Vegas, knew what I was doing.

Whoever he was, Christopher or Christophe, he was a complex being, probably supernatural, and he wanted something from me I wouldn't freely give. So he was just Cicereau in mime make-up as far as I was concerned.

I made sure to hit the Inferno the next night long after the show, when the sweat of performance and the sweet brain-freezing liquidity of the Brimstone Kisses were history. I wondered if he was affected at all, felt anything profound himself. Nah. Most womanizers weren't that sensitive.

I donned a royal blue poplin suit I'd used for attending political lunches for WTCH-TV and hot pink fifties pumps. The silver familiar apparently approved of the footwear, because it immediately slithered up my arm and down my side and leg to become a slender ankle bracelet. Call my look Business Brazen.

Nick Charles offered me an Albino Vampire at the bar, but I declined. Didn't need any high-octane oral stimulants tonight.

Snow showed up in black this time: slacks, jacket, silk shirt, and sunglasses. Maybe he homed in on my silver accessory, which still sported buttoned lip charms. Like his lips were sealed. Right.

Snow gathered me into a half-time rumba. He'd been expecting me. So I got right to the point.

"Why do you do it?" I asked.

"Dance?"

"Snow all those women."

"Because I can?"

"So. You're a human drug."

"Who says I'm human?"

"I wish you were."

"Why?"

"I might like you. A little."

He stepped back and stood apart from me, holding my hands in the extravagant open posture of a dance that had frozen in time. "I like *you*. A little."

"Then we're even."

"No. Never even." He smiled and swept me into a *Dancing with the Stars* gallop around the dance floor. I felt quite breathless, but then I always felt breathless with Snow.

"Are you Christopher?" I asked in hard inquiring reporter mode.

"Who is Christopher?"

"A saint."

"No."

"A sinner?"

"Sometimes."

"A user?"

"Even you say I'm a drug. Not a user."

He was too right. I tried another tack.

"I'm searching for a killer."

"You're a hunter. And a victim. And a—"

He stopped speaking. I really wanted to know what his third evaluation of me was. I wanted to know as badly as any Snow groupie wanted a Brimstone Kiss. So of course I couldn't let on.

And I was . . . a woman who needed answers. To puzzles, to people, to unhumans.

"Snow. You both hinder and help me. Why?"

"Perhaps you need both."

"That answer stinks!"

"Then why are you here?"

"I need to know what Las Vegas vampire got it on with a werewolf mob boss's daughter in the late forties."

"You want me to just give it to you?"

"Ah, what are we discussing?"

"Your perennial caution flatters me. What I'm saying is, you don't want to work for it. You don't want to cheat me out of it, you just want me to hand it to you."

"I don't want that. I *need* that. I don't have time for games."

"Want and need. Interesting concepts. Close, but very different, after all. What if I said that I needed you to beg for what you want?"

"I'd say, Styx it!"

He laughed. "You're clever, if lazy. Your blundering investigation happens to have hit upon the moment when the werewolves won the Werewolf-Vampire War. Neither side will thank you for exposing that long-buried secret."

"I don't like either side."

"I'm sure the feeling is mutual and will become even more intense, given time. All right. You have knocked over all my defenses. I am helpless. I'll give you what you want, although it most certainly will *not* be . . . what you need."

Somehow this easy, even indolent, capitulation got my pulses throbbing in all the wrong places, as it was intended to.

"I know who she was, the dead girl in Sunset Park," I added. Fiercely.

The fact was, I *cared* about who she was. And I cared about who she could have been had someone not decided to staple her sternum with silver bullets. Even if she had been a werewolf. Everything alive started out as innocent and trusting and helpless and deserving as any human baby. Even wolves. Maybe even me.

Not Snow.

"You know who she was," Snow repeated, sounding interested and alert. Obviously, he didn't, and wanted to. "Can you prove it?"

Dammit, no. But . . . soon. "Yes."

"Then you need to have proof of her partner in crime, and punishment. Of a sort."

I nodded.

Snow turned and strode through the tourist-clogged casino.

I trotted behind to catch up. Interesting. No one reacted to him. Onstage he was instant opium. Offstage, mingling with the hoi polloi, he was invisible. Except to me.

He didn't take me to his office, but to a private bullet elevator to the sky.

Could you say Hyatt? The elevator was all glass outside and all mirrors inside. The sight of Snow reflected into eternity unnerved me more than visions of Lilith and me repeated into infinity. I exercised my new mirror magic and turned the surface to a golden autumnal color with falling leaves and lots of golden Lhasa apsos and taffy-colored spaniels capering.

Snow saw that and touched my arm. "Delilah. No need to fight me. I'm giving you what you want."

He'd made me think that I was a sell-out. I felt tears as hard as amber forming.

"My quarters," he said, preceding me out of the elevator.

What a Snow groupie wouldn't give for this moment! I thought about what I was giving up by relying on his inner knowledge of Las Vegas. I'd rather be working this out with Ric. I should have told him where I was going, what I was doing. But Lilith's trail was my own particular obsession, and Snow understood obsession, at least from being the object of it.

The double doors to his domain were white-mirrored Plexiglas, in which he was a looming black-and-white presence and I was the humble goose girl. The white tiger from his office sat on its huge haunches before the door.

"Grizelle, my guest and I need privacy and a couple of your best Albino Vampires."

The tiger's growl almost deafened me, but its stripes became narrow and then vertical and the huge green eyes tilted and shrank. A black woman over six feet tall with snow-white hair and emerald eyes stood before us, her ebony skin tattooed with charcoal stripes like watered silk and barely covered by a high-fashion black leather miniskirt and halter-top outfit, probably Thierry Muglar and about eight thousand dollars. But maybe she had mugged the hot European designer for it.

"Sure, boss," the were-tiger bitch said, eyeing me like an invading ant she'd like to use to spice her cocoa.

Beyond the doors everything was white except for the black night-view from a wall of windows. Whereas the Paris restaurant window's framed a view of the Bellagio's dancing fountains, this penthouse looked down on the periodically exploding artificial volcano at Steve Wynn's Treasure Island setup. Fire, flame. Orange and crimson damnation. A roar like a pep squad of distant lions, or tigers.

Snow's Man in Black outfit made him the central attraction even in his colorless color scheme. His shirts always opened to the brink of his hip-slung belt and I noticed with surprise for the first time that his chest was hair-free, but was emblazoned by a vertical and horizontal slash of feathered scarring, as if a lightning bolt or Jack Frost had struck him cold dead.

Were these the scars from the finger of God casting him from Heaven to Hell? Adam on the Sistine Chapel ceiling had been lounging, languid, and an easy mark for the touch of the energized forefinger of God.

Lucifer would have been active. Aggressive. All pride and archangel flight against the light. It would have taken a divine body blow to send him down, down, spiraling into Hell, or into Hell on earth. He would bear divine scars for his rebellion.

I was unaccountably curious about those marks, but they were not my mission here and now.

Grizelle, indeed lean and lanky in her human form, brought in a silver tray with two Albino Vampires on it. I didn't reflect in the tray, and she smirked as I observed that. Were my powers muted here? Or did she just want me to think so?

Like Madrigal's familiars, Snow's right-hand assistants didn't like me.

But then, whoever had, and I'd survived them all.

"You found the chip designs in my office," Snow noted, sitting and sipping like any busy chief executive taking five.

"Right. The Inferno has a history in Las Vegas. It was just . . . cut short."

"The founding father disappeared. You were right. He was a vampire. I find it hard to believe he ever became the lover of a naïve werewolf girl, a mixed-blood Mafia princess—"

"Some very powerful individuals like naïve girls. Must make them feel potent."

Snow's lips twitched, rather than smiled. Behind his opaque black sunglasses his eyes were the usual mystery.

"And vampires like to prey on the innocent," I added. "Makes them feel *bad*."

"Quite true. Opposites attract. The alliance of werewolves and mob bosses was unfortunate for the Blood Immortals. They must sleep, and sleep makes one vulnerable."

I could second that statement. Sometimes I wished I never slept, never dreamed.

"Do you sleep?" I asked.

"Soundly," he said. "Eight hours like ordinary humans."

"You're not an ordinary human, if you boast about that."

"No. Are you?"

"Mostly."

"What parts are not?"

I didn't answer because I didn't know. "Can I prove who the dead man in Sunset Park was?"

"Have you talked to the coroner?"

"Not yet. I don't know what to ask him."

"Ask if the male victim's heart had mesquite slivers in it."

"A stake?"

"Or your lover's dowsing rod splinters. The wands peel free of bark when they dowse. That very power drives deep beneath the surface, finding and altering, perhaps."

"You're saying Ric accidentally staked the male victim, decades after the original crime?"

"Possibly. Not knowing. Not all of us know our own powers. Not all of us control our powers."

I sipped the pallid cocktail. It was delicious, if I did say so myself, down to the liquor-soaked cherry in the bottom, which was still sweet.

Ric. Did he dowse for more than he knew? Did the act of dowsing change what the rod found? "*Not all of*

us know our own powers." Snow had seemed to sweep
Ric and myself up in his mystic trail of bewitchment and
hidden purposes.

"Will solving the identity of the dead couple in Sunset
Park achieve anything?" I asked.

"It will win you Hector Nightwine's regard. It will
upset various powerful and vicious personages around
town, which will make you someone to reckon with, and
possibly destroy."

"And you?"

"It may suit me very much, as you do, Delilah Street."
He lifted his Albino Vampire and ticked rims with mine.

"I don't like being used."

"No one does, you more than most, but one day you
will beg me for a Brimstone Kiss."

"Not damn likely."

"No, merely certain." Those cold white lips drew in
more of my own creation, the Albino Vampire cocktail.
"Check with the coroner on the boy's body. It wouldn't
hurt to cultivate the coroner, as only you can. You'll be
seeing a lot of him from now on, one way or another."

CHAPTER FIFTY-ONE

As usual, Snow had implied more than he gave away. The next day I looked up the address of the coroner's office. Most municipalities had medical examiners nowadays, but Vegas still called its head man for dealing with dead bodies a coroner.

An online map site showed the Clark County Coroner's office located on a two-block-long street north of busy Charleston Boulevard, the east-west street that also featured a lot of vintage shops, I noticed as Dolly and I cruised along Charleston with the top down.

I figured I'd need fresh air coming back from the county morgue.

Pinto Lane was not far from Our Lady of Las Vegas Convent school. I was reminded of poor Father Black. Imagine if he saw me driving Miss Dolly these days! My vintage Caddy was as long and black as a hearse, but the red interior and white ragtop gave her a jaunty rather than a funereal look. Still, I could smuggle a few dead bodies in her huge trunk, if I wanted to.

Smuggling dead bodies made me think of Ric. I didn't know if he'd be proud or annoyed that I was taking the investigation by the horns and waltzing right over to interrogate the coroner himself. Having been a reporter gave me the nerve to ask anybody anything, but without official credentials, I wasn't sure that nerve alone would work.

The low-profile morgue building had sculptural brushed aluminum lettering on the outside. I made out the name, Grady Bahr, Coroner.

Dolly dwarfed the other cars and vans in the lot. I slammed the door with a satisfying thump and went in through the glass door into a lobby that looked like a dentist's office waiting room.

A young woman at the walk-up window eyed my blue suit and hot pink pumps. I figured Business Brazen would work on coroners as well as rock stars.

"Delilah Street, PI," I said. "I'd like to see Dr. Bahr."

Darn, I needed to run some pro-looking business cards on the enchanted cottage computer. Maybe pixies would do the graphics for me.

"You don't have an appointment."

"Like death, investigative matters have a way of just cropping up."

"I'm sorry, Miss Street, but the coroner is a busy official. You can't see the coroner without an appointment."

The bland blond wood door to my left opened. A guy who had enough rusty-gray eyebrow hair to go to Halloween parties as a caterpillar couple peeped through.

"Fortunately, Miss Street, I can see *you* via the lobby surveillance camera." The sharp pale hazel eyes behind half-glasses eyed my shoes, and then my calves, including the sweet silver ankle bracelet of dangling . . . skulls. *Oh, Snow.* "Come right in. I have a few moments. It's fine, Stephanie."

Stephanie rolled her eyes at having her pronouncements ignored, but I was through the door.

Dr. Bahr was a big, vital man in the expected white lab coat; he bustled me to an empty conference room.

"I don't get a chance to see many attractive *live* young women," he said, collapsing into a wheeled leather chair. "What totally inappropriate information did you want from me?"

"No more than you want from me," I grinned back.

We grinned at each other like a pair of jolly death heads.

I'd run into his type before: late middle-aged authority figure who liked to ogle the ladies but meant no harm.

He was pleased that I recognized we could deal.

"I need information on the old murder in Sunset Park."

"*Hmm.* Now that's a sensitive case."

"I helped find the bodies."

"You?" He was looking suspicious for the first time.

"And Ric Montoya."

The eyebrows reached for the sky. "So you're an associate of the Cadaver Kid? Why isn't he here?"

"We're not married, Dr. Bahr," I said coyly. "He's been in Mexico a lot lately."

"What else is new?" His mouth seesawed left and right with indecision, then the flat of his hand slapped the bare conference table. "All right. I'll answer what I can, but if one word appears in or on the media—"

"Off the record, I swear."

"Can't be too careful. We had to shield all our windows from paparazzi and morgue-robbers. You from Vegas?"

I shook my head. "Kansas."

"You'd be amazed what folks in this town would do to get a hold of a piece of celebrity bodies."

"Nothing amazes me, but the truth."

"Ah. One of those. All right. Ask away."

"The age of the skeletons—"

"Dead and buried and left alone for sixty-five years or so. That's a good record for undisturbed graves in Vegas, especially now that all the supernaturals are coming out of the closet."

"Their age at death, I meant."

"Young. She was about seventeen. He maybe twenty."

Her Romeo and Juliet, yes!

"And they weren't killed the same way."

Bahr herded his caterpillars into a unibrow frown. "No. Now how did you know to ask that?"

"Just a suspicion."

"You have good suspicions, Miss Street, is it?" He leaned around the conference table corner to eye my ankles again. "And a rather grisly taste in jewelry."

"I thought grisly was up your alley."

"And down my Street, maybe," he quipped, laughing. "Okay, since you suspect so darn much I'm gonna make it easy for you. Normally I'd take you on a tour of the facility first. We have an outstanding decaying corpse room, and a state of the art body parts storage system."

"I don't have time for the Grand Tour. Maybe another day. I want to know about the thirty pieces of silver, the gambling chip, and the causes of death."

"You *were* there." He was impressed. "That's all top secret. But there were twenty-nine pieces of silver scattered over the bodies."

"Twenty-nine? Was the gaming chip supposed to be thirty?"

"Or thirty-four pieces of silver if you count the pancaked bullets."

"Silver bullets?"

"Yes, ma'am." He leaned close to whisper. "You don't seem too surprised."

"Her. The bullets were for her."

He nodded.

"And the man?"

"Too young to be considered a man. The bone growth showed him to be twenty, but the age of the bone would have better come from a catacomb."

I felt a chill in the super-cool air-conditioning. For the first time I detected a fruity scent of decay overlaid by a wave of bitter orange.

"What killed him?"

"Not who?"

"That's for me and Ric to find out."

"'What' may describe it better. There were thirty pieces of silver. Silver dollars. You were right. But only twenty-nine in the grave. The last one was in the jaws of the man, and he was killed with an axe. Spinal cord severed at the neck."

Now I frowned, and Bahr leaned close again. "One old world method of laying a vampire to rest forever. Coin in the mouth; head cut off, buried for eternity. Except you and Ric came along. You have the Kid's same . . . knack?"

"No," I said, a bit stunned by my instincts turning out to be true.

"Good. I find it rather creepy."

I sat stunned, then laughed! Trust a coroner to find dowsing for the dead "creepy." He was first and foremost a doctor, a scientist.

"We work together," he added. "He had to tell me how; otherwise, it would have hampered my reports. I'm surprised he let you in on his facility."

"You let me into yours."

"Ah." He nodded. "Anything else?"

"It was suggested to me that Ric's wooden dowsing rods could act as a sort of psychic stake."

"You mean kill, as well as find?"

I nodded.

"Interesting theory, but I doubt it."

"What do the police know?"

"Shot and axed. That's all they want to know at the moment. These Millennium Revelation changes have freaked out the criminal justice system. It's just been a few years; the laws are a patchwork that's being fought out in the courts. I hope I've been of service."

I stood. "Very much so, Dr. Bahr." I held out my hand for a shake and he took it in his big paw.

"Call me Grisly. All my friends do. Not that there are very many of them in my line of work."

I worked it through. Grisly/Grizzly Bahr. "Black humor gets us all through."

"You sound like you know a little of what I'm about, Miss Street."

I nodded.

"Bring Ric the next time you come. Not that I'm eager to share the riches, but he's spending too much time in Juarez. He needs a social life and less morbid atmosphere."

And then he laughed.

So did I, so I left.

DRIVING DOLLY HOME from Pinto Lane, I had the white top down so the wind would freshen my hair and dispel the orange-scented decay of the coroner's facility.

That's when I noticed a huge billboard above the Strip advertising Madrigal's show at the Gehenna.

I'd seen lots of photos of the Strip featuring similarly huge billboards of Siegfried and Roy and one of their white tigers before Roy's tragic accident shortly after the Millennium Revelation. (White tigers are magnificent creatures but they don't hold the same allure for me now that I've seen Snow's shape-shifting bodyguard-cum-personal assistant, Grizelle.)

I'd probably driven by this and matching billboards a dozen times since coming to Vegas, never noticing the striking image of Madrigal posed with a delicate and fey familiar assistant on each brawny bare shoulder. What almost made me make Dolly shriek to a sudden stop was the image of my own airbrushed face behind the trio. And the words: NIGHTLY: MISS MAGGIE, DEAD AND ALIVE, ONLY AT THE GEHENNA.

The frenetic Strip traffic flow doesn't allow for gawking, so I drove on, stewing. Why not paste up a giant WANTED: DEAD OR ALIVE! poster of me all over town? Every Maggie freak around would be hunting me everywhere. The

Rococo lettering style actually read "Margie," but you had to look really hard to see that. I was sure Nightwine's non-CinSim lawyers would make hash of that dodge, but legal action could take years.

So it was up to me to provide some illegal action. I had to get that semi-CinSim of myself off the stage and the billboards and out of the Gehenna for good. Pronto! I gunned Dolly onto a side street and headed us overland to Nightwine's place. My place.

When I got there, Quicksilver was out and Ric still wasn't answering his cell phone. I'd tried calling repeatedly to tell him the news from the coroner's office.

I left a message that I had business at the Gehenna. That worried me a little, both of them being out of touch, but I faced a bigger worry: Margie at the Gehenna. There was a slice of me still there and I had to get her out somehow. Right now!

While I paced the cottage living area, I noticed how sparkling clean everything was. I never caught my cleaning crew in action. The place was indeed enchanted, as Godfrey had said. I could use some enchanted good ideas about now.

Only one idea occurred. Could I sneak into the Gehenna's theater before tonight's first show, avoid Madrigal and his creepy-crawly assistants, and do something about Margie?

I went upstairs to change into black cat-burglar clothing, just in case.

I headed down the upstairs hall and turned off into my bedroom.

I stopped.

Walked back into the hall.

It was always in shadow, being an interior passage with no strong lighting source, so the mirror at the end of the hall was always murky, useless for checking how you really looked. You'd only get an approximation.

Only now I got . . . nothing. No image. No reflection. Nothing.

For a moment I stood frozen. I hadn't reflected in the silver tray at Snow's, either. The old legends said vampires couldn't reflect in a mirror, but that was then and the Millennium Revelation had rewritten the rules. I hoped so, because I definitely didn't want to be a vampire. Anything but that! Well, anything but a werewolf.

I went to the kitchen, got my flashlight, and returned to the hall. I turned on the strong beam and walked toward the eerily empty mirror. The flashlight reflected like the one-eyed headlight of a locomotive rushing toward a film camera.

But *I* didn't move a muscle, according to the mirror. *I* was invisible. Not there. At all.

I think my heart stopped at what that meant. Was I now locked out of my own medium, the silver-backed mercurial magic of a mirror?

Oh, my.

I'd come up nose-to-nose with the glass. It wasn't the front-surface mirror Madrigal had showed me, the mirror that I'd been able to walk through with the assistance of his magical powers. Yet I couldn't *see* that this wasn't that kind of mirror, because no matter how close I came, I saw nothing of myself. No reflection.

Because I had been separated from my reflection. My reflection remained behind at the Gehenna, just barely a material girl, a . . . zombie animated by Madrigal. My God, maybe that was my soul! It was *me* . . . certainly, a part of me.

I shuddered at the implications: yet another me out there, to be used and manipulated.

No way.

My fingertips felt the cold smooth surface of the mirror, even if the mirror didn't trouble to reflect them back. This was an enchanted cottage. The mirror must be enchanted too. Maybe I could use it.

I pressed my hot, anxious cheek to the icy surface. It was there. Only I wasn't. Jeannie hid somewhere behind it. Margie could be there too, especially since she was a part of me.

Mirror, mirror, on the wall, who's the realest of them all?

"*You,*" a voice whispered back to my unspoken question.

I stood there, shocked. Maybe I was hallucinating. The word conveyed no particular gender, and it sounded so distant that it echoed a bit.

I swallowed, playing this by ear, by my ear pressed to the cold glass. I thought I could feel a slight pulse, like a heart beating. Weird.

I pulled back. "Then let me see myself," I said aloud.

No answer, but my fingertips felt the icy glass warm beneath them. First fingerprints formed where I'd touched the surface, blackened whorls that looked like they'd been inked by an old-fashioned police process.

Behind the reflected fingerprints an image assembled bit by bit.

Flattened pink pads, curved gray nails . . . claws. A vague, two-legged shape. Then a fanged, terrifying face, half pale flesh, half gray fur with gleaming blue-green eyes backlit by carnivorous yellow.

The mirror was making me into a monster, assembling a werewolf version of myself . . . or connecting me with a supernatural shape-shifter inside it.

I pulled my fingers away, but they were bound as if by Superglue. I really wasn't this appalling vision! I pulled harder. My flesh seemed to peel away, leaving glowing raw pink spots. Had the mirror changed into an acid pool that had eaten off my own fingerprints?

With a sizzling, hissing sound, the monstrous reflection vanished.

My fingertips felt as raw as open sores. Had there been any decent light in this hallway, I probably would've swooned to see the damage. As I watched, the mirror bulged out in the same starfish spots that my fingers had touched.

Blue-white hands came reaching through, stretching the mirror's surface like Saran Wrap. Those cool blue hands were the color of Madrigal's front-surface glass. Now the entire mirror surface was a cool blue lake. I plunged my throbbing, skinned fingertips into it, as into ice water.

I felt a bracing tingle, and then *she* assembled before my eyes, in the mirror, my severed self, naked where I was clothed, serene where I was battered, soothing where I was agitated.

When her full figure was visible, I stepped away and broke our contact.

Her silhouette wavered, flashed through a rapid-fire of alterations from demon to the dead girl of Sunset Park, and ended by reflecting me entirely, dressed as I was, looking as I did now.

I stepped even farther back, exhausted.

Somehow I knew that no mirror image of me-made-flesh existed at the Gehenna anymore. All those expensive billboards would have to be painted over.

Madrigal's act would be all Sylphia's and Phasia's again.

Cicereau would be furious.

Nobody would be able to explain it.

Not even me.

At least that left only one dangerous mission to accomplish onsite at the Gehenna.

I had to break back into Cicereau's office to copy the photo of his dead daughter. That would be proof enough of the old-time crime victim for Nightwine, and my own satisfaction. Getting back in shouldn't be a problem. For now, the ghost of myself was still supposed to be alive and well and performing nightly. It was still five hours to show time.

Masquerading as my own reflection, as Margie, I'd be in and out of there in a heartbeat.

CHAPTER FIFTY-TWO

Ric would have been worried that I was off and running without waiting for him, but there were lots of things I didn't want to explain at the moment. Like my mirror-split personality.

Quicksilver was still out on big doggie business, so no one witnessed my exit from Nightwine central. I'd used Godfrey's codes to disable the security cameras when I came home. I didn't want anybody in the main house to tumble to my intentions and try to talk me out of them, or any record of my criminal intent.

When I departed again, I was, in fact, as good as a ghost of myself.

I wore a black leotard and Spandex leggings. My black ballet slippers and best vintage black satin opera gloves had rosin on the soles and fingertips to give them more traction. I was entering a reptile-arachnid world and I needed to slither with the best of them, even if only by artificial means. I'd removed the thin sterling hip chain I wore for Ric—it was fragile and might snap during exertion, but I worried about the glaring reflectivity of the silver familiar. It could really cook my cat burglar act if it migrated somewhere obvious at a key moment! But, not to worry. The prescient thing had instantly morphed into a duplicate of the sterling chain and settled on my hips. One might think Snow had intentions of usurping Ric. At least I knew this chain wouldn't snap . . . although it might bite.

This time I parked Dolly two long Las Vegas Strip blocks away from the Gehenna, where nobody bothered with security cameras, and retraced my escapee steps. Into the laundry Dumpster and up the chute I went, crawling like an insect. I passed the churning central mechanical systems and finally arrived at the theater's backstage area.

The first show wouldn't open for more than three hours. It was late afternoon. Everything and everybody unloosened their corsets and breathed at a major hotel and casino during the hours that change over from day to night.

I prowled the deserted backstage area, feeling an unhappy twinge of homesickness. My reflection had adapted quite well once I was gone. I sensed that. Madrigal had been thoroughly pleased at this outcome, also his pets. They had liked the Stepford Wife me, tamed, predicable, not upsetting the status quo.

Too bad. Stepford Divorcee was here now and this was Splitsville.

First, I had to confront the blue-toned front-surface mirror in which I'd split in two.

The mirror surface was inert, as it had always been. When I touched my black-gloved fingers to their reflection, my whole hand plunged right through. Whole. Uncorrupted by debased mirror images. I stepped through again. *Presto-change-o*, I was in Cicereau's office, the slim flash drive case flat against my hip inside the leotard, concealed. The drive was memory overkill—I was only after one image—but a CD was more difficult to conceal in Spandex and I could hardly email that damned and damning file to myself from his machine.

The trouble with breaking physical barriers is that you can't scout ahead. Even as my body emerged crouched on the wet bar, I saw that the joint was jumping.

Not only was Cicereau present, and his butch bodyguard Sansouci, but my most non-favorite wanta-meet, Detective Hardboiled, Half-balled Haskell.

At the moment I was a scintillating reflection in a dozen silver surfaces. Maybe if I kept the dazzle going, I'd be overlooked.

"You've been useful before because you were human, Detective Haskell," Cicereau was saying. "Now you are neither flesh nor foul, but a freakish half-breed. You don't even know which super bit you, half-werewolf or debased vampire or something worse."

There was something worse?

"I'm a half-were now." Haskell spat the words through distended fangs. He looked a mess. Everything human about him had degraded and mixed with the worst of beastliness. "I can do even more special work for you."

"Such as?"

"I know where to find that meddling Maggie you're missing."

"Madrigal has been here having a fit when you arrived because she'd disappeared, and I admit I'll drop a bundle in advertising, but I don't want her, Haskell. She's more trouble than she's worth. Just get out of here."

Sansouci made it happen in one muscle-bound moment.

One down, two to go.

"Scum," Sansouci said, wiping his hands on his black denim thighs. "Now half-breed scum."

"Agreed." Cicereau smiled. "Still, scum is always useful, always has been. No trace of my Margie?"

"Your little Margie has left the building. Gone." Sansouci sat in the swivel chair before the desk, then swiveled my way. I thought, *Sparkle, sparkle, little reflective star. Hide me.*

"Think that Madrigal had anything to do with it, despite his indignant act?" Cicereau asked.

"No. He had the perfect new trick worked up. I saw it in rehearsal. It rocked."

"Yeah, it did, didn't it? What hooked you, like, as just an audience member?"

So I had to listen to Sansouci rave about me being swathed in silk and then naked in serpent coils and elevated into thin air and having a rhinestone apple sucked out of my throat. These mob guys made a fanged Howard Hughes look enlightened, but what the hell else did they have to do?

"We're still probably better off without Margie," Cicereau concluded. "Dames will always turn on you and then you have no choice but to off them, which makes you feel bad."

I shuddered to imagine Cicereau's farewell speech to his own daughter sixty-some years ago, if he'd even bothered to be in on the kill.

"I'm gonna check on the high-roller baccarat tables." Cicereau rose from his desk and from behind his restored computer.

"I'll hold the fort, boss," the black-and-silver haired Sansouci said, standing.

He would make a damn impressive werewolf, and I didn't even want to tangle again with him in human form. I hoped "the fort" meant more than this office.

Apparently it did, for Sansouci eyed everything, then slipped out the door. I heard the security system beep into action after he left.

It hurt to stretch myself back into unmirrored form, but I hopped from the wet bar onto the floor and made for the computer on Cicereau's desk.

The flat-screen monitor showed the same wallpaper as before, a Disney forest scene teeming with rabbits, squirrels, and deer, all great prey for wolves.

I moved right to Photo Album, found the deeply buried family pic from 1949 and copied it onto my flash drive.

The drive whirred as happily as Jiminy Cricket for a second or two. I was ready to chirp myself when I tucked the earring-sized portable drive into my Spandex tights.

Everything was going perfectly until all the power in the room went out, which meant all the lights too. Trouble was, I needed light to see a reflection to walk into. While I froze, being a thinking being, and realized someone must have rigged the power outage from outside the office, a huge heavy web fell atop me. *Boobytrap!* Also triggered from outside. A net seemed hokey for the Cicereau operation, so who would have motive or opportunity, and the nerve to use Cicereau's office for his or her own purposes? It sure wasn't Sylphia's web, not these scratchy rope fibers. I fought the cumbersome netting, and was still fighting it when the lights and power came back on.

The office door opened and in walked . . . Detective Haskell in all his half-were glory.

CHAPTER FIFTY-THREE

Talk about a list of people you'd most like *not* to meet in heaven, or hell; Haskell was now *numero uno* in my book.

The lights showed that I was tangled in a huge, heavy-duty fishing net. The more I thrashed, the more tangled I became. This must have been rigged after my first break-in. Still, I didn't see Sansouci or Cicereau racing back to gloat. Believe it or not, that tightened the sulfuric acid knot in my stomach behind the hidden drive even more.

Haskell grinned, showing yellowed teeth between a pair of rusty red fangs. You could have nicknamed him Canadian Sunset. Then he spoke.

"Our friends here at the Gehenna underestimate you, and they sure underestimate me, Miss Delilah Street."

I jerked in distaste to hear my name on his peeling, blackened lips.

"You know from how I cracked Nightwine's fence security that I have my little ways of coming and going in the most unexpected places in town."

I glanced up, examining the ceiling as I hadn't before. A dark pattern of rugged wood beams suggested overarching forest branches. The net would have been invisible up there. And Haskell probably had something on a lot of local security firm personnel who would do him favors. Even now, he was exulting in what he had on me.

"The minute I saw those new Gehenna billboards, babe, I knew it was you."

He circled me and the desk, checking to see that I was tightly wrapped. Thank God I'd quit Photo Album, although Haskell might have been too stupid to figure out what I'd been doing.

"I suppose," Haskell went on, as the seldom-listened-to invariably do, "you read about my near-fatal mugging in the Sinkhole and thought you were done with Irving Haskell."

Irving! I'd forgotten it from the newspaper article. *And who wouldn't?* Irma asked. *Not an A-list first name.* No wonder he had issues.

His fingers prodded and poked me through the webbing, which made me feel even more like a snared fish.

"Thing is, girlie, does it pay me better to let the management know I got you, or are they tired of you and I can take you home and keep you all to myself?"

I didn't answer. I didn't breathe. I knew which alternative I preferred. So I screamed. I thrashed, even though it was useless. I threw my full weight on Haskell and managed to kick his feet out from under him so we were rolling on the floor together.

He actually seemed to enjoy this version of dry mud wrestling, but it was worth the nausea if I could get the big boys back in here to play. Against them I had a chance. Slim, but a chance.

I heard the office door slam against the wall. In an instant, Sansouci hauled us both upright and slammed us against the nearest wall. He hit a button on the desk, then sat against the edge, arms crossed, biceps bulging impressively, eyeing us both.

I knew what he was thinking: *Which of these two would I like to skin alive the most?*

From the quick glance he gave my Spandex cat burglar outfit I could tell that he liked me best, and in my skin.

Everybody hates a loser, and Haskell was a loser born, whether human or unhuman.

On the other hand, I'd made Sansouci look bad to Cicereau, and no guy likes a woman who shows him up to his boss.

I shrugged and did a little Mae West CinSim. "Get this slug off me and I'll run away with you to the Clark County jail."

"Don't listen to her!" Haskell screamed. "She's the Devil in a black Spandex catsuit."

Actually, that description didn't hurt me with Sansouci one damn bit.

He sighed, got up, wrenched the netting off us both, kicked Haskell in the stomach, and spun me against himself one-armed while he pulled the handcuffs from Haskell's belt. In a thrice I was cuffed behind my back. Sansouci pushed me up against the wall solo while he rolled Haskell into a fishnet rug on the floor.

"Mr. Cicereau," Sansouci said, "will decide what to do with both of you." He glanced at me. "Sorry that's not up to me, Snow White. The Clark County jail sounds like a nice peaceful getaway for us both about now."

As if cued, Cicereau bustled in, the busy, pudgy executive on a heartburn roll. "So what's this now?"

Sansouci stood to attention. "Haskell caught her and I caught them both. We throw 'em both over Hoover Dam, or what?"

Sansouci had not been kidding when he'd told me he was sorry! I must be losing my Maggie charisma.

"*Hmmm.*" Cicereau strolled over to me. "She *is* quite a draw."

"I caught her, boss," Haskell panted from the floor.

"But you *got* caught." Cicereau prodded him with his Gucci-shod foot, and then lashed me with a glance that was half-murderous, half-paternal.

I guessed he'd made a very similar decision decades before.

"You did okay," he told Haskell grudgingly. "You're still on the payroll. Now make like a wart hog and vanish. We'll call *you*."

Sansouci unrolled Haskell from the webbing with one long gesture. Haskell spun so fast he must have gotten rope burns as well as dizzy.

Haskell rose and wobbled out.

As soon as the door shut behind him, Cicereau turned to Sansouci. "Take her to Starlight Lodge. The moon's about to go full. I'll decide about her then and there."

I breathed a sigh of relief to be rid of Haskell until I saw Sansouci's impassive face flinch slightly. The expression was gone before he pulled me away from the wall by one arm and hustled me out.

I'd been working my black satin wrist-length gloves off behind my back since I'd been cuffed and now was glad I had them to leave a trail. What good that might do was another matter. Quicksilver could follow the scent maybe, if anyone knew where to start looking for me.

Ric might.

Going through the office door en route to the mysterious Starlight Lodge, I felt a sharp, quick pinch on the butt.

Sansouci? He was looking way too grim to indulge in anything as playful as butt pinching.

But somebody wasn't.

Like it says in the old song, "Somebody Loves Me."

The next line is even more apropos to this situation.

"I wonder who?"

CHAPTER FIFTY-FOUR

My chauffeurs to the Starlight Lodge were my not-so-old friends, Chartreuse and Flamingo. They drove a van marked "Hazardous Material."

That worried me a little. Okay, a lot. What also worried me was I'd been unable to feel my friendly neighborhood familiar. My body heat had warmed the hip chain and it was too delicate to sense.

The boys were pretty tight-lipped. It was full dark by the time we'd wound our way up into the Spring Mountains. I didn't see any signs for Los Lobos, but I did see billboards advertising the Paiute Golf Club and its famed fifteenth hole of the Wolf Course.

"Hey," I said, "you guys know a dance club called Los Lobos?"

"Not on this part of the mountain," Chartreuse said. "Sorry."

The funny thing is, he really sounded sorry. Very sorry.

"Say," I said, "you think you could get me out of these handcuffs? They kind of hurt my shoulders and wrists."

"That's for the bossman to okay," Flamingo said. "Sorry."

He too sounded very, very sorry.

Okay. What was the Starlight Lodge?

The pink-and-green watermelon boys had joked about Quicksilver being sent there the first time they'd kidnapped me. Apparently it was a perennial send-to place. Maybe it was like the Post Office. If you got sent to the wrong address, you never got returned.

But when the van drove up to a lighted porte cochère, the place looked like a five-star retreat, rustic but posh. The boys let me out of the van. One produced a key and handcuffed my hands in front, at least.

"Hope you enjoy your stay, miss," Chartreuse said, exchanging a glance with Flamingo. Then they both teared up like the doorman to the Emerald City in *The Wizard of Oz*.

I got it. It was "Surrender Dorothy" time and I didn't even have a straw man, a tin man, a cowardly lion, or a valiant little Lhasa apso on my side.

I walked into the place alone, head high.

I entered the ultimate National Park lodge, all soaring wood and gigantic balconies, fireplaces and leopard skin rugs. (I didn't approve of walking on dead pelts, but no one had asked me). And heads were mounted on every wall. Lions and tigers and bears. Deer. Buffalo. Even otter, beaver, and fully mounted squirrels, the cowards! Their bright-eyed animal profiles all looked way handsomer and nobler than Homo sapiens.

But this was where the wolves lived, not man. Quicksilver's ancestors had run down deer and boar and I suppose even humans on occasion.

A LATINA SERVANT GIRL showed me to a room. Yeah, a servant girl. You or I might have called her a waitress or a Mexican maid or even a concierge, if we wanted to get fancy. She thought nothing of my handcuffs and even less of my requests. A phone. A computer. TV remote? None of these transmitted in the mountain air, she said. Sorry.

I was really getting tired of people who had jobs that made them "sorry" all the time. Had they never heard of the union movement? Apparently not.

Time flew, as it always does when you're not having fun. I'd watched the day darken into night from the window of

my room, which wasn't merely locked, but sealed. There
had been only a medicine cabinet mirror in the bathroom,
although lots of polished marble. The cabinet was empty
and so was the mirror. It reflected only me, looking worried. I tried my silver medium touch to turn it into an escape
route, but it resisted me like Snow did: cold, hard, giving
nothing back. Maybe my mirror powers had been enhanced
by Madrigal's magic or presence, or the mirror itself, and
didn't translate to other mirrors, other places. Darn!

Otherwise, the suite was palatial, but not my style.
The long-haired white goatskin rugs on the exotic wood
floors, the black mink throw on the California king-size
bed and pillow shams were all too furry for me, though
they reminded me that I was in the hands, or soon-to-be
paws, of predatory carnivores, not just your run-of-the-
mill ruthless mobsters. In the ranks of villainy, these guys
offered a fabulous two-fer.

I stood, still handcuffed, on the balcony of another huge
room, but more intimate than the vast main hall. Below
me gathered a company of men, drinking and smoking
and talking. I recognized Cicereau and Sansouci, but
none of the others.

Two half-were "escorts" had hauled me before them
like a delinquent daughter. Maybe I was playing the role
of Jeanie with the light brown hair from my enchanted
mirror and from less enchanted Sunset Park, at least for
Cicereau. Or Norma Jeane. Or even St. Jeanne d'Arc.
Think of every female martyr on the roll call of saints and
sinners, and I was probably a stand-in.

No thanks.

While on trial, I noticed some things I hadn't before.

If the Starlight Lodge was a luxe hideaway for high
rollers, it was indeed huge and luxurious. But it was the
heads on these particular walls that bothered me. Sure,

hunting was a long-time necessity and then a sport in the West, but . . . *people's* heads decked these walls, going back to what was labeled as First Kill. I recognized him from my online info search into the kingpins of early Las Vegas development: Bugsy Siegel.

So he'd been hit by the werewolf mob, not the Chicago "Outfit." *That* had caused a lot of bloody retaliations on the wrong parties. Thinking of wrong parties, I sure was one here and now. And it wasn't much of a party.

While I tried to avoid eye contact with my eye-level predecessors—this little balcony was apparently a prime viewing station of the mountees—a lively debate was going on below. About me.

My captors were clearly torn about my fate. All agreed I was too hard to control to have a future as a major Strip hotel attraction, no matter how hot the Maggie mania.

Some of Cicereau's party wanted to keep me prisoner as a lucrative source of black market Maggie tapes. This would require impressing me into the blue-movie industry, and require a lot of nude lying around on dead animal skins on my part. Among other things I didn't want to think about.

Some wanted me dead but killed in a way to fill the ravening coffers of the snuff film industry. Slowly and gruesomely. Some of the werewolves actually objected to that solution on moral grounds.

Others just plain wanted me dead the way all of those sent to Starlight Lodge become dead: because the moon was full and they craved chasing down fresh human meat on the hoof. This place was, after all, a retreat-cum-holding pen for mob enemies or turncoats. After living in pampered luxury until the next full moon, the "guests" would be turned loose in the surrounding mountains for the werewolves to hunt down. Call it the ultimate in extreme sports for harried executives needing to unwind.

Unlucky me, the moon was already full, so I won't get much luxurious living time before being hunted down.

What could I do? I'm stuck in future tense, very tense, no matter what. Ric hadn't answered his cell phone and must still be in D.C. (and incommunicado) on the Juarez business. Nightwine and Godfrey sure didn't know I'm not snoozing at home in my cozy little cottage. My desire for discretion and hatred of being monitored now looked foolish. Quicksilver was out on the town on big dog business, the last I knew.

These mob chieftains have me trapped and bound here, security cameras rolling, debating whether I'd work best as an enslaved slasher/porn-movie star or as . . . just plain dead and forgotten. Or maybe resurrected somehow later for whatever they might have in mind.

Just plain dead and forgotten looks kinda good from here.

The majority concludes that too.

My two hairy guards march me back to the huge curving redwood staircase to the main hall and then out onto a main-floor balcony six feet above the ground, facing the great American Western night. Huge torches flutter with the sound of eagles' wings on either side of the lodge doors. By their light I see that Sansouci isn't here. Neither are Flamingo and Chartreuse. Maybe they've "changed" already. Or maybe only strangers will be in for the kill. Maybe even werewolves observe the niceties.

The mountains around us loom dark, rocky, empty of everything but a hoot owl's cry.

Before I know it, a pack of half-weres have gathered below me, including Haskell, whose now-elongated jaws are slavering silvery strings of spit like a born lycanthrope. Cicereau must have decided he deserved a piece of the action, after all. My mind flipped back to Los Lobos. They'd be dancing the Change there now, the awed tourists watching the werewolves two-stepping themselves into their four-legged selves, howling for freedom. But those werewolves were a different breed, and probably didn't hunt humans.

That's not a problem for my circle of furry admirers. A mob of full werewolves gathers, also slavering, beneath my balcony. I feel like Evita. *Don't weep for me, Argentina, send reinforcements!*

Haskell's police department issue handcuffs still bind me. Just when I'm hoping for a silver accomplice, an innocuous wrist bangle suddenly wreathes my wrist. Before my eyes it changes back to a charm bracelet of keys! I struggle to manipulate one into the cuff lock without attracting too much attention.

Snap! One cuff loosens into the palm of the other hand, but by now the werewolves are snuffling and whining with canine excitement and hear nothing. If only Quicksilver were here! Maybe he'd somehow sensed something wrong and had secretly tailed me to the Gehenna. Maybe he'd run alongside the van, unseen, the whole way here . . . Maybe pigs like Haskell could fly as well as slobber.

On a higher balcony, as if enjoying box seats at a theater of blood, Cicereau and a few still-human guests are sipping red wine (I hope) while I wait to be signaled to run for my life.

I unsnap the second cuff and hold it one-handed so I can swing the other cuff as a weapon. *The best defense is a good offense,* Irma whispers. Right. I bound over the balcony into the midst of the werewolf pack, slinging handcuff.

I'm on my back in a pile of scrabbling curved claws. Glad I wore long sleeves and pants. The deep, burning scratches even penetrate my nylon Spandex. Whoever thought trendy workout togs would get a workout like this?

I grab wolfish ears and struggle to my feet, avoiding the huge snapping muzzles.

Amidst my enemies, my handcuff sling looks as threatening as a linked pair of sleazy big-hoop earrings.

And then I feel the silver charm bracelet icing down one wrist, streaking over my shoulders and capturing the other wrist.

In the wavering torchlight I see silver cuffs three inches wide on each of my wrists, linked together by a piece of Quicksilver's heavy pet store chain. Shackles! I've now got metal-cuffed wrists with a two-foot-long swag of thick chain between them, which make even better bonds than police-issue handcuffs. Now I'm handicapped big time.

Damn Snow! His freaky invasive "gift" is gonna bind me for the kill.

Which is even now heading this way.

As the rising werewolves scrabble for purchase so they can press in to devour me, their combined meaty doggie breaths are enough to knock over a bank. I dodge, turn, elbow their jaws and rib cages, kick their knees and knee their furry little balls . . .

Wait! A half-were charges me, fanged jaws wide. I raise my shackled hands without thinking to defend my neck from a fatal wound. He bites down, hard, on industrial-strength chain and howls with pain. I lift my hands over his shaggy, fanged head, cross my wrists to circle his furred throat with chain, and *presto!* He falls, throttled. I've got a built-in garrote.

Someone . . . something . . . grabs me from the rear.

I feel a swift, cool, dry tremor down my legs . . . suddenly I have silver spurs to kick out and back with. Screams from my attackers are followed by a warm thick bloodbath on my ankles. I'm so grossed out at the idea of wading through blood that I literally climb over the oncoming half-were and werewolf forms, momentarily standing on free ground again.

I turn. Three of the half-weres are down and howling, but most of the werewolves throng me again. The shackles are gone but I feel something cold flooding over my chest—not a touchie-feelie diamond necklace in the night, but enough snaky metal tendrils to form a Victorian rainfall necklace over my entire chest. Very vintage.

Snow and his heavy metal games! This is no time to go vintage and cop a feel! Oh. Wait. This damn metal necklace is prickling, not tickling. It's icy cold, like someone's reputed prick.

I glance down. Silver martial arts hurling stars dangle from every multitudinous chain of my sudden new necklace.

So. Live, learn, and kick butt. I pluck those saw-edged stars off that new hanging arsenal one by one, and send them slicing into oncoming furred throats, chests, and femoral arteries.

That's enough to halt the werewolves. I run into the darkness, my thin-soled ballet slippers finding every sharp rock. Heavy panting, wet slobbery breaths, and frenzied whining barrel right behind me.

Where do I think I'm going, and why? Muscle stitches scream in my side and scratches burn everywhere. I'm finding that the terrain is rarely flat and always ends in rocky walls not even rosined soles can climb.

AND THEN THE BULLETS START FLYING.

Oh, my lucky throwing stars!

I spot a human on two legs, standing on a rocky rise holding a big black semiautomatic-something with a lot of rounds, treating the packing werewolves like ducks in a carnival shooting gallery.

It's Ric!

His white shirtfront is like a feral grin in the moonlight. How on earth did he get here? Never mind. I can use the distraction, and hopefully his shooting-gallery aim. Hey, my ballet slippers have sprouted silver pitons. Wings would be better.

With the harsh stutter of the semiautomatic gun, and silver bullets striking werewolves and even the ground near me, the scene is all gunfire, screams, and confusion. I hurl silver stars at the fallen wolves as Ric pauses to pump in more ammo. The werewolf pack retreats behind rocks. Ric empties his weapon again, then throws it into a knot of standing werewolves.

Ric races down the incline to me as the survivors reassemble and we escape onto the dark, cool night.

Together again.

But the full moon pins us in a relentless spotlight and night creatures see well in the dark. Howls and whines echo from the rocks all around, concealing their direction.

The howlers are closing in, packs of maddened, frustrated, rabid wolves and half-weres. They're beyond the control of the mob bosses who run the lodge, who've sent delinquent gamblers, failed hit men, and their rival mobs' soldiers here to die for decades.

This is a killing ground where the unhumans take out the humans. Every time.

Ric pulls a nine-millimeter pistol from his belt.

"Too bad you had to ditch the big gun," I say.

"Silver bullets aren't exactly sold at Wal-Mart, and I didn't have much notice, but I've got a bunch of rounds left for the hand-gun. So you run. I shoot."

"No!" I don't want to leave him.

But the wolves keep coming, centering on me. I'm suddenly standing on silver platform boots, ready to race into the raw desert for my life.

"Ric?"

He's not looking at me. The semiautomatic pistol clasped in both his fists looks pathetically small. He's a dead shot. When he shoots, a werewolf drops, but two will spring up in its place.

How many shots does a dead-shot have before he's dead?

"Run, Delilah!"

I do, sobbing with frustration, grinding harsh sand beneath my impervious silver soles, my all too-pervious soul yearning to be behind myself, with Ric. Shots echo. And stop. I pause. Why go on? I'm penned in another natural arena of rock. No place to climb, to turn and retreat.

I turn anyway.

There's a star high in the sky. I recognize the brightest star in the heavens, Sirius in the constellation of Canis Major. Sirius, that forms the Big Dog's eye, known as the Dog Star, just off an invisible line drawn to the belt of Orion, the heavenly hunter. Sirius is seriously out of season, being a fall-winter constellation. Seeing it now seems a sign of hope. I think of Achilles, my first guard dog, small but fierce.

Some women have always loved cowboys, but I've always loved canines. Dogs. Not wolves. Dogs.

Time seems collapsed. I trip. I stumble. Sage stalks break to scent the night. I stop, exhausted.

And then I see the wolves. Real wolves as they once were. Not *were*. Strong, wild. Their eyes blaze with the crimson light of the Dog Star. Their fur rises on their hackles in a corona of lightning. They've come to stand against the degraded of their own kind.

And the werewolves rush us, dead and alive, old and new.

Maybe true wolves can't out-dog their own supernatural kind, but I believe in them, whether I survive or not.

We all brace to fight the dark and hope for the coming of the day. I look for Quicksilver, but these are full-blooded wolves, not tame at all.

They stand with me only because I'm bait. I'm the target of all the oncoming werewolves.

CHAPTER FIFTY-FIVE

The moon is as pale as a fingernail tip in the black, starry sky.

The battle has come down to two forces: the double whammy of ruthless human mobsters unleashing their lethal animal natures, and me surrounded by wolves who should be extinct, and maybe are spirit wolves. I don't know. Those moonlit fangs look pretty solid.

So far I'm safe within a circle of the spirit wolves with their eerie lightning halos snapping and crackling. Thoughts of Ric dart through my every move as the wolves and I leap to repel any were that reaches us.

Still, several werewolves dance two-legged toward this intruding wolf pack, but retreat from that cold blue burning aura and the snarling jaws on four paws with hunched backs. Their fur is matted and gray, and now red-streaked, but the werewolves seem beyond pain, determined to reach me no matter how wounded.

The battle is an endless draw. What we need is the cavalry, not that ghostly desert wolves are anything to sneer at.

Instead, by the light of my guardian wolves, I see one man marching up an incline into view.

For a moment I think I see Ric, but it's not him. It's a man, weaponless, walking tall on two legs, coming on strong, not hesitating, making not for us, but for the werewolves!

In the moonlight, as I watch, another dark head breasts the rise forty feet behind the first man. Our reinforcements number two! Or are these unchanged mob bosses come to insure my end? Something relentless and swaggering drives their gait, a sense of arrogant, accustomed power.

Yet another dark head crests the hill and stalks onto the killing ground.

And another!

It's an army of heads, their eyes gleaming white and fixed on their objective.

Me!

Where's my silver familiar? I try to sense its place on my body, and fail. Has it deserted me? As good as! No, it's still here, all right, coiled into a girly, spindly "Hello Kitty" bracelet around my left wrist. Not only girly, but also juvenile. Child's play.

Rather like Snow and his games.

I try to rip it off out of sheer betrayed fury, but the thin chain cuts my fingertips, so I channel my rage forward and wade through the wolves. Impressive ghosts can't help me either.

I walk *through* them as into a mirror, I wade through a warm mist past their snapping jaws that give me mild electrical shocks. My electric personality doesn't deter the latest wave of werewolves, which leap for me with huge bounds now that I've left my charmed circle of conjured wolves.

I see a wolfish snout howl and then plummet from sight among the mobster pack, as if trampled. Another goes down screaming, under the wave of wolfish muscle and bone and fur and ferocity that is Cicereau's human-killing pack. The full moon illuminates the scene like liquid silver.

On the edges, on the fringes the oncoming forces wear . . . business suits and camo-pants and leather jackets. They sport razor haircuts and ponytails. I'm seeing corporate headhunters side-by-side with gang-bangers. And they all wear faces as white as Snow's.

It can't be just the ghostly moonlight playing tricks on my vision. What are these things, besides eager-beaver werewolf-beaters?

Someone brings up their rear, comes charging over the incline, then stops to watch them. Supervise them. Herd them.

The dazzling moon glow reflects off the only white shirtfront in the vicinity to spotlight a familiar face.

Ric! Still alive! Then I shout it aloud. "Ric!"

His hands hold something dark as he watches from above, a general who's loosed the dogs of war and now sees his orders unfold. These must be Feds, FBI men and undercover agents, mustered from the Mexican border operations and flown in.

"Ric!" I wave to show him I'm all right.

I doubt he even heard me. He's intent upon the actions of his troops. The reinforcements who, coming closer, grim and expressionless, give me the chills.

These aren't faceless bureaucrats and cookie-cutter agents.

They're our *new* supernatural allies in the Werewolf-Law Enforcement War. Finally I understand who they are, *what* they are.

Zombies!

What perfect soldiers they make, the empty dead-eyed, implacable, endlessly moving. Harried and confused werewolves turn and leap upon them as if expecting Happy Meals. These terrifying killers fall beneath the undead strength of the oncoming zombies' limbs. The werewolves' attacks leave shredded skin but can't stop the marching legs and feet, the dead-zone zombie eyes, zombies as relentless as robots. Mindless. Soulless. Heartless.

Werewolves retreat before them. Some seemed to have vanished. The gray spirit wolves surround me again, howling like Quicksilver at the full moon. I look up at that always-present wonder. It's no longer totally full and round, but slightly lopsided, the way I feel right now.

It's waning. Only the merest sliver of a wane, but it's waning!

At that moment everyone, everything halts. Some unseen celestial director who had cast every creature here into the same terrifying, fatal script, has shouted, "Cut!"

Everything takes new measure of the fading night. Every entity, unhuman or human, sees the delicately withdrawing moonlight, ebbing like a lady inching a long white skirt across a black marble floor far away and high above.

The night itself declares a truce.

The wolves that circle me push inward no farther. Such beautiful creatures! All lean, lovely legs, all wise yellow eyes. Ghosts. Sages. Friends and lovers.

Why did I think that?

As I watch, they dissipate into silver fur and golden eyes flashing through a silvery sagebrush mist.

And the silver snake that made like a kiddie bracelet? I sense a metallic chill somewhere. Oh. It's now just a thin chain at my neck, a docile barrier, all sterling and no snap. Right.

The zombies have dragged down or run off all the werewolves. Now they're heading unchallenged toward me.

I lift my dukes, stomp my feet, hiss like an angry lynx. They split when they reach me, and make a second circle around me. This is when I get a good look at them. Not your ordinary working stiffs, for sure. I spot some famous faces, a couple from the silver screen. Most reek of mob muscle or street gangsters.

Then I get the full, ghastly picture.

What kind of living dead would surround the Starlight Lodge? Previous victims of the werewolves. It didn't pay to skip out on your gambling debts or irritate a mob boss in Vegas once the werewolves won the Werewolf-Vampire War. Instead of getting concrete booties in Lake Mead, you'd get sand between your dead toes in the desert. I was witnessing eighty or ninety years of anti-werewolf troops in the making, dead and buried all around them, just waiting for the right opportunity, the right moment to dig out, stand up, and take no prisoners.

Maybe not even me.

Something has stopped the zombie march, not just the retreat and defeat of the werewolves.

The zombies were waiting, unknowing, like I was, for just the right man.

I hold my breath.

Ric's finally walking all the way toward me in the moonlight.

When silver bullets weren't enough, he'd known just where to find fresh ammunition. Under the desert sand and rocks, waiting for a liberator. Like I had been.

"Ric! My God, Ric, we're safe. You did it."

I eye the zombies, their expressionless faces. Some are . . . more realistic than others. More whole. But, hey, handsome is as handsome does, and these guys have saved my butt, my bacon, my life. Nice of them, since they won't ever have any life again themselves.

Ric's face is strangely transfixed too.

His eyes focus on me, only me, and in them is recognition, triumph, and despair.

"I'm okay, Ric. Let's bid our underground buddies goodbye and get off this mountain. The weres didn't touch me, hurt me. Honest."

Well, they had, a little, but why dwell on the negative?

Ric stopped in front of me, his eyes on my face, as mine had fixed on his since he'd appeared again. In some deep part of my mind, I'd given him up for dead. I couldn't believe we'd made it. That we had both survived and still had each other, give or take a few dozen zombies.

Something more touched Ric's expression, something more than all the good things I had read. There was one bad thing I hadn't read, hadn't wanted to read.

His face, his body, had adopted some of that zombie rigidity, something so new for Ric of the flowing words and gestures and emotions that had given my own zombie heart a new Latin beat.

I eyed the dark thing at his center, his waist, where his hands held not a gun anymore but a dowsing rod. Right?

It wasn't the shadow of night and dark deeds I'd seen, sensed in him.

It was the shadow of suffering.

Below the elbows, his dark suit coat, probably donned for a quick trip to D. C., was sopped with a deeper darkness. . . blood. His hands bore a simple tri-limbed object. And they, his hands and arms, the dowsing rod, were drenched in blood.

A follow-spot of moonlight poured down on that red ruin, painting it black, the black-and-white of a vintage film.

I shrieked.

"It's all right," Ric said. "The zombies drove off the werewolves. Anything human remaining ran."

"Zombies. Our allies. How?"

"I dowsed for them, one by one." He spoke with slow, almost painful reluctance. "I swore never to do that again. Once I raise them, they obey me until I release them."

He moved past me, gazing at his fresh-raised troop.

"The killing dance of the werewolves roused them, the scent of fresh, flowing blood. You have no idea how many souls are buried out here, burning for vengeance. This is just a fraction of the dead bodies out here." He was keeping cool, removed, instructive.

"Your . . . hands," I said. "The blood."

Ric was still lost in explaining everything, almost to himself.

"That's what I realized when the ammunition ran out. They had to be here for the raising. The werewolf mob was shortsighted, so secure in being killers in both human and wolf form. They'd defeated the vampires, the undead, decades ago. What could the dead do to them? No one knows how the dead wait. Unseen. Unremembered. Think how many there are, just a few feet under this shifting sand. Just a few clawing handfuls from resurrection. We're all so quick to forget those we've wronged. Now, after the Millennium Revelation, all bets are off. The walking dead and the dead walk. All I had to do was dowse for their gravesites, call them up, and they came. I could have raised more."

"These were enough, Ric."

As we spoke, the zombies ranged around the area, lifting dead werewolves now metamorphosized into a half-were form, wrenching off arms and heads with a sort of aimless curiosity. I looked away from them, shuddering.

"What happened to your hands?" I asked Ric again. "Did it take shedding some of your blood to raise them?"

Ric lifted the raw pieces of meat at the ends of his jacket sleeves and I felt myself grow faint.

"Only a drop of blood needed. This was overkill. I guess my hands got chopped up a little."

"Ric! What on earth! Tell me! What did this to you? Why?"

He shrugged. "Once I ran out of ammunition, I needed to raise the zombies to fight the werewolves. They were killed by werewolves, so now they're invulnerable to them. I needed a dowsing rod to do that. This is high desert. There's nothing suitable out here I could find but barbed wire."

Oh, my God! "You dredged up zombie after zombie with barbed wire?"

"Not enough maybe." He looked around, dazed and self-critical. "These were all I could bear to raise."

Nothing I'd said so far had seemed to get through to him, but what he said just now wrenched me to the core.

I felt every searing instance of it. Ric moving methodically over the desert ground, waiting for the dowsing rod to burn through his palms and point downward. The twisting, intense force grinding the rusty barbs into his hands . . . Each zombie clambering out of the ground, eager to follow Ric to the person . . . creature, who had put him there. Ric, dripping blood onto sand and scrub, moving to the next spot where the barbed wire would tear at the hearts of his hands to tell him a zombie lies there. And on to the next.

I pulled his jacket shoulders down on his arms, and eased his hands as carefully as I could out of the sleeves. He hardly seemed aware of that, but stood there docile as a child. I should have recognized shock: blood loss and horrendous pain. I hung the jacket over one arm and took hold of his upper arm with the other hand.

"I'll get you to an emergency room, a hospital, a micro surgeon."

That snapped him out of his daze.

"No! Can't go to the ER. That gets on the record. None of this can be on the record."

I sighed my extreme frustration, which was a form of fear. We were alive, but what did that mean if Ric was mangled?

The hair-snake was still sleeping and had nothing to offer. The gray spirit wolves of an older era had melted into the dark, for wolves had been hunted to extinction in this part of the country for decades.

So where else could I go for help? The cottage. Godfrey. Hector might know a good star-quality doctor from the silver screen days. . . .

"Just get us out of here," Rick said, sounding a bit more like himself.

I guided him down the steep trail. "Where's your car?"

"Below the lodge in a stand of firs just off the road."

Madame Moon was generous with her light, even though her lopsided face made it look like she'd taken her lumps tonight too.

I ached in more places than I knew I had. Ric's right arm across my shoulders was heavy enough to drag me down and dripped blood onto my breast, but we tottered down the empty mountain to the road. The lodge was lit, but deserted, and the stillness was eerie. I wondered where the surviving werewolves and mobsters had gone to ground and what the zombies would do now that they were free.

The Corvette was well hidden, so low it blended with a stand of sage, but Ric guided me to it. I wrestled him into the passenger seat. My usual place. I wrapped his black, bloody hands in his lap, using his jacket like a muff. His Washington-white shirt was now spattered with blood.

I caressed his face once he was seated, and felt his lips kiss my fingertips in passing. At least he was conscious. At least I *have* fingertips. Tears seared my cheeks.

Above us, the sloppy-drunk moon was grinning down. The moon had to answer for a lot of crimes against persons tonight.

When I lowered myself into the driver's seat and started the powerful engine with a peace-shattering rumble, I could turn on the interior lights. I could see his face well now, but not his hands.

"How bad?" I asked. "The cuts."

Ric winced. "To the bone, I think."

"*Madre de Dios!* You must have the *cojones* of a *chupacabra.*"

His look was rueful but his skin-tone was a sick sepia color. "That street Spanish book is improving your vocabulary, *mujer mia.*"

Mujer mia. Woman mine. All right. What was I going to do about this? Ric's hands. With which he dowses for the dead. No more. Those hands, with which he dowses for my heart. No more.

"How do I drive this thing? I haven't driven stick shift for almost ten years."

Ric smiled, palely. He told me what to do and I did it. A couple minutes later we were barreling down a narrow mountain road in the dark in third gear. I tried to coast and ride the brake, but momentum pushed us faster and faster.

I looked in the rear-view mirror. The steel-toothed grille of a HumVee was barreling wildly down the mountain road after us. Suddenly I didn't dare brake at all anymore. I steered for my life. Our lives.

The needle pushed up to ninety as we slithered down that mountain road. I was trapped in a nightmare video game, moving my eyes and arms by raw instinct. Dodging and swerving until we skidded onto flat straight highway, where I put the car into fourth gear and spurred the Corvette up to one-twenty in no time. The highway was flat and straight and no lumbering HumVee would catch this baby now.

Maybe a state trooper would spot us and pull us over, then see the emergency and escort us, siren shrieking, to safety.

No. No one was out here in the desert tonight but ghost wolves and werewolves and zombies, oh my. Also a lot of enemies and damn few and very dicey allies. Now no one could help us but me.

CHAPTER FIFTY-SIX

The bright lights of Vegas in the distance seemed to mock our dark, desperate circumstances. I tried to take Ric's mind off his injuries by keeping him talking.

"How did you know where I was?" I asked.

His head lay against the headrest as he watched the off-full moon race us through the blue-tinted glass roof panel.

He smiled, thinly.

"When I could check my cell phone, I found your message and was alarmed enough to go to your guest house on Nightwine's premises."

I smiled. *Premises*. He still talked law enforcement despite being a free agent now.

"It's a cottage."

"Whatever, it still has the Hound of Hell for an unwelcoming committee of one. He was howling and snarling and bounding at the front door. I was standing there about to get out a credit card to B and E into the place—"

"Break and enter? Could you?"

"Sure. This CinSim in black tie and tails who talks like a British butler shows up, only he's American. He lets me in, then orders 'Master Quicksilver' back from the door and into the closest corner to be 'a good bad dog.' Then he tells me he's 'most concerned.' Seems a cousin of his at the Inferno has a friend who sometimes hangs out at the Gehenna. He told him that 'Mr. Cicereau and some of his less savory associates have taken our Miss Street for a ride' out to someplace called the Starlight Lodge near the Paiute Golf Club on Spring Mountain, and that it would 'behoove' me to look into that 'post haste.' "

"The butler dude was Godfrey, Nightwine's major domo. He looks after everything around the estate, including me."

What I don't explain, because I can't just yet, is how and why the CinSims have a secret communication network. Nor can I imagine why an Inferno CinSim would haunt the rival Gehenna, but I know who it was. That farewell butt pinch on being escorted from Cicereau's office makes sense now. My really, *really* secret admirer and the CinSim tattletale had been Claude, the Invisible Man. Curiouser and curiouser.

"I'm glad you looked me up," I told Ric, eyeing his face as the city streetlights swept it rhythmically.

His normally warm complexion was still a cold gray color as the Corvette slowed to the speed limit and lurched onto Sunset Road under my iffy in-town shifting, although the knack was coming back fast. I knew if I pulled up to an emergency room Ric would never forgive me and I didn't know where any were in this town, anyway.

There was no place to go but home.

Wait! Shouldn't that mantra be: there's no place *like* home?

I finally punched in the security code to my private entry gate and drove into Nightwine's ultra-secure estate. Ric could barely walk into my enchanted cottage, and I could barely hold him up. Like head wounds, hand wounds bleed profusely, and the flesh on Ric's hands had to be hash.

Not one freaking grumpy helpful domestic dwarf was in sight. Things could be worse. I was alive when I wasn't supposed to be, but the only person I deeply cared about was damaged beyond repair.

Ric swayed as he stood in the entry hall, dripping blood on the slate tiles. He was still shaky, more cream than coffee in his face color.

Before I could install him on the couch and call Nightwine to send a doctor, I heard a thump at one of the cottage's windows. Next came a scrabbling sound, and then Quicksilver bounded into the main room, limping and looking ragged.

Not another victim to tend simultaneously!

Before I could even acknowledge his presence, Quick made one great arching leap toward Ric, knocking him onto his back on the floor. Ric lifted his crossed arms just in time to keep Quicksilver from lunging onto his neck, taking the brunt of the dog's weight on his forearms.

Oh my God! Two wounded alpha males, still at each other's throats! Just what they, and I, didn't need!

"Get this monster off me, Del!" Ric yelled through gritted teeth. "This damn dog has never liked me and now that I'm down—I can't use my hands to fight him off!"

I was crawling on top of Quick, grabbing for the dog's massive shoulders, ordering him to *leave* Ric, to get *off . . . ! Bad dog!*

Quicksilver ignored me. He was too busy sniffing at Ric's bloody hands, a true bloodhound, and whimpering at me in-between, licking my hands with soft wet swaths of tongue. One canine swipe managed to give Snow's bracelet such a thorough slobbery bath that it migrated to my upper arm and coiled there like a scared snake.

I grabbed Quick's collar; if I half-throttled him the dog would have to back off.

My fingers curled around the thick black leather, over the round silver medallions circling it like little moons. Before my eyes, those medallions, as liquid as quicksilver, changed shape, going slightly off circle. Like they were . . . waning. With the moon! Of course!

Quick probably did have wolf in him. Which made him . . . what? Lethal?

Before I could get clear on what this might mean, the silver snake on my upper arm split into dozens of hair-fine chains and slithered back down to my wrist, binding my hands. *Why?* I didn't know, but I sensed intent and urgency. Was this familiar mine, or Snow's? For me or against me? It had never hurt me, although it had taunted me. Okay, so who am I to argue with a silver-tongued Devil?

"Ric! Give Quicksilver your hands." I can't believe I'm urging this.

"Are you crazy?"

"No. Maybe. Moon madness. Give Quicksilver your hands. That's what he wants, what he needs."

"Del, he wants to *eat* me!"

"He's not that kind of wolf. He's a wolf*hound*. Unless you're a closet werewolf, let him at you."

Ric, shocked, stared into my eyes. In that strange, mesmerizing moment, Quicksilver slipped my grip on his transformed collar and strained forward to lick a swath up Ric's raised right hand.

Somehow moonlight had entered the room, maybe when Quicksilver had busted through his usual window. A silver aura blossomed in the air. The unearthly light made Ric's bloodied white shirt fabric gleam again like chain mail. It made my bracelet of many chains lightning-bolt bright. It made the off-round metal moons on Quicksilver's collar glow in the semi-dark.

I heard a ghastly searing sound of flesh melting. *No! What have I done? What have I permitted to be done?*

Ric's hands burned white-hot under the passage of Quicksilver's fire-red tongue. He screamed, despite himself and probably a lot of training.

My tears must have looked silver as they sizzled down my face. I screamed too.

The only one who didn't scream was Quicksilver. He was busy licking Ric's hand, as dogs will.

Even shouts of pain and dismay were not enough to express our human anguish at this ignorant assault. The gruesome dog-lapping sound stopped as the silver effusion of moonlight faded. I gazed at Ric's mutilated hands, cringing. One palm gleamed with saliva where Quicksilver had licked. The skin was . . . fresh, unbloodied. Whole.

Ric saw where I was looking, at what I had seen.

He eyed Quicksilver's muzzle, as big as a young bear's, all white fangs and overheated red tongue, all grin that can be either canine friendliness or canine threat.

Ric bit down hard on his lower lip and nodded.

The moments of uncertainty were over. Time was moving again. The minute frozen in a net of quicksilver slipped into a new minute.

I sat back on my heels, exhausted by fear and wonder, to watch Quicksilver lick Ric's wounds clean, stroke by stroke, banishing bloody silk and shredded flesh, leaving healed skin behind.

"Dogs lick their wounds," I told Ric, I told me, told the damn dog who knew better than both of us combined what had happened here. Maybe it wasn't any of us, but the enchanted cottage. Then there was the rational explanation, and I'm sticking to it. "There's a bacteria-banishing element in dog saliva. It works in the wild."

"On dogs and wolves," Ric pointed out.

The skepticism told me his hands were feeling better.

"Maybe you've got some canine DNA."

"No." Ric sat up, pushing Quicksilver back on his haunches. Dogs always overdo it. Ric wiped his hands on his shirttails. They came away clean, whole, perfect.

"Ick! Poison dog lips!" I said, quoting Lucy from the Charlie Brown strip for comic relief. Charles Schulz was with us again. The Kennedy Center Awards now reanimated a "national cultural treasure" each year as well as honoring those in their first lives.

"Right." Ric was watching Quicksilver wash his own hairy body with an amazingly large, supple tongue, especially the private area.

I moved to help Ric up. Instead, he pulled me down against him on the floor for a long, penetrating kiss. He wasn't too shabby in the tongue department either.

I heard a faint, muffled growl.

"Ric. The dog might be . . . um, you know. Jealous."

Ric's hands on me were strong and certain. "He doesn't like this, I don't like his public grooming habits. He'll just have to get used to it."

"Maybe you'll have to get used to each other."

"Yeah. Maybe." Ric's voice had become a soft, possessive growl.

I heard the click of Quicksilver's nails fade and then thump as he leaped out of his doggie door. This scene was obviously way too mushy for a wolfhound to witness.

Ric ran his hands down my arms, relishing their flexibility and strength as much as the feel of me. That had to stop. Right here, right now. I took hold of his wrists.

"You need to rest those hands. Recover."

"They're fine now. I'm fine."

I didn't answer, just pushed his wrists to the floor above his head and held them there.

He stilled beneath me, his eyes questioning.

"Rest," I said. It was an order. I must have developed this irresistibly firm bedside manner since my brief stint as a nurse.

"I'm fine, Del. No one laid a finger on me when I showed up with the reinforcements. My hands only caught it from holding onto a whirligig of barbed wire for so long."

"Are you sure you're fine? Everywhere? I'll have to see. Just don't move."

I felt a triumphant surge of life restored in every cell. I felt strong and alive. I felt . . . very hot. I had to have something right now, and I knew what it was. And according to Ric, it was fine.

I rolled over to wriggle out of my black stretch leggings and pull out the precious Cicereau photo saved on the small flash drive, which had stayed put and come through everything without any visible damage. Spandex rocks!

I rolled back over to straddle Ric's hips and unclasped his belt, unhooked his pants, ripped down the zipper, pushed all that aside, and pulled what I wanted through the slit in his silken shorts. It was still in that delicious state of becoming all that it could be, but I was far from through.

I lay atop him and stopped whatever he'd been about to say or do with a fingertip to his lips. Despite all he'd been through, only his top shirt button was undone. I undid another two and put my left hand over his heart. My right hand pushed the shirt collar aside until I could see the faint blue bruise at the side of his throat. When I'd exposed it, his heart rate quickened.

"Tell me about this," I whispered, stroking it with my forefinger.

"It's a love bite. You ought to know. You did it the first day you met me, *mi tigre hembra*."

Calling me "tigress" was only inciting me tooth and nail. "Why is it such a turn-on for you, *mi hombre*?"

"Lord, Del, you were there, in the park when that bolt of sheer sex coursed through us. You didn't even remember turning your head into me and biting my throat. That made me come. No woman's ever done that, given me an orgasm that way."

"I must be pretty potent." I ran a fingernail over the mark and felt his heart leap against the palm of my hand. Something else leapt against me.

"Del—" His voice and breath were ragged.

My own pulses thundered to feel him ready but pinned beneath me. But he kept his arms and hands still, giving me the lead I'd asked for. Demanded.

"We know now it was earth magic," he said, "borrowed lust, but it worked to bond us."

"No woman has ever bitten you in passion before? Anybody or any*thing* else I should know about?"

He smiled slowly, flirting in foreplay. "I said no woman had ever bitten me *there* before."

I let my fingernail trail hard over "there." His heart rate doubled again, fluttering like a caged hawk in my hand.

"Who has then?"

"Are you jealous?"

"Madly. I want to know why you want what you do, so I can give it to you better."

His face sobered. No more teasing evasion. I took my finger from his throat, my hand from his heart, kissed the flutter, and laid my head on his chest to hear the deeper hollow thud of his heart through his body.

"I was a boy," Ric whispered finally, though we were alone and Nightwine's devices were disabled and no one else could overhear. He was speaking from a place he'd never wanted to go back to. I knew that place well.

"In Mexico. Dirt-poor Mexican desert. Still, there were cattle, burros, goats, and peasants to try to live off the bitter land. I was . . . an orphan, like you. I slept with the burros at night. I used to see visions of Our Lady of Guadalupe sometimes. I could even smell the roses that are her sign. She comforted me like a mother come to give her son a goodnight kiss.

"I never could remember such a . . . legendary thing as a kiss. I grew up among evil men and brutalized animals. But I was on the fringe of manhood, maybe twelve. One night the burros were restless. I slept and dreamed and something came to me and kissed me on the neck. My first kiss. It was long and sweet and I sensed it in my sleep and didn't ever want to wake up. When I did, my neck and throat ached. I was glad to feel that, to prolong the mother's kiss I longed for. I touched the place, the site of the miracle, of the Virgin's compassion, smelling roses. My fingers came away wet with my own blood."

I'd heard this with tears welling behind my eyes—who would dream that Ric Montoya's successful, attractive present was built upon such a barren, hurtful, lonely past? His last sentence chilled my soul, though, and even my surging libido.

I jerked my head up to face him. "You'd been visited by a vampire!"

My heart almost stopped. *No!* Once vampire-bitten, a human was forever susceptible to the breed's spell. It couldn't have been worse if he'd told me he had cancer.

He nodded, and lifted an arm to catch my first falling tear on a fingertip. "Yes, Delilah." He smiled tenderly. "But it was a vampire bat."

"A real bat?" What did that mean? Was that better or worse? "Are you sure it was the real thing?"

"In the Chihuahua desert? What else? It was a bat, the same blood-sucking parasite that was named after real vampires, a Mexican bat. There are millions of them. I was mistaken for a burro, probably because my hair was uncut and covered my neck."

"Then you're not . . . infected by an undead human vampire bite?"

"No." He stirred under me, lifted his hips and my weight with the move, the gesture saying sexy things again.

"No. But the next night I was visited by a vision of a dancing girl with writhing hips and naked breasts and she kissed me on the neck in that very same spot, and I had become a man."

I got it. That had been his first turn-on. Wet dream. Weird maybe, but harmless, right? And my heart ached for the lonely boy in the desert, sleeping with donkeys and goats. There must be more, much more, to Ric's story, but this whispered confession had soothed my immediate panic.

He watched me accept that and put his arm back down. I wriggled up his body and placed my hand on his heart again. The rate had quieted nicely and he was half-soft between my legs again. If pseudo-vampire dancing girls and vampire bats did it for him, I was ready to throw myself into the part.

I breathed hotly on his neck, my hand gauging his pulse rate. I ran the tip of my tongue over the bruised spot, and then my lips. My many kisses added up to a month of goodnight visitations. He was breathing hard and his heart was racing, boy and man ready for so much more. So I bore down hard and sucked a series of moans out of him, then teased his skin with my teeth. I was a very *bad* batgirl.

"*Delilah!*"

I sat up and pushed him into me and tore my Spandex top over my head. Luckily I was wearing a bra I'd bought during my post-Sunset Park shopping spree. I have to admit that Irma's taste has always been way sleazier than mine, and she'd been in firm control that day. Ric's hands twitched, but remained out of play. I was in control now, in control of the vertical. I moved up and down slowly, my body swallowing that tantalizing length again and again, rocking and rolling.

Ric was gasping. "You've never been so aggressive before, *mi tigre hembra*."

"I've never almost lost you before."

"It was worth it, then. We'll have to do that again," he panted, caught between a moan and a laugh.

"I'll have to do this again too."

I could feel him on the brink of explosion; I collapsed down upon him, sinking my teeth hard into the vampire bat spot. My spot.

We came together, I screaming, Ric adding an inciting basso of satisfaction to the clan vocalizations. Los Lobos had seen to it there'd always be a call of the wild in our encounters.

I pushed myself back up finally, looking down at him. And he finally moved his arms, his hands on my hips, his fingers toying with the thin sterling silver hip-hung chain I wore for him under everything, impaling me gently down deep onto him one last time. For now.

Sweat evaporated slowly and sweetly on our bodies. Ric's face gleamed like a golden idol's in the funky old-fashioned cottage lamplight. I could feel him softening in me, a sensation as engaging as a thick milk chocolate bar melting in your mouth.

Ric reached a hand up to brush my hair off my damp neck. "*Te amo*," he said softly.

I'd never said, "I love you" to another person, only to Achilles.

And I'd never yet said it to Quicksilver, although I did.

I'd always had a mental block about saying it and had never had anyone much worth saying it to, except for the occasional transient stranger in my life who might have done me a small, unexpected kindness, and saying that would have been overkill, although I did silently love him or her for it.

Ric had done far more for me than that, but I still had a block about saying the words now. *I love you*.

"*Te amo*," I heard myself telling Ric, smiling. In Spanish the words came much more easily. *Te amo, te amo, te amo*, I thought.

We stayed there, locked together, smiling at each other for a long time.

Like gourmet coffee and chocolate, it was almost better than sex.

CHAPTER FIFTY-SEVEN

Okay. Woman. Man. And Dog. Silver mirror-medium, corpse-finder, and walking, trotting first-aid kit. I guess we're the new Triad in town.

Las Vegas, place your bets, figure your odds, and hang on to your secrets as best you can, because we are here to break your bank!

That's what I thought when I woke up alone in my cottage bed the morning after the face-off in the Spring Mountains. Ric had left long before morning. He needed to get back to the mountains by night to round up his zombies.

"They only respond to me for now," he explained. "I don't want any zombie wranglers capturing them. In the old days, they had to be fresh. Then the big combines had them flash-frozen and shipped to the States for assignment."

"Like fish sticks?" *Euww.*

Ric nodded, steel-jawed. "Today the Immortality Mob has preservatives for the harvest. They scour mass death sites, preferably those due to natural disaster. War and massacres tend to chop off limbs. It gets more expensive."

"Who is the Immortality Mob? Nightwine used that phrase."

"We don't know. We can guess. Listen. I've got to go. I shouldn't have left them there unclaimed earlier tonight. But—"

Now the zombies sounded like lost luggage. I could understand Ric's fury in wanting to end this trade in human skin and bone if not souls.

388   CAROLE NELSON DOUGLAS

"Can't you . . . put them back?"

He took my hand, held it to his beating heart. "There's no going back. For any of us."

I CLOSED THE COTTAGE DOOR behind Ric just before Quicksilver returned from his run nattily groomed and not limping any more.

Ric had noticed the rakes on my legs and arms before he left and said, "If Wonderdog wants to lick you all better, I don't want to be here to see it."

I hadn't considered substituting Quicksilver's healing tongue for Neosporin, but did after Ric left. Quick sat quietly, gazing limpidly at me with those Tiffany gift box-blue eyes. Maybe his healing gift had been exhausted on Ric and himself. His tail dusted the floor with a touch of eagerness. Maybe I'd better let Quick keep his tongue to himself in my case.

I took a shower, anointed my wounds and hit the bed, dreading nightmares.

They came with a vengeance: a harrowing rerun of vamp boys with my blood on their fangs, of me/Lilith levitating nude and snake-bound and vampire-bit, of running, running, running through a rocky wasteland, of hurting, burning, falling, of a Paiute Indian shaman bending over me, chanting alien words and dripping the soothing, warm balm of a dessert succulent plant on my wounds. Weren't they the tribe that invented the famous and ultimately tragic Ghost Dance?

I awoke and stretched, determined to think only of the happy outcomes of the night before. Despite the nightmares real and dreamed, this one morning all was right with my world.

Snow's silver familiar chose that moment to make its move from a limpid chain around my neck into a cold silver garter at the top of my right thigh.

Garter belts and silk stockings, Snow? You and Howard Hughes wish! It'll be a cold day in Hell.

Which I am really looking forward to making come true in your case.

But first I had to report to my boss, Hector Nightwine.

THE BLACK-AND-WHITE PHOTOGRAPH of Cicereau with his teenage daughter occupied the huge center screen of Nightwine's media wall.

"Excellent," he gloated. "That copyright-stealing thug! Try to rip off my rights to Maggie, will he? I'll smear Cicereau's messy supernatural private life all over the world's television sets. Child murder is not popular anywhere, even these days."

"We have no proof," I pointed out.

He hauled out a pair of half glasses with iridescent frames, and then snapped off the enlarged image I'd taken from Cicereau's computer.

"*Las Vegas CSI V* is a fictional show," he said.

"You're as liable for being sued as anyone, and Cicereau might go farther than that."

Nightwine chuckled and grabbed a fistful of what looked like mixed nuts from a crystal bowl on his desk. "Have some?"

"I'm on a new diet."

My new diet was based on eating food that didn't try to crawl away on you.

"*Tsk.* You certainly don't need to lose an ounce. I managed to get some black-market footage of your act at the Gehenna."

"What!"

"You can never underestimate Maggie fans. I must watch them like a hawk. They were ready to burn a million DVDs and hustle them internationally. Naturally, I waited until their job was done and unofficially seized the lot. They'll go like hotcakes and Cicereau can't do a thing about it."

"*Hector!* I haven't given permission, and I never will."

"Who's to say it wasn't really Lilith herself? I'd give you a generous cut, of course."

"I've gotten enough cuts in your service, thank you. No. Absolutely not, not if you want any more work out of me. And don't whine. I also want the recording of Rick and me in Sunset Park. The enlarged, closeup and personal version you made from the distant spy camera footage."

"Have mercy, Delilah. That is one of the best cinematic 'meets' ever, and I did the final cut on it. Let me keep a copy for my private collection."

"No."

Actually, I think he liked it when I put my foot down. He pouted instead of whining and slaked his congenital greed with three fistfuls of nuts. They crunched like walnuts, but I didn't like the jointed black leggy "crumbs" that fell to his desktop.

"Agreed on the recordings," he grumbled through his gluttony. "For a yummy-soft bit of female you drive a hard bargain."

"Back to the case," I said. "We don't know everything yet."

"Of course not, but I can go to script on this. The existence of a series of Inferno chip designs prove *someone*—if not Christophe himself—was keeping the concept alive all these decades. I love the hunky vampire prince getting whacked and someone else getting the Inferno hotel and casino off the ground decades later. A real weeper for the supernatural set."

"This is all still speculation, Hector. Christophe may not like that."

"I'll make the Inferno owner black, maybe a warlock, and call the place the . . . the Snake Pit. As for the true facts, what else is there to know?"

"There's got to be more to it, that sad hit and secret burial of two young lovers. Cicereau didn't banish all the vampires just by killing a couple of lovesick kids, even if one of them was his own. And why kill them?"

"He's a very, very bad man, and wolf?" Hector asked archly, cracking open a nut with his teeth and gobbling the wriggling white meat inside. "But I like it, Delilah. You think like a movie mogul."

So I started thinking like a screenwriter. I stared at the photo of Cicereau with the daughter who had come calling in my cottage mirror ever since Ric and I had found her body, but whose name I didn't even know. Yet. She deserved a name on a gravestone.

The shock of Cicereau's paternity had kept me from even noticing others in the group shot until I viewed them life-sized on Nightwine's seven-foot screen.

The three guys in pinstriped, broad-shouldered suits were obviously nameless bodyguards, two in fedoras. The young one with the slicked back dark hair and pencil-thin mustache had a roguish Clark Gable forelock falling onto his forehead. Close-up, I spotted a thin streak of silver running through it. One-two-three, *woof!* Sansouci didn't look a day older today, except for the heavier silver streak job. *Hmm.* He'd shown me a flicker of humanity. Him I might be able to deal with.

And since when had werewolves become so long-lived? It was much easier to off a marauding werewolf with silver bullets than to find a vampire's sleepy-time lair, dig him or her up by night, and then do the stake routine. Everyone figured that nowadays full-blooded werewolves were rare, shot to extinction all over the globe like the wolves themselves, rather than dying of old age. But what if they weren't?

At the photo's edge stood one of those tall, glam chorus-girl types as common to Las Vegas as palm trees and with about the same IQ I tended to notice them as much as I do the trees. But her clothes were a hoot.

She wore a long white crepe gown. Its huge forties shoulder pads sparkled with rhinestones. The neck was high . . . but a narrow open slit ran from the hollow of her throat to her waist, and I bet the back was wide open. The skirt was draped toward her left hip in the Grecian goddess style popular in that era, and a spangled dark crimson flower pinned it there. A matching exotic bloom nestled above her right temple amid her elaborately upswept dark hair.

That's when it struck me that a lot of women in the forties looked like the Black Dahlia, that I could do a great job of it myself. *Hmmm.* Samba, rumba, tango. Chichi Latin dances and clubs. I bet Ric would flip if he saw me in that getup.

Look at you! Irma interrupted. *Used to avoid your own image in mirrors and dress only for work. Now you're walking through mirrors and morphing into the Vamp of Las Vegas. You go, girl!*

Hector too was gazing on beauty bare and having his own private thoughts, which he now said aloud.

"I've decided to launch a new spin-off," he announced. "*Las Vegas CSI: The Vintage Collection.* It'll unearth all the unsolved crimes of the Werewolf-Vampire War era, use the music of the period."

"That's such a rip-off of *Cold Case*," I pointed out. The crime show was in its umpteenth year.

Hector's huge shoulders shrugged off my comment. "I can do an extended miniseries too. *Dead and Alive: The Making of Las Vegas.*"

I turned to stare at him.

"Don't look so surprised, Delilah. Your vintage clothing has inspired me. You dig up the past crimes; I film 'em. I could even cast you in some juicy bit parts."

I sure hated to hear the words "juicy bits" and me in the same sentence from Nightwine. Still, the role of Delilah Street, Paranormal Investigator, on and off the screen appealed to me.

"It'd pay way better than a non-speaking role." His rum-raisin-brown eyes gazed dreamily into the distance. "A cameo role would keep Lilith's image alive."

And such a role would perpetuate the obsession of the creeps who were out to capture, debase, and destroy her. No wonder she'd gone missing, if she wasn't already really and truly dead, and I had my doubts. On the other hand, my doing this for Hector might draw out Lilith . . . . I was curious about her. Surely she'd be curious about me. Meanwhile, Hector was screenwriting aloud.

"You'd be . . . the Black-and-White Dahlia, a misty, mysterious glamorous noir film dame glimpsed in distant shots, like Alfred Hitchcock always showing up as a passing extra in his films. All you'd have to do is look good, do some moody voice-overs, and float around."

"I'm not Hitchcock and I doubt you are, either."

"Who could be? He was the master of nuanced black-and-white film suspense and even managed to do some fairly interesting things in color. And, Delilah, I could hire your dead-dowsing swain as a consultant. Might reduce those pesky out-of-town trips of his, *hmmm*? Keep him here in town more."

Okay. How did Nightwine know about Ric's trips? The charming vintage cottage dial-phone must be tapped! Fine. Ric and my calls would be all-cell phone all the time from now on.

But Hector's grand vision had hit a nerve with my reporter's instincts.

Everybody accepted Las Vegas as a fantasy destination, as larger than life. Nobody had reexamined the city and its tawdry criminal past since long before the Millennium

Revelation, when the addition of supernaturals to the landscape had seemed like just another entertaining Vegas excess.

A Cirque du Soleil for creatures of the night.

"You don't have to okay the whole vision just now, Delilah."

I could hear Hector crunching contentedly on something disgusting behind me.

"If you reveal their past to the public," I turned to point out, "every shady human and unhuman in town will be out to get you. Me. Us."

"Just keep looking at what's going on, what went on, and you'll find something I can use on my shows."

"Or . . . something really, *really* bad will find me."

Nightwine shrugged and smacked his lips.

"Every modern girl's looking for Mr. Right."